# Keeping THE Score

## BRANDY PELLETIER

Developmental editor: Melanie Yu at Made Me Blush Books

Copy/line editor: Beth Lawton at VB Edits

Formatted by: Kristen Hamilton at Kristen's Red Pen

Cover design: Lorissa Padilla Designs

*For my inner circle.*
*Thank you for being zero-judgment friends, for second-hand therapy,*
*and for always being my safe place to land.*
*I love y'all more than my luggage.*

# ALSO BY BRANDY PELLETIER

*Between the Lines*

# AUTHOR'S NOTE

Dear reader,

*Keeping the Score* is intended for adult readers (eighteen and older.) It contains adult language and open door spicy scenes.

There are a few content warnings I'd like you to also be aware of. If any of these are sensitive topics for you, please put your mental health first.

- death of a parent (not on page—happened in the past, but mentioned throughout the story)
- cancer diagnosis of parent (happened in the past; character is in remission when story occurs)
- cheating (not by either MC and happened in the past)

Happy reading!

# KEEPING THE SCORE PLAYLIST

"Blue Ain't Your Color" - Keith Urban
"The Story of Us" (Taylor's Version) - Taylor Swift
"New Town" - Smithfield
"I Can See You" (Taylor's Version) - Taylor Swift
"American Girl" - Tom Petty and the Heartbreakers
"There's No Way" - Lauv feat. Julia Michaels
"Kiss You Tonight" - David Nail
"Tiebreaker" - The Head And The Heart
"Keeping Score" - Dan + Shay feat. Kelly Clarkson
"Heartbroken" (Jessie Version) - Diplo & Jessie Murph
"Sure Thing" - Miguel
"Pink" - Julia Michaels
"Never Til Now" - Ashley Cooke
"Beautiful War" - Kings of Leon
"Tell Me What We're Gonna Do Now" - Joss Stone feat.
Common
"Coming Back to You" - Sara Bareilles
"Let's Stay Together" - Al Green

# PROLOGUE
## MEL

*Ten years ago...*

"I'll have another," I tell the bartender, holding up my nearly empty glass of Blue Moon. As he refills it, I study my reflection in the mirror behind the bar for the first time since I stepped foot in here half an hour ago.

My dishwater blond hair is smoothed into an elegant updo, nary a strand out of place. My makeup is flawless. Even though it's more than I normally wear, I look good. Put together.

Though nothing could be further from the truth.

My big brother Mark is a married man as of five hours ago. The ceremony went off without a hitch. He and his new bride are no doubt enjoying each other before they leave tomorrow for a week in the Bahamas.

*Eww.* Nope, I definitely don't want to conjure a mental image of Mark and Lisa on their wedding night.

I'm proud of and happy for them. They are one of *those* couples. They're one another's missing piece. My brother is incredible on his own, but with Lisa, his Mark-ness is elevated to max capacity. And it's the same for her, too.

They are each other's safe place to land.

I sigh as images from the wedding and reception flit through my mind. When the doors opened at the rear of the sanctuary and every eye turned to the bride, I was watching my brother. His handsome face, a younger version of my dad's, crumpled with emotion for a few seconds, and his eyes went shiny with unshed tears. The happiness radiating from him made my eyes burn, too. And Lisa? She beamed when she entered the church on her father's arm; her huge smile lit up her face like she was under a spotlight. Their first dance was swoony. Strains of Tim McGraw's "My Best Friend" created the perfect moment.

I danced with my parents, posed for an obscene number of pictures, and even caught the damn bouquet, all while maintaining a perky, happy, sister-of-the-groom smile.

But my heart? It hurt like a bitch all damn day.

Now, I'm alone in a dive bar in Americus, two beers in. Feeling sorry as fuck for myself and my current life status. When considering where to drown my sorrows, I crossed Fuzzy's, our hometown bar, off my list first. I've only *legally* been allowed to drink for two months, and stepping foot inside makes me feel like a kid caught with my hand in the cookie jar. Finding this joint on my way out of town felt serendipitous, even though I can't let myself get as tipsy as I'd like to, considering I still have to drive home. Well, to my parents' home. Which is also my home these days.

Living with my parents, with no solid plans on the horizon, is far from where I expected to be at twenty-one.

*Fucking Nick.*

Just thinking his name causes a low growl to escape my lips.

"Can I get a Terrapin, please?" A masculine voice pulls me out of my Nick-haze.

On instinct, I glance at the newcomer, then do a double-take.

It's Cordell. *Cordell Freaking Watkins.*

What the hell is he doing *here*? I mean, his mom still lives in Bennett, so he's probably visiting her. But Americus is forty-five minutes from our hometown.

He takes a stool to my right, leaving an empty one between us. Try as I might, I can't take my eyes off him. He's wearing a gray T-shirt and black basketball shorts with an LSU ball cap pulled down low. Almost as if he's trying to hide.

I take a swig of my beer for courage, then blurt out, "Terrapin, huh?"

He swivels his head and catalogs my face, all made up and still pristine after hours. Then he gives me a once-over, taking in the cutoffs and Birks I changed into after the big send-off.

"When in Rome," he says, his deep baritone making my insides quake. "What do the pretty Georgia girls go for these days, beer-wise?" he asks, nodding at my glass.

I squash the instinct to get all twitterpated over a throwaway compliment from Cordell Watkins.

*Play it cool, Mel. Cool and aloof.*

"Blue Moon, sans orange wedge."

"You don't like oranges, or..." He trails off.

"They taste too much like sunshine and happiness."

"And those are bad things?" He cocks a brow at me under his cap. In the dark bar, it's difficult to make out his features. Regardless, Cordell is fine as hell. The moment I started thinking about boys like *that*, he occupied a starring role in my spank bank.

"I'd need *way* more of this before we get into *that*." I tip my beer in his direction, then face forward again. My insides jumble like a scurry of rabid squirrels at a rave—Cordell Watkins is talking to *me*?—but I don't let it show.

"I'm Cordell," he says, extending his hand for me to shake. As if anyone in a sixty-mile radius doesn't know all about him and his career. He's been our town's golden boy for years.

Cordell ended his third season in the NFL a few months ago. His team made it all the way to the wild card round of the play-offs and finished the season with a ten-and-six record. He ended the year with forty-seven receptions and 616 receiving yards.

Not that I keep track of that kind of stuff or anything.

"Mel."

His huge hand swallows mine, and his face lights up in a megawatt smile that makes my knees go weak.

Even when I'm seated on a damn stool.

I tilt closer and keep my voice low. "I know who you are, by the way."

Both of his brows raise until they're no longer visible under the brim of his cap. "Don't hold that against me." The huff he lets out is soft, like he's aiming for self-deprecation, but there's a hint of emotion hidden beneath the humor. Fear maybe. Or vulnerability.

With a smile and a silent nod, I turn back to my drink. We're both quiet for a few moments, but soon, I can't help but pipe up. "What's your favorite sports movie?"

He doesn't even hesitate before he answers. "*Remember the Titans*."

"A football movie, of course."

"Of course," he says, lifting a shoulder. "Not only is it my favorite sports movie, but it's my favorite *movie* movie. My dad took me to see it the night it premiered." He looks away then, and before my eyes, sorrow creeps over his face.

Hoping to make that look of despondency go away, I change the subject. "My brother, Mark, married his college sweetheart today. It was perfect."

In my periphery, the corners of his eyes get these cute little crinkles when he smiles big. Cute little crinkles that make my tummy flip-flop.

Briefly, he inventories my perfectly coiffed hair, then scans my bare legs. "Is that right? You on the lam from a bridezilla situation?"

"Oh, definitely not. Lisa, my new sister-in-law..." A gooey warmth floods my body. She's a *real* part of my family now. The smile that spreads across my face is unbidden. I love that girl. "She was very chill about the whole thing. She's amazing."

"How'd they meet? Mark and Lisa." Cordell's face is filled with nothing but genuine curiosity.

I like how he uses their names, like he wants to make our conversation more personal than that of two strangers shooting the shit in a bar.

"They met during their freshman year. Like two weeks after classes started. They were at a party and locked eyes across the room. Boom. That was it." I can't help the wistfulness that creeps into my voice. Better that than the bitterness that would dominate my tone if I mentioned *my* brief college romance.

"That was it," he repeats, assessing me. He scans my features and pauses on my lips.

My cheeks heat at his steady gaze. Gah, he's freaking *hot*. I fight the urge to fan my armpits.

"To Mark and Lisa," he says, holding his glass up.

"To Mark and Lisa," I repeat. I tap my glass to his and bring it to my lips. The cold beer, blessedly, tempers the heat from Cordell's stare. My lips tingle like his dark brown eyes brushed them with more than just a glance.

*What the hell is happening here?*

"Do you have any siblings?" I ask, even though I already know the answer.

"Yep, an older sister." He bobs his head, but he doesn't elaborate. "Are you from around here?"

I flinch a little. Shit? How honest should I be? Do I tell him that we grew up in the same small town? I'll definitely keep my years-long crush to myself. But should I mention that my mom has been his family's physician for years?

Thinking total honesty might make him clam up, I go with a vague reply. "Oh, my people have been around here since before the war."

"Which war?"

"Take your pick."

His lips curve up at that. I like making him smile.

"But yeah, I'm Georgia born and bred."

"You could be from worse places." He takes a long sip of his beer and sets the empty glass on the bar top. "My family moved to the area when I was seven. It was a good place to grow up. Small town. Friendly folks." He's giving me soundbite answers now. Probably out of habit. The media training he's endured since his time playing in college is no doubt deeply ingrained. But I want him to be *real* with me, for him to give me his truth.

"C'mon, what do you *really* think about your hometown?"

"You don't want to ask me about football? About being drafted?" He lets out a disbelieving chuckle, then holds up a finger to signal the bartender for another beer. Once he's got it in hand, Cordell turns on his stool to face me, so I follow suit. He's so tall that, even sitting, I have to tilt my head to give him my full attention.

"You don't want to ask about my *way* more famous team-mates? My QB? My money?" That last question is spit out with a bitterness I wasn't expecting. I can't imagine what his life is like; how hard it must be to feel like the people around him are only interested in his status or what he can do for them. To feel as though he can't trust people because there's a good chance they're only after a piece of him.

I could give a flying fart about his status. Sure, I'm starstruck—he *is* a famous local celebrity, after all—but I'm not interested in Cordell Watkins's fame or fortune. I've been inter-ested in *him* for as long as I can remember.

"I want to ask about *you*," I confess. "I want to know what you really think about your tiny map dot."

Cordell crosses his arms over his broad chest. The move makes his biceps bulge and stretch the cotton of his T-shirt. "Who *are* you, Mel?" he asks softly, tilting his head like he's really inspecting me, searching for an ulterior motive. Eventually, though, he surprises me by answering my question. "I think my hometown is the smallest small town on the planet. It's full of people who are scared to venture into the big, wide world and experience different cultures. But," he pauses and cocks a brow, "it's the place that welcomed my family with open arms when we moved to town. It's the place where my sister and I grew up, where my mom is surrounded by friends who would give her the shirts off their backs." The passion in his voice reserved for the place that built both of us sends an overwhelming wave of homesickness washing over me. This is the real Cordell Watkins. "It's the place where I met my best friend."

"Sounds like a great place. But it's not Americus. I—I mean, I'm assuming." *Whew. Nice save.* "So what are you doing *here*?"

He brings his beer to his lips and studies me over the rim of the glass for a long moment. "I don't want to sound like an ungrateful jerk, but sometimes I just need to get away. Have time to myself, where there are no demands. It's hard to do that where I'm from. It's like the whole town gets an alert any time I show up in public. It's exhausting." As soon as the final word leaves his lips, his eyes widen in surprise, like he didn't intend to get that candid with me. "I made a good choice coming here tonight, though," he says, one side of his mouth lifting.

Is it my imagination or has he moved closer? The air in here is stifling, even though the air conditioner is running. "Oh, yeah?"

"Yeah. I've got peace and quiet." He waves an arm around, gesturing at the bar. It's empty save for us and a bartender who is more interested in playing Candy Crush on his phone. "There's no one around to butt into my personal space or ask for a picture or an autograph. Cold beer," he says, raising his glass. "Plus, I met this pixie of a girl who intrigues me." He gives me a ghost of a smile. "That'd be you, by the way."

"Me?" My question is accompanied by an unfortunate snort. "Why in the world are you intrigued by *me*? Because I'm not in your personal space?"

He regards me, his brown eyes narrowing. For a fleeting moment, I panic deep down in my soul. This man might possess the ability to see the *real* me.

And it's terrifying.

"First of all, I wouldn't mind *you* in my personal space. At all."

My heart trips over itself at his flirty answer.

"But," he says, wearing a hint of a smirk like he knows exactly how he affects me, "you intrigue me. Because under that updo and makeup highlighter, I think you're sad. You're trying like hell not to let it show, though. And I know a little something about the outside not matching the inside."

I force a tough swallow and keep my expression neutral. Damn, I do not like how close to home his observation hits. To distract him, I scoff. "Highlighter? How do *you* know about highlighter?"

He points at his chest. "I have a sister, remember?" His smile fades then. "I'm right, though, aren't I? You're sad, Mel. And the question is, what do you want to do about it?"

I scrutinize him, taking in his features—his dark irises, thick brows, and the lines around his mouth. I can't figure out what the hell his intentions are. He's spot-on—my brother's wedding to the love of his life has only validated what I've secretly suspected for the past year and a half: that true love is not meant for me. That I'll never again allow myself to believe in pretty words and fleeting emotions. *Never again.*

But maybe Cordell is suggesting something I *can* have. For a night, at least.

"I want to forget," I tell him. Brazen. Confident. Maintaining eye contact, I watch for his reaction, hoping he's offering what I think he is.

Maybe all he wants is to get laid, to earn another notch in his belt. But right now? Maybe that's what I want, too. I haven't been with anyone since Nick, and tonight, I want nothing more than to forget.

"I think I can help you with that." His deep voice alone is a seduction that has my lady-bits snapping to attention.

Oh my God, my grandma calls them *lady-bits*. They've been neglected for so long, I'm invoking her at the most inopportune moment.

With a shake of my head, I clear Glamma from my thoughts.

Cordell licks his lips and pulls the full bottom one between his teeth, causing all sorts of heat to gather between my legs. Then he angles in closer. So damn close his scent invades my senses and makes me a little dizzy. "Let me help you forget, Mel."

With my heart pounding its way out of my chest, I nod. I probably look like a damn bobblehead, but I've lost all my cool.

Cordell waves at the bartender, silently signaling him to close our tabs, then he grasps my hand and pulls me from the stool. He threads his long fingers between mine and gives me a gentle tug to get me moving. I swear I take two steps for every one of his on the way out the door and into the almost-empty parking lot.

On our journey, I covertly take him in. Now that we're standing side by side, the difference in our sizes is evident.

He's taller than Nick, that's for damn sure.

Ugh, no. No thinking about Nick. *Especially now.*

My car is parked close to the door, and there's a dark SUV to the right, facing the woods that line the property. That vehicle is our destination, I infer, when Cordell presses a button on his key fob and the lights flash once.

Instead of opening a door and ushering me in like I'm envisioning, he pockets the fob and swings me around so that my back is pressed against the cool metal of the SUV. His chest rises and falls in rapid breaths so close to mine they almost touch with every inhale. I place my palm against his left pec, soaking in the warmth of him beneath the cotton, and my stomach flips at the feel of his heart beating as furiously as mine. He rests his hands against the car, caging me in.

"You have a condom?" I manage through a fog of lust.

Shit. *Slow down, Mel.* We haven't even *kissed* yet.

Cordell dips his head and licks his lips again. His eyes dart to my mouth, then back up. "I do."

Of course he does. He probably fucks girls in his car on the regular.

"Then make me forget, Watkins."

He pulls up to his full height and flips the brim of his cap backward before sliding his hands down my hips. So quick the move catches me off guard, he grips me under the ass and lifts me so we're eye to eye. I'm hardly off the ground when his lips crash into mine. Our kissing is frantic, all lips and tongues and teeth. Without my permission, my legs encircle his torso and my ankles lock together to hold on tight.

Damn it, he smells and tastes so freaking good. A heady combination of beer and man and sweat and cologne.

After a moment, the initial frenzy of our kiss wanes. Cordell slows the pace, languidly sliding his tongue against mine and pulling my bottom lip between his. I moan at the sensation, hoping like hell the way he's dipping in and out of my mouth is an accurate simulation of what he'll be doing with another part of his anatomy very soon.

Oh my God, I bet he's *huge.*

I jerk back at the thought and pull in a sharp breath. He

uses the move to his advantage and trails kisses along my jaw and down my neck. With a soft moan, he pauses to suck at my skin until I feel a slight sting.

*Oh my God*, Cordell Watkins gave me a hickey.

Then his mouth is on mine again. We kiss until I'm certain I'll have red marks on my chin from his stubble. With a pained groan, he finally lowers me to my feet, making sure to keep me close as I slide down his front, right over a very hard, very large appendage. My legs wobble a bit, and he holds me steady until I can lock my knees to hold myself up.

"I want more." I force the words out before I lose my nerve. As we stand chest to chest, catching our breath, I tilt my chin high and thrust my shoulders back. The responding gleam in his eye reassures me that he won't deny either of us what we want.

"I'll give you more." He steps impossibly closer, crowding me, and reaches around my body. Smoothly, he opens the back door and pulls me by the arm so he can climb in first. I'm still standing outside the SUV when he hunches over the center console and pops the glove box. The silvery condom wrapper flashes as he settles his tall, powerful body on the leather bench seat.

I pause in the open door and worry my lower lip as he takes off his shirt. Damn, what I can see of the expanse of smooth, brown skin in the dim glow of the lone streetlight is absolutely mesmerizing.

My heart takes off at a gallop, even faster than it's been pounding since the second he put his lips on mine. Because I'm about to *do it* with Cordell Watkins.

Mel, ages fifteen to eighteen, would be on the ground, kicking her heels and squealing with delight. Twenty-one-year-old Mel, who's had a crappy couple of years and needs a win, climbs on in.

As soon as the door clicks shut behind me, I'm shimmying

out of my cutoffs. I leave my pale pink thong in place as I toss them to the floorboard and lift my chin. "You fuck girls in your back seat often, Watkins?"

His pupils blow wide, eclipsing his dark irises, but he quickly recovers. "Believe it or not, you're the first."

"Then let's make it memorable," I say as I straddle him. A shiver skitters down my spine when I brush the hard length pressing against his roomy shorts. "How's this for personal space?"

We waste no time getting back to making out. Cordell's hands roam all over me, and I rake my nails over his skin as our lips and tongues go at it.

How our interaction in the bar escalated to *this* is beyond me, but I won't look a gift horse in the mouth. I quickly force those thoughts to take a back seat so this hot man can take *me* in the back seat. My impulsiveness has bitten me in the ass before, but this is pretty low stakes compared to one certain rash decision in my past.

Cordell's thighs are like granite beneath me, and everywhere I touch is hard and muscular. But his hands are gentle, even when he's kneading my ass or tilting my head to get a better angle. As he smooths them from my shoulders down to my wrists, I break our connection to lean back and whip my tank top over my head.

When I'm bared to him, his hands fall away, palms up, and he freezes. For an instant, what looks like panic flashes in his eyes.

"They're not much to look at, but they're enough to grab on to." To prove my point, I grasp his wrists and place his hands on my breasts. He's so still, I'm about to ask him if he's ever touched a set of boobs before, but before I can spew the words, his rigid posture sags and he starts kneading and squeezing.

I take that as my invitation to pay some attention to the stiffness in his shorts. I roughly palm the hard outline of his dick over his clothing, and in response, his breath hitches. With a groan, he pulls my hand away and lifts his hips to yank the shorts and his underwear down his thighs. As he does, he jostles me, and my head bangs into the headliner above me.

"Shoot, I'm sorry." Instantly, he's got a gentle hand on my head, and he's stroking the top of my updo. His lips stretch down in a grimace, showing off his perfect white teeth.

"'S'okay," I giggle, reaching up to free my hair from its pins.

"Here," he says. "Let me help." Gingerly, he helps me pull the bobby pins out. When most are removed, he massages my scalp, and holy hell, does it feel good after it's been up all day. The tender gesture causes tears to prick my eyes. I roll my lips and focus on my breathing to stave off the emotions coursing through me.

What started as a quick hookup in the back of a professional athlete's car is turning into a much deeper interaction.

"You're beautiful, Mel," Cordell whispers, bringing his lips to mine.

Not wanting him to see the vulnerability that's got me in a chokehold, I cast my eyes downward, but when I take in what's standing at attention between us, my lungs seize.

"Holy shit!"

I've only seen one other penis in my life, but I have no doubt I'll never see one this size again. Cordell laughs as he takes in my shocked eyes and round mouth.

"It's not funny." I swat at his shoulder. "There's no way—"

"It'll fit," he growls. "I'm going to take care of you. I promise we'll make it fit."

The authority in his voice sends sparks dancing through me. Desperate for that sensation to continue, I surge forward and slam my mouth to his in another searing kiss. While we go at it, I wrap my hand around his hard length. My heart trips over itself when I *feel* his girth. I'm about to arch back so I can examine closer when he pulls my thong to the side and his fingers find my wetness.

The heat there ignites at the touch, and all coherent thought leaves me.

"Mel," he whispers as he slides his digits through me, forward to circle my clit and then back again. Then he's pushing two fingers inside and pressing his thumb firmly against the spot that makes my eyes roll back in my head.

I have to clutch to his biceps to keep myself upright as the sensation overtakes me. Cordell shifts forward and guides me back until my shoulders hit the front seats. In this position, my back is arched and my breasts are on full display. Angling over me, he takes one of my nipples into his hot mouth and flicks his tongue over the sensitive tip in time with the pulsing of his fingers between my legs.

"This feel good?" he questions when his lips let go of one boob before moving to give the other some attention.

"Mm-hmm."

"You gonna come on my hand, Mel?"

Words fail me. A breathy moan is all I can manage. In response, he increases the tempo of his fingers and sucks on my left breast *hard*.

That's all it takes. A tremor courses through me, and the ripples of my orgasm take my breath away.

I haven't come in eighteen months.

Not that I've been counting or anything.

As the aftershocks fade, I peel my eyes open and find Cordell's attention locked on my face. It's dark in here, but there's no mistaking the hunger in his expression.

"You're breathtaking when you let go." He plants a soft kiss on my shoulder and then my lips.

Gah, he's being *sweet*. He's being sweet, and he's nowhere near as suave as I'd have imagined him to be. The combination of his genuine kindness and charm is like a warm blanket draped over my cold, dead heart.

*No, Mel. No time for stupid feelings. Stay on task.*

He's made me feel good. Now it's his turn.

I snatch up the condom from the seat beside him and sheathe his dick, determined to lead him to losing himself in the pleasure in the way he's done for me. Our breaths are labored, and we've both broken into a sweat. Already, the tinted windows are steamed up. Pulling my teeth between my lips, I tilt to one side and use my finger to draw an M on one. When I do the same to the happy trail below his navel, his lips tip up in a smile.

"Making your mark, huh?"

"Making it memorable." With that confession, I rise up on my knees and position myself to slide down his condom-covered length, still not certain it's possible to take all of him. Cordell keeps a tight grip on my hips, supporting me and encouraging me as I ease my way down a few centimeters at a time. The way he stretches me and the responding burn is almost cathartic. Like the sheer size of him will rid my vagina of the lingering traces of the man who occupied it last.

As I work myself lower, rocking my hips a little to accommodate him, Cordell hisses out a breath that turns into a grunt.

"Mel. You're so tight, babe."

A shot of anger hits me at the endearment, swirling with the desire still simmering in my belly in the most contradictory sensation. I open my mouth, ready to tell him that I'm no one's *babe*, but the sheepish smile he gives me is so sweet and unexpected I roll my lips between my teeth and swallow my retort. He gives me another tender kiss and slides his hands up my back to hold me in a hug, squishing my boobs into his hard chest.

This man feels so good, so different. Suddenly, I want to weep.

Instead, I grind my hips back and forth. He's still not fully seated, but the length I've managed to take will do. He lets me work myself over him, clutching his shoulders for leverage. His big hands grip my ass cheeks to guide my motion.

Then it's all instinct and flashes of heat. His hands on my hips. On my breasts. In my hair. Me setting the rhythm, panting, chasing that high once again.

After we both come—me first, because he's a gentleman like that—we quickly dress in silence. We part with one lingering kiss. There's no need to exchange personal information or to plan for future rendezvous. We both knew what this was from the moment we decided we wanted it.

"Thanks for helping me forget." I stand before him with my sandals dangling from my fingers and my head tilted back. My hair is no doubt a wreck, messy in that freshly fucked way.

"No problem, little pixie." One side of his lips quirks up, and he tosses me a wink.

At the last second, I do something reckless. Without letting myself think about the foolishness of it, I dig through my bag. I find an old receipt and a pen and jot my number down.

"Just...in case." With a trembling hand, I hold it out to him before I lose my nerve. "No pressure, you know?" I clear my throat of the vulnerability threatening to choke me, hoping beyond hope that he didn't pick up on it.

Keeping his attention trained on me, Cordell hits me with one final breathtaking smile and folds the receipt and slips it into the pocket of his shorts. "Thanks for making it memorable."

With a small smile in return and a tip of my chin, I spin and head toward my waiting car. Back to my life. Back to the uncertainty and sadness. Back to the defeat I can't shake.

For a little while tonight, I got to escape. These memories are a tiny light tucked deep inside my heart, giving me the smallest reprieve from the darkness that haunts me. As I slip into the driver's seat, I vow I'll keep that flame lit. I'll carry the experience with me always.

I'll forever cherish the memory of a sultry June night outside a dive bar in central Georgia, when I let a stranger who's not really a stranger shake loose the cobwebs on my soul. And on my lady-bits.

And hell, was it memorable.

# CHAPTER ONE

## MEL

I fell in love with Cordell Watkins for the first time on the sunbaked blacktop of Bennett Elementary, in tears over a skinned knee. Shawn McManess, notorious playground bully, had pushed me down after I refused to leave the four-square I was playing in. I was eight and small for my age, and Shawn was terrifying to most average-sized kids. That day, I got it in my head that I wouldn't back down. I'd been minding my own business, playing a made-up game in the four-square space after being abandoned by my brother and other friends the moment Shawn and his cronies entered the playground.

"Hey, McManess. Leave her alone."

Tears streaming, I looked up from where I was sprawled on the concrete, shielding my eyes from the sun.

"Here." The tall shadow looming over me held out a brown hand. "You okay?"

He pulled me to my feet, and as I found my balance, a sharp bolt of pain shot through my knee. Shifting most of my weight to my uninjured leg, I dipped my chin and assessed the wound. The scrape was embedded with dirt, and a small trickle of blood was running down my shin.

With a whimper, I turned to my knight in blue-jean armor, and only then did I realize who he was. My stomach bottomed out, and heat crept up my neck and into my cheeks. Angling myself away, I scrubbed my hands over my face, trying to erase the evidence of my tears. I did *not* want Cordell to see me cry like a baby over a little skinned knee.

It must've been lunch period at the middle/high school down the street. Sometimes the big kids came over to our playground with their lunches to sit at the metal picnic tables bordering the blacktop. Cordell stood tall, facing down Shawn with his arms crossed, angled so his body shielded mine from the bully.

"C'mon, Melanie. Let's get you a Band-Aid from the office." Luke Shipley, Cordell's best friend, stepped up and placed an affectionate hand on the top of my head. As I hobbled along beside him, I peeked over my shoulder at my hero. He was still puffed up, and he was leaning in close to Shawn's ear. I couldn't hear what was said, but the horror-filled look on Shawn McManess's face made it clear that he wouldn't bother me again.

A deep guffaw pulls me from my walk down memory lane. I straighten in the cushioned Adirondack chair and blink back to the present.

Turns out, that guffaw came from the subject of my nostalgic reverie.

Cordell is lounging in his own chair on the other side of the firepit in the Shipley backyard. He's got his elbows on his armrests, and he's laughing along with his mom and Luke's mom. With a long pull of my lukewarm beer, I shoot daggers at him. When he notices my attention, he has the audacity to grin and wink at me.

The look is an arrow to the chest every time. It's the same damn look he gave me when I left him in the parking lot *that* night.

Ugh. I refuse to give in to his charms.

Not that he's charming or anything.

The sun has almost gone to bed for the evening. Soon it will be hard to see each other. The firepit isn't lit, seeing as it's the end of May and already hot as balls, but Mrs. Shipley has arranged citronella candles within the circle to keep the pesky mosquitoes at bay.

"No questions about favorites tonight, Marshall?" Luke sits in the chair to my right.

His wife, my best friend, is perched on his lap wearing a serene smile, and he's rubbing soothing circles on her pregnant belly. Tessa's got one arm looped casually behind Luke's neck and both of her bare legs draped over one arm of the chair. They're ridiculously, disgustingly in love. And freaking adorable.

Without my permission, my eyes dart over to Cordell again. He's still watching me.

I empty the last dregs of my beer and set it on the ground beside my chair. "The inspiration hasn't hit yet." I rub my lips together and consider my options. The Favorites Game is my go-to when there's a lull in a conversation or to defuse a difficult one. It started in college as a way to pass the time on road trips with…

*Nope.* Not going there.

Going *there* will make me think about the postcard that's currently shoved between a stack of bills on my kitchen counter.

I've become a firm believer of the *out of sight, out of mind* mentality and an experienced practitioner, so there's a decent chance that postcard will stay hidden until I get around to paying those bills.

Which will be at the very last minute. Then I'll be forced to shove that damn postcard into the shoebox hidden at the back of my closet. With the rest of them.

"C'mon, Marshall. You haven't exhausted the list of possible categories after all this time, have you?" Cordell asks.

I give him a fake smile and follow it with an eye roll for good measure. "The possibilities are endless, Watkins."

In my periphery, Luke and Tessa are eyeing each other, but I ignore their scrutiny.

Cordell's hitting me with that stupid smirk again when Hannah shouts across the backyard. Luke and Tessa's seven-year-old is standing on the small pier that juts out into the Shipleys' pond. "Look, everyone."

Luke's dad is on the pier too, lighting leftover New Year's sparklers for her to twirl through the evening air.

"Careful, Banana," Luke hollers.

"I know!"

"Favorite patriotic movie?" Cordell questions the group. My heart squeezes a little painfully in my chest, and I tip forward in my seat.

I'm about to berate him for stealing *my* game when his mom, Ms. Rhonda, shouts, "*Forrest Gump.*"

"Nice, Ma." Cordell gives me a gloating smile that makes my blood boil.

I mean, it's not really *my* game. When my friends suggest categories, I never think twice about it. But he's doing it to ruffle my feathers, and like a sucker, I've played right into it.

"I'm going with *Air Force One.*" Mrs. Shipley sighs. "Harrison Ford is a dreamboat."

"Better not let Mr. Tom hear you say that, Ms. Marj." I regard Cordell and scrunch up my nose in a *so there* gesture.

I refuse to take his bait tonight.

"Hmm." That damn deep drawl is directed at me, but he pivots quickly. "What's it gonna be, Shipleys?"

"*Independence Day* for me. What about you, Mrs. Shipley?" Luke asks Tessa. His eyes are warm and so full of affection as he dips close to place a quick peck on her cheek.

See what I mean? Disgusting. And adorable.

Tessa tilts her head and purses her lips. She always has a hard time choosing, bless it. "Can I say *Legally Blonde*?"

Lighthearted groans and exclamations ring through the twilight sky.

"Baby," Luke chuckles, "how in the world is *Legally Blonde* a patriotic movie?"

"You know that scene in the movie where Paulette tells Elle that she looks like the Fourth of July?" She scans the circle in search of support. "C'mon. When she tells Elle that she makes her want a hot dog *real* bad?"

The entire group is silent, brows raised and breath held. Then, all at once, we fall into fits of laughter, Tessa included. The sound prompts Hannah and Mr. Shipley to start up the pier toward us.

When the laughter dies down, Tessa gets a far-off look. "A hot dog does sound good right now." She's absentmindedly rubbing her bump. "How am I already hungry again? We just ate two hours ago."

"You're growing a human, sweet girl." The look Ms. Marj gives her daughter-in-law is full of fondness.

"I'll fix you a hot dog, baby." Luke grasps her hips, ready to shift her off his lap.

"No, don't get up. I got you, T." I jump to my feet before she can stand from his lap. "Just ketchup, right?"

"Right. Thanks, Mel." She blows me a kiss.

I survey the group to see what else I can bring back for them, then I head up the wooden steps and cross the deck to the Shipleys' sliding door. The second I step into the cool house, gooseflesh pops up along my bare arms and legs.

The kitchen smells like the remnants of the Memorial Day meal Mr. Tom and Ms. Marj prepared for us. The food was covered and brought in from the deck before we ventured farther into the yard, but it's all sitting on the kitchen counters, so I find the leftover buns and get started on Tessa's request.

I'm reaching for the ketchup when the door slides open and Cordell steps into the kitchen.

My hackles raise instantly. I can't help it—my body goes into defensive mode in proximity to his.

"You need something?" My voice is snappy and sharp. I turn back to the plate I'm making for Tessa. I refuse to look at his gorgeous face for longer than I have to.

"Ma wanted potato salad." He's still standing just inside the door, not making any effort to go about getting it.

"I got it." With a huff, I uncover the bowl and heap a spoonful onto a paper plate, then wordlessly shove it across the island.

He doesn't pick it up. Instead, he slips his hands into his pockets and chuckles deep. "No red, white, or blue hair dye available for today?"

Ugh. The *nerve* of him. He teases me about my hair color relentlessly.

I tuck a bubble-gum pink strand behind my ear and get back to my task. I snatch up a handful of barbecue chips—Tessa's favorite—and drop them onto the plate.

Surely she'll want chips with her hot dog, right?

Cordell mumbles under his breath, the words too low and grumbly for me to discern.

"Excuse me?" I snap, squirting a line of ketchup along Tessa's hotdog a little too aggressively.

When I peer up at him, he's got his arms crossed and one hip propped against the other side of the island. He doesn't repeat himself. No, he just stands there, all tall and muscly and *infuriating*, and tips his lips in a smile that both enrages and hypnotizes me.

And now we're in a stare-off. Gah, I hate when we do this.

But I refuse to fold first.

I refuse to pull my focus from him and let him win, but his brown orbs soften as they roam my face and dip down to my red tank top. They harden when he locks eyes with me again, and a muscle in his cheek tics, like he's grinding his teeth.

Stalemate. Most of our stare-offs end this way.

A laugh from outside pierces the silence, and Cordell swivels his head that way, thus losing the contest. It takes all my self-control to not yell out a *ha!* He turns back to me and pulls in a breath like he's gearing up to speak, but I'm not interested in what he has to say, so I busy myself with straightening and rearranging the dishes on the counter.

Several silent seconds pass. I'm about to snatch up Tessa's plate and head back outside when he whispers "*Remember the Titans*" in a voice so low I almost question if I imagined the words.

All the air rushes from my lungs, and the plastic lid I was holding clatters to the island. The look on his face, the pleading eyes and the furrowed brow and the downturned mouth that's always smirking when he's focused on me, is now open and vulnerable.

That can't be right. I tilt my head, puzzled and still fighting to take in a full breath.

"My favorite patriotic movie. And my favorite sports movie."

*And your favorite* movie *movie*, I want to say.

My heart beats fast. But it feels heartsick, too. Like I've been punched in the chest by a weak man.

"I remember," I whisper.

His Adam's apple bobs with a heavy swallow as he regards me, and I'm transported back to that night. To his back seat. When I kissed that neck while I rode him.

When he helped me forget for a little while.

And then, quick as a blink, the memory of the very *next* time I saw Cordell Watkins flashes through my mind. It's enough to make me repeat, louder and harsher, "*I remember.*"

"Mel," he says. My name is a plea. He *never* calls me Mel. It's always Marshall or some exasperating term mocking my five-one height.

But no. I will not let him soften me. Not about *this*.

"I remember, Watkins. Unlike *some* people." Snarky Mel is getting her mojo back after a momentary slip.

"Your hair was *magenta*, for Christ's sake." Ah. Now Irate Cordell is joining the party.

"I don't care if it was *rainbow*." I fist my hands at my sides.

He tracks the movement, and his lips twitch, like my anger entertains him.

The *nerve* of this guy. My pulse throbs so hard my ears pound with the rhythm.

I refuse to let him laugh at my indignation, damn it. It's beyond childish, but nevertheless, I react, using ammunition within reach. I dip my hand into Ms. Marj's bowl of potato salad and fling it across the island.

The moment I release it, I suck in a sharp breath.

His eyes widen in disbelief and his jaw unhinges.

With my clean hand, I cover my mouth to stifle the cackle that threatens to escape. The glob of potato salad smacked him on one side of those damn kissable lips and caught on the roughness of his short beard.

"Did you just. Throw. Potato salad. At my face?" The movement of his lips causes a chunk of potato to drop onto his pristine red Eagles football T-shirt.

A squeak of laughter sneaks through my fingers. Garnering all my control, I inhale through my nose, lower my hand, and adopt my most stoic expression. I can't hold it for long, though. Not at the sight of his indignation. So I roll my lips together and give my head a little shake.

"You little—" He grabs a bottle of mustard and aims it at me.

With a stomp, I shake my head. "Don't you *dare*."

Cordell barks out a menacing laugh and squeezes the bottle, sending a stream of mustard shooting across the island. His aim is true. The sludge hits me in the chest, covering the *Firecracker* emblazoned across my tank top.

"You did *not*," I say through clenched teeth. The scent of mustard fills my nose, and I try not to gag.

I *hate* mustard.

"I totally did." He lifts his chin, smug.

In retaliation, I snatch the bottle of ketchup and step around the corner of the island, getting in closer range. Cordell holds both hands up in surrender, but I give that damn bottle a violent squeeze and take delight in the spurt of red that shoots out and covers his shirt.

I throw my head back and crow at the murderous look on his face. That is, until something cold and slimy hits my chest and slides down the neck of my tank top and into my bra. With a gasp, I snap my neck down, eyes wide. Cordell's hand is hovering over a pan of red Jell-O.

"You. Ass."

From there, it's a free-for-all. I fling a handful of baked beans, and he lobs marshmallows from the S'mores we made on the grill. When he runs out of that ammo, he resorts to shaking a can of whipped topping and rushing me. He gets close enough to squirt a dollop on my face before I chuck sliced pickles and tomatoes at him.

We're so caught up in our quest to one-up each other that we don't hear the sound of the back door sliding open. Only Tessa's "Oh!" is enough to startle us out of our madness. My best friend's eyes are the size of saucers as she inspects her in-laws' trashed kitchen. Shame instantly sours my gut. In what feels like slow motion, her face crumples, and tears stream down her cheeks.

*Oh shit, oh shit, oh shit.*

Tessa's disappointment in me is like a knife to the heart.

The only thing worse is the disappointment of my parents and my brother.

Struggling to breathe through the self-disgust that swamps me, I sneak a peek at Cordell. His head hangs and his shoulders slump. He looks as disgraced as I feel.

"Tessa, baby, did you—" She turns toward the sound of Luke's voice. At the threshold, he freezes and scans her tear-stained face. "Why are you crying?" Without waiting for a response, he pulls her into his arms and murmurs in her ear. When he looks up again, ready to search for the cause of his wife's devastation, I'm sure, his face morphs from concerned to shocked. "What. The. Fuck?"

If looks could kill, his best friend and I would be six feet under.

"Luke, Tessa, we're so sorry." Cordell is so damn sincere I can't even balk when he has the nerve to speak for me. His eyes are glassy and his face is etched in painful regret as he lowers his chin to his chest. "We'll get it all cleaned up."

Tessa steps back from Luke, wiping her cheeks. "Hormones." She shrugs and pastes on a watery smile. "I need a minute in the restroom."

Luke squeezes her shoulders, looking torn between following her and staying to read us the riot act. He settles for kissing Tessa's temple and letting her go.

Silently fuming, he tracks her movement, and once she's out of earshot, he scrubs a hand down his face.

"Please explain to me what—"

"Dad, Nana sent me to check on y'all." Hannah's eyes almost bug out of her head as she surveys the scene. "Whoa."

"Banana, go check on your mama in the bathroom."

She snaps to it, likely understanding how serious her father is based on his dark tone and murderous expression. She does sneak a wide-eyed peek at our mess as she heads to the hall, but she doesn't dawdle.

"Luke—" I start. Damn it. There is absolutely no good excuse for what we've done. I look at Cordell again, but he's watching his best friend like he's waiting for the hammer to drop. I take a careful side-step toward the hallway, then another. I'm about to make a run for it when Luke's gruff voice stops me.

"Uh-uh, missy, you're not going anywhere. Please tell me *why* my parents' kitchen looks like a couple of three-year-olds had a food fight."

Cordell clears his throat. "Marshall and I got into an argument, and we both reacted childishly. It escalated." He sweeps a hand out. "But I assure you that we will clean up every drop of this mess, and we'll never let something like this happen again. I'm so sorry, man."

"Y-yeah." I swallow past the lump in my throat. "So sorry, Luke. Really." I'm so distraught over upsetting Tessa that I might cry. And I haven't been a crier in over ten years, so...

Luke heaves out a sigh and drops his chin, shaking his head. With his hands on his hips, he pins each of us with a stare. "You guys are our best fucking friends. We love y'all like family, but *this*"—he waves a hand—"is ridiculous."

"You're right," Cordell agrees without delay.

When Luke raises his brows my way, I nod.

"Now." He huffs a breath. "I'm going back out there to make sure my parents, and *your mother*," he emphasizes, homing in on Cordell, "don't come in here."

I can't look at him any longer. His disappointed frown is like an anchor tied around my neck, pulling me down. So I turn and get to work cleaning. Cordell does the same.

After what feels like an eternity, Luke speaks again, breaking the silence. "Listen."

With a roll of paper towels in hand, I turn.

"I mean it. Figure your shit out." He gestures between us

with his hand, then with another deep sigh, he exits through the sliding door.

The silence returns. I wordlessly hand Cordell the broom out of the Shipleys' laundry room before I find the disinfectant wipes under the sink. We work quietly but efficiently, and the kitchen is almost back to normal by the time Tessa and Hannah return from the bathroom, hand in hand. Tessa gives me a weak smile as she places a package of baby wipes on the island on their way to the door, but neither of them says a word to us as they join the others out back.

I owe her a *huge* apology. And a hot dog. Or twenty.

I'm loath to show my embarrassed face outside, so I put the leftovers away. Cordell follows suit. We don't speak. I can't even bring myself to look at him, but we manage to get the room cleaned up. The only things left on the island are the cupcakes I brought and Ms. Rhonda's Crock-Pot of Rotel dip.

"Marshall." Cordell finally breaks the silence. "He's right, you know."

I jut out a hip and cross my arms. "I *know*."

*Gah, grow up, Mel.*

*Why* is it so hard for me to take the high road with him?

He nods a couple times, his lips pressed together. Then he opens the package of baby wipes Tessa left for us. He removes one and slowly approaches me. He keeps his hands out in front of him, as if I'm a wounded animal and he's showing me he's not here to hurt me. When he's within arm's reach, he gently takes hold of my right bicep, which forces me to relax my stance. Then, he wipes the remnants of our food fight from my arm. The cool, wet cloth sliding down my skin makes me shiver.

Or maybe it's the heat of his touch?

I blink at his food-stained T-shirt. Why is he being so nice to me? Even with our friends' admonishment and our own shame hanging over us, I'm surprised he could find it within himself to help me.

My breath stutters as he moves the cloth to the skin above my tank. He's focused on his task, but when he steps closer, his warmth soaks into me. After a moment, he swallows thickly and drags his attention from my chest up to my face. We make eye contact for a second, but I don't linger there. On those dark, soulful irises.

They see too much.

He sighs, his warm breath brushing my skin, and tips my chin up. At the contact, another shiver racks my body. "You got something...right...there," he whispers, wiping at a spot on my jaw. His hand falls away, but he doesn't step back as he searches my face for more stray smears. We lock eyes again, and like that night so many years ago, when his gaze dips to my lips, my *lady-bits* sit up and take notice.

*Shit*. Glamma again. I'm going to demand she start using a better euphemism.

But I'm not the same girl I was ten years ago. I force a swallow and take a much-needed step back.

"Thanks." I intend for the word to sound genuine, because that's how I mean it. But in response, Cordell's jaw tightens and he returns to the other side of the island.

A safe distance away.

He reaches for one of the strawberry shortcake cupcakes I made for the cookout and downs it in three bites. "These aren't half bad."

I snort. "Gee, thanks again." I want to follow up with another snarky comment, but I think better of it. Not after the shit we just pulled.

"Marshall." His deep, gruff voice vibrates through me. "I have a proposal for you."

My heart stutters at that word, but I chide myself for even going there.

Not *that* kind of proposal, idiot.

"I propose that you and I," he flicks his wrist between us, "spend some time together."

I open my mouth to protest—

"Just..." He sighs. "Just as friends."

My chest aches at the thought. Friends? How is that even possible? "Why?"

A humorless laugh escapes him. "So we don't have a repeat of *this*."

"Well." I'm feeling petulant again, but I tamp it down. "I need more details."

His lips curve in a smile, like maybe he's pleased, and a little surprised, that I'm willing to hear him out. "The two of us will spend some time together. Nothing extreme. Just a cup of coffee or a beer at Fuzzy's. We get to know one another a little better."

It takes all my self-control not to remind him that we already know each other *biblically*.

"And hopefully we find some common ground so that our friends don't disown us."

I chuckle. "You mean like Joey and Janice's Day of Fun?"

He cocks a brow. "What?"

"From *Friends*?" How does this man not get that reference? *Everyone* gets a good *Friends* reference.

"Ahh. Yeah, not a *Friends* watcher, I'm afraid." He shrugs.

"Well," I scoff. "You're missing out."

"You're a big fan, huh?"

"Sure. I fall asleep to episodes every night. It's a comfort thing for me." The words are out before I realize who I'm confessing them to, and my stomach sinks. Shit.

He shoots me one of his signature smug smiles. But before I can snark about it, he says, "So tell me about Joey and Janice's Day of Fun."

I give him a brief rundown of how Joey doesn't like Chandler's girlfriend, so he agrees to spend a day with her to get to know her better. I leave out the part where Joey still hates Janice by the end of the day. No need to taint our tentative truce with bad Janice juju.

When I'm finished, he says, "So yeah. Like that. Let's do this for our friends, Marshall. Luke's right—we need to figure this out, especially with baby Shipley's debut right around the corner."

Joy crashes over me at the mention of the little one. I love that baby already, even if I am hella frustrated that the little goober's parents are waiting until the birth to find out its sex.

"So, olive branch?" He extends his hand. His eyes are sparkling, full of too much mirth.

I have a sneaking suspicion that I'll regret this, but for Tessa, I'll do just about anything. Including agreeing to an armistice with the guy who's been a thorn in my side for years. "Olive branch," I huff, giving his hand a begrudging shake.

He holds on longer than necessary and uses my trapped hand to pull me closer. "This is gonna be fun, Marshall." With a wink, he steps back, and before I know it, he's laughing with the others in the backyard while I'm standing alone in the Shipleys' kitchen with my jaw on the floor.

# CHAPTER TWO

## CORDELL

"**C**oach, you're staring at that phone like you've got woman trouble."

I look up in time to catch the teenager who's too nosy for his own good get elbowed in the ribs by one of his teammates as they make their way around the track.

"Mind your business, Jones. And that'll be three extra laps for you." Clay, my assistant coach, huffs out an impatient breath and turns back to me. He assesses me until the last of the boys are out of earshot. "Is it?" He leans in close. "Woman trouble, I mean?"

I give him my best *are you serious* face. "Like I'd tell you."

"Ain't that the truth. You're like freaking Fort Knox." He gives me a wry smile, but his tone is easygoing. He knows better than to push about my romantic pursuits, even though we're good friends. Unfortunately for Luke, he's the only friend I trust to carry that burden.

Even if I haven't been all that forthcoming regarding a certain *encounter* in my past.

"You think Phillips will give track to Thompson now that Coach Pruitt's retired?"

"You gonna tell her you want it?" Clay's got a family. I have no doubt he would appreciate the extra stipend.

"Psh." He snorts. "Frannie would kill me. She thinks I'm gone too much as it is."

I dip my chin. "I get it." Even if I can't empathize with trying to keep a wife happy.

I'm thirty-six and have never been married. Much to the dismay of my mother and my sister.

Coaching in a small town is a heck of a lot harder than most people think. And it's especially hard on those who have families. Scheduling time—for strength training, practice, drills, maintenance, travel—all while trying to balance a healthy home life, is difficult.

Clay goes back to observing the boys on the track, and while his attention is trained somewhere other than me, I take the opportunity to return to the text message that's been bugging me since I received it five minutes ago.

The sight of Mel's name on my phone's screen stirs up all sorts of emotions, most of them confusing. Even now, several days after the incident, a wave of mortification still hits me when I think about the way we engaged in an actual food fight like a couple of bratty, obnoxious children. We haven't spoken since, even though we're supposed to be finding a peaceful way forward.

Clay blows the whistle, and the boys head for the locker room.

"Jones!" I holler. "You heard Coach Reeves. I believe you owe us some extra laps."

Darius hangs his head but trots back to the track without argument.

"The attitude on that one might be the death of me." Clay slaps my shoulder, then jogs toward the field house. Halfway there, he turns, but he doesn't stop moving. "Before I forget," he yells, "Frannie's making lasagna on Thursday. You in?"

"You know it." Heck yeah, I'm in. Frannie's homemade lasagna might be the most delicious thing I've ever put in my mouth. My mouth waters just thinking about it.

As I amble back to the field house behind Clay and the boys, I pull my phone out of my pocket again and navigate to Mel's text message. The name I've listed her under in my contacts makes me snicker every time. I check on Jones's progress and stop at the sidewalk that leads inside.

ANGRY PIXIE

I guess we need to make good on our promise. Even though your face makes me want to pluck my nose hairs out one by one.

So much for olive branches.

Mel Marshall remains a contradiction, just like her appearance that June night all those years ago. Part of me wishes she would *get the hell over it* already and forgive me. But I can't deny that I love to rile her up, to see that fire in her eyes. I'm never more alive than when she's spitting mad and lobbing insults at me. Going toe-to-toe with her appeals to my competitive nature. And I'll take her venom over the sad, lost look she had in her eyes in that bar. I can take whatever she wants to hurl my way.

Except this time, our friends got caught in the crossfire. The memory of the looks on their faces still makes me sick with regret.

I've sent numerous *I'm sorry* texts to Luke and Tessa since Monday night. Shoot, I've even considered writing a formal apology to Ms. Marj and Mr. Tom, even though I'm pretty sure Luke didn't fill them in on what went down in their kitchen.

Let's meet for a beer at Fuzzy's. Tonight. 7 p.m.

> And your face makes me want to run
> backward through a cornfield.

So flipping childish, I know. These text insults started up a couple of years ago, when Mel was desperate to help Tessa mend a breakup with Luke. She'd been forced to contact me so we could coordinate a plan to get the two of them to speak to each other. Ever since, we've gone back and forth, sending the most elaborate and detailed insults we can come up with.

ANGRY PIXIE

[middle finger emoji]

By the time Darius Jones is finished running his extra laps, I'm stepping into the field house with the hope that the rest of the day passes quickly. I can't wait to face off with the woman who drives me to madness.

~

Fuzzy's Tavern is surprisingly crowded for a Tuesday night. Even so, I secure a booth along the wall. Before Mel arrives, I order drinks—Terrapin for me, Blue Moon with an orange wedge for her—and sit back.

She's going to be late. She's always late, but with me, she'll be ridiculously late.

I scroll through social media to kill time, stopping at the new pictures my sister has posted of her wife and kids. Cass and Kelly have been married for almost ten years and are the proud adoptive parents of a boy and a girl. They live in Atlanta. They're only three hours from Bennett, but Ma and I don't get to see them as much as we'd like. Thank God for the technology that keeps us connected even when we're not together.

I'm commenting on a picture of my eight-year-old nephew Ryan—he's grinning at the camera with his hands covered in paint—when I feel a presence beside me. I check the time on my phone. Seven twenty-three.

"Don't even say it, Watkins."

She's still on her feet, so I finish typing out my comment, hit submit, and close down the app before acknowledging her.

Letting her stew in her annoyance.

Noting the way my heart rate increases.

The sensation that floods me in her presence is the same one I used to get when I stood in a huddle with my teammates before a game. That thrill of adrenaline coursing through my blood, the nervous energy ready to be converted into pure power—ready to absorb every hit, make every catch, beat every opponent.

"You're late." I say it anyway.

"*Ughhh.*" She drags the sound out.

Only then do I turn my attention to her.

Mel stands by the table, hands on hips in her ready-to-fight stance. Her left leg is straight and planted out to the side.

I school my expression as I give her a once-over, being sure to telegraph pure boredom, knowing that will fire her up even more.

Dang, she's so fun to piss off.

Her tiny toenails are painted a neon orange and sticking out of her beloved Birks. She's wearing a pair of plum yoga tights that accentuate every curve of her small frame and a loose black tank top that says *Zen AF* above a minimalistic lotus flower. The straps of her lilac sports bra peek out from beneath. I swear those straps will be the death of me. The light dusting of freckles across her nose and the apples of her cheeks are evidence of time spent in the sunshine, and the tiny gold loop in her left nostril flashes in the dim lighting as she releases an angry breath.

"Sit, Marshall."

Her eyes narrow as she flings her patchwork bag onto the

seat and slides in after it. When she notices the orange slice on the rim of her glass, she huffs. "No orange wedge."

"I remember. Sunshine and happiness, right?"

She removes the fruit and chucks it at my beer. My reflexes are primed, so I yank my glass away before she can make the shot. But my motion causes some of the beer to slosh over the side and soak my hand.

"Ha!" she crows.

I roll my eyes and hunch forward to lick the beer off my hand with a swipe of my tongue.

Mel's eyes track every movement. Her throat bobs in a hard swallow, and she nervously tucks a strand of her shoulder-length tickle-me-pink hair behind an ear that holds a couple of small studs and a tiny loop at the top.

I give her a satisfied smile, and then it's her turn to roll her eyes.

"Didn't you learn your lesson about throwing food the other night?"

"Didn't *you* learn that you're about as useful as a screen door in a submarine?"

"I bet you've been saving that one for days. Probably have a list copied down from the internet." I pluck a napkin from the dispenser on the table and clean up the rest of my spill.

Mel juts her chin. "Let's get this over with, shall we?"

"Why the rush? Got a hot date later?"

She crosses her arms over her perky breasts. "Like my love life is any of your business."

An irrational spike of jealousy stabs at me at the thought of Marshall having a *love life*. She brings her beer to her lips and raises a brow, daring me to comment. I won't give her the satisfaction.

So I issue my own challenge. "Go fishing with me."

Her mouth falls open. "Wh-what?"

Now it's my turn to hide behind my beer glass. To keep her waiting. To keep her guessing.

To shore up my bravado.

"Go fishing with me." I affect a confident yet nonaggressive tone.

"Why?" She's popped up so she's sitting ramrod straight with her hands at her sides. If I had to guess, she's sitting on them. She's flustered. It's almost as adorable as when she spits nails at me.

"We told our best friends we'd try to find some common ground."

She's wearing a confused frown now, but she hasn't shot me down yet, so I continue.

"Let's share our favorite hobbies with each other. It'll be like..." I snap my fingers when it comes to me. "Like Cordell and Mel's day of fun."

Mel crosses her arms over her chest and scrutinizes me. It takes all my self-control not to let my eyes wander down to glimpse what this position does to her cleavage.

"What do you say?" *Please say yes, please say yes.*

"You think I'd let you take me out in your boat so you can throw me to the gators?"

A niggle of disappointment worms its way in. "C'mon, Marshall. Don't be so dramatic."

A little too loud, she scoffs. "Dramatic?" She snaps her mouth shut and peeks around, sheepish. "I'm not *dramatic*."

"Exactly what a dramatic person would say."

"Okay, fine," she relents. "Maybe I'm a little—"

I raise my brows and open my mouth, ready to correct her, but she extends a pointer finger in my direction as a warning.

"A *little* dramatic." It's pretty dim in the bar, but I swear her lips twist up in a smirk that wants to be a smile.

*Dang, that feels good.*

"Maybe a little. But it sure keeps life interesting." I fight the urge to wink at her.

She takes inventory of me, her striking hazel eyes roving over my face. Finally, she takes a deep breath and blows it out again. "If I agree to this fishing time, do you promise not to throw me in the water, even if I piss you off?"

"Marshall, I have no doubt you'll piss me off." When she scoffs, I rush to continue. "But of course I wouldn't throw you in." And I swear to God, I *can't help* but follow that with "because the gators would instantly throw you back."

Mel sits still as a statue, but with the way her eyes flit back and forth, it's clear her gears are grinding for a comeback. I love the look in her eyes when her brain lands on the right one. But instead of saying it out loud, she snatches her phone out of her bag and gets to tapping on the screen. Moments later, my phone buzzes on the table.

ANGRY PIXIE

Your face makes me want to slather myself in chum and dive into a gator congregation headfirst.

"Congregation?" I question.

"That's what a group of alligators is called."

I cock a brow at her ridiculousness.

She drops her phone into her purse again and holds her head high. "Look it up if you don't believe me."

I close my eyes and pray for the patience I need to keep this from escalating. We were on the precipice of coming to an agreement about fishing, and I *had* to ruin it.

"Cupcakes."

That one word brings me back to the moment. I open my eyes, instantly focusing on her heart-shaped face. "What about cupcakes?"

"That'll be my activity. We'll bake cupcakes together."

"Can I pick the flavor?"

"Of course not," she huffs. But she twists her lips, again trying not to smile.

"You promise you won't put something gross in mine? Or something...that would cause issues...after?"

"Like a laxative?"

My stomach sinks just a little. "It's scary that your mind instantly landed *there*."

"My mind can be a scary place, Watkins." She smirks again. "But yes, I promise I won't poison you."

"Okay, then. So on Cordell and Mel's day of fun, we'll start the day on the river and end it with a baking lesson."

"Okay," she breathes. "Deal." Her eyes sparkle as she rolls her lips together.

I lean back and relax my shoulders, relishing the sense of accomplishment filling my body. We sit in tentative silence for a few minutes, enjoying our beers and the people-watching that is the prime draw of a small-town bar.

"When are we doing this?" Mel breaks the silence, twisting her almost-empty glass on the wooden tabletop.

"Sunday?" Her yoga studio is closed on Sundays, and I don't have any weekend plans.

"This Sunday?"

"Sure." That familiar prickle of excitement that hits when I know she'll be around courses down my arms.

"Early, I'm guessing?" She watches me over her glass as she downs the last swig of her Blue Moon.

"Yeah." I dip my chin. "We'll have to go early if we want to catch something. It gets too hot midday at this time of the year."

"What time, exactly? And don't tell me a fake time thinking it'll keep me from being late."

A bark of laughter escapes me. "I know you're going to be late."

She gives me a half-hearted eye roll. "Ugh. *Fine*. What time do you want me to be there so I can be sure to arrive thirty minutes later?"

"I'll pick you up, Marshall. Be ready at six."

"*Six*?" She shakes her head. "Fuck a duck." The second the words leave her mouth, she flinches and dips her chin.

I tense, too, instantly hit with a memory of a night long ago. Her hazel eyes raise to mine, swimming with a mixture of hurt and disappointment.

My natural reaction is to apologize, but I don't want to relive the memories of the reason we've been sniping at each other for the last nine years, and I can guarantee she doesn't either. We need to move forward rather than wallow in the past.

But if she doesn't forgive me for that one moment of idiocy, I don't know that we can ever truly move on.

Mel clears her throat and looks everywhere but at me. "I think it's time for me to head home."

I need to let it go. For tonight, at least.

"Yeah, I'm right behind you."

She gives me a smile that doesn't reach her eyes. "I'll see you at six thirty on Sunday morning, right?"

I release a breath. She's not backing out of our deal. The wave of relief that hits me keeps me from making an issue of her little time change. "Yeah, sounds good, Marshall."

Mel stands, but she hesitates by the booth, like maybe she has something more to say. Instead, she pulls out her phone. "Later, Watkins." With that, she heads out of the bar.

I watch her every step, admiring the way her tight backside looks in those painted-on leggings. I'm only pulled out of my stupor when my phone buzzes on the table.

ANGRY PIXIE

Thanks for the beer. [middle finger emoji]

I tap out a reply.

> Your face makes me want to take a bath in jalapeño juice.

I expect a quippy comeback, but I'm pleasantly surprised—shocked, really—when her response pops up.

ANGRY PIXIE

> Nice one. [thumbs up emoji]

But then she follows that up with another text.

ANGRY PIXIE

> Jerkface.

Ah, well. Progress is progress, I guess.

# CHAPTER THREE

"No running by the pool, boys."

I lower my shades to watch my father sweep one boy up into his arms while my brother goes after his twin. Ollie makes it a couple more feet before Mark reaches him. The loud giggles he lets loose as his dad swings him up into the air brings a goofy grin to my lips and causes a dull ache in my chest.

Three-year-old twin boys are a good time.

Especially because they're not mine.

"If he barfs that sandwich all over you, don't come cryin' to me." Betty Jane Marshall, better known as Glamma, oversees the chaos from her shady spot.

With a chuckle, Mark continues the game of toss-the-toddler.

"Me, too, Pop Pop. Toss me." Never one to be left out, Owen wiggles in my dad's arms and begs him to copy Mark's motions with Ollie.

"I'll do you one better, little man." Dad laughs and swings Owen toward the pool, where my mom is ready to catch him.

After a count of three, Dad tosses Owen into the water,

where his gigi is waiting with open arms. Mom sticks close to him as he dog-paddles through the water.

"My turn," Ollie shouts. Mark hands him over to my dad, then takes a running leap so he can do a cannonball into the deep end, making sure to splash Lisa and me.

"Mark." Lisa sits up straight on her pool lounger and scowls.

My brother breaches the surface and blows his wife a kiss. "Love you, too, babe." With a grin, he makes his way to the middle of the pool so Dad can toss a surprisingly patient Ollie to him.

"Ugh, your brother," With a grunt, Lisa settles on her lounger again.

I hide a smile behind my hand. She always refers to him that way—*your brother*—when he's being irritating.

With a sigh, I revel in the way the sunshine warms the cool droplets of water on my skin, content to let the sounds of a family pool day carry away my stress.

"How's Tessa doing?" Lisa asks. "How far along is she now?"

"She's great. She's five and a half months, I think."

"And they're still team green?"

I press my lips together and give her a deadpan look. "Unfortunately." I'm still salty that Luke and Tessa are making us wait to find out if baby Shipley is a boy or a girl.

Lisa chuckles. "What if Mark and I had gone that route? Can you imagine what your brother would have been like if he couldn't plan out every last detail?"

"I would've disowned y'all, for sure," I tell her. "I can't believe it's already been three *years* since those sweet boys arrived."

She adjusts the tie holding her light brown hair in a messy bun on the top of her head. "Sometimes it feels like yesterday. And then other times it feels like a lifetime ago. Especially when I think about how much they've changed." Her voice takes on that nostalgic tone all moms get when lamenting their children growing up.

"And you're sure you're done? Please, *please* give me a niece," I whine.

The snort she lets out in response is unladylike. "There's a chance you'd end up with *two* nieces, and you know Mr. Cautious isn't one to play the odds. I'm afraid you'll have to be the one to give Pop Pop and Gigi a granddaughter."

I shoot her a glare, but she can't see it behind my Ray Bans. "There's a greater chance of Glamma giving them a granddaughter at this point."

"C'mon, Mel." She sighs. "You'll meet that special person and have a family. I know it."

"Not happening, LiLi. We've been over this a million times. That life is not for me."

Lisa crosses her arms over her blue one-piece. "I refuse to accept this."

"Refuse all you want. It's not happening." I can't keep bitterness from bleeding into my voice. Even though I decided many years ago to never let myself fall in love again, the ache has never gone away.

"Are you still seeing Mikey what's-his-name?"

"We were never *seeing* each other. It was a mutually beneficial arrangement," I remind her. "But we decided to move on a couple months ago." The friends-with-bennies situation with a Bennett firefighter had run its course. We both got what we needed at the time—no-strings-attached hookups a couple of times a month. Enough to scratch the itch. There were no feelings involved, on either side, but Mikey's cousin wanted to set him up with her neighbor, and he didn't feel right continuing our trysts. I was completely fine with moving on.

"Let me guess: he got too clingy."

I can't blame her for her assumption. That specific quality has caused me to end a few of my arrangements in the past.

"Nope. It had just run its course." I drop my head back against the chair and watch as Owen jumps off the edge of the pool into my dad's arms.

She picks up her tumbler and takes a sip of water. "Now what?"

"Now Fernando will have to work overtime."

Shocked, she spits the water out with so much force a couple drops land on my arm. "Fernando," she whisper-shouts. "I *forgot* about him. He's still kicking?"

"He is," I chuckle. I probably shouldn't have told my sister-in-law that I named my vibrator. I blame that little confession on too many daiquiris. Regardless, her reaction brings me back to the contentedness I'd found sitting out here in the sun, surrounded by the people I love.

We settle back into silence. The heat of the day lulls me into a drowsy state. My eyelids become heavy, and my limbs relax. About the time I'm starting to drift off, I'm assaulted by a giant splash of cold water. I jolt upright and scramble to wipe the water from my shades, sputtering the whole time.

Mark is laughing his head off, leaning both arms on the edge of the pool, as we grumble in annoyance.

"Not cool, bro." Swiping up the towel I was using as a pillow, I pat my arms and legs dry.

"You two looked way too cozy over here." He grins at his wife and takes a step back. "Our sons have requested your presence in the pool."

"Duty calls." With that, Lisa is up and out of her chair.

Remaining upright, I watch my brother and his precious family play together in the water. It's then that I realize my parents have disappeared. Ugh. I roll my eyes at the thought. It's become somewhat of an unspoken family joke that if Greg and Beth Marshall disappear from a family function at the same time, they'll reappear in about twenty minutes, flushed and giggling.

"Melanie. Come keep me company."

My eighty-two-year-old grandmother whisks a Greg Marshall Realty fan back and forth in front of her face. She's wearing sunglasses and a wide-brimmed sun hat even though she's sitting under a large patio umbrella. Across the width of the pool, she purses her coral-painted lips in annoyance when I don't immediately hop to it.

I haul myself out of my chair, slip on my flip-flops, and join her at the table. "You're not too hot are you, Glamma?"

"I'm fine," she huffs. "I'll go in when your parents come back out." She tilts her head in a knowing way that makes me grin. "What were you and Lisa up to over there? Girl talk?" Her nosiness makes my grin grow wider. One of our favorite pastimes is gossip and girl talk.

"Auntie Mel, look it," a tiny voice yells from the pool.

Mark's family is now engaged in a game of chicken. The boys are each perched on the shoulders of a parent, and they've got their hands locked in battle.

I'm not sure which twin demanded my attention, so I take a gamble and holler, "You can take him, Whosie," using the nickname I gave Ollie when he was a tiny, wrinkly baby.

"Dat was me, Mel-Mel!" Owen shrieks when his brother pushes him with enough force that he loses his grip on Mark's hair.

"Sorry, Whatsie."

Both boys burst into giggles.

"Tell me what boy has your eye these days, Melanie." Glamma's demand has the smile slipping from my face.

Glamma is the only person who's called me Melanie since I was ten and insisted on going by Mel only. If anyone else tried, they'd get a swift punch to the bicep.

"No boys, Glam. I'm flying solo, as usual."

Though she's familiar with my philosophy on finding love

and settling down, she continues to try her damnedest to convince me otherwise.

"Flying solo is a lonely life, dear." She places her soft, papery hand on top of mine on the table. My eyes burn at the tenderness of the gesture.

What the *hell* is wrong with me these days? This is the second time this week emotions have almost gotten the best of me. With a thick swallow, I force them back to where they belong—dead and buried.

I turn my hand over and lace my fingers with hers. "I don't need anyone else when I've got you. And those knuckleheads." I tilt my head toward the pool. "I'm set for life, Glam."

"Melanie," she tuts. "You know in your heart of hearts that won't be enough."

I open my mouth to protest, but she jerks her chin in silent command not to interrupt.

"I won't be here forever. Nor will your parents. Mark and Lisa will always want you around, but they're each other's safe harbor. Who's going to be yours, darling?"

With a familiar stubbornness settling over me, I keep my jaw locked tight. She won't buy what I'm selling anyway. For eleven years, I've been determined to not let myself get swept away by the idea of loving another person again. I *do* believe that some people are meant to fall in love and spend their lives together. How could I not when I've spent my life watching my parents? Mark and Lisa are fortunate in that way, too. Hell, I had a front-row seat to Tessa and Luke's love story. But I've learned the hard way that love doesn't guarantee a happy ending. That some people will not get the white picket fence.

Mark and Lisa haul the boys out of the pool and bundle them up in big, fluffy beach towels to join us at the table. My chest heats and expands when Owen rests his head against his dad's chest, his light brown hair sticking in clumps to his soft ivory skin.

"You gonna join us for breakfast before we head out tomorrow, Mel-Mel?" Mark asks. "Mom's making pancakes."

My mouth waters at just the mention of my mom's perfectly fluffy buttermilk pancakes. My heart aches then, when the last part of his question hits me. My brother and his family are leaving after their over-too-soon weekend visit.

I want to soak in all the time I can with them, but tomorrow is Cordell and Mel's day of fun. I owe it to Tessa to not back out.

"I can't, I'm sorry." I hold my breath, hoping like hell they won't ask why.

I should know better.

"What big plans do *you* have on a Sunday morning?" My brother regards me from across the table, rubbing both hands up and down Owen's arms.

I can't lie to them. Glamma can spot a fib at fifty paces, and Mark has always had an uncanny ability to tell when I'm bending the truth. He never let me get away with mischief when we were kids unless he was involved in it with me.

I tilt my chin, hoping nonchalance will deter my family from probing deeper. "I'm going fishing."

Mark's not having it. "*You?* Fishing?" He barks out a laugh. "With who?"

I look from Mark to Glamma to Lisa. They're all homed in, expectant.

Shoulders slumping, I sigh. "With Cordell Watkins."

"The coach?" Glamma asks.

At the same time, Mark says, "The football player?"

"Yes?" I don't mean for it to come out as a question. Nevertheless, my voice pitches high at the end.

Mark narrows his eyes, assessing me. Glamma sits straighter. Her expression is inscrutable behind her sunglasses. Lisa hugs Ollie close, her lips twisted like she's trying not to smile.

I need to nip this in the bud ASAP.

"We're friends—"

"But you're *not* friends." Lisa knows about my contempt for Cordell and the reason for it. She *doesn't* know, though, that it's ramped up since Luke and Tessa's relationship has forced us to interact more.

"We're friend-adjacent," I insist, tugging my ponytail tighter.

Lisa's blue eyes track my movements, and I swear to God, they freaking *twinkle* in amusement.

"Why aren't you friends?" Mark asks, clueless.

Lisa swoops in for the save. "I was just teasing her, babe." She shifts Ollie in her lap.

The sweet little guy's eyelids are heavy, and he's snuggled into his mama, moments from conking out. Owen's already snoozing, his body starfished against my brother's chest.

"Fishing," Glamma says. "Just the two of you?" I wish I could see her eyes. I bet they're slitted with doubt.

"Yep." Before anyone can probe further, I blurt the first excuse that enters my mind. "I lost a bet, okay?"

My brother snort-laughs. "A bet? Over what?"

I'm sucking in a breath, ready to dig my hole of lies even deeper, when my parents appear. A blush stains my mom's cheeks, and my dad's salt-and-pepper hair is standing on end.

"Hope you two had a pleasant romp," Glamma says, her mouth a flat line. "Melanie needs our best fishing advice, so pull up a chair and let's school her before her date with that hunky football coach."

There's a brief pause, followed by an eruption of questions and comments.

∼

I'm going to need toothpicks to hold my eyelids up.

Tense with annoyance, I stomp down the narrow stairwell.

When I heave the heavy metal door open, an unseasonably cool gust greets me.

It's six thirty, and Cordell's Land Rover is idling in the narrow alley behind my building. His shiny blue boat is hitched to the back.

I pull a deep breath of air into my lungs and yank open the passenger door.

"That's what you're wearing?" he asks.

I dip my chin and assess my outfit. Pineapple-print running shorts, Birks, and a halter-tied yellow tank with a flannel button-down. The flannel is open and I've rolled the sleeves to my elbows, although now that my arms are covered in goose bumps, I'm seriously considering rolling them down. A green trucker hat will keep the sun off my face today, and my pink hair is pulled into low pigtails.

I peer at him with narrowed eyes and point to the slogan on my hat.

"*Don't talk to me.* Well, that should make for an interesting day." Cordell is far too awake for such an early hour. Awake *and* cheerful.

I want to stab him with a thousand tiny toothpicks.

With a grunt, I pull myself up into his vehicle. Instantly, I'm assaulted by the man's scent. I don't know whether it's a cologne or a body wash, but either way, I want to purchase stock in it and spray my sheets with it every night.

It's freaking manly. And so *him.*

I open my mouth, ready to smart off again but swallow my sass when he places a steaming to-go cup of coffee under my nose. DejaBrew isn't open this early on Sundays. He must've stopped at the convenience store at the edge of town, but it's too early to be picky. If anything, the gesture fills me with a kernel of hope that maybe today won't be so terrible.

"Late night?" he asks, chipper as fuck.

Forget that kernel of hope.

I side-eye him across the console and bring my coffee to my lips. A spark of joy ricochets through me when my tastebuds are not met with the bitter black I was expecting. It's just how I like it—a little sugar and a lot of creamer.

"Not awake yet, huh?" He gives me a full inspection, a smirk taking shape on his luscious lips.

"How long until we get there?" I croak.

"About twenty-five."

"Great. For the next *twenty-five*," I sigh, "don't talk to me." My chest squeezes when the harshness of my command hits me, so I lighten my tone and add a whispered "please."

Cordell lifts both hands from the steering wheel in surrender and mimes zipping his lips. His easygoing smirk sends a wave of relief through me. I haven't pissed him off yet. With a small nod, I relax into the seat's supple leather and sip my coffee, letting the caffeine work its magic.

We don't make it more than ten minutes before he heaves a deep sigh. "Sorry, Marshall, I can't do silence in the car." He pushes a button on the steering wheel, and a Taylor Swift song blares from the speakers. After a few ear-splitting notes, he manages to get the volume down to a tolerable level.

I turn my head, keeping it pressed against the headrest, and cock a brow at him. "Seriously?"

He shoots a quick glance at me and turns back to the road. "What?"

"Taylor Swift?"

"You don't like her?" A small smile creeps up his face.

"I like her just fine. Just didn't take you for a closet Swiftie, Watkins."

"Oh, there's no closet involved," he chuckles. "I am a *loud and proud* Swiftie." And to prove his point, he proceeds to sing along to "Cardigan."

He knows every damn word.

*And* the bastard has a lovely singing voice.

Ugh, I want to stab him with a *million* tiny toothpicks. Tipped in jalapeño juice.

By the time we pull into the boat launch, I'm awake and mentally prepared to be trapped in the middle of the river with Cordell.

Once the boat is loaded, he gives me a quick rundown of how to back it into the water so he can navigate the Land Rover down the ramp and then park it once the boat has been launched. After my life flashes before my eyes and I take a solid five minutes to panic, I follow his instructions. Miraculously, I steer the boat to the side of the adjacent pier without any mishaps, and I preen when he praises my steering skills. In the next heartbeat, he refuses to let me drive into open water, and I'm scowling again.

The Flint River is quiet this morning. According to Cordell, that's typical for the weekend after a holiday.

For the first several minutes, we're silent. Cordell heads to one of his favorite spots, and I take advantage of the opportunity to study him. His tall, imposing figure looks right at home behind the wheel; he uses those large, capable hands to casually steer us around bends and debris. The way the muscles in his forearm flex is hypnotizing. I have to shake my head a couple of times to pull myself out of the daze I've fallen into. He's wearing khaki cargo shorts and a short-sleeve button-down fishing shirt. The teal color looks amazing against his brown skin. A gray boonie hat rests on his broad back, the straps flopping in the wind.

Once we're anchored, he tosses a bottle of sunscreen to me. "Here, put this on." He adjusts the hat on his head and tightens the chin straps as I strip my flannel shirt off.

The temperature has warmed since the sun is finally out, making me grateful that I chose the cropped halter instead of a T-shirt. As I apply the sunscreen to my arms and legs, I have to ignore the added heat of Cordell's attention. His eyes are hidden behind a pair of sunglasses, but that doesn't lessen the way his focus sears my skin.

"Let me get your back." The deep timbre of his voice sends an unwanted shiver across my skin.

"O-okay." The heat of him engulfs me as he steps close. I have to fight like hell not to let his touch affect my body in any noticeable way as he uses his strong fingers to rub the sunscreen into my skin above and below the halter ties. When it feels like he's being a little *too* thorough, I turn my head to one side and huff, impatient.

The breath from his low chuckle stirs the strands of my hair that have escaped the pigtails and sends a tingle rippling down my spine. "Don't want to miss a spot," he says, all gravelly. "Don't want to damage this flawless skin." It's a whisper, so low I wonder if I imagined it.

The warmth behind me disappears then, and I turn to find Cordell applying the sunscreen to his arms. After he finishes and drops the bottle back into his bag, he readies the bait and poles like he could do it in his sleep. I jerk my hat back on my head, irrationally irritated all of a sudden.

Irritated because I *like* his hands on me.

When he starts digging around in a Styrofoam bucket of dirt, I shudder. "I thought you fish with those shiny lure things." I cross my arms. *No way* am I messing with worms.

"We do." One brow lifts behind his sunglasses, but he doesn't turn his focus away from the bucket of dirt. "Luke and I use them when we're fishing for bass. Today, we're going old school. Nightcrawlers and minnows." He removes his sunglasses and holds a reel out to me.

I keep my arms tucked tight and take a step back.

"You're afraid of a little worm?" He grins big, showing off perfectly straight, blindingly white teeth.

Makes me want to shove that carton of worms in his face.

"I'm not *afraid*," I sneer, sticking my chin out. "I'm just...
against animal abuse."

"I've watched you eat an entire rack of ribs. By yourself."

"Food-shaming is rude and damaging."

"I'm not food-shaming you, Marshall. Hell, I love it when a
woman has a big appetite."

I rack my brain, flipping through my mental Rolodex of
retorts, but I come up empty. It's still too early.

He holds my gaze, challenging me. Always challenging me.

Infuriating man.

"Ugh," I groan. "Fine. I don't want to touch the damn
worms."

With a grin, he baits the hook, then passes the reel to me.
"Was that so hard?" he teases.

Churlish, I huff and cast my line. When the bobber is
floating on top of the brownish water, I settle in one of the
seats.

Cordell does the same. From the corner of my eye, I watch
him—the way he slowly reels his line in before casting it out
again. He repeats this sequence several times, never getting
frustrated when it returns empty. Me? This is torture. I'm
having a very hard time sitting still. And being quiet. As a yoga
instructor, still and quiet is my MO, but in his presence, the
dead calm makes me twitchy.

Finally, the silence gets to me. "Watkins?"

He keeps his eyes on the water. "Hmm?"

"I know talking scares the fish off and all, but aren't we
supposed to use this time to *get to know one another*?" I attempt
to use finger quotes on that last part but end up almost
fumbling my rod into the river.

Cordell rolls his eyes. "We can talk, Marshall. Just quietly."
He casts his line out again. "We're not going for a tournament
catch here."

"All right. Tell me about fishing," I prompt. "Why do you enjoy it so much?"

He's quiet for several moments, never taking his eyes off the water. "I feel closest to my dad out here."

My heart pangs at his response. Cordell's father passed away when he was younger.

"It was our favorite thing to do together. He'd take me and Cass out on the water every chance he could." His Adam's apple bobs as he takes in the scenery. "As we got older, Cass joined us less and less. She was too busy with her friends. So it was just the two of us most of the time. We'd sit out here for hours just soaking up nature. And each other."

Damn it. My eyes start to burn as he continues.

"He'd always say 'Never be too busy to slow down now and then.' Said it helped you appreciate the little things in life." He clears his throat. "After he died, I didn't fish for a year. Mr. Tom invited me out all the time, but I couldn't do it. Hurt too dang much, the thought of missing him out here."

"What changed your mind?"

His sigh is heavy, and his shoulders slump. "I knew he'd be pissed if I gave up something that brought me so much peace. It had always been *our* thing, sure, but I realized after a while that the lack of his physical presence didn't change that. It's still *our* thing."

A warmth settles over me at the concept. At the love and devotion he still carries. "I love that."

Cordell turns to me, his lips parting, then closing again. Then a smile spreads across his handsome face, making those little crinkles by his eyes prominent. "Check your line, Marshall."

I've been so caught up in his story that I've completely neglected my rod. The bobber is jumping up and down on the water's surface in a frantic dance.

"Oh!" I shout, grasping for the reel and getting to work. When there's a tug on the line, I instinctively jerk it back.

"That's it," he coaches. "You've set the hook, now reel it in." He comes to stand beside me at the back of the boat, but he doesn't try to take over.

Damn. Why is it hot that he's letting me try it alone? If I need help, I have no doubt he'll offer it, but his confidence in me is making me even more determined to pull this catch in by myself.

When silver scales appear among the churning water, I know I've got it. But when I finally reel the fish out of the water, I gasp.

"That's *it*? All that tugging from *that*?"

Cordell laughs, deep and low. "That's it. Even the tiny ones put up a fight."

I jerk around to face him so fast I'm sure I'll have whiplash.

Because that statement was about more than the damn fish.

He's unaffected, though. Without a word, he moves to the side of the boat and snags the line. He waves me over and holds it out until I take it from him.

"We've gotta get a pic of your first catch." Grinning, he pulls his phone from his pocket.

After he's snapped the picture and returned the phone to his pocket, he grips the slippery fish in one broad hand and detaches the hook.

"What now?" I ask.

"Now." He leans over the side of the boat. "We do a little catch and release."

I shuffle up beside him and watch the silvery streak dart beneath the surface. "Well, there goes our dinner."

"Yeah, I wouldn't want you to turn me in for *animal abuse*." He snickers.

We spend the next couple of hours in *mostly* companionable

silence, both piping up here and there with random questions or observations. About midmorning, he presents me with a variety of snacks he's packed. I go to town on teriyaki-seasoned beef jerky, feeling more friendly toward him than I have in years.

After he's reeled in a decent-sized catfish, the only other bite we get, he insists I reapply sunscreen.

"Can't keep your hands off me, huh, Watkins?" I taunt as he returns to his seat at the front of the boat. *The bow?*

"Psh." His denial is loud and obnoxious. "Excuse me for ensuring you don't burn out here. I couldn't stomach carting a cranky lobster back home."

I drop my reel and stand, hands on hips, battle ready. It feels good to slip back into the state of annoyance I typically live in when he's around.

But he's focused on the river, not paying me a bit of attention.

I'm thinking through suitable retorts when he adds, "We both know you're still carrying a flame for me after all these years."

My heart drops into my stomach, but I recover quickly. "Ha!" I scoff. "You. Are. Delusional."

He shrugs, still focused on the water. "You can admit it, Marshall. We'll keep it between me and you and the fish."

"I am *not* hung up on you, you ass."

He still won't look my way, won't acknowledge the contempt rolling off me. No, he's sitting there wearing a damn smirk I'd like to slap off his perfect face.

"In fact, to prove to you how much I am *not* harboring any kind of feelings for you, how about this? I'm going to set you up."

He lazily cranes his neck my way. "Like on a date?"

"Yep," I say with a pop.

"You think you know my type?"

"I *know* I do."

He snorts and returns his attention to the water. "And just where would you find this mystery woman, huh? Swimming in Bennett's deep dating pool? Like our town is ripe with eligible singles."

I wince. He's not wrong. Bennett is as dry as the Sahara when it comes to single people under the age of fifty. Hence why I pounced on Tessa when she moved to town and demanded that she become my best friend.

My bookish bestie is always trying to convince me to read these small-town romance series that feature five hot, broody, single brothers. Who all find their soulmates at the county fairs and shit. Pfft. That's so far removed from *real* small-town life it might as well be in outer space.

Pretty sure there are outer space versions of those books, too.

Regardless of the lack of fresh meat, I won't be deterred. She only needs a pulse and an interest in dating a former NFL player, right?

Easy-peasy.

"You let me worry about that, *friend*," I tell him. "In fact..." Maybe I'm getting too big for my britches, but like usual, I can't stop myself. "I'll bet that I find you *the one*."

His brows are in his hairline. "The one?"

I nod vigorously. No going back now. "Yeah, *the* one. *Boom*." I hold my fist out and open it, palm down, mimicking a mic drop, even as the callback to that long ago June night causes a pain to flare in my sternum.

I hold a hand to my chest in an effort to soothe it.

His full attention is on me. His jaw clenches, like he's gearing up to tell me to shove it. "Let's make it interesting," he says instead, shocking the hell out of me. He swivels in his chair so he's facing me full on. "I bet I can find *your* future husband."

"Nope." I flick a hand. "I'm never getting married, so you can for—"

"What do you mean?" His spine goes ramrod straight and his eyes round.

"I mean what I said, *Coach*. I'm not going to get married."

"Why?" He's leaning forward now, frowning.

"I have my reasons." I cross my arms.

He's silent for several beats. I'm about to snap my fingers in front of his face to pull him from his stupor when he clears his throat. "Fine. Not your future husband, then. But someone compatible with you. I'll set you up with someone who knocks your socks off."

"What are your terms?"

"For the bet?" When I nod, he presses his lips together like he's truly thinking through options. "We'd have to agree to more than one setup. It takes time to find someone truly compatible."

"That's fair."

"And you'd have to agree to be *honest* about how you feel. No denying your feelings just to spite me."

I rear back, insulted. "I can do honest."

He drops his chin.

"What? I *can*."

He shakes his head, but I plow forward.

"So, the first to find the other a legit compatible match will be the victor? What will I win?"

"Aww, Marshall, I would think bragging rights would be enough."

"Fine. Bragging rights, then."

"We'll meet up after each date. For a..." He tilts his head to one side and scans the water, then snaps his fingers. "A debrief. To hash out how they went."

*Mental record scratch.* It's so deafening I check our surroundings in search of the source. But nope—no surprise river DJs to be seen.

He wants to have "debrief" sessions? Spending even more

time with Cordell is a double-edged sword. A sword meant to slice me right down the middle *and* humiliate me in equal measure. And yet...the idea of these debrief sessions makes my pulse race. And not in a *you need to see a cardiologist because something is terribly wrong with your heart* kind of way.

He's focused far too intently on me. His whole body is rigid, like he's waiting for my reaction to his suggestion. He's upped the ante, and he'll be absolutely insufferable if I don't agree. When his tongue darts out to lick those damn kissable lips, I feel like the mouse caught in the lion's net.

"Deal," I proclaim. Unwilling to let him see the way he affects me, I thrust out my hand.

He stands and slowly makes his way to me, the lion stalking his prey. His warm hand engulfs mine, and we seal our fate once again.

Two handshakes with Cordell Watkins in a week's time? That better earn me extra best friend brownie points.

# CHAPTER FOUR

## CORDELL

With a deep breath in, I knock on the door.

I'm ten minutes early, which will get under her skin.

The thought sends a tiny thrill through my body.

It's been six hours since I dropped her off at home. We agreed to meet up again at seven for cupcake baking. I can still feel the silky smoothness of her skin under my fingertips. I can still see her in that dang lemon-yellow halter like the image is tattooed on the backs of my eyelids. All morning, that scrap of fabric teased me with glimpses of her skin while hiding the parts I'd love to get my hands on again. Those tiny pineapple-print shorts showed off perfect suntanned legs that seem to stretch on for miles even though she's a good foot shorter than I am.

Deceptively seductive. That's how I'd describe Mel's look today.

Or every day.

I anticipated going straight from the river to the baking, but she insisted that she needed a few hours to "get stuff done." So I dropped her off and went home to shower and to torture myself with mental replays of our time on the water. Our conversations, her expressions, my restraint. The adorable smile that lit up her face when she reeled in that white perch.

*Even the tiny ones put up a fight.*

Yeah, Mel is like that fish—small, but mighty. She's been fighting me for years now.

And Jesus, I've relished every dang one of her swings, all the while mentally drop-kicking myself for ruining the chance to have her.

That one flipping moment of idiocy ruined any chance I had at winning her heart.

Losing my shot with Mel is just one instance in a long line of *so close, but yet so far* moments in my life.

Then, to make matters worse, I suggested a competition to find compatible companions for one another. What the hell was I thinking?

Another flipping moment of idiocy, I'm sure.

But she was so vehement when she swore she no longer had a thing for me, so my stubborn, wounded pride demanded that I up the ante. That I box up any residual longing and ship it off to parts unknown.

Because it was one thing to agree to let her set me up. I will still be in control of that situation, ultimately. Yes, I'll have to endure a bad date here and there, but at the end of the day, I don't have to agree to more with these women. But to volunteer to find dates for Mel, to sit on the sidelines and watch her date random dudes? The thought makes me nauseous.

Yet, I'm the idiot who suggested it.

And I can't give her the satisfaction and forfeit. No, I'll have to set her up, and my choices can't be throwaways. I can't fumble this. The men I choose must have legitimate potential, or she'll see right through me.

I refuse to let her win this competition. But at the same time, I don't want to lose *her*.

Even if it's pretty dang clear I lost my chance with her ages ago.

Call me an optimist, but I'm not ready to give in and resign myself to a life without her.

When she finally opens the door, her brows draw together as she eyes me up and down. She doesn't immediately step aside to usher me in.

I check my watch, noting that she's kept me waiting out here on the landing for nine minutes. Typical.

She opens her mouth, like she's ready to take the first shot. Instead, she cringes, then takes in a deep breath. "Did you close that door all the way?" Looks like she's going with civil, though it obviously pains her. "You have to pull it hard sometimes to get it to shut." She's referring to the door downstairs that leads to the alley behind her building. Mel's apartment is on the second floor above her yoga studio and the town coffee shop.

"I did."

With a subtle nod, she steps back and gestures for me to come in.

Though I've known her for years, this is the first time I've been inside her place. Immediately, I'm drawn to the huge window that overlooks the main drag through town. From this vantage point, Ruth's Diner and Ms. Rita's thrift shop across the street are visible. To the left, Crazy Daisy's floral shop is nestled beside Mel's dad's realty office.

"This view is pretty great."

She steps up beside me. "It is." Her surprisingly soft tone pulls my attention away from the street below.

She's studying me, her hazel eyes a kaleidoscope of warmth. The outer ring of her irises is an olive green that lightens to a deep goldenrod at the center. They're mesmerizing.

Gone are the pigtails and trucker hat from this morning. Now, her tickle-me-pink hair is tousled in soft waves that skim the tops of her shoulders. I fight the urge to push a strand behind her ear. She's changed into teal leggings and a fitted gray T-shirt that says *Stevie Nicks is my Fairy Godmother*. Her face is fresh and makeup free, and her nose and cheeks are slightly pink from the sun today, even though I was diligent about sunscreen.

I yearn to kiss her, to feel her perfect, pouty lips brush against mine. Softly, at first. Then harder and more demanding...

Mel clears her throat and steps back. "Are you ready to get started?"

"Sure." I take a deep breath, count to three, and exhale.

The kitchen is set back in the corner, next to the door. As I follow her to it, I survey the rest of her home. The apartment is open concept, one area blending into the next. The majority of the space is dedicated to the kitchen, living room, and an office area outfitted with a desk and corner bookshelves. Along the left wall is a doorway into a bedroom; centered against a wall of exposed brick that I'm sure is original to the building is an unmade queen-size bed.

Mel hands me an apron, then dons her own. Hers reads *'Bout to Stir Up Some Shit* while the one she's handed me looks like it came from the girliest shop on the planet. It's tiny and covered in a pastel floral pattern, complete with hot-pink polka dot ruffles along all the edges.

She raises a brow in challenge, and that one little gesture makes my heart race and my blood heat. I love feisty Mel. Now I'll have to fight for the rest of the night to keep myself from picturing her in nothing but this tiny floral apron.

I call her bluff and don the ridiculous scrap of fabric like it was made for me. The intense satisfaction I feel when her skin flushes makes me pull my shoulders back and puff my chest in victory.

My smugness evaporates at the brush against my calf. At the sound of a soft *meow* near my feet, I jerk back.

"Oh, that's Mouse." Mel picks up the gray cat and nuzzles into its soft fur. "He's harmless."

She then holds him out toward me. Tentatively, I brush the cat's back. When it doesn't immediately hiss or sink its teeth into me, I scratch behind his ears. His fur is thick and soft, but not long, and his eyes are bright green. His tiny dark gray nose sniffs the air around my hand as I pull it back. She kisses his head once before gently placing him on the floor. With another meow, he struts into the living room.

"How long have you had Mouse?"

Mel swipes her hands down the front of her apron, then goes to the sink to wash them. "About six years. I'd just opened up the studio when Ms. Daisy found this gray fluff ball behind her shop one evening, all alone. No mama cat or siblings in sight. He was just a tiny little thing."

I follow her lead and wash up, and our fingers brush when she hands me the towel to dry off. In that instant, I make myself a promise to touch her as often as I can tonight.

Her touch leaves me feeling untethered, and I hope like hell she feels the same way.

The counter space is crowded with mixing bowls, utensils, measuring tools, and canisters.

"What's the flavor tonight?" I've been wondering since she mentioned baking cupcakes together; Mel is well known in town for her delicious, if sometimes unconventional, flavor combinations.

"Ginger molasses. I already peeled and minced the ginger. You want to start mixing the dry ingredients? I'll talk you through each step."

I flip my cap backward so I can see, and we begin. I combine the flour, baking soda, and salt while she creams the butter with sugar. As we work, she calls out each measurement without consulting a recipe. As she tips the measuring cup of molasses into the metal bowl, the thick substance oozes its way into the mixture. The slow, sultry stickiness is captivating in a way I never would have expected. I look to her to gauge her reaction and find her attention already fixed on me. The charge between us is electric. My pulse quickens as her striking hazel eyes roam my face and pause on my lips. Her thick lashes flutter.

I blink and clear my throat. "You've made these before?"

She nods and turns back to the measuring cup. "They're my grandma's favorite." With practiced efficiency, she scrapes the remaining molasses into the bowl with a spatula. Then she flicks on the mixer.

One at a time, she adds eggs to the batter while I place the liners in the muffin tins. Her brow is set in concentration as she alternates adding dry ingredients with a dash of hot water. She takes the bowl off the mixer stand and scrapes the sides, then adds the minced ginger, giving the batter a few firm, quick stirs. It's like watching a maestro conduct the sweetest orchestra.

"Batter check." She dips her pointer finger into the bowl and comes back with a dollop. But before she can bring her hand to her mouth, I take her wrist.

I expect her to resist. Instead, her lips part, and when I close my mouth around her finger, her eyes widen. As I lave at the sweetness, she angles closer. I suck on her skin for longer than I should, then pull her finger out slowly and release it with a pop. The responding fire in her eyes is equal parts anger and desire.

"Delicious."

With a sharp breath in, she comes back to herself and yanks her wrist from my grasp. She then presses it to my chest to give me a weak shove. "Ugh, Watkins." Her features twist up in that angry pixie scowl I'm so familiar with. When she swivels on her bare feet and saunters toward her bedroom, I can't help but home in on her shapely backside. "I'm going to wash away your *germs*. Don't touch anything," she scolds over her shoulder.

I chuckle and drop my elbows to the counter nearest the door. It's clearly her catch-all—cluttered with stacks of mail, a jumbled set of keys, two purses, and various hair ties and makeup items. A colorful piece of mail lodged in the middle of one of the stacks catches my eye. The bright blue of an ocean and white sand of a pristine beach peek out amid bills and junk mail. I'm nosy. My mom and sister call me out for it every chance they get. I glance back at the doorway Mel disappeared into at the distinct flush of a toilet. I have to be quick.

I know it's wrong, but I pull the bright piece of mail out from the stack. It's a postcard. A picturesque aerial beach photo with *Panama City* printed across the bottom in tangerine block letters. I flip it over, my curiosity getting the best of me.

It's addressed to Melly and contains a single line of text in slanted, messy handwriting: *Your sunshine skin in my melancholy days*. The angular handwriting looks like it belongs to a man. There's a single name scrawled at the bottom. Nicky.

Who the *hell* is Nicky?

The sound of a door opening jolts me into action. I shove the postcard back into the stack of mail, making sure the corner is sticking out like it was before I snooped. By the time Mel walks through her bedroom door, I'm propped up against the counter that holds the baking supplies, looking down at my phone. When I drag my gaze up to her, she's squinting at me in suspicion. With a tip of her chin, she glances around the room. Then she settles her scrutiny on me again.

"Ready to bake these things or what?" I return the phone to the pocket of my shorts and stand tall.

"Yep." With that, she picks up some kind of scoop and dips it into the batter.

As she fills the muffin tins, I pose the same question she asked me earlier about my favorite hobby. "So...baking. Why do you enjoy it so much?"

She pauses her scooping and peers out the window, her

brow furrowing. "I guess because it's pretty low stakes. If I mess up a batch, I can throw 'em out and start fresh. But when I get it right, my creation has the ability to bring joy, even if it's only for a little while. Plus, I like being in control of every step in the process."

There's a lot to unpack there. I clear my throat, ready to ask about the control thing, but then my brain gets stuck on another point, and I pivot. "Low stakes appeals to you?"

Never have I pegged Mel as the kind of woman who plays it safe. Her audacious hair colors, her outspokenness, her brazen personality. She's a bold palette of colors in a world of neutrals.

She juts her chin and pops one hip. "Not always," she says. "I'm here with you, aren't I?"

My heart lurches in my chest, but I keep my expression easy. "Oh, we're high stakes, huh?" The *we* hangs heavy in the air; the implication that we're more than we are makes me burn from within. Thank the stars my brown skin makes the flush creeping up my cheeks almost imperceptible.

"The stakes are *high* because I could skewer you with a sharp utensil at any moment, Watkins." Her nostrils flare as she huffs. She spins and places the tray of cupcakes in the oven. When she straightens and turns back to me, her features have evened out. "I guess I'll leave the skewering to another time."

Crossing my arms, I relax against the counter again. "Have you always liked baking?"

"No, not always." She copies my position across from me.

"When did it become a passion?"

"At a time when I needed it the most." The words are quiet, almost like she didn't mean to speak them aloud. But then she presses the heels of her hands into the counter on either side of her and owns it. "I started when I was twenty."

"You were in school? Where'd you go again? UGA?"

"I started there, yes. But I didn't finish."

I want to ask her what made her leave, but I don't want to

imply that she's lacking because of that choice. Lots of people don't finish college. Or never even attempt it. But man, am I curious. What happened to twenty-year-old Mel that forced her to find comfort in baking, an activity that, according to her, she can control? Why'd she quit school and move home?

What led her to that dive bar that warm June night?

And, again, who the *hell* is Nicky?

"You want a beer?" Mel's voice pulls me out of my head. "It's not a Terrapin, but..."

I offer her a smile. "Sure."

She collects them from her refrigerator and pops both tops.

Blue Moon. Of course.

I take a deep pull, savoring the zest of the orange notes. "Look at us. Still alive."

She gives me a wry smile, then tilts her head toward the living room area. "We've got a few minutes until those are done."

"Do we need to make icing?"

"No, I just squirt a swirl of whipped cream on these and call it a day."

I nod and follow, breathing deep in hopes of tamping down the whipped cream fantasy my brain is conjuring.

*Unsuccessfully, I might add.*

I fold my body on the couch, and she curls her legs under her in one of the patterned armchairs.

"What made you pick a burnt sienna couch?" I rub my hand along the orangish-brown fabric next to me.

She sputters, almost spitting out a mouthful of Blue Moon. "Burnt sienna? That's an oddly specific color choice."

I lift a shoulder. It's not the first time someone has given me hell about my color descriptions. "What can I say? I was obsessed with my sixty-four pack of crayons when I was a kid. Like, *obsessed*."

The grin that lights up her face makes me feel like I've won the lottery. "What do you mean, *obsessed*? I need examples, Watkins. And, you know, *reasons*."

I shrug. "My mom bought Cass and me our own boxes one summer. For what felt like the first time, I didn't have to share with my sister; the crayons were all *mine*. I memorized every dang color in that box. I thought they were so cool, those names. Brick red. Cornflower. Timber wolf. Burnt sienna." I pat the couch cushion again. "That's much better than brownish-orange, don't you think?"

"You were a *nerd*!" she laughs. But her teasing is softened with a hint of affection.

"No doubt." I chuckle. "I even collected those paint swatches you find in hardware stores." The memory, one I hadn't thought of in a long time, makes me smile. "Every time I tagged along to Mr. Rusty's with my dad, I left with a handful of new ones. Saved 'em in an old shoebox on my bookshelf."

"All right, Mr. Color Nerd. What would you call this?" She yanks on the throw pillow beneath her thigh and holds it up.

"Robin's egg blue."

Her nose wrinkles in a laugh, but her eyes remain cool. "What would you call my hair color?"

I answer without hesitation. "Tickle me pink."

She tilts her head, and her lips part, another challenge on her tongue, but then the oven timer goes off, and she pops up out of her chair. "Hang on. These have to cool a while before we whip-cream them."

*Whip cream fantasy number two, coming right up.*

On her way back to the couch, she turns on a lamp. A glance outside confirms that the sun has retreated for the night. When Mel settles in her chair again, Mouse appears and jumps onto the back of it, rubbing his head against hers for attention. She scoops him up and deposits him in her lap, where he curls into a boneless heap.

"What about Mousers? How would you describe his color?"

"Timber wolf gray."

"Hmm." She presses her lips together and contemplates the room around us, absently twirling her hair. "Tickle me pink," she says as she rubs the strand between her thumb and pointer.

I finish the last swallow of my beer and cant forward to set the bottle on the coffee table. "You thinking about changing it again?" I ask, dipping my chin in her direction.

She frowns at me, puzzled.

"Your hair. Time for a change?"

"Oh. Maybe..." She trails off as she inspects the wave of pink closer.

"I've seen you with this—tickle me pink." I hold up a finger. "It's been lavender, though I'd categorize it as more of a wisteria." I put a second finger up. "One time you did a turquoise. Then there was the mauvelous." I swallow before the next one, my heart in my throat, but say it anyway. "Magenta..."

She closes her eyes for a couple of seconds, and when she opens them again, her expression is hard.

She doesn't want to go *there*, I'm sure. She never does. But I need to.

"Marshall, I'm so sorry—"

"No." She stands abruptly, sending Mouse leaping to the floor.

I stand, too, and hold out my hands. "Listen to me, please. If I could go back and erase that whole encounter, I would. In a heartbeat. You've gotta believe that."

"I don't have to believe anything, *Coach*."

I wince. She only calls me Coach when she's really pissed.

"You know what? Let's get this topping on these cupcakes and call it a day." She spins and stalks back into the kitchen, leaving me defeated once again. How I wish I could fix this rift between us. And throw in a do-over of that night, too.

Sometimes I think it's ridiculous for her to still be *this* upset after all these years. But then I remember that I'm the jerk who made her feel insignificant when she was vulnerable. The cause of that vulnerability still eludes me, but the look of devastation on her face that night still replays in my mind on a loop.

By the time I join Mel in the kitchen, most of the cupcakes are topped.

"Can I help?"

"I've got it." Her voice is calm, subdued. There isn't a hint of anger or snark.

Once she's done with the whipped cream, she splits the batch into two plastic containers. She hands me one and smirks, though she won't quite meet my eyes. "Cordell and Mel's day of fun is complete. With no fatalities."

Many possible responses roll through my mind, but in the end, I settle for something simple. "A win is a win, Marshall."

After a quick goodbye, I drive out to my place on the outskirts of town, letting the events of the day replay in my mind like a highlight reel. The Mel in every scene blazes in pops of color—lemon yellows and pouty pinks and hazel greens and molasses browns.

I turn onto the road that leads to my property and wind my way to the garage. I'm still sitting in the car, lost in thought, when my phone lights up in the cupholder.

ANGRY PIXIE

Ok, Watkins. I've got your first date lined up.
Just name the time and place.

My gut twists. She's already found someone? When did she hunt this person down? Wouldn't she have mentioned it when I was over there for hours this evening? Or did our time together spur her into action?

My heart races, but I type out a response.

Oh yeah? Who is this willing participant?

ANGRY PIXIE

Her name is Darcy. She's a teacher. My SIL
Lisa used to work with her. She lives in
Columbus.

Great. Shoot me her number.

In seconds, my phone pings again, and I've got her contact information. I drop my head back against the seat and groan. I'm not looking forward to an awkward first date. At all.

But once I set Mel up with someone, we can have our first debrief.

Another text lights up the dark interior.

ANGRY PIXIE

For realz, today wasn't the worst day I've ever
had, even if your face makes me want to kiss a
jellyfish. [Jellyfish emoji] Props for not throwing
me to the gators.

A laugh escapes me as I respond.

There's always next time…and your face
makes me want to staple my tongue to a
moving train. [Train emoji]

ANGRY PIXIE

Ha. Night, Watkins

Night, Marshall

# CHAPTER FIVE

## MEL

"I now call this meeting of the Bennett Business Babes to order." Ms. Daisy raps the plastic novelty gavel on the glass-topped coffee table.

"Oh, didn't we change the name at our last meeting, per Mel's suggestion?" Ms. Rita's voice is soft, as always, when she pipes up.

"You are correct, Rita." Ms. Daisy clears her throat. "I now call this meeting of the *Badass* Bennett Business Babes to order." The owner of the flower shop shoots me a wink over the bottles of wine and snacks cluttering the low table. "Shame your mama couldn't make it tonight."

"She sends her love and said we should FaceTime her if anything important is decided." As the town's only doctor and owner of her own practice, my mom is one of the founding members of the BBB. Technically, I suppose it's the BBBB now. Even so, she couldn't pass up the opportunity to drive to Columbus to babysit Whosie and Whatsie so Mark and Lisa could attend a dinner with friends.

"Thanks for hosting this month, Ms. Daisy." Jane rounds the table, filling our mugs with wine. As the newest member of our little group, she's not as vocal as the rest of us. She owns our little town's only clothing and gift boutique and does a steady business despite our small population. She looks like a Barbie, with her long, straight blond hair and perfect makeup, and she's as sweet as pie. Not to mention she's closer to my age than the rest of the women in our group.

"Don't mention it, doll." Daisy holds her Crazy Daisy's mug high, then brings it to her lips. She special ordered mugs for all the business babes' establishments and gets them out specifically for our meetings. When she's not the host, she shows up at each of our houses with her box of mugs.

"The peach cook-off is coming up." Ms. Rita is good at keeping the rest of us on topic, even though she's the most reserved of the bunch. Her thrift shop has been in Bennett for as long as I can remember. It's Glamma's favorite spot in town.

Like any respectable Georgia town, Bennett loves to celebrate our state fruit. The annual peach cook-off happens the third Saturday in June, rain or shine. As a three-time winner, I've been planning my entry for weeks.

"Yes, I've already talked to Buck about the location for the business booths." Daisy dips a cracker into the cream cheese and pepper jelly dip. "I told that boy he better have our canopies in the same place, or so help me..." She pops the cracker into her mouth. Only Daisy could get away with calling our well-into-his-fifties mayor "boy."

"Do we know who the judges are this year?" I scoot back on the couch with my plate of goodies in one hand and my *Go with the Flow-Ga* mug in the other. Technically, the identities of the judges are supposed to be kept secret until the event, but Daisy's always got inside knowledge. I'm a little scared of her and her ways, if I'm being honest. But I also kinda want to be her when I grow up. She gives zero fucks.

She scowls in response.

*Okay.* Maybe the powers that be have caught on to her sneaky ways.

"I don't have all the names, damn it. *Yet.*" Her scowl quickly changes then, into a knowing smirk. "I *do* know that a certain head football coach is on the roster, though."

She watches me, like she's looking for a reaction, so I work extra hard to adopt a look of total nonchalance.

"What do you think about that, Mel?"

"Good for him," I say, with a pop of a shoulder. "He's done it before, I think." In a town this size, the list of prominent towns-folk eligible to judge the cook-off is pretty short. And honestly, I don't *think* Cordell's been a judge before. I *know* he has. Four years ago, in fact. One of the few years I *didn't* win best in show in the dessert category.

Not that I'm still bitter about that or anything.

I'm bombarded with the memory of Cordell's warm mouth sucking that cake batter off my finger a few nights ago, and I discreetly pinch the fabric of my T-shirt to fan myself. Why is it suddenly ten degrees hotter in here?

"Coach Watkins is such a gem," Ms. Rita says. "He's been so good to my Clayton. And Cole has learned so much from him. We're so blessed to have him here." Rita raised her nephew, Clay Reeves, as well as his brother, after their parents passed away. Clay's oldest son, Cole, will be a sophomore this upcoming school year.

The entirety of Bennett is just as enamored with Cordell. He's every bit the hometown hero today that he was when he was the star wide receiver at Bennett High. Then the LSU standout. Then the NFL draftee with serious potential.

"Chase thinks he hung the moon," Jane gushes.

Cordell's a hit with the under-twelve crowd, including Jane's seven-year-old son. And apparently with the over-fifty crowd, if the shine in Ms. Rita's eyes is any indication.

Pretty sure I'm the only soul in Bennett who isn't a member

of the Cordell Watkins fan club. So what if I revoked my membership out of spite? Someone's gotta keep that man from getting a big head.

Ms. Daisy pours the last of a bottle of wine into her mug. "I have it on good authority that our resident yogi was seen with Coach Watkins at Fuzzy's a few days ago. *Without* the Shipleys in tow." She says that last part like she's sharing the juiciest gossip to hit the town since Bridget Jenkins crashed her car into her cheating husband's auto shop five years ago.

"Ms. Daisy," I admonish, eager to nip this in the bud, "two people can have a beer together without it being a *thing*. Trust me, it's not a *thing*."

"Hmph," Daisy snorts. "I've seen the way you two look at each other, Mel."

My face flames, and I have to fight the urge to duck my head into my T-shirt.

"Ooh, how?" This from Jane.

I narrow my eyes at her, and she shrinks back into her chair, suddenly interested in the snacks on her plate.

"Those two," Daisy crows, "look at each other like they can't decide whether they want to rip each other's clothes off or spit in each other's faces."

Rita and Jane, the traitors, giggle.

"That's how it was for Richard and me," she claims. Richard was her second husband. She's been married four times, but she talks about him the most.

I scoot to the edge of the couch. "I can promise you, there's *nothing* between me and Cordell. Except maybe an intense dislike." I pick up the corkscrew and get to work opening another bottle of wine to give my hands something to do, hoping like hell that if I ignore them, they'll move on from this topic quickly.

"You know what they say." Ms. Rita smooths back her long, gray hair. "There's a thin line between love and hate."

"Yes." Jane claps her hands. "I just read the *best* book with that theme. Tessa called it an enemies-to-lovers, or something like that." Jane has recently become a bookworm, much to Tessa's delight. My best friend shares book recommendations with anyone who will listen.

I give her a half-hearted eye roll, then seize the instant of silence and change the subject. "Have you decided which boutique items you're going to have at the cook-off?"

As I'd hoped, she takes the bait and launches into her plan.

The Badass Bennett Business Babes end our June meeting by going over our plans for the peach cook-off and making decisions about business ads for the upcoming season's football programs.

Once we've picked up Ms. Daisy's living room, Ms. Rita offers me a ride home, but I decline. Daisy's place is only a few blocks from downtown, and when the weather is nice, I prefer to walk. Thankfully, now that the sun has set, the temperature is tolerable. I'm just rounding the corner off Mills Street when my phone buzzes in my bag.

It's an unknown number, which I usually ignore, but I'm just distracted enough going over the plans we made this evening that I click Accept without thinking.

A deep chuckle echoes down the line, sending a bolt of ice through my veins. "Melly." His tone is full of affection he doesn't deserve to have for me.

Stomach plummeting like I stepped off a ledge, I toss my head back in defeat and close my eyes. "Nick. New number, I see." I want to shake a fist at the universe. Then use that same fist to punch Nick's face.

"You won't answer my calls anymore, babe. Had to borrow a friend's."

Garnering every bit of nastiness inside me, I growl, "I'm not your *babe*. You don't get to call me that. You don't get to call me anything."

"C'mon, Melly—"

"*No.*" I lower the phone and seriously consider throwing it into the middle of the street. But that would create a whole new headache for me, and this one is enough for tonight. So I take a calming breath and bring it back to my ear. "What do you want, Nick?"

"I can't call you because I miss you?" He uses that raspy tone that did things to me all those years ago. The one that sent thrills through my body and made pretty promises that turned out to be nothing but lies. The voice that made me stupid.

I know better now.

"No. You can't." I keep my tone flat. I know Nick; there are only two possible reasons for this phone call. He either needs money or he's just shy of drunk and feeling nostalgic. The twang that takes over when he's tipsy is absent from his voice, though, so money it is.

He's quiet for a moment. I consider hanging up and powering my phone down for the night, but before I can, he hums. "Did you get my last postcard?"

I don't respond. I'm not interested in having any kind of conversation with him.

"We played a few gigs in Florida over the past few weeks. You know I can't go to the beach without thinking about that night."

*Damn him.* Damn him to hell for bringing that up.

A disgusted sigh works its way up my chest and out of me. "Just get it over with and ask me, Nick, so I can tell you hell no."

It's his turn to sigh, the sound crackling over the phone. "I miss you, Melly. So much."

Unexpected tears prick my eyes. *Shit.* I haven't cried over this jackass in close to ten years. Why are my emotions blindsiding me lately?

"You don't miss me, Nick. I'm sure you've got a girl in every port to keep your dick wet."

"Shit, Mel." Does he sound offended? That's rich.

"I'm going to hang up now. I'm not sending money. Stop wasting yours on postcards that just end up in my trash can." The lie tastes bitter, but without giving him a chance to respond, I end the call and shove the phone back into my bag.

Ugh. Ex-husbands are a bitch.

That damn shoebox in my closet haunts me once again as I wait for Tessa at Ruth's Diner. It's filled with dozens of postcards he's sent me over the years, postmarked from various destinations all over the southeast. Little coastal towns and midsize college towns and tiny, rural almost-towns where his band has played. On the back of each one, he's hastily jotted down a song lyric in his slanted script.

Lyrics from the songs he supposedly wrote about *me*. Once upon a time.

I can't explain why I've held on to them all these years. Maybe because they're a physical reminder of Nick's betrayal— a reminder to keep my heart locked up tight.

I've asked Tessa to meet me for lunch today so I can come clean to her about my past. About the huge, unfortunate fuckup I made when I was young and stupid. She's my best friend, and she knows everything else about me. A few months after she and Luke moved in together, I even told her about my one-time romp with Cordell. That night, over a couple rounds of Tito's and Sprite, when I explained my extreme scorn for the man, she clutched my hand, looked at me with zero judgment, and told me that she was Team Mel forever. But in her next breath, with her eyes filled with tears, she admitted she had room in her heart to be Team Cordell, too.

"He's just so dang *likable*, Mel," she'd said, her voice cracking.

Rolling my eyes, I trace the condensation on the glass of iced tea with a purple nail-tipped finger. The color is so dark, it's almost black.

What color name would Cordell use to describe it?

Mother trucker, *why* am I thinking about that man again?

Tessa bustles into the diner, flushed and freaking adorable. She's wearing the cutest navy knit dress. The knot tied below her breasts makes her rounded belly more prominent than even a few days ago.

"The bump is bumping today." I can't help the soft smile that overtakes me at the sight of her.

She scoots along the bench across from me. I've scored our favorite booth in the back corner, away from the town nosy-rosies who frequent this place at lunchtime.

"Tell me about it," she says, settling in. "I'm so sorry I'm late."

"Your boobs are huge, T." And I can't help but admire them from across the table. Tessa's got that hourglass figure that men go feral over, and being pregnant has only enhanced her curves.

She rolls her eyes at me, but her face, neck, and chest turn pink. "Gee, thanks for noticing."

I bark out a laugh. "It's hard not to! They're spectacular, by the way."

"Right?" The giggle she lets out is quickly followed by a sigh, though. She drops her shoulders and her chin. "I feel like a whale."

"Stop. You're fucking beautiful, you human-grower. Did everything check out okay?"

I haven't spoken to her since her last doctor's appointment, other than through text.

"Yeah," she says with a wave of her hand. "Dr. Singh said everything looks perfect."

"Did Dr. Singh happen to mention if little goober has a *p* or a *v*?"

A huge smile lights up Tessa's face. "I'm sorry to report that she did not."

"Ugh. Fine."

"I can't wait to see Luke's face when we find out." Her big green eyes shine with happy tears. With a groan, she fans her eyes to stop the flow. "Sorry. Everything makes me cry these days."

"Lisa was the same way." I give her a sympathetic smile. "A strange look from Mark could send her into hysterics." I chuckle at the memories of nine months of bewildered stares my brother gave his wife. "How's Luke?"

Tessa's blush grows darker. "He's good. Busy." She occupies herself with straightening her silverware.

"I'll *bet* he is." I give her a saucy wink. I can't help but tease her. It's so damn easy to rile her up.

"Mel!" She hunches her shoulders and takes a quick peek around. When she's sure no one is within earshot, she grips the edge of the table and leans forward until her bump stops her. "I can't get enough of him these days. I'm horny as a toad." Her voice is barely a whisper, and now her face is flaming. God, she's so cute.

I open my mouth in a silent cackle and shake my head. When I met Tessa, there was no way in hell she'd willingly talk about sex with me. She's come a long way.

*Come.* Ha.

"Stop." She glances around the diner again, still smiling and still glowing scarlet.

Fuck. *Scarlet*, Mel?

I school my features and adopt a serious tone. "Listen, it's just me and Fernando these days."

"You have that date this weekend, though, right?"

Oh yeah. The date—Cordell's first attempt at matchmaking. He texted me a couple of days ago to ask if he could share my contact info with a guy named Rob. Hours later, Rob texted, and we agreed to a lunch date. All I know about Rob is that he's Clay's buddy from college.

"Ah, yes. The date." I've already filled Tessa in on the tentative truce and matchmaking competition with Cordell. "Maybe I'll get as lucky as my bestie this weekend." I waggle my brows.

"Mel." Tessa huffs out a humorless laugh. "It's a serious problem. Poor Luke." She shakes her head, genuinely concerned about her husband getting laid on the regular.

"Pfft. Poor Luke, my ass. That man is living his *best* life, my friend."

She melts. My bestie is so thoroughly loved-up, every inch of her face softens. Tessa and Luke have *that* kind of love—the kind that inspires love songs and poetry and happily ever afters. The kind I've sworn off for the last decade. Because that kind of love is not for me. For me, that kind of love ends with a broken heart.

And I can't get a broken heart if I keep mine protected.

The pure love radiating from Tessa causes a sharp, lancing pain in a place I keep hidden. It strikes me so abruptly that I suck in a breath and clench my fists under the table. And damn it if my eyes don't fill without my permission.

*Mother trucker.* What is it with these unwelcome tears lately?

"Mel Marshall, are those tears?" she asks softly.

"No. No way. Not even a little bit." I swing my gaze to the ceiling and blink my lashes rapidly.

"Oh, honey, what's wrong?" The concern in her voice only makes them well again.

It's time to come clean—to purge this hurt from my heart and confess to her what very few people know.

I swallow hard and dig deep for courage, then I begin. "There's something I've been meaning to tell you. Something from my past."

Her green eyes search my face. "Okay," she says, her chest heaving with a deep inhale. "Zero judgment, remember?"

We declared our friendship a zero-judgment zone over homemade pizzas, back when our friendship was still new and we were tentative with our confessions.

"I remember." I wet my lips and rub them together. Best to rip this Band-Aid right off. "I—I was married before. Back in college." As soon as the words spring free, a weight is lifted.

My best friend's brows draw together, and she lowers her head, searching the table, likely processing my bombshell. When she meets my gaze again, her eyes are shining. And I feel like the biggest ass.

"You...you were *married*?"

"Please, don't cry, T," I beg. "It was so long ago and—"

She swipes away the tears that trail down her cheeks. "But why are you just now telling me?"

*Note to self: do not confess a critical past mistake to a best friend when she's got a shit-ton of pregnancy hormones coursing through her body.*

I close my eyes. I can't stand to see Tessa's hurt expression. It doesn't help. Her little sniffles break my heart. She thinks I've kept a piece of myself from her.

When I force myself to look at her, to take in how I've hurt her, she's pulling a napkin from the metal holder. I place a hand on the table, palm up. Her eyes dart between it and my face a few times before she gives my fingers a squeeze and holds on tight.

"I love you. You know that, right?" I question.

She nods, blinking rapidly.

"I didn't keep this from you because I don't trust you with it." I shake our joined hands. "It's because, honestly, I'm still hella embarrassed about it. I was a young, stupid kid who made a huge-ass mistake. I like to keep it all locked up nice and tidy in a box labeled *regrets*. A box I never open unless absolutely necessary."

"Why open it today?" She gives my hand another firm squeeze before releasing it. Her face is red and splotchy.

I hope like hell Luke doesn't decide he wants Ruth's for lunch today.

"I got an unexpected call from my asshole ex-husband last night." I pinch the bridge of my nose. "He wanted money."

Tessa's eyes widen and her mouth drops open.

"Oh, don't worry—I told him to shove it. I always tell him to shove it, but he still calls every now and then. I blocked his number long ago, but last night he called from a friend's phone."

"He's why you left UGA." She bobs her head and leans forward on her elbows. "Tell me. All of it."

With a deep breath in, I start from the beginning. "I met Nick my freshman year, at a bar. He was there with friends, checking out this drummer they wanted to recruit for their band."

"He was a musician," she says, as if that explains everything.

"Still is," I counter. "His band is pretty well known regionally. They tour around the southeast. They'll never make it big, but they refuse to accept it." Shoulders slumped, I wring my hands in my lap. "Honestly, if I didn't loathe him so much, I might find his unrelenting optimism inspiring."

Ms. Peggy comes to our table to take our lunch orders, and once she scurries away, I jump back in.

"He had this magnetic pull. I attached myself to him so fast my head was in a constant spin. It was an inevitable whirlwind, and before I knew it, I was driving the band to gigs on the weekends, shacking up in hotel rooms with Nick and three other dudes..."

Tessa's mouth forms an *O* and her brows almost reach her hairline.

"No. Not like that." I can't help but let out a laugh. "It was very unglamorous and unsexy, I promise you. Not one of those *why choose* stories you talk about."

Her face grows as red as the ketchup bottle.

"I was an idiot kid in love. I was willing to endure *anything* to be with him. Even put up with gross, smelly bandmates who brought local groupies back to the room to fuck like they were Georgia's version of freaking One Direction."

"Is that the kind of music they play?" Tessa asks as Ms. Peggy places our plates in front of us.

"God, no. They're more like a southern rock version of Fall Out Boy. Total emo with a rock edge." I roll my eyes.

"What's their name?" She tilts her head and bites into a fry.

"The Low Bars."

"Oh!" she splutters. "I've heard of them. They were pretty popular in Athens when I was there. I never saw them play or anything..."

I can't help but smile at her. Of course my bookish bestie didn't spend her free time in muggy dive bars. She takes a bite of her club sandwich and waves her hand for me to continue.

"By Christmas of my freshman year, I was living with him. Along with the rest of the band and another dude who was acting as their manager. Two of the guys had already dropped out of school so they could devote all their time to the band. Nick and the lead singer held out until the end of freshman year before they followed suit."

I blow out a breath, ready to just get it all out, hoping it'll take away some of the disgust churning in my stomach.

"That spring, after a gig in Florida, after fucking me in the sand on a public beach that was, thankfully, unoccupied except for us, Nick proposed. I didn't even tell my parents until after the courthouse ceremony three weeks later."

"Mel..." Tessa is teary again.

I am, too, as I force myself to remember the disappointment

in my parents' voices when I called them hours after becoming a wife at nineteen. They had only met Nick once. I can still hear the despair in my father's voice. It's the one and only time in my adult life that he's called me by my full name. *Melanie.* My stomach roils, and suddenly, the Caesar wrap on my plate is no longer appealing.

"Things between us were strained for a while. They thought I'd made a big mistake, but I wouldn't hear any of it. To me, Nick hung the moon. I was certain we would be together forever. That the Low Bars would hit the big time, and we'd be catapulted into greatness. The one thing that kept my dad from driving to Athens to haul my ass home was my promise to finish school."

It helped my cause that my parents have always let us figure things out for ourselves. They've always been supportive of Mark and me, college elopement notwithstanding. Even when it's hard to do, they let us make choices and learn from our mistakes. But I'd always wanted to set myself apart from my perfect older brother. I didn't see it then, but choosing to marry Nick was partly an act of rebellion, a way to show them that I could make "grown-up choices" as well as he could.

Except my grown-up choice bit me in the ass and broke my heart.

"What happened then?" Tessa's voice is so soft, so encouraging.

"I stayed in Athens for the summer after freshman year. I worked as a waitress at this bar where the guys played a lot. On my off nights, I joined them on the road. I swear I've been to every dingy bar in Georgia, Florida, *and* Alabama." I give her a wry smile. "Nick wrote the lyrics. He swore I was his muse. Vance, the lead singer, wrote the music. We lived in this happy, broke bubble for months, existing on ramen and tip money. Nick tried to convince me to quit school, but I couldn't break my promise to my parents."

Sometimes, when I can't sleep, my mind wanders back to those days. Those carefree, so-in-love days in that run-down house. Hours of the Favorites Game in an SUV barely big enough to haul the band and their equipment. Nights spent wrapped up in Nick's arms in that double bed, confident we would grow old together.

*Fucking Nick.*

Now comes the hard part of this tragic tale. I wait for Ms. Peggy to clear our plates and refill our drinks before I launch into it. "I decided to stay with Nick in Athens for Christmas break of my sophomore year. My parents were hurt, but we were broke, and I was able to pick up extra shifts to cover for my coworkers who were heading home for the holidays." I swallow past the lump in my throat and will my voice to remain even. "Our other roommates went home for the break, too, so it was just me and Nick in the house. I had big plans for us to go at it like animals while we had the privacy." I shake my head. "Well, *one* of us went at it like an animal..."

"Oh, Mel." Tessa's green eyes are wide and full of compassion. She grasps my hand on top of the table, sharing her strength with me.

I blow the wisps of hair that have worked their way out of my ponytail out of my face. "Two days after Christmas, I arrived home to find my husband fucking another woman in our bed. Doggie style, by the way." I force out a laugh, though it lacks humor. "It's the age-old cautionary tale: girl falls in love and gets married at nineteen. Girl discovers her husband is a lying scumbag cheater and gets divorced at twenty."

"I'm so, so sorry you had to go through that," Tessa offers.

I pop a shoulder, going for flippant, but the weight of all the things I haven't told her is strong enough to pull me under. All the details from the end that I skipped over: The moans and grunts that echoed through the house as I walked in the door. The devastation that hit me when I realized I was about to be confronted by something that would alter my life forever. The way I stood in the doorway of our bedroom for two solid minutes, unable to move or speak as Nick fucked a groupie in front of me, her bottle-blond ponytail wrapped around his fist. The sound my bag and keys made when they dropped to the floor, loud enough to garner his attention, for him to finally notice his wife standing stock-still as her world fall apart. The shriek I couldn't hold back after he jerked out of her, closed his eyes, and said, "Shit, Melly. Babe, it doesn't mean anything." The fake tits that came into view as the blonde reached for something, anything to cover herself up. My scramble to pick up my things and hightail it out to the car, with Nick hot on my heels while attempting to pull on a pair of jeans. The three-hour drive from Athens to Bennett in the dead of night, my eyes so swollen from crying I could barely see the highway.

Other visions of that night flash in my mind: Waking my parents up at four a.m. Crying so hard I couldn't get words out. My dad pulling my coat off to check that I wasn't injured and then pulling me into his arms. My mom crawling into bed with me an hour later, holding me close while I wept, her gentle hands smoothing back my hair as I purged my sorrow.

The trip my dad and brother took to Athens the next weekend to pack up my belongings.

I don't mention the way that betrayal has significantly impacted every relationship I've had since. How I built walls around my heart to keep it safe from future hurt, because I'm not sure it can withstand any more damage.

Tessa finally lets go of my hand and leans back. "So when you and Cordell…"

"It was a year and a half later. I was mostly over it at that point, thanks to my family and *several* sessions with a counselor." I take a long sip of iced tea, questioning the truth of that statement. Have I ever *really* gotten over it? "But that night was my brother's wedding, and…"

"And it brought all those feelings up again," she finishes for me.

I sigh. "Yep. I was so freaking happy for Mark and Lisa, but their wedding brought all these residual feelings to the surface. I watched the two of them dedicate their lives to one another, and I knew, without a doubt, that Nick never loved me like *that*. He wasn't capable of loving me the way my parents love each other, the way Mark and Lisa do. The way you and Luke love each other."

Her eyes are shiny again. "Oh, sweet friend. Nick didn't deserve you, obviously, but that doesn't mean there isn't a man out there who does. A guy who will love and cherish you and that big heart of yours."

I bite the inside of my cheek to stop the words from spilling out. The questions that've plagued me since that awful December night almost eleven years ago: What if I'm unlovable? What if the best I get out of this life is a rock star-wannabe fuck-boy?

What if Mel Marshall can't *keep* anyone better than Nick Hayes?

I don't voice any of this to my best friend. I don't tell her that I'm afraid my heart is defective after being walled up for so long.

Speaking of my fortified heart...

"You haven't said anything to Luke about Cordell and me, have you?" The night I confessed to her, I made Tessa swear on her glass of Tito's and Sprite, then pinkie promise like she does with Hannah, that she would never tell her husband about his best friend's dive-bar score.

"I haven't," she vows, holding a hand to her heart. "You know Luke and I don't keep secrets from each other, but I made a promise, and because you're my best friend, I will keep it."

I settle back against the booth and pull my legs up to sit crisscross on the bench.

"But," she starts, "that doesn't mean Cordell won't tell Luke one day."

"I know," I groan. There's no good reason to keep Luke in the dark about this, but the fewer people who know, the better. It's like the more people know, the more vulnerable I feel. It's bad enough that Tessa and Lisa are aware of it.

After we finish our drinks and pay our bills at the counter, we step out into the cloudy June day. The air is so heavy it feels like a cloak slung around my shoulders.

Tessa looks up at the gray clouds and hums. "Luke said storms are moving in tonight."

"Perfect. At least the weather will match my mood."

"I hope you don't regret telling me. About Nick." She squeezes my forearm.

I give her a genuine smile. "I don't regret telling you. Talking about it just puts me in a sucky mood."

She tilts her head and assesses me. "I get it. But I'm proud of you. Thank you for trusting me with this, even if you waited three years to do it." She twists her lips into a smirk.

"I'm sorry, T. Really. It feels good to get it out, though."

"Of course it does. This is what zero-judgment best friends are for. Plus, you know what they say..." She takes a step back, then another, heading down the sidewalk in the direction of the library, her eyes crinkling and her smile bright. "You can't move forward until you let go of your burdens."

She's referencing her own journey, and Luke's, too. How they both fought so hard for the happiness they have now.

We blow goodbye kisses, and then she spins on her heel and picks up her pace.

As I step off the curb to cross Central and head back to the studio, the clouds part for a moment, and a few rays of sunlight peek through the gloom, intense, reminding the world of their presence.

I lift my face to the light and exhale.

# CHAPTER SIX

## CORDELL

The annual peach cook-off is one of the most anticipated events in Bennett. All the parking spots lining the main drag are occupied, forcing me to find one in the library parking lot a couple of blocks from where the stage and tents are set up. As I follow the crowds meandering their way to the center of town, I spot my mother up ahead with Luke's parents, so I jog to catch up with them, dodging townsfolk as I go.

"Mornin', Ma." I give her shoulders a squeeze.

Startled, she jumps like she's been struck with a low-voltage shock. I plant a huge smack on her cheek and loop her arm through mine. Then I pull Ms. Marj in for a side hug and rest my arm across her shoulders. Mr. Tom gives my back a hearty slap as the four of us continue our shuffle down the sidewalk.

"Dell," Ma scolds. "You better get your hind parts up to that stage so they aren't short a judge." She tightens her grip on my bicep.

"Nah," I scoff. "They'll wait on me."

She reacts the way she always does when I pretend to be more important than I actually am. With a playful pinch to my arm, she tilts her head and gives me a mock look of disapproval. "You better watch yourself, now."

"Yes, ma'am." I have to work to suppress a laugh.

Ms. Marj grins up at me, and I give her a wink.

Ahead of us, two of the town's finest are putting up barricades to block traffic from this end of the street. The stage is set with a podium and microphone for the mayor's welcome speech, and there are produce boxes overflowing with the stars of the show everywhere.

The street is flanked with white tents. On one side, they cover a long line of folding tables. This is where the cook-off judging will happen. On the other, local small businesses have set up booths. Ms. Daisy is hawking fresh bouquets. A few tables past her, Mr. Rusty has brought out models of his best-selling yard equipment, and down one more, DejaBrew is selling coffee and drinks. Several booths are dedicated to fresh produce from local farms, the tables laden with homemade beeswax candles and freshly harvested honey, baskets of homemade preserves and bags of boiled peanuts. Everywhere I look, I spot friendly smiles from people I've known all my life.

This is why I chose to settle in my hometown after my football career came to an unexpected end. The slower pace is like a balm to my soul after years of trying to acclimate to the hectic lifestyle of a professional athlete.

"Yo, Coach!"

At the call-out, I turn. A group of teenage boys is heading our way, and when they reach our spot on the sidewalk, each player offers a polite hello and handshake to my mom and the Shipleys.

A surge of pride zaps through me. My job is to not only coach these boys, but to instill valuable lessons that will hopefully stick with them for the rest of their lives. To provide them the kind of role model my father was for me.

Cole Reeves steps around one of his teammates and moves

in close. "Hey, Coach, my mom asked me to remind you to stop by the boosters' table before you leave."

"Tell your mama I won't forget." Frannie recently took the helm of the football boosters, and she's nervous she's going to let us down. Her husband and I have given her numerous pep talks. Frannie isn't capable of disappointing me—unless she forgets to invite me to a lasagna night.

I'm in the middle of goodbye fist bumps when a flash of tickle-me-pink hair catches my eye.

Mel's talking to a group of teenage girls who've gathered around the table she's set up to advertise her yoga studio. At the sight of her, my heart rate accelerates like someone's pushing on a gas pedal. She's wearing a pair of ragged blue jean cutoffs that make her tan legs look like they stretch on for days. I grit my teeth, trying to push away the urge to punch any jerk who so much as looks at those legs for a second longer than is appropriate. She's sporting this year's cook-off T-shirt like all the contestants, but she's cut the neck of it so that one hot-pink bra strap peeks out when she moves. The bottom of the shirt is tied in a knot at her back so a strip of her toned stomach is on display. Her hair is styled in loose, choppy waves with one chunk at the front braided and pinned back.

Like she senses my attention, she looks up and fixes her focus on me. A trifecta of emotions plays across her features—first, her lips part and her eyes widen in surprise, then she smirks and gives me a once-over. She ends with the usual: eyes narrowed in slits and mouth pressed in a firm line. From pleased to attracted to irritated in a matter of seconds.

Dang, she's a firecracker, and I'd gladly let her light me up.

With a glance at my watch, I mentally count the hours until my judging obligation is met and I can go head-to-head with her. We've completed our first round of dates, and she's agreed to meet up for a debrief after the peachy festivities.

"Coach Watkins! The other judges are already on the stage."

I pull my focus off Mel and search for the source of the reprimand. Deedee Kilpatrick, the mayor's wife, hustles over as quickly as her sky-high heels will allow. She pastes on a fake smile as she holds out a hand to me to shake. I have to steady her when a heel gets caught in a crack in the concrete and she almost goes down. Once she's regained her balance, she smooths both hands down her peach-colored dress. "Buck's ready to go, Coach."

With a cursory glance at my mom and the Shipleys, she grabs my arm and tugs me toward the stage.

"I know you've done this before, hon, but we'll go over the judging criteria with y'all before we get started. That will give the contestants a chance to get set up."

Obediently following, I peer over at Mel again. She's standing inside her tent holding a tray of cupcakes, and she's focused on me, too. I send her a quick wink, and naturally, she fights a smile. Deedee's grip is ruthless as she yanks me up the stairs that lead onstage, so I don't get to see whether her smile breaks free.

Mayor Buck Kilpatrick welcomes the crowd and explains the judging process for the three categories: savory, sweet, and swill. Fellow judge Junior Jenkins, Bennett's oldest living war veteran, rubs his palms together when the swill category is mentioned. With an elbow to my side, he angles in close. "Make sure you get seconds of Mabel's peach sangria."

"I'm pretty sure they serve the alcoholic entries in leftover communion cups so we don't get slosh—er, inebriated." I duck my head and take a quick peek around to make sure I wasn't overheard. Fortunately, the mayor's speech drones on, so I'm in the clear.

Junior groans, and the last of our judging trio, elementary principal Rosa Hernandez, smirks at him. "That's correct, Sergeant. The church now uses the prefilled kind, so they donated the leftover communion cups to the city."

"Hmph," Junior grumbles. "I'm eighty-six years old. Get me a Solo cup. I'm ready to get *sloshed* with the coach."

I chuckle right along with Rosa, then offer an arm for Junior to hold as we make our way back down the steps.

"My granddaughter insisted on bringing that damn chair." He flicks his wrist, pointing out a woman pushing a wheelchair our way. "I told her I don't need that damn thing. You'll back me up, won't you, Coach?"

"Yes, sir. But only if you promise to let me know if you get tired. I'd be happy to be your driver for the day."

Junior grunts but nods in begrudging agreement. We shuffle-step to the closest tent and get our first look at the recipes in the savory category. By the time we make it to the end of the table and Ms. Rita's famous peach and whiskey chili, he's decided he wants the wheelchair, so he takes possession of both of our clipboards, and I get to pushing him.

The sweet category always has the most entries, and a quick glance down the table reveals everything from pies to macarons to cupcakes to cobblers. Contestants are allowed to enter the same recipe every year if they wish, and most do. Mel, however, changes things up from year to year. Sometimes her risk pays off and she comes out on top, and sometimes it backfires. The last time I served as a judge, her peach galettes were just a touch overcooked, but if you ask her, I'm to blame for her loss.

We're halfway through the sweet category when we reach her. She's standing with her hands behind her back and her chin jutting out proudly. In front of her is a tiered stand that holds fluffy, scrumptious-looking cupcakes.

Cupcakes. Sticking with her tried-and-true playbook.

"Hey, Uncle Dell!" Hannah's next to Mel, decked out in the same girly apron I wore the night we baked together.

"Banana girl! Did you enter the contest this year?"

She scrunches her nose and giggles in response.

Mel gives Hannah's ponytail a wiggle. "Hannah is my

personal assistant for the judging." Then she leans over to Junior and says, "You're awfully brave to let *this* one drive you around." She raises a brow when we lock eyes. Her lips look extra pouty today.

Junior beams up at her, charmed. "I guess he'll have to do since you're busy, young lady." His laugh deepens the crinkles on his face.

She shoots him a saucy wink. "Next time, Sergeant."

"What do you have for us today, Mel?" Rosa asks.

Mel takes a deep breath and launches into her description. "I'm proud to share my special recipe with y'all—peach pie cupcakes. They're filled with a homemade peach pie filling and topped with a cinnamon cream cheese frosting."

She slices one of the cupcakes into thirds and places each chunk on a plate Hannah holds out for her. Then she lets her little helper pass the plates to us.

As I take a bite of the fluffy confection, I watch Mel. There's a glint in her eyes that screams *I dare you to find these lacking*, yet when she chews on her plump lower lip, nerves filter through her expression. She's so flipping adorable and scathing at the same time. The juxtaposition is a major turn-on.

As I fight the blood that rushes to my groin, the flavor of her cupcake activates my taste buds. I have to stop myself from moaning. They're delicious. The airy sweetness of the cake is the perfect counter to the rich pie filling in the center. And the decadent frosting has just enough cinnamon to enhance the cream cheese flavor rather than overpower it.

This is the best thing I've put in my mouth. Ever.

Can't tell her that, though. At least, not now. I file away every compliment to give to her later. After the contest.

I hold a hand out to Hannah for a high five, then push Junior's chair down to the next contestant. In my periphery, Mel gives Hannah a big hug. They link hands, and with quiet giggles, they hop in a happy circle.

Close to an hour later, we tally our scores, and I make myself a firm promise to stay away from peaches for a hot minute.

Unless the recipe is one of Mel's. She can force-feed me peachy things anytime she likes.

Junior, Rosa, and I stand off to the side of the stage and wait for the prizes to be awarded. Over and over, I'm bombarded with questions about our football program's summer training. The town is chomping at the bit for the season to start since we lost in the first round of the playoffs last year. Bennett is a small school, and we're in a competitive district. I keep my answers vague. I'm not interested in making promises or predictions that might come back to bite me in the butt later.

As I wait, my best friend and his family make their way through the crowds. When they approach, I breathe a sigh of relief. Luke and I greet one another with our typical bro hug, and I lean in to give Tessa a careful squeeze.

"Are you all peached-out, Coach?" she asks while she rubs tiny circles on her baby bump.

I copy her movement, soothing my own belly. It feels like I've gorged on sweets for days. "If I don't see another cobbler until Thanksgiving, I'll be a happy man."

Her husband steps up behind her and pulls her so her back is flush with his chest. She melts against him with a sigh. "How were Mel's cupcakes? She really wants to win this year."

Luke snorts. "She wants to win every year."

"You got that right, mister." Mel appears, hand in hand with Hannah. "I *know* my cupcakes are better than Mary Lou's cobbler, so if I don't win this year, I'm going to demand a recount."

"Mary Lou's cobbler has won the most best in shows in the history of the cook-off," I remind everyone. "And it's flipping fantastic. I swear that woman uses two sticks of butter in her crust."

"Mmm, cobbler sounds so good."

Mel ignores her friend and narrows her eyes at me, hands fisted on her hips. "She uses shortening *and* butter, if you must know. That's why it's so flaky."

"Well, whatever her process, it is *working* for her." I can't help but flash her a smug grin.

Mel's mouth drops open, her lips shaped into a perfect *O*. She's *pissed*. And I'm ready to gobble her contempt right up.

Luke cuts me a dark look.

Right. The truce. I step back and relax my shoulders, content in my knowledge of the winners and looking forward to continuing this sparring session with Mel later.

"Dad, I'm hungry," Hannah pipes up.

"Let's wait until they announce the winners, Jelly Bean." Tessa grasps Mel's hand. "We want to watch Mel-Mel's victory lap."

Mayor Kilpatrick stands at the microphone and announces winners in the three categories. Ms. Rita's chili takes the savory category for the fourth year in a row. When Mary Lou's cobbler is called as the second-place dessert, Mel shoots me a look of triumph and pulls her shoulders back.

"Best in show in the sweet category goes to..." Even though I know the results, the mayor's dramatic pause makes my full stomach flutter. "Mel Marshall's peach pie cupcakes!"

I take a mental snapshot of the grin that overtakes Mel's face and watch her every move as she gives Tessa a quick peck on the cheek and jogs up to the stage to accept her trophy. She blows a kiss to her parents on the edge of the crowd, then shakes the mayor's hand and poses for several pictures. The winners typically don't make speeches, but once the photo op is finished, Mel grabs the mic out of Buck's hand.

"I'm proud to take this home today, my fellow Bennetians. Oh, and remember..." She finds me in the crowd and beams. "Let your haters be your motivators!"

"Those better not be *my* fries, Marshall."

Mel is perched in the passenger seat with one knee drawn up against the door and one bare foot resting on the leather cushion. Her hand is buried in the bag of burgers and fries we picked up at the new fast-food joint at the edge of town. When she pulls a fry out and stuffs it into her tempting mouth, she scrunches up her nose at me.

I have to cut my eyes back to the road so I don't wreck.

"These are not *your* fries, bee-tee-dubs. They're bag fries. Bag fries are fair game."

"Bag fries are *not* fair game. They should be split equally amongst the diners when the bag is unpacked."

"Pfft," she huffs. "That's the dumbest thing I've ever heard, Dudley Do-Right." She sticks another fry between her teeth and chews. "And I've heard some dumb shit in my day."

I park in an empty space behind Mel's building and snatch the paper bag from her lap. "Hey!" she snarls. She throws an arm out, but I keep it out of her reach.

We agreed to meet up around dinnertime so we'd both have time to head home and relax after the peach cook-off. As soon as I stepped up to her door to knock, she swung it open. She had her bag on her shoulder and her keys in hand as she stepped out and informed me that I was buying dinner.

The sun is low in the sky but just as fierce as it was midday, and the air is just as humid as it's been for weeks.

Inside Mel's apartment, the first thing I notice is that the bar that was cluttered with mail and random items the last time I was here has been cleaned off. I place the bag there as she moves one of the stools to the other side so we can sit across from each other.

She passes out our dinner choices, giving me a container of

fries that is most definitely missing quite a few and flashing me an exaggerated smile.

"Fry thief."

She takes a deep draw of her strawberry milkshake, ignoring my accusation, and regards me as I take a bite of my bacon double cheeseburger.

Licking her lips, she tilts her shake toward me. "I'm surprised you eat stuff like this."

I bark out a laugh, wiping my mouth with a napkin. "You've seen me put some food away, Marshall."

"I have. But I'm still surprised. I would think you'd only eat healthy crap, looking like that."

"Looking like what?" I taunt her.

She tips her chin up and huffs at the ceiling. "Don't be a jackass. You have a mirror."

"I love to eat all the things, so I put in all the work to stay healthy. I run at least three miles every day before school, and I lift weights a few days a week, too." I polish off the last of my fries. "What about you?"

Lips pressed together, she searches my face. "What *about* me?"

My snort comes out louder than I intend. "Don't be a jack-donkey. You have a mirror."

"Jack-donkey?" she sputters, twirling her pointer finger at me. "What the hell?"

I shrug. "My ma always had a swear jar for my dad. He had to put a dollar in every time one slipped. I grew up using alternatives. My years in college and in the league kinda corrupted me. When I moved home, I brought that bad habit with me, but Ma wasn't having it." I shake my head with a laugh. "I try my hardest not to disappoint Rhonda Watkins, so I cleaned that mess up real fast. But one will still slip out every now and then when the situation calls for it."

"A dollar a curse?"

"Oh, no. She makes me pay the big bucks. Twenty dollars a pop. Says if I can use grown-up words, then I can afford to pay grown-up money. She uses it to buy her friends rounds at Fuzzy's."

"You two are close," Mel says softly.

"We've always been close." I nod. "After Dad died, and it was just the three of us, I tried to step up, be the man of the house. But that woman *ran* the Watkins household, even before he was gone. She flat-out told me that my job was to grow and learn and enjoy being a kid. Then, when she got sick..." I swallow to clear away the panic that sets in. She's a survivor, currently in remission, but the memories of when she battled breast cancer still haunt me. "Our roles reversed, and she had to rely on me and Cass more than ever. And yeah, we grew closer."

"I'm so sorry she had to go through that, but I'm glad she had the two of you to fight alongside her." Mel tilts her head as she regards me.

I'd love to know what she's thinking. But I don't get a chance to ask.

She shakes her head and claps twice. "First date with Darcy. Let's hear about it." She hops up and takes care of our trash while I collect my thoughts.

"Darcy was..." I search for the best way to describe her. "She was intense."

"How so?" Resting her crossed arms on the bar, Mel tilts forward.

"Don't get me wrong, she's a nice lady. But we're definitely not a match."

"Aww, c'mon, Watkins. It was your idea to debrief. You have to give me more details so I can be informed for future setups."

I heave a heavy sigh. "You're right."

She rears back and gasps.

"I know. Alert the media," I deadpan. But before she can gloat too much, I jump in. "Darcy talks fast. Like, really fast."

"Like *Gilmore Girls* fast?"

"Yes." I snap my fingers and point. "She's like Lorelai-Gilmore-on-a-caffeine-high fast."

"Wait, wait, wait." Mel slams a palm down on the bar. "You've watched the Gilmores?" Her puzzled expression is so cute.

"I have indeed watched the Gilmores."

She sits up straight and waves an impatient hand, signaling for me to go on.

"Ma and I binged it when she was going through chemo." And I'm back to thinking about that terrifying season of our lives. In an instant, my heart feels heavier than a wrecking ball.

Mel's eyes soften, but I don't want to circle back to that topic, so I ask, "Favorite Rory boyfriend?"

"Let's answer at the same time," she challenges, one brow cocked.

When I nod in agreement, she counts down. "Three, two, one—"

"Jess!" we shout in unison.

Mel's eyes widen, but I give her a smug smile.

*This.* I love our dynamic. How quickly we go from sparring to finding common ground, from flirting to fighting, quick as lightning. My chest tightens, because we could be so dang good together. If only she'd give me another chance.

"Back to Darcy."

I clear my throat and put a pin in that thought. "Right. Darcy. We met up at an Italian place halfway between here and Columbus. She talked really fast. I'm pretty sure I annoyed the heck out of her when I had to ask her to repeat herself like three times."

"So...her only red flag was the fast-talking?"

"I'd say that's a pretty big red flag. Kinda hard to communicate with someone if you don't catch half their words. But she also FaceTimed with her dog in the middle of dinner."

"Erk!" The sound Mel makes is like a driver slamming on the brakes. "Pause. Did you just say she FaceTimed her *dog*?" She rests her chin on a fist, totally invested.

"I did. Apparently, her poodle has separation anxiety. So when she's at school or out with friends, she takes him to her elderly aunt who lives a few blocks away. And if Pierre gets anxious, her aunt FaceTimes Darcy, even if she's in the middle of class. Or on a date, I guess."

Mel tosses her head back and cackles. The action exposes the column of her neck, and the sudden urge to press my lips to that soft skin and inhale her scent overwhelms me. I clench my fists against my thighs and will the feeling to pass. She, of course, remains unaffected.

"Please, *please* tell me what she said to the dog."

I hold both hands up. "Listen, I'm not trying to shame a pet parent. And I'm definitely not making fun of having anxiety. But she used *baby talk*. At the table. In front of her date. She totally could've excused herself and taken that call in private."

"*Watkins*," Mel whines. "I need a reenactment. What were her exact words? And don't forget to mimic her voice."

I shake my head, but she keeps on. "*Please*?" she drags out as she lays her upper body along the top of the bar, arms splayed wide.

I want to tell her that I like how she sounds when she begs.

I'm ready to refuse her again, but she pops up and angles herself over the countertop so her face is only a foot from mine. Her eyes are wide in anticipation, making the greens of her irises impossibly bright. I can't deny her. This pixie of a woman has me in a chokehold, and she's oblivious.

"All right." I sigh.

Sitting ramrod straight, she claps and grabs the edge of the bar, rapt.

"She said…" I clear my throat and adopt the highest-pitched voice I can muster. "Hewwo dere, my widdle Pierre puppers."

Mel's laughing silently, her body shaking with pure delight, so I go on.

"Are you being a sweetie-kins for Auntie Gloria? Are you? You're da bestest widdle pupper man in the whole wide world."

"Stop!" Mel howls, bringing a hand to her chest. "She did not!"

My heart feels lighter than it has in years as I watch the way joy radiates off her. I knew within the first ten minutes of my dinner with Darcy that we didn't have a connection. But suffering through it was totally worth it for this reaction.

A breath later, though, my heart sinks, because next I'll have to sit through the play-by-play of Mel's date with Rob.

I rub the back of my neck and drop my focus to the bar. I'm almost afraid to ask for a rundown.

She rubs her nose and hauls in a deep breath, filling her lungs and pushing her chest out in the process. "Oh em gee," she says when she's composed herself. "I don't want to follow that."

We make eye contact and hold it, like the pause before a snap, the connection between us full of potential. She breaks first and shifts her attention to the bar, to my shirt, to her nails, into the distance over my shoulder. Anywhere but where I want it.

"So tell me about Rob," I request, even though I'd rather she forget she ever met him.

"Rob," she begins, "is a total frat bro with a business degree." The exaggerated eye roll that follows that statement means she misses the relief that is surely evident on my face.

She didn't like Rob. Best news I've heard all day.

"I mean, he was okayish, if you're into that whole two o'clock-tee-time,　　let's-circle-back-to-this-so-we-can-go-get-wasted-after-work type. He was kinda handsy, too."

I jerk my head up as icy hot anger grips my body. "Did he try something?" I can't keep the granite from my voice.

Mel lowers her brows, and the tiny wrinkle that forms between them is so dang cute it dilutes that initial rush of rage that courses through me. But it isn't enough to erase it completely.

"No, he didn't." The accompanying shake of her head is resolute. "Believe me, I know how to deal with losers who think they can—"

"You shouldn't *have* to."

"I shouldn't," she agrees. "But that's not the way the world works. A couple of times, he touched me in ways that were mostly innocent but lingered, too. When I asked him to stop, he apologized and said he didn't even realize he was doing it. And he did stop after that."

I bite the inside of my cheek to quell my anger. I've never had to deal with idiots being too pushy with my sister. She came out in high school. Not that women can't be the aggressors in relationships, but fortunately, none of Cass's dates or girlfriends gave off predator vibes.

"I don't get the friendship there—between Clay and Rob— if I'm honest," Mel continues. "They don't match."

"They don't *match*?"

"Yeah, like personality-wise. Clay's a total sweetheart. Rob is...*not*."

"Hmm. Clay did mention that they've drifted apart since college." I make a mental note to tell him he shouldn't act as Rob's wingman anymore.

Mel bounces off her stool and opens a kitchen drawer. She pulls out a notepad and a pen, then returns to her seat. She draws a T-chart and labels the top of each column with our names. Then, along the left side, she writes *Round One* and puts a zero in both columns.

"What's this?"

"For keeping the score." She shrugs. "Each attempted setup will be represented by a numbered round. If the date's successful, we'll mark it with a tally. Obvi, we both got big, fat goose eggs for round one."

"Obvi," I repeat, a wry smile lining my lips.

"Don't worry, Watkins. We'll frame it when I win. You can hang it up so your new girlfriend has a constant reminder of who was responsible for bringing you two together." She crosses her arms and shoots me a smug look. "I expect full credit in the wedding program."

Ignoring her gibe, I take the notepad and pen and flip a few pages in.

Mel leans over the counter to peek at what I'm doing, but I pull the pad away and continue. She huffs but lets me finish without complaint.

When I'm finished, I draw a line under what I've written and hand the notepad back to her.

She squints and tilts her head. "C's round one: Lorelai 'extreme dog mom' Gilmore. M's round one: Touchy McFeely, zero spark."

"This is how we'll document each date. A reminder for why each is, or isn't, a love-match."

"I like it." She shoots me an impressed smirk. It's an expression I've seen before, but it's rarely directed at me.

Gritting my teeth, I take her in. "I have a feeling every date of yours will have 'no spark' listed, though."

Mel scoffs. "Why do you think *that*?"

"Because, Marshall." I take a deep breath and consider whether it's wise to try this path again.

Dare I bring up the elephant that haunts every room the two of us together occupy? She's inspecting me now, waiting for my answer. As I regard her in return, the Mel as she is before me morphs into the woman I met all those years ago, with flickers of her face and body illuminated by a streetlight in the back of a dark vehicle. The night we moved together so perfectly, we created a rhythm all our own.

When she cocks her head to the side and her eyes narrow, the words spew out like water through a burst dam.

"Because, Marshall," I repeat with a huff. "You won't give someone the time of day even when you *do* feel a spark."

At first, her frown is soft and her eyes swim with confusion, but as the implication of my words becomes clear, her nostrils flare and her expression turns to stone. She hauls herself off the stool, then backs up until she's even with the door. Like she's aiming her body for the nearest exit in case she wants to bolt.

I move to the end of the bar, ready to catch her if she tries.

"We're not going there," she says, her voice edgy steel.

"We *are* going there,"

She shakes her head as her chest rises and falls in rapid breaths.

"We're having this out. Tonight." I keep my tone calm but firm.

This was not in my plans for tonight, but being with her, laughing with her, only makes my need for her to move past this wedge she's placed between us more acute.

Closing her eyes, she pinches the bridge of her nose and inhales deeply, no doubt trying to "center" herself—putting those yoga practices to use. When she looks at me, her eyes are slits. "If you're implying that *we*"—she flicks her hand between us—"had a spark—"

"There was a spark, and you damn well know it."

"So much for that swear jar, Coach," she mutters in a low voice. "Even if there *was* a spark—"

"There was."

"Ugh, let me finish, you infuriating man!" she growls, clenching her fists and punching her arms toward the floor.

God, I itch to grab her and toss her over my shoulder like a caveman.

"Even if there *was* a spark," she barks out, "whose fault is it that it never went anywhere?"

"Mine."

She opens her mouth, surely to spew another comeback, but she freezes as the weight of my answer registers.

"The blame lies with me, Marshall. I've tried to apologize to you so many times. But every time I bring it up, to tell you how utterly sorry I am, you run." I take a step forward. When she doesn't retreat, I take another. Then another until I'm so close she has to crane her neck to meet my gaze. "I'm so sorry I let you down," I confess, every word heavy with truth. I want to take her hand as further proof of my sincerity, but, afraid she'd snatch it back, I place one of mine over my heart instead.

She searches my face like she's trying to unravel my apology, but when she sees only truth, her expression goes blank. She shuts down like a shade's been drawn. She clenches her jaw, and through her teeth, she whispers, "I don't run." From the trepidation in her eyes, it's obvious even *she* doesn't believe her own lie. She lowers her chin and fixes her attention on my feet. "I think you should go."

I sigh from deep within my chest and hang my head. We stay that way for several long seconds, neither of us moving. My gut clenches in defeat and in disappointment—in myself, for being such a bonehead back then, and in Mel, for being so stubborn about forgiving me. For not letting go of the past so we can move forward.

Swallowing back my frustration, I stalk to the door. The second my hand touches the knob, she calls out softly.

"Hey."

I don't turn around, but I do pause to hear what she has to say.

"Thank you for dinner. And for today. For giving me such a high score in the cook-off."

I peer at her over my shoulder and lift one brow.

She gives me a sheepish smile in return. "I caught a peek of the scores on the podium when I accepted my trophy."

"You deserved to win, Marshall."

I pull the door open gently and step into the small entry outside her apartment. Just before I close it behind me, she calls out again.

"Your face makes me want to throw myself down a never-ending staircase!"

I'm still chuckling when I pull away from the curb.

# CHAPTER SEVEN

## CORDELL

The early morning sun is blinding as I turn onto the county road that leads into Bennett. I pull the visor down and settle in for my twenty-five-minute commute. And like I do every morning I make this drive, I turn the radio off and talk to my dad.

"Hey, old man," I begin. "Gonna be a hot one. High's supposed to get up to ninety-five. Don't worry, we'll make sure those boys drink plenty of water. Won't work 'em too hard."

I pause, like I always do, imagining how he'd respond. The silences between my words both heal my heart and fracture it a little more.

It's been twenty-three years, eleven months, and six days since my dad left this earth. I've missed him every single minute since.

"The season is shaping up to be a good one." I can't help but smile. "Grady's a junior this year, still starting QB. He's gonna be a great leader for the team. The senior boys will be, too. And Clay's oldest is probably gonna start. He's put on a few pounds since last season."

My dad played football in high school, and our television

was always tuned to a game. Didn't matter if it was college or professional. If football was being broadcast, it was playing in the Watkins' living room. I played baseball, basketball, and soccer as a kid, but football was my first love, and that was largely influenced by my dad's fondness for the game.

I continue our conversation as I round the bend and pass the turnoff to the Shipleys' homes. "Talked to Cass last night. She and Kelly just got home from their annual beach vacay."

Cass's wife is from South Carolina, and they take a week every June to visit her parents in Myrtle Beach. "Ryan got stung by a jellyfish, and Raya was in hysterics, thinking he was gonna die." My heart aches a little thinking about my tender-hearted six-year-old niece being worried about the big brother who torments her every chance he gets.

"Kelly took her down the beach to get a push-pop from one of the vendors to calm her down. I swear she loves those things as much as you did."

My throat burns the way it does every time I think about all that my dad has missed out on with his grandkids. God, he would be over the moon for them. I can picture the pure joy that would overtake his face as they raced to him. How he'd open his arms wide, ready to wrap them up in one of his bruising bear hugs.

"You should be here," I whisper into my empty car. I grip the steering wheel tight and will the grief to drift away like a wave returning to the ocean. "Ma and I are heading up to see them next month, before we start two-a-days. Before life gets too busy."

*How is your mama doing?* That's what he'd ask next.

"She's doing well. She's got her vegetable garden looking real good. Tomatoes, cucumbers, peppers, zucchini." I chuckle. "You'd be after her to make zucchini bread, no doubt. She still gets out and about plenty. Still goes to Fuzzy's with Ms. Daisy and her crew." Here is where my dad would good-naturedly roll his sepia eyes, but he'd be wearing a wide grin. My dad was as introverted as my mom is extroverted. He had a quiet, gentle nature and was content to sit back and let her shine. They shared plenty of life's ups and downs throughout their time together, but they loved each other fiercely.

A few years after his sudden passing, I overheard my sister ask our mom if she would ever consider dating again.

After a beat so long I thought she wouldn't answer, she said, "No, I don't think I will. I had my great love. I vowed to love him until death, and that's what I'm going to do." Neither Cass nor I brought the subject up again.

*And what about you?* he'd ask. *How's your love life?*

My dad died when I was thirteen, when I was smack dab in that awkward phase between boy and man. Needless to say, we didn't have many conversations about the opposite sex. There were times, when my mom was angry with him, that he would tell me his plan to smooth things over with her. "Here's how you keep a woman happy," he would say. Then he'd drop a nugget of wisdom. I can still hear him ask, "How's your love life?" his voice deep and gravelly, a few times in the months before he died.

I was in eighth grade, and I was just beginning to notice girls in that way.

"There's this woman." I press back against the headrest. "I've told you about her before. Mel, remember?" I imagine him nodding, encouraging me to continue. "We're not...anything, really. I don't even know if you'd call us friends. She's maddening, honestly. Yet..."

That word: *yet.*

I sigh. How do I put Mel into words? She's so tough, *yet* so soft. Sassy, *yet* sensitive. Childish, *yet* all woman. Jaded, *yet* endearing.

Not mine. *Yet.*

"I'm convinced she's supposed to be in my life. There're too many signs." I lift my hands off the wheel. "I know that's a bunch of mumbo jumbo. But how else do you explain why she keeps popping into my life? That night, that dive bar? Then *that* night. At Fuzzy's."

My gut twists when the image of Mel and the way her expression changed after my apology last Saturday flits through my mind.

"I've tried to give her space. Which is not exactly easy in a town the size of Bennett. But then Luke had to go and fall in love with her best friend, putting us in each other's orbit again."

My dad would no doubt offer me some sage advice here, and it hurts like hell that I don't know what he'd say. I let off the gas when the Bennett town limit comes into view. I'm almost to the school, so I need to wrap up our chat.

"I'll keep trying with her. That's all I know to do. And I'll keep setting her up with bozos who don't deserve her." I can't hide the disgust in my voice.

I take a deep breath, and I swear my dad asks, *How long do you plan on playing that foolish game?*

"Until she forgives me."

*You think there's a way for you two to make this work?*

"Yeah. I think there might be."

I pull into the parking spot labeled *Athletic Director* and sit for a few moments, not quite ready to say goodbye to my father again. I've been saying goodbye to him for most of my life.

As I sit, several players trickle into the gym, bags slung over their shoulders or strapped to their backs. Clay's truck is already here, but I don't see Eric's vehicle. My other assistant coach consistently strolls in right on time, so he'll be here soon.

"Well, old man, I've gotta go whip these boys into shape."

I imagine his deep chuckle ringing through the air. What he'd say next is the same thing he told Cass and me when he sent us out the door to catch the bus every day. He'd say it before every game or sporting event.

He'd plant his warm hand on the top of my head and wait for me to look him in the eye.

The words settle into my chest, strong and true like the man who quoted them to his children every chance he could.

*Be great today.*

"Will do, Dad. Love you."

*Nine years, four months, and five days ago...*

The air inside the bar is muggy, even though it's February. February twentieth, to be precise.

My twenty-eighth birthday.

The last thing I feel like doing is celebrating.

Luke practically dragged me to Fuzzy's tonight. My mom backed him up, likely as tired of my mopey butt as I am. I argued with her about it; she had another treatment today, and I don't leave her on treatment days unless Cass is in town and can stay with her. Even though she'll sleep the entire time I'm gone, I want to be nearby in case she gets sick or needs help getting to the bathroom. The home health nurse we hired only stops in during business hours.

I hadn't even considered Luke's suggestion to meet up until Ms. Marj offered to stay with Ma. Before leaving, I made her swear to text me if anything changed.

"Relax, bro. Doc Marshall is right across the street. She'd be over in a heartbeat if Ms. Rhonda needed her." Luke and I have been friends for most of our lives. There isn't a soul alive who knows me better than him, and right now, I'm not so sure I like it.

I nod at the bar a few times, but his words do nothing to ease the tension in my muscles. Or the heavy sense of doom that's weighed me down for months.

Gordon, who purchased Fuzzy's from his uncle last year, sets two full glasses on the bar in front of us, along with a bowl of mini pretzels.

Luke raises his beer and turns on his stool to face me. "Happy birthday, bud."

I wrap my hand around my glass, but I can't muster the strength to raise it.

Turning his Braves cap backward, he clinks his beer against mine and gulps it down. He assesses me, studying my face. Then he glances at my beer, a silent plea for me to make an effort.

We've been best friends since my family moved to Bennett when I was seven. We've maintained that friendship over the years, even when I went to college in Baton Rouge. Even when I moved to Tennessee to play for the Tors. He's seen me through the grief of losing my father, and he's been a solid presence since I moved home after my surgery in November. His parents are like my second parents. They'd do anything for me.

"I didn't get you a cake or anything." Luke's tone is full of apology. "But...here." He holds out a box I didn't notice him bring in. "Sorry it's not wrapped. Mom's out of birthday wrap, and I thought reindeer and candy canes would be weird."

His cheeks grow pink above his dark stubble, but it's not like him to be embarrassed over a trivial thing like not wrapping a gift.

Luke swallows, his Adam's apple bobbing, and tips his head at the box. I steel myself with a breath and carefully lift the cardboard lid. Nestled among red tissue paper is an eleven-by-fourteen framed print. Violets and golds and reds and indigos and grass greens stand out in blazing color behind the glass. On the left, surrounded by an abstract crowd decked out in the purple and gold of my alma mater, stands a lone football player, his helmet tucked under his arm. The back of his jersey is a focal point. My last name and an 84 are etched on it in fine detail. On the right, the image is almost identical, except it features the reds and blues of the Tor's team colors. Another football player, another jersey—Watkins, 84. Eighty-four because that was my dad's number in high school. Luke's drawn me tall, proud, and indestructible, standing on the green turf that was my second home for years.

Now his nervousness makes sense. He's worried about how I'll react to this reminder of a time before my dreams were crushed.

But his drawing is incredible. It perfectly captures the on-top-of-the-world feeling football gave me. The joy and triumph and devotion and agony of the experience. My best friend has serious talent. He's loved drawing since we were kids, but he's never given me a piece of his artwork to keep.

I study the intricate lines and precise shading, and a swirl of emotions overwhelms me: pride and love for the man sitting next to me, appreciation and gratefulness for the game that changed my life, despair and heartbreak because it ended too soon. All of those feelings, mixed with the terror from my mom's cancer diagnosis, create a perfect storm that threatens to drown me.

After several moments of silence, Luke clears his throat.

He's waiting for me to react, but the words get lodged in my airway, and my sinuses burn with the emotion.

"I just thought—" Luke sighs and sits a little taller. "I just thought you'd like a reminder of that special time in your life. Even if you aren't playing anymore."

I nod and blink rapidly to stave off the tears.

He clasps my shoulder and squeezes in support.

And we sit with each other like that for a few moments, always each other's safe place.

When I get my emotions mostly under control, I croak out a thank-you. "It's amazing, dude. I love it."

"Yeah?" he asks, his brow still furrowed in uncertainty.

"Absolutely," I confirm. "It'll look perfect hanging above my bureau."

"The fuck is a *bureau*?"

His bewildered expression makes me bark out a laugh, and some of the tightness inside loosens.

"A bureau," I explain, "is a dresser. You know, the thing with drawers your mom puts your folded laundry in, you spoiled ass." I tease Luke about his only-child, still-lives-at-home status every chance I get, even if he's doing it to save money to build himself a place on his family's land.

I have no room to nag him about it now, considering I've been living at my mom's for the past three months.

"I do my own laundry." Luke crosses his arms over his chest.

I raise my brows and pin him with a look. We both know better.

"Fine," he huffs. "I do my laundry *occasionally*."

We both grin into our beers, and pretty soon, we're ready for another round.

Gordo's serving us round two when I feel a presence to my left. A cupcake appears on the bar next to my glass, then there's a hand on my back, patting briskly. Ms. Daisy's face pops into my periphery as she hoists herself onto the stool next to mine.

"Little bird told me it's your birthday today, Cordell." She brushes a hand through her slate-colored hair. She's sported the pixie cut since I was a kid.

"Ms. Daisy, you shouldn't have."

"Oh, I didn't. Believe me, you don't want to taste anything I make. My Richard used to say he should've bought stock in smoke detectors and batteries."

Luke and I chuckle.

"No, that right there was left over from the very first meeting of the Bennett Business Babes." There's a gleam of pride in her eyes. "Doc Marshall's daughter made them. Apparently, she's taken up baking and has turned her parents' kitchen into a cupcake factory. Sorry I don't have one for you, Luke."

He dips his chin and gives her a genuine smile. "No worries, Ms. Daisy."

"Just wait till you bite into that." She nods at the treat in front of me.

Although I haven't had much of an appetite since my surgery, my mouth waters. But before I stuff my face, I survey her, looking for a hint of her motive. "You talked to my mom today?"

They're good friends, Daisy and my mother, and she always takes the time to call and check on Ma after her treatments.

She nods. "I did. She told me Luke had to 'bout drag you out of the house."

I grunt in response and bring my beer glass to my lips. Of course she did.

"You gonna eat that or not?"

Annoyed, I remove the paper wrapper and inspect the treat. The icing is a light spring green, while the cake portion looks to be vanilla. I take a generous bite and close my eyes when the unexpected flavors stir on my tongue. There's vanilla, yes, but also a hint of lime and something else. Tequila?

"Mmm." I can't help but moan.

Daisy slaps her palm on the bar. "Delicious, right?"

With a nod, I take another bite, suddenly feeling a fraction lighter.

"They're margarita flavored. Ain't that the darndest thing? Cupcakes that taste like actual margs. She even uses tequila."

I'm too busy inhaling the remaining chunk to respond. This cupcake might be the best thing I've ever put in my mouth.

"Well?"

I swallow the final mouthful and swipe at my lips. "Delicious. Thanks for thinking of me on my birthday."

She knocks twice on the bar top. "Been thinking about you

for something else, too." She leans in, waving for Luke to do the same, and lowers her voice. "Word on the street is that Coach Rivers is retiring after next season."

Coach Rivers has been the head football coach at Bennett High long enough to have coached generations of families. He's a stalwart pillar of our community and was influential in my decision to pursue a career in football.

Luke snorts a laugh. "'Bout damn time. He's gotta be pushing ninety."

Ms. Daisy gives him a withering glare. "Try seventy-three, boy. And respect your elders." She stabs her pointer finger in his direction.

"Yes, ma'am." Luke drops his gaze to the lacquered bar top.

"Anyhoo." She scoots even closer, pursing her lips. She smells like fresh grass and roses and earth—the exact aroma of her florist shop. "After next season, Bennett High will be looking for a new head coach." She leans back, scrutinizing me.

Like a balloon deflating, I sag. There goes the modicum of cheer I found when I tasted that cupcake.

She's angling for me to apply for the head coach job, but I'm done with football.

I was carted off the field in October after suffering an ACL tear. Three weeks before that, I took a hit that resulted in the second concussion of my short career.

And then five days after the surgery to repair the tear, I got that teary phone call from Cass—the one where she attempted to relay details of my mom's cancer diagnosis through breathless, heaving sobs—and I pledged I'd never step onto a field again.

I've experienced the highest of highs and the lowest of lows wearing those pads and that helmet. Walking away feels as final as a divorce.

I've broken up with the love of my life. I see no need to attempt a reconciliation.

Luke pounds on my bicep with his fist. "Yes. One hundred percent yes."

"One hundred percent no thank you."

"Why?" he asks.

Daisy's standing quietly beside me, watching us with her head tilted.

I open my mouth and search for the easiest way to convince her I'm not interested in the job, but before I can form the words, she holds both hands up.

"My work here is done." Then she scampers off to join her friends at one of the booths behind us.

I turn back to face the bar. "No." I lace my voice with the authority that Ray Watkins used on my sister and me when we drove our mom plumb crazy.

"Dell," Luke starts. "C'mon. This is the perfect job for you."

"I don't want to coach."

"So you're just going to, what? Wallow in misery? Doesn't sound like the kind of life my best friend would want."

"Dude, my mom—"

"I know. Your mom's sick. She needs you right now. You're going to fight right alongside her, every step of the way. But—" He holds up a finger. "Number one—it doesn't feel like it right now, but this battle won't last forever. Ms. Rhonda is going to kick cancer's ass and keep the two of *us* in line until we're old and gray. When she takes her victory lap, and she will, where does that leave you? You need something to fall back on."

He heaves in a deep breath.

"That brings me to number two—Pop is always telling Mom that she can't pour from an empty cup. She has to have things in her life that fill her up outside of being a wife and mother."

"Pretty sure having a full-time job while taking care of my sick mother would keep my cup pretty dang empty," I counter.

"That's why you need to fill it with something that's just for *you*."

I purse my lips and start drumming my fingers on the bar, ready to move on from this conversation.

Luke grimaces. "What I mean is, your cup should be filled with shit that gets you going, that lights you up. Sure, you'd be busy. Juggling coaching and helping your mom wouldn't leave a hell of a lot of leisure time. But." He takes a hearty swallow of his second beer and wipes his mouth with the back of his hand. "There's nothing in this world that lights you up the way football does."

Four months ago? He'd be right. But at the moment, there's nothing in this world that brings me down lower than football. Or, more specifically, the end of my career.

"Coaching would give you the opportunity to be a good role model for idiot teenagers, the way Coach Rivers was for us."

Luke drones on about idiot teenagers and mentoring and football, but I tune him out and consider what it would be like to be a coach. I never considered what I'd do after playing. Until a few months ago, I thought I had a decade before I'd have to worry about life after the NFL.

I thought I'd build a respectable career I could be proud of. A career my father would have been proud of. I made every decision with the Watkins name in mind. I never put a toe out of line. I always showed the utmost respect for the game, the coaching staff, my teammates, the organization. Arrived on time and stayed away from the women and the flash and the drama. Refused to blow my money on frivolous things. Other than my car, my only splurge was the house I bought for my mother in Bennett's only gated neighborhood.

I hustled from the minute the ink was dry on my rookie contract. No, I wasn't winning rookie awards or blowing up the stats, but I worked hard, believing that success would come over time. I just had to stay focused, mind my business, and put in the effort.

Life can be a real kick to the nuts sometimes.

Luke presses his shoulder into mine, pulling my attention back to the bar. He leans in and lowers his chin. "Hey, this is from work. Can you tell me what it says?" He slides his cell over, and I discreetly rattle off the details his manager texted.

His shoulders are hunched when he tucks the phone into his back pocket. Every time he has to ask, he folds in on himself and refuses to make eye contact with me.

Me? I silently berate myself. My gut churns when I think about how I've let him down. My best friend can't read. He always struggled. From the day we met. And instead of going to a trusted adult with this knowledge, I helped him keep it a secret. I helped him sweep it under the rug, provided him with answers, and completed assignments for him. There were times I tried to tutor him, but he would shut down so easily. I was afraid I'd lose my best friend if I pushed too hard, especially after my dad died. I'd lost one of the people I loved most already. I couldn't lose Luke, too. So I became complicit in his deception.

At a loss for what to say, I study his profile. I don't know how to make it right. When I bring it up, he's an expert at changing the subject. His parents are aware, I think, but they probably feel as helpless as I do. It's heartbreaking to watch him struggle with a basic life skill.

Ms. Daisy's words float back through my mind: *After next season, Bennett High will be looking for a new head coach.*

Had Coach Rivers known about Luke's illiteracy, he would've intervened. He'd give guys rides after games, and he bought sneakers on more than one occasion when he found out a player's family was having financial difficulties. He organized a meal train when Seth Petrie's mother passed away, and he required his players to volunteer in the community. As cheesy as it sounds, Coach Rivers was a difference-maker.

*Maybe I can be one, too.*

Maybe I can ensure that kids like Luke don't go unnoticed.

My stomach sinks. Am I *really* thinking about getting back into football?

"A pool table just opened up." Luke's voice cuts through my brain fog. "I'll snag it. Get us another round?"

As he stalks away, I push off my stool and turn back to the bar to signal Gordo.

I snag our third round of beers and spin, only to crash into a woman rushing past. The impact causes both beers to slosh over the sides of their mugs, drenching me and my fellow crash victim.

"Fuck. A. Duck."

A short, magenta-haired girl shakes her arms, flinging beer droplets onto the concrete floor. Her white shirt is soaked. So soaked the whole bar can now see her turquoise bra through it.

Like a creep, I take her in, letting my gaze linger there a little too long. Shaking out of my stupor, I drag my focus up to her face. She's assessing the damage, her head tilted low, but when she finally looks up at me, the fury in her gaze softens in recognition.

Her lips, painted in a bold plum, part as she takes a step back. "You..." she breathes.

Ah. She must be a fan.

"I'm so, so sorry, ma'am." I set the now half-empty glasses back on the bar and wipe my hands on my jeans. "Would you like an autograph? Or a selfie?"

She presses a hand to her stomach and takes another step back. "Wh-what?" I swear a look of hurt flashes across her face. The expression urges me to study her more closely. Her eyes seem familiar, maybe? But they're so heavily lined it's hard to tell.

"A selfie," I repeat. "Or I'd be happy to sign something for you."

Her hazel eyes go hard and her nostrils flare, making the tiny gold hoop on one side catch the light. "Are you fucking kidding me?"

"I'm sorry about your shirt. Is it dry-clean only or something? I'll pay—"

"Unbelievable." She pulls in a deep breath and fists her hands on her hips. She's angry, but I'm just baffled. "No, I don't want a damn selfie or an autograph, asshole." Her eyes narrow to slits that slice right through me.

If looks could kill, I'd be DOA.

Her blatant disgust makes me antsy. Where is it coming from?

Even though it'll probably fan her flames, I lean in. "I'm sorry, do I know you?"

A guttural groan escapes her lips as she steps toward me. For a moment, I think she's going to take a swing. Instead, she reaches around me, picks up one of the glasses I just set on the bar, and thrusts with her whole body. I'm cognizant enough to close my eyes a split second before cold beer drenches my face and hair.

Gasps echo around the bar, and there's a "Damn!" from somewhere nearby. Even a cackle from the back that sounds an awful lot like Ms. Daisy. I wipe my eyes and blink a few times to clear the burn. By the time my vision comes back into focus, the tiny woman is gone and Luke is standing next to me, pool cue in his hand.

"Damn. What did you do to Mel Marshall to make her do *that*?"

*Mel.*

A reel of flashbacks plays in my mind. A cute-as-hell bridesmaid on a bar stool, whose sad, mesmerizing eyes drew me in and prompted me to offer her an escape. A sexy pixie of a woman, head thrown back, grinding her hips as she chased her release in the back seat of my Escalade. The brazen confidence that revealed itself as we fumbled our way through a quick, hot hookup.

*I want more.*

*Then let's make it memorable.*

Standing in the middle of my hometown bar, as beer drips from my chin onto my already-soaked T-shirt, I swear I feel the sensation of her finger tracing an M on my body. Marking me to ensure she'd be memorable.

Luke and I turn to face the door Mel just stormed through.

Even though I've already worked out the answer, I swallow a lump and ask, "Mel, as in *Melanie* Marshall? Doc Marshall's kid?"

"*Yep.*" He drags the word out, his lips popping the final sound.

*She looks so different.* I stare at the empty space inside the door. Her hair—longer and dishwater blond that night—is now shorn to her shoulders and dyed an aggressive magenta. Her makeup is darker, angrier somehow. The nose ring is new. Even her clothing is a different style. Tonight, she was wearing a plain white tee tucked into tight, black shorts layered over black fishnet stockings. Black Chucks. All her colorful softness has been leached from her body, leaving behind a monochrome palette accented with harsh pops of color.

What caused such a drastic change?

An unwelcome thought hits me like a middle linebacker: Maybe her encounter with *me* caused this?

Another flashback: Mel, biting her bottom lip as she scribbled her number on the back of a receipt. A number I never used. I wanted to, but I was in Tennessee and she was in Georgia. It wouldn't have been fair to either of us to pursue more than that one night. Even though the memories of it have kept me company often.

I close my eyes as the weight of my mistake presses down on me. I have royally effed up.

"You still want to shoot, or…"

I exhale a deep, chest-burning sigh and turn to Luke. "Nah, I think I'm gonna head home." I wave a hand down at my sodden clothing.

"Yeah," he nods. "Helluva memorable way to end your birthday, huh?"

I can only nod as I grab the gift from him and fish my key fob out of my pocket.

*Memorable*. That word is sure to haunt me for a long while.

# CHAPTER EIGHT

## MEL

*The blame lies with me, Marshall.*

*I'm so sorry I let you down.*

Those words have run through my mind on a loop for the past two weeks. His tone was sincere. His expression was earnest. His words were heartfelt.

So why can't I get the hell over it?

He *did* let me down when he didn't remember me. And it hurt like a motherfucker.

I looked different, I can give him that, but there wasn't even a glimmer of recognition.

I left the back of his SUV that night feeling *seen* for the first time in more than a year.

It became clear that night at Fuzzy's—with that *I'm sorry, do I know you?*—that I was only a random hookup to him. I'd thought I was more than that. He made me *feel* like I was more than that.

Girl hooks up with a celebrity (or celebrity-adjacent) horndog and expects it to be the meaningful encounter that changes his life, only to find out she's nothing special. Tale as old as time, right?

After Nick's betrayal, Cordell was the first guy I felt a visceral connection with. We *did* have an undeniable spark that hot June night. He's not wrong. That's what compelled me to offer him my number.

Maybe if he were anyone other than the guy I'd crushed on for most of my adolescence, I could've moved on ages ago. Chalked it up to a learning experience.

But it was *him*.

And he offered me a fucking *selfie*. Like I was nothing more than an infatuated jersey chaser.

I avoided him for years. It was easy enough. We'd run into each other occasionally. Sometimes I'd see him outside his mom's house after she moved in across the street from my parents. But it wasn't until Luke and Tessa started circling each other that we were forced to interact on the regular.

Being in Cordell's proximity makes me feel *things*. Things I'd thought I had shoved into those internal boxes ages ago. He also pisses me the hell off, with his stupid hot body and stupid handsome face and stupid kind heart.

"Whoa, what did that computer do to you?"

I stop my aggressive mouse-clicking and look up, a little startled. Jane is standing on the other side of the counter, looking like Workout Barbie in hot-pink leggings and matching workout tank. Her blond ponytail is at the perfect height to ensure maximum bounce when she walks. If I didn't like her so much, I'd hate her.

"Sorry." I search the corner of my screen for the time. "I was just...are you early or am I late?"

"I'm early." She gives me a sweet smile. "I needed to get out of the shop. If Bailey asked me one more question, I was gonna scream." From the stories she tells, Jane's new part-time employee is not the typical flighty teenager who spends most of her shift scrolling on her phone.

Her complaints reinforce my choice to operate as a one-woman show. With the exception of Christine, who drives over from Oglethorpe three times a week to teach our Inferno Hot Pilates classes.

I close out of the spreadsheet I've been updating and turn back to Jane. "I guess it's better that she asks too many questions than not enough."

"True," she concedes, looking up at the class schedule posted above my head. "Flow is your last class of the day, right?"

"It is."

"Want to grab a drink after? Chase is spending the night with Josh's parents." Her eyes are bright and her smile is so wide and hopeful.

So I feel like a jerk when I decline. "Raincheck?"

Her shoulders slump.

"I have a date!" I blurt, as a consolation prize.

She perks back up at that tidbit. "Ooh, a date? Details, please." She props her elbow on the countertop and rests her chin in a palm, showing off the shimmer of her perfectly manicured nails.

I avoid sharing details about my personal life with anyone other than my family or Tessa—and Cordell, I guess, which is ridiculous—so I hesitate.

"Don't hold out on me." Jane's blue eyes widen in anticipation. And is she holding her breath?

I sigh. Fine. This won't kill me, right?

"It's a setup."

She opens her mouth, but before she can ask, I go on.

"Mutual friends. It's not a blind date. We've seen each other's pictures, but we've only communicated through texts. He's a music teacher in Americus. His name is Drew. We're meeting at a park over there for a picnic—his idea, not mine." Why the hell am I babbling like this? And does my voice sound squeaky? I wipe a thin layer of sweat from my hairline.

Jane places a hand over mine. "Breathe," she says. "I swear I don't think I've ever seen you like this. It's okay to be nervous."

Only I'm not nervous about the date. I eat guys like Drew for breakfast. I'm sweating bullets because of the inevitable debrief after the date. I haven't seen Cordell since the night he apologized, and I'm not sure I'm ready.

Jane offers me first date advice, and soon, people trickle in for the afternoon class. I get through the instructions and poses without any further thought of Cordell, Drew, first dates, or apologies.

When I'm finished for the day and the studio is spotless, I lock up and head upstairs to shower and change. On my way up to my apartment, my phone buzzes in my bag.

COACH ASSHAT

Drew will meet you at the gazebo in Rees Park at seven tonight.

I shoot off a quick reply.

Got it, boss.

Then another:

Has your face scared any small children today?

Once I'm in my apartment, I fill Mouse's bowl with kibble and riffle through the stack of mail I stuffed into my bag this morning. Bills, bills, and more bills. An ad for Mr. Rusty's hardware store. A coupon for a new nail salon a town over—I'll save that for Glamma. Near the bottom of the stack, a small, bright piece of mail slips out and drops to the floor. My heart pounds against my ribcage as I bend to pick it up.

A postcard of the Atlanta skyline at night.

Atlanta is close. Too close. I can shake off the dread when

it's Florida or Mississippi or South Carolina. But Georgia...

I flip the card over and read the words Nick's scribbled on the back in blue ink: *Let's bask in the wild infinity.*

It's a line from the Low Bars' song "Meditations on a Doomed Romance." A song he wrote, ironically, the week after we got married. We had a good laugh at that song title. If only I hadn't let love blind me so damn much.

I storm into my bedroom and rip the closet door open. With a huff, I yank the lid off the shoe box and stuff the Atlanta postcard in with the rest of Nick's lies. The glimpse I get of the previous postcard sends an icy sensation trickling down my spine. He sent it just over a month ago. Usually, I have three or four months of reprieve between surprises. Why did he send another so soon?

Ignoring the trepidation settling in my stomach, I shove the shoebox back onto the shelf at the back of the closet.

"Out of sight, out of mind," I whisper.

I hum the tune of "Since U Been Gone" and go in search of my phone.

Let's have a phone debrief tomorrow after your date.

I've set Cordell up with a girl my brother dated in high school. I'm seriously running out of options. Tomorrow is the only day that worked for both of them, so they're meeting up for lunch, even though it's a holiday.

COACH ASSHAT

No dice, Marshall. We already agreed to meet up after the [fireworks emoji]

Ugh. I'm not ready to spend significant time in proximity to him. Not so soon after his apology and the shock of Nick's postcard.

I roll my shoulders to release knots of tension.

Fine. Don't expect me to be in a good mood.

COACH ASSHAT

I never do. [winky face emoji]

COACH ASSHAT

And be nice to Drew. He's a good guy.

[middle finger emoji]

I'm ready in record time. It's a forty-five-minute drive to Americus, and if I know Cordell, he's warned Drew that I'm forever running late. Dressed in my summer uniform—cutoffs, a graphic tee, and Birks—I lock up and climb into my car.

I pull into an empty spot at Rees Park twelve minutes after the time we agreed on. To my left is the large gazebo where Drew should be waiting. Since it's after seven, the only souls here are a few dog walkers scattered along the paved walkways through the park.

The scent of freshly mowed grass fills my nose as I make my way up the sidewalk to the gazebo. As I approach, a man stands from one of the benches lining the inside of the structure.

"Mel?" he asks, rubbing his right hand against his jeans.

"Yeah. Drew, right?"

He nods and lets out a shaky laugh. When I reach the top of the brick steps, he offers his hand, and I place mine in his. Instead of shaking it, he lifts it to his mouth and kisses my knuckles.

"You're adorable," he says, breathless.

Taken aback, I fight the impulse to cringe. "Er, thanks."

He's not a bad-looking guy, just vanilla. A dime a dozen at any sporting event or concert. He's taller than me—c'mon, who isn't?—and has neatly trimmed light brown hair that's parted on one side. His full cheeks are clean-shaven, and his eyes are a golden brown. The sleeves of his light blue button-up are rolled to his elbows, and sensible brown loafers peek out from below the hem of his jeans.

Loafers. In July.

"I see no good reason to act my age."

His voice pulls me out of my assessment, and for a minute, all I can do is blink at him. Until I realize he's reading the words on my gray T-shirt.

"That's funny."

I let out a breath. "Oh, uh, thanks."

God, this is awkward.

"Sorry I'm late, by the way."

"Um, no problem. Cordell mentioned that you might be running a few minutes behind."

See? I had no doubt he would.

"So, you and Cordell met at a conference?"

"Yeah, last summer. It was a professional development seminar on trauma-informed education practices. We were paired up for a presentation and hit it off. Imagine that, huh? The band geek and the jock being friends."

He pauses like he's waiting for me to react, so I force a laugh. I want to tell him that I *can* imagine it, because Cordell is the type of man who'd befriend anyone. But I keep that thought to myself. With my luck, Drew would tell Coach Asshat that I complimented him.

I rock back on my heels, at a loss for what to say to keep the conversation going. Drew stands in front of me, smiling.

When it becomes clear that I'll have to move this along, I did deep for a topic that'll get the conversation flowing.

"So, you brought stuff for a picnic, huh?"

*Wow, Mel. Incredible.*

"Oh! Yes. Sorry." He crouches low and pulls a wicker picnic basket from under a bench.

"Wow, that's a legit basket. Did you borrow it from your mom or something?"

"No," he answers, but doesn't elaborate. I stand awkwardly at the entrance of the gazebo as he spreads a colorful quilt over the concrete floor.

I'd kill for an adult beverage right now.

With a sigh, I plop down next to where my date is kneeling and pulling items out of the basket.

"I wasn't sure what you'd like, so I packed a bunch of things."

When he holds up a container of potato salad. I'm struck with the memory of slinging a handful of it at Cordell on Memorial Day. I roll my lips to tame the smile that wants to break free.

"And crudités. I brought deli meat, cheese, and bread to make sandwiches." He hands me small bottles of mustard and mayonnaise. "Three kinds of chips. Drinks." He pulls out bottles of water, Sprite, and cola. "And for dessert...banana pudding."

This guy has gone to so much trouble. Damn it. Guilt swirls in my gut because we'll probably never see each other again after tonight.

We build our sandwiches and spoon the potato salad onto the sturdy paper plates Drew packed. I pluck a snack-sized bag of barbeque kettle chips from the selection he laid out and take a huge bite of my turkey and Swiss.

"Cordell tells me you own a yoga studio," Drew says, setting his sandwich on his plate. "How long have you been open?"

I swallow and wipe my mouth with a napkin. "It'll be six years in January."

"Is that something you've always wanted to do?"

"God, no," I snort.

He watches me, brows lifted in curiosity, like he's waiting for me to elaborate, so I take a swig of Sprite and give him an abbreviated Mel history lesson. "I didn't finish college, and when I moved back home, I drifted from job to job for a while, looking for something that didn't suck the life out of me. I waitressed, worked retail, delivered flowers, spent two weeks as a receptionist—you name it, I probably did it." Every job I tried after moving home from Athens felt like wearing clothing a size too small. "One weekend, while I was visiting my brother in Columbus, my sister-in-law convinced me to go to a Saturday morning Flow class with her. I was hooked. Spent the rest of the weekend on their laptop, researching how to become a certified instructor. I continued working rando jobs as I earned my certification hours, and when I was finished, I opened my own place."

"That's impressive, Mel."

I bite the inside of my cheek. His expression is so unguarded and genuine. It's hard not to like this guy.

Ready to move on, though, I shoot him a smile and pick my sandwich up again. "So...music teacher. Is that something *you've* always wanted to do?"

He shakes his head and points at his chest. "Band geek, remember?"

"What did you play?"

"Alto sax in high school and college." He leans in and brackets his mouth with a hand. "Don't worry," he whispers, "I practice *safe sax*."

I snort. Did he *really* just say that?

Drew's silent laughter and pink cheeks charm me. Just a little.

When he's composed himself, he continues. "With my musical background, becoming a music instructor was really a no-brainer. Not to mention teaching is the perfect dad job."

"Dad job, huh?"

"Yeah, think about it." He brushes breadcrumbs off his shirt. "I'll have summers off to spend with my kiddos. Not to mention all the same holiday breaks."

"I see. And when do you plan to have these kids?"

"I mean, are you free for the next eighteen-plus years?" He slaps his knee and throws his head back.

Oh, holy hell. He's obviously joking, but my armpits are suddenly extra damp. And it's not from the summer evening.

"Drew?"

"Yes?"

"Maybe don't ask a first date to be your baby mama," I suggest.

"Right." He clears his throat. "You're right. I'm sorry. It was a bad joke." He dips his chin, suddenly very interested in the banana pudding on his plate, fidgeting with his plastic fork and refusing to make eye contact.

Shit. Was I too harsh?

"Listen."

He looks at me with wide Bambi eyes, and my sandwich turns into a boulder in my stomach.

"There's nothing wrong with wanting to be a parent, but I don't know if I even want kids." The moment the words leave my mouth, a picture of a grinning little boy with tawny skin and curly brown hair strikes me like a bolt of lightning.

Where the fuck did *that* come from?

"Can we rewind this conversation? To before I made an ass of myself?" His expression is so hopeful and genuine.

Cordell's texts from earlier come to mind.

*And be nice to Drew. He's a good guy.*

"Fine. Yes, let's forget about it."

His shoulders lower, and he breaks into a smile. "How long have you had the pink?" He nods at my space buns.

"For a few months. I went with pink when my best friend told me she was expecting. I'm manifesting a girl." I squeeze one of the twisted buns, only to panic when I realize I've steered our conversation back into procreating territory.

Thankfully, it seems as though Drew has learned his lesson. "What color was it before pink?"

"Oh, uh, it was lavender for a while." I kept it that way for a long time to spite Cordell. Simply because he *claimed* to not like purple. Liar. He went to LSU, for fuck's sake.

"I like that you express your individuality that way."

I refrain from rolling my eyes. Cordell would be so proud. I've been coloring my hair vibrant shades since shortly after Mark and Lisa's wedding, but it's never been about expressing my individuality. No, it's been a way to distance myself from the girl I was *before* my life fell apart—the girl who fell in love with a wannabe rock star and had her heart smashed to smithereens.

Of course, I don't divulge any of this to Drew.

After a few more minutes of surface-level small talk, we clean up. Drew talks a little about his siblings and his nieces and nephews, as well as his dog, Scout. Baby mama joke notwithstanding, Drew really is a nice guy.

But there's no spark. Not even a flicker. I picture Cordell's smug, handsome face, and I clench my fists.

The sun is low in the sky; the last remaining hour of daylight fades as a symphony of cicadas suffuses the air. I'm running through my list of "let him down gently" speeches, ready to choose the best one for this situation, when Drew clears his throat.

"Um, I have a little surprise for you, if you don't mind."

He looks so hopeful, so I don't have the heart to deny him, even though I'm probably going to crush his spirit in the next five to ten minutes.

Immediately, I regret giving him the opportunity. Because with a nervous smile, he pulls out a fucking acoustic guitar he had stashed behind one of the benches.

Every cell in my body goes on high alert. Instead of running for the hills like I should, I'm frozen on the quilt, my heart thudding against my ribs. I'm assaulted with memories of Nick, guitar in hand, strumming the chords as he worked to match Vance's new melodies to the lyrics he claimed I inspired.

Drew returns to the blanket and strums the strings. My mind is screaming to ask him to stop, to tell him that this whole thing is making me uncomfortable, but I've lost the ability to speak.

"Thought we could use a little mood music," he says as he gently plucks at the strings.

I arrange my face into something resembling a smile, though the closest I can get feels more like a grimace.

He doesn't notice. "This song is from one of my favorite Georgia bands. I discovered them when I was in college."

*Holy. Shit. Fuck all the damn ducks. Is this really happening?*

My thoughts are a series of creative curses, one after the next. I cycle through the list, then tell myself to calm the fuck down. There are dozens of regionally popular bands from Georgia. What are the mother-trucking odds that he's about to play a tune from the Low Bars?

But as Drew plays the first chords of "Hymn of Youth and You," I know the mother-trucking odds are *not* in my favor.

Does he know? Does he know that the lyrics he's warbling were written the morning after guitarist Nick Hayes fucked his then-girlfriend for the first time? Does he know that the line "from innocence to passion, unveiling a new reality" refers to me? To when I gave my innocence to a man who would end up crushing me?

Then another thought, one much darker, has my turkey and Swiss threatening to make a reappearance: Does Cordell know? Did he put Drew up to this?

But *how* would he know? Tessa wouldn't divulge the secret of my failed marriage, even to Luke. I trust my best friend implicitly. Despite how small our hometown is, news of my quickie marriage and subsequent divorce didn't spread like gossip normally does here. Since it all went down in Athens,

Bennett was a safe bubble for me back then, a refuge from pitying looks and *bless your hearts*. Or maybe I was too caught up in my devastation to notice.

The one person who might know is Ms. Daisy. That woman knows *everything* about everyone in Bennett. Maybe she shared the news with Ms. Rhonda. They're close, so it's not a stretch to imagine whispers of my embarrassment being passed along like some fucked-up, small-town game of telephone.

I force my lids open and study Drew, searching for signs that he's playing some cosmically horrible joke on me.

But he's lost in the melody, crooning the words in his soft, pleasant voice. If this was a prank, he'd be watching my reactions with vested interest, right? He does watch me as he reaches the bridge, and the shy smile and pink that stains his cheeks indicate that he's likely blameless.

Drew may very well be an innocent participant in my distress. But what about Cordell?

Both my stomach and my heart are heavy. Could he be behind this? Because despite the arguing and food fights and forgotten identities that define our relationship, when all is said and done, he *is* a stand-up guy.

But if he's behind this...

Drew finishes the song with a flourish. Miraculously, I find my voice and thank him for a nice evening. When he asks if he can call me again, I let him down as gently as I can. I don't mention that his serenade was akin to torture.

Halfway home, my phone lights up. It's a text from Cordell, but I don't bother to read it. I'll hold on to my anger like a life preserver while I work up the nerve to confront him about tonight's date.

If it turns out he did suggest that performance to Drew, I'll stiletto his balls and never speak to him again.

# CHAPTER NINE

MEL

I sleep in on the Fourth of July, and when I finally haul myself out of bed, I discover four new text messages from Cordell. I refuse to text back. The conversation we need to have is one best done in person, so it will have to wait until after his lunch date and the town fireworks show.

Mark, Lisa, and the boys are coming over from Columbus to spend the weekend, thank God. Otherwise, I may just stay in bed all day.

Mouse lets out an angry meow when he's jostled by my movement, but he's quick to forgive me when I scoop him up and scratch his ears. His fur is soft against my cheek, and his whole body vibrates with deep purrs.

After a scalding cup of coffee, I pack a bag and head over to my parents' house for the day. When I arrive, Glamma is the only one around. She's on the back patio, shelling peas, her white hair perfectly coiffed.

"Melanie!"

"Hey, Glam." I close the patio door behind me and give her a quick peck on the cheek. Her familiar scent—a combination of rosewater and White Rain hairspray—wafts into my nose. "Traded the coral for red today, I see." I gesture at my lips.

"Yes, yes. Your father said the same thing. It's America's birthday and I'm eighty-two years old. I can change my lipstick, darling."

"Of course you can." I plop down on the cushioned patio chair next to her. I can count on one hand the number of times I've seen Glamma not wearing her signature coral.

The day is already hot, and it's not even noon, but the shade of the patio and the two ceiling fans set on high provide us a little reprieve.

"Your parents are picking up last-minute groceries, and Mark and Lisa should be here soon."

Focused on the blue pool water, taking in how calm its surface is, I nod.

"Go get another pan. You can help me finish these purple hulls," she orders. "We'll have some with the roast on Sunday and freeze the rest." My parents are busy professionals and typically stick with last-minute dinner plans, but they insist on having a sit-down dinner every Sunday evening.

Once I have the pan in my lap, Glamma hands me half of her unshelled pile of peas, and we fall into a companionable silence. I've been shelling peas with my grandmother for as long as I can remember. The rhythm of the routine is ingrained. All the tension flows from my body as I split open each pod with a thumbnail and slide it through the husk to scrape the peas into the pan.

My fingertips have grown pruney by the time Glamma decides she's ready for girl talk. "How are things going with that coach?"

That question is enough to jolt me out of the peaceful trance I'd fallen into and jump-start my heart. "What *things*?" I frown at her. "There are no *things*."

"Melanie, darling, you know better than to try to bullshit me."

I can't help the grin that breaks free. Cussing grannies are my favorite.

Glamma's brow wrinkles as she narrows her eyes at me. "Something's there. Mark my words. I've heard things."

My smile fades and I swallow hard. I've been worried that the rumor mill would start churning with speculation about Cordell and me. We've been seen together, just the two of us, several times—at Fuzzy's, riding in his SUV, at the fast-food drive-thru—and it doesn't take much to set tongues a-waggin' in this town. If people think we're dating, that will make our whole matchmaking competition difficult. The pickings are already slim.

"We're just friends. Sorta," I insist, even though I know damn well she won't be fooled. "We're actually in a competition to see who can find a suitable match for the other first."

"A competition, you say?"

"Yes, ma'am. We set each other up on dates and then meet up to talk about how they went. That's why we've been seen around town together."

Glamma's hands still over the baking dish she's using to collect peas. "And how's that going so far?"

The buoyed pride I felt after my confession deflates like a flat tire. "Uh." I clear my throat and lower my voice. "Not so well."

"Hmph." My grandmother goes back to attacking the pea pods like they've wronged her somehow. "And do you know *why* it's not going so well?"

"Because dating in Bennett is like searching for a unicorn in the forest?"

"No, darling. If Daisy Crawley can live in this town and find four husbands, then geography isn't the problem." She leans closer, a sharp glint in her eyes. "I reckon your little competition is going ass-backward because, deep down, you don't want him to find someone else."

"That's ridiculous. Why wouldn't I want him to find someone?" I scoff. I suddenly feel like I swallowed a handful of cotton balls, but my focus remains on the pea pods in my lap.

Glamma gives me a thorough once-over before she finally speaks again. "Melanie Jane Marshall, look at me."

I bite the inside of my cheek and lift my lashes. Her eyes, the same color as mine, are shining with so much love and wisdom. I grip the edge of the pan so hard my knuckles cramp.

"My beautiful girl." Her chin quivers a bit, but she composes herself quickly. "I don't think what you're choosing for yourself is what your heart really wants."

She sees all of me. She always has. I want to tell her she's right, that I want to let my heart lead the way again, but that I'm afraid I won't survive another heartbreak. That it's easier this way, keeping the walls and internal compartments fortified.

I'm terrified she's right about Cordell. That subconsciously, I don't want him to find someone.

And suddenly, I think it's time to confess these things to her. I take a deep breath, ready to pour out my truth, but my lungs lock up at the sound of excited little voices coming from inside the house.

Glamma and I finish our shelling, then join the rest of our family for a day full of splashes and giggles and snacks. Once we've vacated the pool for the day, Dad and Mark grill hamburgers while Mom helps Lisa bathe the boys and get them dressed for the fireworks show. I hop in the shower to wash the chlorine from my hair and body and change into cutoffs and my red *Firecracker* tank top. It's the same shirt I wore the day of the food fight. The day that started this whole arrangement with Cordell.

My family—minus Glamma, who opts for an early bedtime —loads up in two vehicles and heads for downtown a little after eight. Mr. Rusty, owner of our town's hardware store, has been in charge of the fireworks show for as long as I can remember. In the last few years, his grown sons have helped him set it off without a hitch.

Central Street, downtown's main drag, has already been closed to traffic, so we park at the library and lug our folding chairs to where the crowds have gathered. The majority of the town has claimed spots in the middle of the street; chairs and blankets and beach towels dot the asphalt, all facing the south end of town where the fireworks show will commence above town hall.

I'm leading the Marshall crew through the front of the viewing area when Tessa calls out to me.

I shift direction and head toward her voice but stop short when I reach where they've gathered. The Shipley, Watkins, and Reeves families are grouped together. The adults are lounging in chairs while the kids are seated in a circle on a blanket spread on the ground. Hannah and several other kids are in the middle of a game of Uno, squinting through the last dregs of sunlight to identify their draw-fours and wilds.

After a round of handshakes and hugs, my family settles in. Cordell is watching me as I open my chair next to Tessa's, but I refuse to look his way out of fear that I might blurt out an accusation while surrounded by the whole damn town.

In less than five minutes, my parents are enveloped by Bennett townsfolk. Mom is listening to lists of ailments and tolerantly agreeing to examine a weird rash. Dad is being grilled about a property in their neighborhood. My patient parents give everyone their full attention. Mark and I make eye contact and shake our heads. Our parents have been ambushed like this all our lives. It comes with the territory for the only doctor and realtor in town.

As the last dusky pinks and oranges are leached from the sky, we stand and place our hands over our hearts, and the high school band plays a wobbly rendition of "The Star-Spangled Banner." Then quiet descends on the town as we wait for that first rocket to light up the sky.

Halfway through the starbursts of red, purple, blue, and green, I scan our group. I take in the joy on my nephews' faces as they *ooh* and *ahh* at the illuminations from the safety of their parents' arms. The way Hannah giggles at something her dad whispers in her ear, her attention locked on the sky and her small hand nestled in Tessa's. At my parents' serene faces. They're standing, wrapped together. Mom's resting her head against Dad's shoulder. I sneak a glance back, just over my left shoulder, to where Cordell stands, hoping for a chance to discreetly admire the way the colors highlight his features. But he's not watching the fireworks.

His dark eyes are on *me*.

I jerk around fast enough to cause whiplash. The heat that flushes my body from head to toe has nothing to do with the temperature. Two warring emotions, irritation and satisfaction, settle deep in my bones.

The show lasts a grand total of twenty minutes, and when the finale is over, we all pack up. The Reeveses bid us all good night and go in search of their teenage son, who's been occupied with his friends and teammates tonight.

I'm just slinging my chair cover over my shoulder when Cordell steps over. "How about that beer you owe me, Marshall?"

The crowd around us freezes. Even the kids.

I gape like a fish as I grapple for a response. "Uh, I have to ride home with my parents. My, um, car is at their house." Yes, we had a plan to meet up after the fireworks, but I didn't expect him to ask me about it in front of my whole family.

"You can get it tomorrow," Lisa chimes in, very unhelpfully.

"We can meet you for breakfast at Ruth's. One of us can drive it into town then." She's giving me a shit-eating grin and not-so-subtly elbowing Mark. Like the good husband he is, my brother blinks a couple of times and nods.

"Great. Your car is covered," Cordell states.

I glare at him for a full ten seconds, mostly so I can check him out. His red Eagles football T-shirt is snug. The fabric stretches across his pecs in a way that should be illegal when he puts his hands on his hips, like he's waiting for me to offer up another excuse. He's paired the casual shirt with red, white, and blue madras shorts. He's wearing leather slides, and to complete the look? A blue ball cap. Turned motherfucking *backward*.

"What about your mom?" I'm grasping at straws now. "Don't you need to drive her home?"

"I drove myself, hon," Ms. Rhonda says with a kind smile. "He's free as a bird."

I offer her a weak smile. Of course he is.

"I could go for a beer." Luke cuts his eyes from me to his best friend. In fact, every eye in the circle is ping-ponging between the two of us like they're spectators at Wimbledon.

"You and Tessa go on and join them," Ms. Marj offers. "June Bug's staying with us tonight anyway."

Luke looks to his wife for confirmation, but Tessa's watching me as we communicate silently, the way only best friends can. After a few seconds, she gives an infinitesimal head bob. "Sure, let's go for a little while."

I exhale the breath I was holding. Cordell won't want to talk about the setup competition in front of our friends, so maybe I'll be able to convince him to have a phone conversation after all.

"You know what?" my brother pipes up, "if y'all are okay with taking the boys home..." He turns to my parents.

He doesn't have to finish the sentence. "Absolutely." My mom beams. "You kids have fun."

My dad takes Owen from Lisa's arms while Mark and my mom trade key fobs.

"C'mon, Rhonda. We'll walk you to your car," Luke's dad offers.

With a pat to her son's abdomen, she turns and loops her arm through Mr. Tom's.

The six of us stand in the middle of Central and watch their procession until they reach the corner that leads to the library.

"Thank God for grandparents," Mark mutters.

Lisa and Luke reply simultaneously. "Amen."

"First round's on Watkins." I smirk at him, then turn and make my way to where Fuzzy's neon sign beckons.

The bar is crowded tonight. We find an empty pub table, but there are only four stools, so Luke goes in search of spares, while Cordell heads to the bar to order water for Tessa and beers for the rest of us. When they return to the table, they refuse Mark's offer for the final stool. My brother shrugs and plops down next to his wife.

The crowd is lively, and Tom Petty's "American Girl" is blasting from the jukebox. We settle in, and the guys get caught up. Mark was a freshman when Cordell and Luke were seniors, so their high school experiences overlap a little.

When there's a lull in the conversation, I take advantage. "All right." I slap a palm on the wood tabletop. "Favorite ice cream flavor?"

"You haven't asked this crew that one before?" Lisa asks, her brows high on her forehead.

"She hasn't," Cordell answers before I can. His tone is confident, like he remembers every category I've ever suggested.

I give him a sarcastic smile, and in return, he just blinks. When I turn back to the group, Lisa is watching the two of us. She wags her brows at me and toys with her ponytail.

Crap. She'll never let this go.

Tessa's the first to answer. "Mint chocolate chip."

"That's Lisa's favorite, too." Mark narrows his eyes at his wife. "Do you know *my* favorite?"

She scoffs. "Of course I do. Rocky road."

Mark clinks his bottle against hers and plants a quick kiss on her lips.

Luke sets his beer down. "I'm going with Neapolitan."

"Of course you are," I tease.

"What? It's like the grand slam of ice cream flavors."

I lift my palms. "If you say so. My favorite, by the way, is cereal milk."

Mark rolls his eyes, and both Tessa and Lisa wrinkle their noses.

"That's not a real flavor." Cordell stands tall, crossing his arms over his chest.

I absolutely do not gawk at the way his biceps bulge with the movement.

Instead, I lift my chin, preparing for a squabble I'll most certainly win. A small thrill courses through me and settles in my stomach like a fizzy soda. "It most certainly is. We can consult my friend Google if you'd like me to prove it." I'm already reaching into my bag to dig out my phone.

"It very well might be a *thing*, but it's a novelty flavor. You can't just waltz into any ole ice cream shop and order cereal milk." Like a judge banging a gavel, he pops his right shoulder —case closed.

"Doing a lot of waltzing these days, are you?" I can't help the haughty quality of my voice.

One corner of his mouth twitches, but he schools his features with a swallow. "Waltzing requires a partner, so...no."

When he raises his bottle to his lips, my mouth goes dry. Damn it. I'm instantly entranced by the way they part and purse as he takes a sip. And at the way his index finger and thumb are loosely wrapped around the neck, lifting it like it weighs nothing. Maybe he pregamed before the fireworks, because he is ridiculously laid back tonight.

Tessa turns to Cordell. "What's your favorite flavor?"

He licks his lips, his eyes locked on mine. "Vanilla."

Our friends all razz him, talking over each other to give him grief about his boring choice, but the two of us remain trapped in each other's stares.

I clench my thighs under the table and anchor myself to the stool, like I'm in danger of melting right off the damn thing. Thirty-one is too young for menopause, right? Because the hot flash that heats my body has me questioning what I learned in biology.

The sounds of the noisy bar fade away as rapid-fire questions ping through my head: *Why did he say* vanilla *while looking at me like that? Does his beard seem longer tonight? Is he growing it out? What would it feel like against my skin? No. Why am I imagining how it would feel against my skin? Did he encourage Drew to sing that song? Does he know about Nick and the Low Bars? Did I put on deodorant after my shower? Have I been abducted by aliens, and if so, are they hot like the ones in Tessa's sci-fi romances?*

*Silly rabbit, there's not a hot alien in the universe who could hold a candle to the hunk of a man standing two feet away.*

I shake my head when a masculine voice pulls me out of my Cordell haze. How long did my out-of-body episode last? They've changed the subject, and I think Luke's asking Mark about his family medicine practice.

"It's nice to have a partner. Takes a little pressure off. I can't imagine carrying one on my own like Mom does."

"I'm surprised you don't get accosted around here like she does." Cordell finally, *finally* pulls his gaze from mine.

My brother is a general practitioner in Columbus; he knew from an early age that he wanted to follow in Mom's footsteps.

Lisa laughs. "Me, too. That poor woman can't enjoy a meal

in town without having pictures of ingrown toenails shoved in her face."

"She's so lovely about it, though," Tessa says.

My chest swells, and Mark and I exchange proud grins. Our mom is the freaking best.

"Speaking of moms, I see Ms. Daisy's crew back there." Luke tilts his head toward the booths along the wall. "I'm surprised Ms. Rhonda didn't join them."

Cordell rolls his eyes, but he's smiling, too. "She wanted to get to bed at a reasonable time. She's going junking with Ms. Rita early tomorrow morning."

I continue my study of him. Damn it. I still can't decide whether he would really suggest the Low Bars' song to Drew. His dark eyes are on me, roaming my face like he's committing every feature to memory. In a blink, his brow furrows and he clenches his jaw. I swear my insides flutter when his head slants in a tiny, almost imperceptible nod—as if he's made up his mind about something. Is he issuing a challenge?

*Shit*. Why am I a fucking nervous wreck?

He swats my brother's arm with the back of his hand to get his attention. "Did Mel tell you she went on a date with a buddy of mine?"

My lungs seize and my mouth drops open as four pairs of eyes bore into me for the second time tonight.

Like the flick of a switch, my lusty thoughts morph into angry ones. Why is he bringing this up *now*, in front of my family and our friends? My pulse races to what has to be an unhealthy level. Mark might need to check my blood pressure before this night is over. He also might have to perform CPR on the man standing across from me after I choke him. Maybe Tessa's estranged lawyer parents can represent me in court. And I'll definitely make Cordell's ghost post my bail.

My brother rakes a hand through his light brown hair. "She

did not. Mel, you have something you want to share with the class?"

Tessa gives me a sympathetic smile while Lisa props her chin on her fist, ready to soak up every detail. And Cordell? By the cocky head tilt, I imagine he's thinking *Your move, Marshall.*

My only choice is to deflect. "Only that Cordell went on a date with Valerie Bordelon earlier today." I puff out my chest.

Cordell's eyes dip down and back up to my face, where I make sure my smuggest smile is waiting.

"Valerie Bordelon? Where've I heard that name before?" Lisa pipes up.

"She was my high school girlfriend." Mark scoffs. "And I use the term 'girlfriend' very loosely. We went on, like, four dates, and we went to prom together." He eyes me suspiciously. "Does this mean you two set each other up?" He waves a hand from Cordell to me.

Luke's dark brows shoot up under the bill of his Braves cap.

"Yep. We've got a friendly little wager going on." Might as well spill all the beans. No way am I backing down now. "To see who's better at finding a compatible match."

I don't know why I wanted to keep this a secret; the looks on our friends' faces are giving me life. Confusion mixed with intrigue and humor, and maybe even a little horror thrown in for good measure. My inner chaos addict preens.

"I think I've read a book with this plot before." That comment comes from Tessa, obviously.

High on the adrenaline rush of calling his bluff, I glare at Cordell. "Did you tell Drew to sing 'The Hymn of Youth and You' on our date?"

My brother mutters "Shit," but I keep my attention glued on the man across from me.

For a couple of heartbeats, he blinks rapidly beneath furrowed brows. Then he barks out a humorless laugh. "Wait. He *sang* to you?" He's incredulous. Not guilty in the slightest.

Relief floods my body. Thank fuck this stool is holding me up.

Luke cuts in. "Wait. I'm missing something."

I scan Cordell once more to confirm his innocence, then turn to Luke. "My date was with a music teacher who thinks girls swoon over being serenaded with mediocre love ballads by mediocre college bands." I take a gulp of liquid courage, then I drop the bomb. "He played me a song written and recorded by my ex-husband's band."

Their reactions do not disappoint.

Cordell barks out a deep "What?"

Luke gasps. "You were *married*?"

Lisa grabs Mark's arm, and my brother rubs a palm over his face.

Sweet Tessa's shiny eyes make me want to scoop her up in a hug.

"Oh, spoiler alert: *Mel Marshall* was *Mel Hayes* for about a year in college." I lift a shoulder in a half-hearted shrug, but my chest is tight. God, it hurts to speak that name. I haven't uttered that combination in a decade.

*Fucking Nick.*

Mark, Lisa, and Tessa—who knew about the Nick debacle before tonight—are indignant for me; Cordell and Luke remain shocked at my revelation. By the way they work their jaws and survey me, it's obvious they're dying to ask questions, but they're gentlemen enough to refrain from pressing for more.

"Mel, I'm so sorry." Cordell steps closer to the table and presses both palms to the top. "Please believe me, I had no idea. Even if I had known, I *never* would've put him up to that." His voice is soft and contrite.

His dark eyes bore into mine, telegraphing his apology straight to my soul.

I tip my head to acknowledge his innocence and give him a small smile.

He lowers his shoulders and presses his lips together. Beside him, Luke looks all sorts of uncomfortable. They eyeball each other for a few moments. It's cute—their own version of bestie eye-speak.

I sigh, still full of trepidation. But now that it's out there, it would be easier to get it *all* out there and move on. "My ex-husband Nick was in a band. They were popular mostly in college towns in the region for a couple of years." I wave my hand, going for nonchalant, when, in reality, talking about this always puts me through the emotional wringer. But maybe, since it's been the topic of conversation twice recently, I'll discover it doesn't hurt as much anymore.

"What's the band?" Cordell's posture morphs from laid-back breeziness into a hard-as-granite mountain of tension in a heartbeat.

It's fucking hot.

I clear my throat. "The Low Bars."

"The Low Bars?" Luke frowns at his beer. "I think I remember them. They had that one song—" He snaps his fingers. "Something about a cheerleader—"

"Cheerleader Burn Book," Mark and Lisa say in unison.

I roll my eyes. I hate that damn song. Girls would wear cheerleader uniforms to their shows sometimes.

"That's the one," Luke says, pointing at them.

I'm ready to move on from this topic, but they need some closure, so I might as well jump to the ending. It hurts, like pressing on a bruise over and over, but I inhale deeply and let it go. "I caught him cheating on me with a groupie."

Cordell's jaw is clenched tight, and his eyes are blazing. The sight of him makes my chest ache.

"Rat bastard," Mark grumbles, lifting his bottle to his lips.

A surge of love and appreciation for my big brother threatens to overwhelm me. To keep the tears of gratitude at bay, I squeeze my hands into fists so tight my nails dig into my palms. He notices, though. He sees every part of me, too.

He reaches over and tousles my hair. The move is affectionate, but then he slides his hand to the back of my neck and gives me one comforting squeeze. "I'm sorry, Mel-Mel."

My responding smile is watery.

Lisa and Tessa are both on the verge of a meltdown. We need a mood-lifter, stat.

I tip the last of my Blue Moon back and nod at Cordell. "I can't believe vanilla is your favorite. That's such a...*vanilla* choice."

The table erupts with laughter and better alternatives to vanilla, but he gives me a genuine, breathtaking smile, one that says *I see every part of you, too.*

And that smile makes me equal parts mesmerized and terrified.

The topics return to safe territory and remain there, but it isn't long before Tessa opens her mouth wide and lets out a yawn.

Luke scoots closer and kisses her temple. "Let's get you home, Mrs. Shipley. You want me to go get the truck, or do you feel like walking?"

"Let's walk." She smooths her bump with one hand, and her husband takes the other to help her off the stool. "This was fun, y'all."

Luke shakes Mark's hand and gives Cordell a final bro backslap.

Tessa blows me a kiss, and then the Shipleys take their leave.

Cordell spends the next few minutes recounting his lunch date with Valerie. Apparently, the woman is on the prowl for husband number four.

"Just think, you could've been her leadoff hitter," Lisa teases Mark.

According to Cordell, Valerie is perfectly nice, but she's looking for something serious right away, and he's not. I won't let myself acknowledge the satisfaction I took from that one statement.

After a second round, Lisa declares that it's way past her bedtime, so she and Mark get to their feet.

"You want to ride with us?" Mark asks.

"We're bringing her car into town in the morning, remember?" Lisa's tone is all innocence, but she shoots me a wink. When she hugs me goodbye, she whispers, "For the love of God, you've been eye-fucking each other all night. Go. For. It."

I choke on air, and she smacks my back.

Ever the big brother, Mark looks to Cordell and says, "You'll make sure she gets home safe?"

"Will do."

He sizes Cordell up for a second, like he hasn't known him all his life. He must approve, though, because he nods and extends a hand.

And then there were two.

While we finish our drinks, he watches me. His face is open, expectant. I could interpret this expression a dozen ways. There are a hundred things we could say to each other right now. But I fall back on our default. It's safer this way.

"What?" I ask, tipping my chin up and going for icy.

His lips twist like he wants to smile, but he smooths them out and clears his throat. "You were married."

"Ugh, old news, Watkins. I don't wanna go there again."

"We're going there, Marshall." His tone is resolute.

I cross my arms, shields up. "There's nothing more to say."

"He's why you were sad that night, isn't he?" He pulls his lower lip between his teeth and nods like he already knows the answer. "At the bar in Americus."

Like he even needs to clarify. I know what *that night* refers to every damn time those words leave his tempting lips.

My chest is tight and my hands are a little shaky, but I keep up the act. "Don't worry. You didn't fuck a married woman. We were good and divorced by then."

"Jesus, Marshall." He pinches his lips together, then blows out a sigh. "Would you talk to me about it like an adult, please?"

I want to screw my face up and stick my tongue out to show him just how "adult" I can be, but being childish with him gets me into trouble. So instead, I do the only other thing I can to maintain my walls: I run.

Snatching my bag from where it hangs on my stool, I storm out of Fuzzy's. I'm three steps into the parking lot when a large hand grasps my bicep and halts my momentum.

He gently pulls me back so I have no choice but to face him. "I promised your brother I'd walk you home," he explains. "I don't break my promises."

"No, you just bang girls and break their hearts when you forget they ever existed."

"Marshall." He steps closer, so close I have to crane my neck to meet his eye. He loosens his grip on my arm and slides his hand down to just above my elbow. Tingles erupt along my skin everywhere he touches. "I'm sorry. I'm so dang sorry for that night. Like I told you before, I take full responsibility for being an idiot. And not to make excuses for myself, but I need you to know...I was in a bad place then. I was still recovering from surgery. I'd lost my dream job. My mom was going through chemo. It was an awful time."

And with those few sentences, I soften toward him, letting little chinks splinter through the walls. I've been so caught up in my own hurt, I never considered what he might've been dealing with back then.

"I'm still so mad at myself for how I reacted that night. For making you doubt how memorable you are. Because you, Mel Marshall, are exceptionally memorable."

His words make my heart pound so hard I'm afraid it'll beat

right out of my chest. Maybe I should have forced Mark to stay. I might need him to perform CPR on *me*. We're standing so close that with one deep inhale, my boobs would brush against his abs.

How do I handle this intense moment? We know that answer by now: I run.

This time, I sprint away as fast as my Birkenstocks allow. He catches up to me on the other side street.

"Not so fast."

I let out an *oof* as his hard shoulder presses into my abdomen, and I'm suddenly airborne. It takes a second to get my bearings, and when I do, I'm hanging upside down, staring at Cordell's ass. He squeezes my upper thighs right below the hem of my cutoffs.

"Put me down, you oaf."

"Nope. You're not running away from me again."

God, he smells good—like fresh laundry and body wash. I pinch his waist hard.

"Ouch!" he bellows, gripping my thighs tighter. "Do that again, Marshall, and I guarantee you won't like how I retaliate."

Images of him smacking my ass flood my brain, tempting me to fuck around and find out.

Instead, I groan. "Ugh, you're infuriating."

"Right back atcha."

"I don't like being manhandled, Watkins. Put. Me. Down."

He turns the corner and stomps toward the alley at the back of my building.

"You might not like being manhandled by most people, but I'd be willing to bet I'm not one of them."

"You arrogant piece of—"

He stops beside the metal door that opens to the stairway to my apartment. "Here's what's going to happen." His voice is all coachy and masculine.

I hate it. Sorta.

"We're going to update the setup scores, and then we're going to talk—like adults—about everything."

"Everything?" I squeak, my heart lurching.

"All the things," he says, no nonsense. "About your ex and that night at the bar and this competition. All of it." He jostles me a bit, emphasizing his resolve. "I'm going to put you down, but so help me, if you run again, I will chase you. And I'll catch you. Every. Single. Time. I ran a four-four forty."

I harrumph. "Maybe in your prime, Gramps."

He growls out a warning. "Marshall..." Standing stock-still, he waits, holding me like I weigh no more than a sack of feathers.

I consider refusing his high-handed demands so I can see how long he'd hold me like this before giving up, but the blood pooling in my head is making me dizzy. "Fine," I snarl.

I brace myself to be plopped down like a rag doll, but instead, Cordell eases me down his front, keeping our bodies flush. Every part of my torso touches every part of his. When he has me at eye-level, he stops, and I dangle a foot off the ground. I kick my feet, trying to jostle my way out of his hold, but it's no use. The man is a statue.

Our faces are so close, his every exhale warms my skin, so I arch my back to put some distance between us. I realize too late that all it does is cause my stomach to press harder into his, which makes him grin like a Cheshire cat.

He's so handsome it hurts. His strong, sculpted jawline is hidden under the black beard he usually keeps trimmed short. But my earlier observation was correct—it's a little longer tonight, and a tad unruly. An imperfection. Proof that he is *real*, not some artificially generated former football stud. His lips are full and a dusky rose. I have to fight the urge to trace his cupid's bow with the tip of my tongue. The corner of that sublime mouth tips up at my examination.

"I'm in your personal space, Watkins," I whisper.

"Pretty sure I've told you this before...I don't mind you being in my personal space." His hoppy breaths heat my skin as he takes in every detail of my face, pausing to linger on my lips when I lick them.

For moisture. In this hot climate. Not to entice him or anything.

In fact, the last thing I want Cordell Watkins to do right now is kiss me. A kiss would be the gateway drug that would inevitably lead to climbing him like a tree.

My tank top rode up on my slide down Cordell Mountain, so there's nothing between his fingers and the skin at my waist. He slips his pinkie into the waistband of my shorts, a soft brush of skin that has all cylinders firing.

I've got to get myself out of this mess before I do something I can't take back. Before those cracks in my walls expand and cause a whole damn collapse.

"I don't want you to kiss me."

"Why? Because *you* want to kiss *me*?" he asks.

"No," I scoff. *The nerve.*

His lips twitch. "Then why can't I kiss you, Marshall?"

"Because kissing you is like making out with hot dog water," I lie.

He lets out a deep laugh, his chest shaking in a way I feel all the way to my toes. How is he still holding me up like this? His muscles aren't even straining.

"Hot dog water, huh?"

"Yep."

He runs the tip of his nose along my cheek and inhales. His chest expands deeply, like he's breathing in as much of me as he can. I fight to hold in the whimper pressing against the backs of my teeth. Words are impossible at this point. If I open my mouth, I have no doubt he'll seize the opportunity to dive in for the kiss.

"I probably shouldn't do this," he confesses, pulling back to meet my eyes. "But you know what?"

I shake my head.

"Fuck it." He crashes his lips to mine.

# CHAPTER TEN

CORDELL

She opens for me instantly, her tongue ready to spar with mine the second our mouths meld. Our kiss is punishing, fraught with the tension that's been building between us all night. Heck, it's been building for weeks.

Her mouth is hot and needy, and she tastes like citrus beer and heady desire. All thoughts but one flee my brain. The sole remaining? I'm finally—*finally*—kissing Mel Marshall again.

She angles her head and lets out a throaty whimper that makes my knees quake. For a second, I worry I'll have to lower her to the ground and break our connection. But like her body is already in tune with mine, she wraps her legs around my waist. I slide my hands to her butt to support her. Like muscle memory, our bodies line up the way they did all those years ago.

She glides her hands from my nape to rest on the top of my head and props her elbows on my shoulders. The move fuses her body even tighter to mine. She digs into the material of my cap when I nip her pouty lower lip. Our lips continue their sensual dance, twisting and pressing and caressing, while our tongues explore.

We break apart, our breaths mingling as we heave in air to slow the heavy thrumming of our pulses. Mel's striking hazel irises are bright, and a hint of vulnerability surfaces in their depths.

"This mouth," I groan, taking in her reddened, ravaged lips. It spews the harshest, most biting words, yet tempts me to distraction every minute I'm around her. It's breathtaking in its contradictions. I'll take everything this mouth wants to give me.

Right now, those delicious lips part and lift at the corners. It's not quite a smile, and it's not quite a smirk. In an instant, she surges in again for round two.

This kiss starts off slower, flirtier. Teasing pecks that lengthen into languid pulls of lips and tongues. I break away to trail a line of kisses from the corner of her mouth down to her jawline and across to below her ear. In response, Mel tilts her neck in offering. Horny as a teenager, I suck on her skin. I want to mark her like a barbarian. If I do, she'll probably knee my balls, so I settle for coasting my lips up the column of her neck and back to her chin. Then I take her mouth again.

She bucks against me with a moan, seeking friction. I squeeze her perky backside, wishing on every star in the Georgia sky that I could feel the softness of her skin here rather than the denim between us. She digs her elbows into my shoulders to hike herself up again, desperate to relieve the ache between her legs. Her breasts rub against my chest as she does it, and I'm instantly hard. Hell, I've been sporting a semi most of the night.

It was hard not to with the looks she kept throwing my way. Though the expression on her face when she sprang the ex-husband bombshell on me had the opposite effect. That was a plot twist I did *not* see coming. But now that I know she married young and went through a traumatic breakup, so many fuzzy details about Mel have been cleared. Like those first few blinks after I put my contacts in, when the world slides into focus.

*Nick.*

Like missing a step on a staircase, my stomach plummets. Because the memory of that name comes along with a mental picture of the beach postcard I uncovered at Mel's last month. The blocky blue letters that spelled out *Nicky*. Why is he sending Mel postcards *now*, over ten years after their divorce? Does she maintain a relationship with the cretin who cheated on her?

I'm inclined to end this kiss right now, to relinquish my grasp on her perfect rear end and return her feet to the earth so I can demand she tell me why he's still in contact with her. But another whimper from her is all it takes to table that discussion for now.

She returns her hands to my shoulders, and we pull apart, breathless once again. I have the strangest desire to kiss the tiny gold hoop in her nose, but that feels too intimate. Even if we did just maul each other like animals.

"Down, please," she whispers.

Obediently, I loosen my grip on her bottom so she can lower her legs and slide down, but when her feet touch the ground, I don't let her step away for fear she'll take off again.

She peers up at me. Her expression is so unguarded. She hasn't looked at me with such openness in a decade.

I tuck a strand of her hair behind her ear and duck low to whisper. "There's that spark you've been missing, Marshall."

As I straighten, her expression shifts from interested to irate.

"*Ugh.* You *ass!*" Jaw clenched, she pushes against my chest with both hands. Even though her muscles are honed from years of yoga, the action does little to shift my stance. And that angers her even more. "I *have* been abducted! Aliens have scrambled my brain!" She spins and stalks toward the metal door to her apartment's stairway.

I cross my arms over my chest and enjoy the show. I'm familiar with this reaction. She isn't mad about the kiss; she's mad because she felt what I felt, and I called her out on it.

It takes her three tries to get the key in the lock. All the while, she slings verbal arrows at me. I catch phrases like *arrogant jackass* and *never again* and *hot dog water*; it's all I can do to keep from grinning like a devil. My blood hums when she gets this riled up.

When she finally wrenches the door open, I prowl her way. No way am I letting her shut me out. She glances over her shoulder and rushes over the threshold like she's going to slam the door behind her, but my hand is there to hold it open before she gets the chance.

"You can leave," she huffs, those perfect pouty lips twisting up in a sneer.

I clench my other fist so I won't reach out and smooth them with my thumb. "What did I tell you?" My voice echoes in the empty stairwell. The tone is the firm one I use on the field. "You and me? We're having a conversation. And we're updating the score. Still tied, zero-zero."

Her eyes flash with anger. God, I want to snatch her up and kiss her again some kinda bad. She opens her mouth, surely to spew more venom my way, so I pull in a breath and tilt my head, ready to take it.

Instead of curses, the only sound that leaves her lips is an emphatic groan.

I refuse to be the one to back down from this standoff, and I'm done letting her get away with these antics. I don't know whether it was at the bar, when she told us about her past, or whether it was on the walk over here, when I had her slung over my shoulder, but sometime between the fireworks and now, I formulated a game plan. The objective: Making Mel Marshall mine.

It'll take finesse. I suspect she's using this dating competition to deny what's been brewing between us, so I'll run interference on her attempts to hide from the truth.

Because the truth she doesn't want to face? It's that she and I are inevitable.

We have been since that fateful night in Americus.

My reverie is cut short when my angry pixie huffs an impatient breath at me. "Well?" she asks, arms crossed. "Are you leaving or not?"

While I was lost in perfecting my play, she must have issued another demand for me to vacate her presence.

"Not." I boop her on the tip of her nose, then dart up the stairs.

On the landing outside her apartment door, I lean over the railing. She's still down at the metal door, shooting daggers at me.

"Marshall. Get up here."

She pinches the bridge of her nose, then shakes her hands as if she's flinging off water. After a deep breath, she stomps up the stairs, making sure every footfall reverberates.

When she's three steps from the top, her expression goes eerily calm, and when she speaks, her tone matches. "You know, some might call what you're doing *trespassing*."

"You gonna call Chief Reeves on me?" Bennett's chief of police is Clay's older brother.

Nose wrinkled, she elbows past me and unlocks her door. Instead of opening it, she drops her keys into her bag and turns, arms crossed. Ready for the next round.

"That," she points downstairs, "won't be happening again."

"Why?" I stuff my hands in my pockets and take a step closer.

Mel retreats until her back meets the door. Her expression

is pinched and her shoulders are tense. I resist the urge to massage the tightness out of her muscles.

"Is it because of Nick?" I crowd a little closer. So close the toes of my slides bump her Birkenstocks. The anticipation makes me want to hold my breath until she responds, but I keep my limbs loose and my breathing even.

"Nick?" She lifts her chin, defiant as ever. "You didn't even know Nick existed until an hour ago. And not that it's *any* of your business, but no. I'm not hung up on my fuckwad ex-husband. I never would've agreed to a damn matchmaking competition if I still had heart eyes for him."

"Is he still hung up on *you*?" The words escape before I think better of them. I have no right to question her about him, but I need the intel.

Her eyes narrow. "I don't care what Nick does, where he lays his head at night, who he fucks, or what he eats for breakfast. That's the beauty of a divorce—his business is no longer mine."

*Then what's with the postcards?* As much as I want to ask, I know better. But it eats at me, nonetheless. He's kept in touch with her all these years. Is he trying to win her back? Is it a control thing? Regardless of his reasoning, it's clear he has unfinished business with Mel.

"Let's go inside and talk, Marshall." We're both stretched taut with the tension we've hauled upstairs like luggage after a two-week vacation. It's heavy and needs airing out.

The defiant set of her chin makes me grin, and that only stokes her fire. "There's nothing to discuss. I'll note the goose eggs for this round of dates and text you when I've found another warm body willing to sit through mediocre dinner conversation with you."

"Mediocre, huh?" I've got over a foot on her in height, so when I brace an arm on the doorframe above her, she has to crane back so far to meet my eye that the crown of her head bumps the door. Unable to help myself, I twist my fingers in a few strands of her tickle-me-pink hair. "You and I both know that's the wrong m-word."

Her chest heaves. I bet her heart is galloping like mine. I'd love to press my fingertips against her neck to check her pulse. The contempt in her eyes is contradicted when she grabs a fistful of my shirt. She doesn't push me away or pull me closer. Her indecision is clear as day. If it's up to her, we'd maintain this holding pattern she's trapped us in.

"Wh-what word would be better?" Her voice is breathy, and her focus strays to my lips for an instant. But in a blink, those eyes are narrowed in anger once more.

"*Our* m-word." I drop her hair and grab the doorknob. I'm going to kiss her into this apartment and make her forget why she's been pissed at me all these years. My lips are millimeters from hers when I whisper the word. "Memorable." At the same time, I turn the knob and push the door open. The move causes Mel to totter back, but I grab her hip to keep her upright just as a streak of gray darts out the door like a shot.

"Mouse!" she shouts, dropping her bag and taking off after the gray blur. She's halfway down the stairs before I realize her cat's escaped.

I take the stairs two at a time and push through the heavy metal door into the alley. Mel's already outside. She has her hands on her head, her elbows out, turning one way, then the other, searching for him.

"How'd he get out?"

When she turns to me, her cheeks are wet. My heart cracks at the mix of sadness and fear in her expression.

"The door. Damn thing gets stuck sometimes and you have to pull it closed."

"That's not safe."

She glares up at me. "It's Bennett. And I'm usually good about making sure it's closed all the way, but you and your damn kissing and your damn m-words..." She trails off and swipes at her cheeks. "He's spooked by loud noises. The fire-works. I didn't even think..." She blinks out a fresh set of tears. "Mouse!" she hollers, but her voice is garbled by her crying.

"Hey, hey." As gently as I can, I place my hands on her shoulders and give them a squeeze. "We'll find him."

She peers up at me, and my heart lurches again. She looks so broken. Nothing like the Mel I know. I haven't seen her this despondent since the dive bar.

"He—he got out once before. Took me hours to find him," she hiccups.

"There are two of us this time. We'll split up. You head down that way. And I'll go back toward the other end."

With her lip pulled between her teeth, she nods.

"Where did you find him last time?"

"He was in a box near the dumpster behind Ruth's. He likes enclosed spaces."

"Okay. Let's start here. We'll work our way to the end of the street and regroup out front. If we still haven't found him, then we can switch to the other side of Central."

Mel nods again, a lone tear slipping down her cheek. I brush it away with my thumb and fight the urge to haul her into my arms.

I offer one last encouraging "We'll find him," then we start our searches.

Softly, Mel calls, "Here, kitty, kitty. Mouse?" as she makes her way down the alley toward the street that crosses in front of Fuzzy's.

I mimic her words, keeping my voice soft and my tone light. I check inside the empty boxes and behind the wooden crates leaning against the dumpsters that line the alley. I almost yelp like a little girl when I bump a box and an actual mouse scurries into the brush and brambles that run parallel to the buildings.

"Wrong Mouse," I mutter.

When I turn to check Mel's progress, she's a speck in the distance and her arms are empty. Unlike the others, the dumpster behind Mr. Rusty's is set on wheels, so it's set off the asphalt by a few inches. I drop to my knees on the rough blacktop, determined to check every nook and cranny until we find him. I have to rest my cheek on the ground to scan under the dumpster. Sure enough, a pair of chartreuse eyes glow in the darkness. Lord, I hope it's Mel's cat and not a stray.

"Hey, Mouse. Here, kitty." He's huddled against the wall of the building where I can't reach. I'd probably spook him if I could anyway, so my best bet is to coax him out. "Your mom's looking for you," I tell him softly. He meows back but doesn't move. "She's really worried about you, bud. Here, Mouse."

Unsure of how to entice him out, I lay my arm on the ground with my fingertips extended into the darkness under the dumpster. I stay very still, hoping the old saying about curiosity and cats will work in my favor. We eye each other warily, our only movements the blinking of our eyelids. After what feels like an eternity, the glowing eyes inch closer.

I hold my breath when I feel Mouse's wet little nose sniff my fingertips, afraid the slightest flinch will send him into panic mode. He inches even closer, and soon, he pokes his gray head out. He pauses there, assessing me, and with a meow, he slinks out from beneath the dumpster. Still, I remain frozen so he can investigate me. He sniffs his way up my arm, and when he's comfortable enough to rub his head against my shoulder, I let out a long breath.

"Hey, buddy. You ready to go home?" I croon.

At his answering meow, I carefully scoop him under his belly and stand. My muscles creak in protest after being prone on the hard ground for so long. But when Mouse curls into me, safe in my arms, I forget all about the aches and pains.

When I don't see Mel, I round the building to where we agreed we'd meet after finishing our search of the alley. Sure enough, she's pacing in front of the coffee shop several store-fronts down.

"There she is," I tell Mouse, scratching behind his ears. His gentle purr stirs up the warm fuzzies inside me. I can't wait to witness this reunion.

The moment Mel turns and sees me with her cat in my arms, her face brightens, and she dashes our way.

"You found him." Her voice is full of wonder as she pulls him into her arms. The volume of his purring increases as she buries her face in his fur. "I'm so sorry, Mousers," she whispers.

He answers with an aggressive head rub along her jaw.

"Where was he?" Her hazel eyes shine with gratitude.

I'm gobsmacked by her once again—how she can be so fierce one minute, yet so soft the next.

I clear my throat. "Under Mr. Rusty's dumpster."

Closing her eyes, she rubs her cheek against his head again. "Thank you. For finding him."

I only nod, unsure of what to say. The momentum that had us storming up the stairs and had me getting in her personal space morphed quickly into panic when Mouse escaped. Now that our searching is over, I'm as wrung out as she looks. All the things I wanted to talk about tonight—the ex-husband, the matchmaking, the kiss—can wait.

*Wait.* It's a word I've associated with Mel for years. A day or two more won't hurt.

As if she's reading my mind, she speaks up. "It's late."

"Yeah. I'll walk you back."

We're silent on our trek back to the faulty door. I don't follow her upstairs this time. Instead, I pull the door open and hold it for her. "I'll make sure it closes this time."

She nods, and when she crosses the threshold, she turns. "Thank you again. For finding Mouse." Hesitating, she presses her lips into a line, like maybe she has more to say. But after a moment, she shakes her head and moves toward the stairs.

"We'll talk soon, Marshall," I vow.

Before she has a chance to argue, I push the door closed. I wait outside, on alert for the telltale snick of the lock.

After several long moments, it slides into place. I smile to myself when her muffled "Good night, Watkins" echoes from the other side of the door.

"Jones was late again today." Clay makes himself at home in one of the chairs facing my desk. "I gave him a talking-to about it. That kid, I swear..." He shakes his head.

"How do you want to handle it, Coach?" I question.

Darius Jones is a starting cornerback, and a talented one. Since Clay coaches the defense, I let him make the calls with his players and only step in if I need to. As the head coach, I have many irons in the fire, but Clay has my implicit trust with these kids. He's been my assistant coach since the day I took over the program.

He exhales a weary sigh. "Honestly? I don't know. The kid has a rough homelife. But he's got so much potential."

"Is transportation an issue? Henderson lives on the same street."

"I asked him about getting a ride with a teammate. Hell, I even offered to pick him up myself. He just gave me a *naw*, like usual." He rolls his eyes.

Jones's one-word answers drive both of us nuts. The kid is absurdly mouthy around his buddies, but when he's getting a lecture, he's monosyllabic.

"I'll talk to him," I promise. "He doesn't want to lose his starting status. I know that much."

He stands and runs a hand down the front of his shirt. "Doesn't look like we're gonna get on that field today."

I swivel my chair so I can look out the small window for

what's got to be the tenth time today. A rare storm is keeping us from running drills. If it was just a downpour, we'd take advantage of practicing in rough conditions, but the lightning and thunder that have shaken the building all day have forced us to stick to the gym and weight room.

"Naw," I drawl, grinning. "Tell Eric they can leave after weights."

With a nod, he knocks on my desk twice, then heads out.

Before I return to the paperwork I've got to tackle today, I check my phone, but I don't let it distract me for long. Paperwork is my least favorite part of the job. Being athletic director means I have to analyze and approve the budgets for every sport. I'm also tasked with ordering equipment for all the teams and organizing fundraisers for the football program. It's almost impossible to find time for these duties once the season starts, so every summer, I check off as many tasks as I can.

I check my phone again and inwardly groan. Maybe I should shove the thing in a desk drawer so I won't look at it every couple of minutes like an addict. It's been almost two weeks since the night Mel and I kissed. She disappeared after that, obviously back to avoiding me. Until this morning. She texted as I was toweling off after getting soaked in the deluge on my way into the building.

ANGRY PIXIE

Got your next date lined up. Her name is Destiny. She's gorg. I have a really good feeling about this one!

When I read the words, I wanted to sink to my knees and throw my phone across the room. Stupidly, I thought we'd turned a corner, and I'd assumed that the matchmaking idea was fizzling. A funny story we could tell our kids one day. *Did I ever tell y'all about the time your mom and I set each other up with random dates even though we were insanely attracted to each other?*

Instead of sharing Destiny's contact, she started a group text. She dropped a few winky emojis and a *Y'all are really going to hit it off*, then promptly removed herself from the conversation like some matchmaking ninja.

Back on our text thread, I sent Mel an honest question and hoped for an honest answer.

> Why are we still doing this? [sparkle emoji]

I've gotten nothing back from her. Hence the obsessive phone checking.

The last thing I want to do is go on a date with Destiny, or any other woman, for that matter, unless it's the one currently driving me crazy, but it appears as though I'll be forced to call her bluff and go on the date anyway.

Maybe this is the wrong play to call, but I'm going with my gut.

I'm more than ready to put an end to this matchmaking foolishness and skip to the good part. The part where Mel and I give this thing between us a chance. But I've made a million wrong calls in the past where she's concerned, and I'm scared to push too soon. I have to treat her like I did her cat that night in the alley. I've got to be patient and wait for her to come to me.

Scrubbing a hand down my face, I open a drawer, ready to shove my silent phone and thoughts about my angry pixie out of sight, when the device lights up.

It's not Mel calling, but I grin at the screen anyway.

I slide my thumb across the screen to accept the call, put it on speaker, and set the phone on my desk. "Well, if it isn't Racy Lacey."

His responding chuckle is gravelly. "Dell. How's it going, man?"

It's good to hear from him, but his tone lacks its usual ebullience, putting me on edge instantly. "Good, brother. How about you?"

A heavy sigh crackles through the speaker. "Same old."

Now I'm worried. My former teammate never sounds less than enthused, even on a bad day.

But I keep my voice light and continue, hoping he'll come out with it quickly. "Tell me what's new, then."

Another sigh. "Team let me go. Found out yesterday."

My stomach drops, and I can't stop the sharp intake of air. Griffin Lacey is one of the most talented and successful tight ends in the league. He was instrumental in helping the Tennessee Tornadoes earn two national championships. He's a fan favorite and an NFL superstar. Yes, he's nearing the end of his career at the ripe "old" age of thirty-four. And yes, he finished this past season with a shoulder injury that required surgery, but he's by no means ready to be put to pasture. He's been with the Tors his entire career and was hopeful that he'd retire with them, too.

"Crap, Griff, I'm so sorry. What does Kevin say?"

Kevin Donahue is Griffin's agent. He's brutally honest, but cutthroat for his players. I'd know. He represented me once upon a time, too.

He grunts. "Kevin might be dead to me. He suggested that maybe it's time for me to hang up my cleats, look into broadcast bullshit."

I almost bark a laugh at the thought of Griffin Lacey's potty mouth on network TV. He'd owe thousands to Ma's swear jar.

"But you still want to play?" I already know the answer, but I ask anyway.

"Fuck yeah, I want to play."

"How's the rehab going?"

"On schedule."

I can't help but frown. He's never been this succinct. I'm still reeling from the news that the Tors let him go, and that another team hasn't snatched him up. He's a dynamic player, both on and off the field. Sure, he might only have a season or two left in the tank, but he could easily be the ingredient that pushes a team into the playoffs.

"Where are you rehabbing?" He's not making this easy on me, so I dig deeper. "Home or Nashville?"

For several seconds, the only sound is his breathing. Finally, he huffs and opens up just a little. "The surgery was in Nashville. I stayed there for the initial recovery. I've been home for about five weeks now."

The Tors' season ended with a heartbreaking loss in the AFC championship game in January. Griff's surgery was in February. If he's been hiding out at home for five weeks, then he spent four months rehabbing in Nashville. His team must've been happy with his progress if they agreed to let him finish rehab at his family's farm.

"Enough about my sorry ass. How's coach life treatin' ya?"

"It's good," I say. "Living the dream."

We both chuckle at that. Living in my hometown and coaching a team full of hormonal teenagers is the last thing I thought I'd be doing when Griff and I played together.

I clear my throat and go for honesty. "Life definitely has a way of keeping us humble. It's not what I thought I'd be doing after the big show, but I can't complain. Call me crazy, but this slower pace agrees with me."

"Hmm" is his only response.

"Has Kevin gotten any offers?" I can't fathom there not being teams out there interested in Griff.

"*Kevin*," he says, voice full of bitterness, "claims he's only heard from Washington, and the offer was insultingly low."

"How low are we talking?" If he's desperate to keep playing, he might have to accept a contract well under what he's worth.

"Like right above rookie contract low."

I whistle. "Dang. Don't lose faith, brother. I refuse to believe that's the only one you'll get."

"It fucking might be. Maybe I *am* done…"

His defeated tone breaks my heart. It's how I sounded when I was forced to walk away from the game I'd devoted my life to.

Clay stops in the doorway, a stack of papers in hand. I wave him in, and once he's set them on my desk, he thumbs over his shoulder, silently gesturing that he's heading out for the day. Then he's gone.

I pick up the papers Clay delivered and shuffle them into a pile with the others still waiting for my attention. As I do, a bright red corner catches my eye. I pull out the flier, and an idea takes root.

"Hey, Griff, how would you feel about getting away from home for a little while?"

"Don't fuck with me, Watkins," he growls. "You know my mom is hovering like a goddamn helicopter."

"You quit that nonsense right now. Donna Lacey is a queen among mothers."

"You're right." He blows out a breath. "But Dad's jealous of all the attention she's lavishing on me. Damn, it would be good to get away. Maybe a little sun and sand? Can you take a trip this late in the summer?"

I hate to burst his bubble, but the more I consider this idea, the more excited I get. "I can't get away." There's a muffled *fuck* on the other end of the line, but I press on. "And I can't offer you sand. But there's plenty of sun to be had."

"What's cooking in that brain of yours?" Good. I've piqued his curiosity. And he's finally beginning to sound like himself.

"Promise me you won't say no right away."

"*Okay…*" His voice rises on that last syllable.

"How would you feel about spending some time in a real friendly small town in Georgia and helping a high school football coach and his team run a summer camp?"

"Wait." He huffs out a laugh. "Are you serious? You want me to leave one podunk town for another? To help with a *camp*?"

Sure, the image of two-time Super Bowl champion and seven-time Pro Bowler Griffin Lacey volunteering at a football camp in Bennett, Georgia, seems ludicrous. But the more I think about it, the more it seems like a perfect fit. His affiliation would bring serious clout to our annual camp. My team could learn valuable insights from him, and it would take his mind off the possibility that his career is over.

I'm sucking in a deep breath, gearing up to launch into my best sales pitch, my *what do we have to do to get you in Bennett?* speech, but before I can form the words, he groans. "Fine. I'm in."

Dropping my elbows to my desk, I angle in closer, afraid I'm hallucinating.

Griff's deep voice snaps me out of my shock. "I'll have Seth contact you for the details. He'll send you my travel itinerary after he gets things set up."

Seth. Griffin's personal assistant. *This is real.*

"Um, yeah," I sputter. "Sounds good."

"I'm assuming there are no four-star hotels in your hometown—what's it called again?"

"Uh, Bennett."

"Right." I can almost hear his smirk through the phone. "How are Bennett's accommodations these days, Watkins?"

Decidedly not up to the standards of any NFL player I've ever encountered. That's how they are.

"You can stay with me." It's maybe not the most appealing idea for me, but my options are limited. "Seth, too. My place is big, and it's secluded. Five bedrooms on thirty acres. It's just me there, so..."

"Cool. It'll just be me. When does this thing start?"

"A week from Monday. The twenty-eighth."

He grunts to confirm.

"I can't tell you how much this means. Really. Thank you for agreeing to this harebrained idea."

He's quiet for so long I tap my screen to make sure we haven't been disconnected, but finally, he lets out a sigh. "I'm happy to help. It'll be good to clear my head for a few days and let the people I pay to worry about my career do their damn jobs. You were such a fucking help to me during my rookie season. For real. Showing me the ropes, being a listening ear. This is the least I can do to repay you."

My heart aches at the genuine sentiment behind his words. I didn't go out of my way to help expecting any kind of reciprocation. I did it because it was the right thing to do. It was what my father would've done.

Griffin and I exchange goodbyes, and once I've ended the call, I lean back in my chair, satisfied with all I accomplished today. The feelings are gone in an instant, though, when my phone buzzes on my desk.

Every time something good happens, the universe has to swoop in and balance the scales.

ANGRY PIXIE

Why wouldn't we still be doing this?

ANGRY PIXIE

Waiting for my next date, coach! [middle finger emoji]

Griffin's face pops into my mind. I know exactly which play I'm going to call next.

# CHAPTER ELEVEN

## MEL

The July meeting of the Badass Bennett Business Babes is already underway when I arrive at Ms. Rita's. To be fair, I'm perpetually late for most things, but I try my damnedest to make these meetings on time. These women are precious to me. Plus, my mother is in attendance tonight, and I don't want a lecture on punctuality.

Nor do I want to divulge the reason I'm late.

*Fucking Nick.*

He called as I was locking up. He called from yet another friend's phone. Probably since I blocked the last number he used. I mentally swore a blue streak when his voice registered, but like an idiot, I didn't immediately hang up. Apparently, I'm a glutton for punishment. Every time he calls, I tell myself that the next time, I'll hang up on him. I'll push that *end call* button with all the vengeance I'm owed. But then the next time comes, and I don't. Am I forever destined to repeat this vicious cycle?

I don't even want to venture into *why* I can't hang up on his ass. I have no qualms about it with anyone else stupid enough to wrong me. But Nick?

Why can't I ignore that fucker the way he deserves?

This time he called to tell me about a job he's got lined up in Athens. It's exactly the kind of respectable job he's proven himself to be allergic to over the years. I don't need a crystal ball to predict his future. He'll quit in a couple of months because the responsibility of it "stifles his vibes" and "drains him of his creative juices."

The prospect of Nick with a real job is laughable. If only I felt the same about the frequency of his calls recently. No, that's far more alarming. For a decade, he's called every few months, but lately, like with the time between postcards, the stretches of time between the calls have decreased.

I resolve to rid my brain of Nick Hayes as I bounce up the steps to Ms. Rita's front porch. I let myself in with an apology ready on my lips. As soon as I step through the foyer and into the living room, the tightness in my shoulders melts away.

Mugs are filled, and the room echoes with shouted greetings. My mom is set up on the well-worn floral couch, so I drop down to the cushion beside her. As I'm slipping off my Birks to sit crisscross, Ms. Daisy appears in front of me with my Go With the Flow-Ga mug filled with rosé.

I take a healthy swallow and sigh. "What'd I miss?"

Ms. Rita places a tray of soup crocks filled with her famous peach chili on the coffee table. When I pump my fist, she smiles warmly. I freaking love when she hosts. She feeds us well, and I never get tired of browsing all the treasures in her house. It's chockfull of antiques and knickknacks. Her walls are covered with paintings and framed prints and random ancient baskets and tools and vintage advertisements. It looks like a Cracker Barrel in here.

The hallway wall next to the stairs is a shrine devoted to her nephews, Chris and Clay—the boys she raised after their parents were killed in a car accident. Every one of the boys' school pictures plus team photos, sports medals, wedding photos, and framed newspaper clippings are on display.

I close my eyes and take a moment to breathe in the savory aroma of the sweet and spicy chili before I dig in. Sure, it's ninety-seven degrees outside, but I'll hear none of that "soups are for cold months" slander. Soup and chili are year-round foods for me.

We're several bites in when Jane pipes up. "I can't believe he's coming *here*. To our little neck of the woods!"

I set my spoon in my bowl and tilt my head, clueless as to what she's going on about.

She smiles at me, obviously noticing my confusion. "We were talking about *Griffin Lacey*. He's coming to Bennett!"

Ah, yes. The town's been buzzing for days.

Griffin Lacey—also known as *Racy Lacey* due to his good looks, his speed on the field, and his exploits off the field.

Cordell and Griffin played together for one season, but if the frequency of their appearances on each other's social media back then was to be believed, they formed a fast, solid friendship that's still going strong.

Not that I keep track of that sort of thing.

"Cole is beside himself." Ms. Rita is beaming over her bowl of chili. "I'm pretty sure that nephew of mine will be starstruck, too."

"It's all Chase has talked about for days. He's Christmas Eve-level excited." With a giggle, Jane scoots forward in her chair to refill her mug. "I'm so glad they run this camp for the young ones."

"Oh, me, too. Those little guys are going to soak up every word out of his mouth."

I smirk into my bowl. *Racy Lacey* is also known for requiring frequent bleeps during televised interviews.

"Ooh, Mel!" Jane gasps. "You should come with me when I take Chase to camp!"

"Those stands will be packed." Mom nods. "I better remind

Frannie and the boosters to have lots of water available for spectators."

"Why don't we donate cases of water and bags of ice? We could set up a watering station for the fans and media and list our businesses as sponsors on a sign at the table." Daisy, ever the businesswoman, is pulling a pen and notepad from her bag to take notes.

From there, we divide up the responsibilities—purchasing the water and ice, setting up, manning the table, and tearing down. After that order of business, we get started on our agenda for the evening. We discuss the annual fall carnival at the elementary school and how we can best serve the community while also promoting our businesses. Our July meetings are traditionally short; it's too hot for outside events, and the holidays are too far on the horizon. We usually spend most of the meeting deep in gossip, so it's inevitable that we circle back to the news that an NFL superstar will be in our midst in a matter of days.

"I wonder if he's still dating that supermodel. What's her name again?" Jane's getting to work opening a new bottle of wine. Riesling this time. Rita only serves alcohol that starts with the letter *r*. Her legendary Christmas parties are so rum-soaked, most partygoers adopt a pirate accent by the end of the night. It's my favorite Bennett event, hands down.

"I'm sure this one knows." My mom gives my knee a squeeze. She's relaxed, nestled back into the poofy pillows that line the back of Rita's couch, though the skin under her eyes bears deep purple circles.

I make a mental note to ask her if she's getting enough rest.

Every eye is on me when I finish my assessment of my mother and turn back to the group.

"Oh. Um, he was dating Kate Volkova. But they broke up last year." I shrug. So what if I spend my free time prowling the celebrity gossip sites?

"You should have Coach Watkins introduce you to him. Go out there and 'shoot the shots,' as the young folks say." Ms. Rita gives me a knowing grin. Lord. I press my lips together to trap the cackle that's tickling my throat.

She's clearly been around her nephews' teenagers recently.

She presses on, unaware of her blunder. "You never know when a love connection will happen. I'm serious. Ask Coach. Or I can ask Clay if you'd like. Give my boy a few days to warm up to having a celebrity in town, then I'm sure he'd be happy to make the introduction."

"Rita," Daisy barks. "I'm certain Coach won't be going out of his way to introduce our Mel to a hunky football player."

Beside me, my mom's lids are heavy, and she's got her head tipped back against the sofa. She must be listening, though, because she stretches her arms over her head and, mid-yawn, says, "Why do you say that?" Except it comes out garbled and sounds like "Wah ooh ay at?"

Ms. Daisy locks me in her shrewd gaze and purses her lips.

My heart stutters. That look never means anything good.

"His arms are full these days."

No one but me catches her covert wink.

Damn. That means that, somehow, Daisy saw Cordell stroll down Central like a caveman with me slung over his shoulder. I swear the woman has hidden cameras set up all over town. I've done many a recon mission at her house under the guise of bathroom breaks in search of a control room with a wall of monitors.

I have yet to find it. Nevertheless, I'll persist.

Cordell and I have been communicating through text only since *the incident*. It's by design, because my brain's still muddled from the whiplash of emotions he stirred up inside me. What would I say to his stupid, attractive face if he was standing right in front of me anyway?

*Hey, thanks for kissing my face off, but eff you for reminding me that no one else has ever kissed me that good and probably never will for the rest of my days?*

Or how about *You can shove that motherfucking* spark *bullshit up your ass, but also, you're my hero; thanks for rescuing my fur baby and being so gentle with him?*

And there's always the question that's haunted me for years: *Why do you have the ability to turn me on one minute and unmoor me the next?*

I must've wool-gathered right through the adjournment of our meeting, because when I blink myself back to the present, Daisy, Jane, and Ms. Rita are collecting empty bottles and dishes from the table. I stand to help the ladies with cleanup, and my mom raises her arm and swats me gently. Taking the hint, I clasp her forearm and tug to help her stand.

"Want me to drive you home? Dad can bring me back."

She shakes her head and stretches up on her tiptoes. "No, I'll be good once I start moving. Rita's marshmallow pillows are so dang comfy." After another good stretch, she wraps her arms around me and pulls me in tight. I freeze for a moment, but when she holds me tighter, I relax into the warmth of my mother's embrace. She smooths a hand down my hair and whispers, "I'm so very proud of you, my girl."

Tears prick my eyes as I squeeze her back. "Mom…" I croak.

"Shh. I just wanted you to know. I don't tell you nearly enough. But I am. Very proud."

I have amazing parents. I've never doubted their love for me, and I've never worried too much about whether they were proud of me. It's always been a given. But I must be in need of affection tonight, because those words are a balm I didn't know my battered soul needed.

We pull away, and when she notices tears have snuck past my defenses, she swipes them away with her healer's hands and kisses my cheek.

I swear I've cried more in the past two months than I have in the past ten years.

"I think I'm having hormonal sympathy tears for Tessa." I lift one shoulder in a shrug. "Ugh, enough." I fan my eyes.

Mom rubs my upper arms. "Let's start helping." She picks up the remaining dishes and starts for the kitchen. But when she steps into the hallway, she casually peers at me over her shoulder and smirks. "By the way, what's going on with you and Cordell Watkins?"

Mother Nature is being kind to central Georgia today. The temperature outside is a downright "breezy" eighty-five. For a Saturday in July, it's unheard of. And I get to spend this glorious day with two of my favorite people on the whole damn planet.

So what if they're three?

I canceled my senior yoga class this morning so I could keep Owen and Ollie. The twins are here all weekend since Mark and Lisa are in Atlanta for a medical seminar, but my parents both had work commitments come up at the last minute—Mom's fulfilling clinic hours in Oglethorpe, and Dad's attending a day of golf and schmoozing that's masquerading as a realtor retreat.

Our morning is chock-full of toddler-friendly activities. We eat breakfast, have a living room dance party, and color at the kitchen table with Glamma. After a quick lunch, the boys start bouncing off the walls, so we head out to the playset my parents set up for when the twins visit. Before long, though, they're tired of swinging and sliding, so I strap them into the double stroller and take them for a walk around the neighborhood. When Ollie announces that he has to use the bathroom, we make a beeline back to my parents' house for a potty break, where Glamma insists that I look "run ragged." Secretly feeling that way, too, I lie on the pallet we made in the living room with the boys, and the three of us take an hour-long nap.

Double the trouble. Double the fun. Double the exhaustion.

I haven't kept both boys by myself since before they were mobile. Either Mom or Dad is usually around to tag team.

The boys wake in foul moods, and I can't help but laugh at their grumpy, wrinkled faces. They're exact replicas of their father first thing in the morning. My crazed laughter quiets their whining, and their identical bewildered expressions make me laugh even harder.

After I lighten their post-nap moods with a tickle fight, we toddle out to the driveway to eat popsicles. Never let it be said that Aunt Mel-Mel won't spoil her little loves with sugary treats.

I'm sprawled out on the concrete, watching Owen and Ollie play their version of catch with a small bouncy ball, when a familiar dark gray Land Rover pulls into Ms. Rhonda's driveway across the street. I hold my breath when he steps out, hoping he won't notice us out here.

The air escapes my lungs in a whoosh when he doesn't even look our way before he enters his mom's house.

I consider rounding the boys up and taking them inside before he reemerges, but their little faces are lit with so much joy as they wander over with their ball that I can't bring myself to disrupt it. Instead, I shift so that my back's to the house across the street and send up a prayer that when he exits, he doesn't spot me.

Minutes later, there's the scuff of footsteps on the concrete, and a looming shadow falls over me. I shield my eyes when I look up, and instantly, I'm transported back to that long ago school day when he rescued me from the playground bully.

Cordell's standing so close I could reach out and grab his calves.

Both boys freeze and crane their necks.

"Marshall," he says in greeting. "And I'm guessing these two are Whosie and Whatsie." He crouches, though even on his haunches, he still towers over us. "Let's see, I bet you're Whosie." He points at Ollie. "And you're Whatsie."

Owen wrinkles his nose and giggles shyly at Cordell's correct guesses.

"Yep!" Ollie chirps, jumping as high as his little legs will take him. "Who are you?"

He brings his hand to his heart, and in a voice more tender than I knew he was capable of, he says. "Me? I'm Dell."

My nephews stare at him with the same look of hero-worship most kids have when they talk to him.

"Can we be buds?"

"What's buds?" Ollie, the more outgoing of the two, frowns.

"Buds are friends, little man."

"I not little man, I Ollie," my nephew states solemnly.

"You're right. Ollie." Cordell's brown eyes twinkle.

He gives Owen, who's positioned himself a step behind his brother, a small smile and holds a hand up for a high five. After a moment of hesitation, my sweet nephew musters up his courage and lands a smack to his huge palm. Cordell shakes his hand like it stung, making Owen cackle with glee.

In seconds, he's won over my nephews.

"How's Mouse doing?" He drops down to the concrete beside me and stretches his long legs out, crossing them at the ankles. He's inches away, but his body heat warms my whole right side.

"He's good." I tuck a strand of pink behind my ear like a nervous ninny. "Thanks again for finding him."

"Sure thing," he says, like it was nothing for him to dig through trash in the dead of night to find my runaway cat.

We sit in silence and watch Owen and Ollie chase after their ball. When Owen kicks it too hard and it bounces off the backyard fence, he runs as fast as his short legs can carry him, one arm drawn up tight while the other pumps sideways for speed.

Behold the toddler run. It's my favorite. Right behind cussing grannies, of course.

Cordell and I snort-laugh in unison. Once we've settled, he clears his throat. "He's got good form."

I throw my head back and cackle this time. Cordell doesn't laugh. No, he's watching me far too intently. The scrutiny makes my face heat.

When Ollie returns with the ball, he holds it in my face. "Mel-Mel, up, up, up!" He points at the basketball goal that's stood sentinel at the edge of this driveway since my brother was in high school.

"Oof, sorry, Whosie. Mel-Mel can't reach that like Daddy and Pop Pop can."

Cordell nimbly gets to his feet. "I got you, buddy." He bends forward and holds his arms out, but he waits for Ollie to make the move. Ollie glances at me, but before I can give him an encouraging smile, he wobbles into Cordell's arms. A tightness lodges in my throat as this gentle giant carefully lifts my nephew high enough to dunk the ball. The pure joy that lights up his little face makes me feel like a balloon floating skyward.

As soon as Ollie's feet touch the concrete, he darts toward me and leaps into my lap. With his pudgy arms around my neck, he squeezes tight and shouts right in my ear. "You see me, Mel-Mel?"

"Sure did." I tilt my head, hoping the damage to my eardrum isn't permanent, and laugh.

Owen collects the ball his brother abandoned and focuses his baby blues on Cordell. He's too shy to ask for a turn, but he doesn't like being left out. I spin Ollie around and plop him in my lap, ready to ask Owen if he wants a turn, but before I can, Cordell takes the lead.

Of course the man has the uncanny ability to read a room—or driveway.

"You wanna try, little man?" He crouches low again, keeping some distance, giving Owen time to warm up to the idea.

"He not little man. Dat's Owen," Ollie explains, waving a hand like Cordell should know better already.

"So sorry, Ollie." A corner of his mouth lifts. "Owen. Do you want to try?"

My heart expands in my ribcage at the sight of my nephew's shy little nod.

Cordell doesn't swoop in right away. No, he lets Owen come to him, then he repeats the slam dunk assist. In my lap, Ollie claps and cheers for his brother. Then he turns and places his sweaty little palms on my cheeks. "Mel-Mel. We go waw now? See da rudder fry 'gain?"

I'm still working the words through the toddler translator in my mind when Cordell steps up to us, once again casting me in shadow.

"You saw a butterfly today?"

Mouth agape, I drop my head back and blink at him. "Since when do you speak three-year-old?"

His answering chuckle causes a caress-like shiver to travel down my spine. "I have a nephew and a niece, remember? I've been adept at deciphering toddler-speak for a few years now."

"Mel-Mel, go waw?" Ollie asks again.

"You guys want to walk *again*?"

Nods all around.

Giving Ollie a little tickle, I look up at Cordell. "We took a walk after lunch, and these eagle-eyes found a huge blue butterfly hovering over Mrs. Gregory's lantana."

"Lantana? Now who's speaking another language?" he teases.

I can't even think of a snarky comeback. Maybe it's exhaustion; I've been chasing after a pair of three-year-olds all day.

Maybe it's because he and I sucked face the last time we were together. Or maybe it's something else I don't want to consider. Whatever the reason, I don't have the energy to fortify my walls today.

"Glamma," I offer. "She's a nature enthusiast. Has a thumb greener than that grass."

"Ma loves to garden, too. She's got a whole spread back there."

Suddenly, Owen is hovering at my side. "Can we, Mel-Mel?" His plea is so damn sweet. "Wanna go for a wawk."

Cordell extends his hand and raises a brow. "Let's go for a walk, Marshall."

I let him pull me up, but I release his hand once I'm on my feet. No way will I let myself marvel at how his touch tingles.

I leave him in charge of the boys while I retrieve the double stroller from my parents' garage. Once the boys are buckled, we trek down the sidewalk in search of *rudder fries.*

The two of us remain silent while the boys chatter to each other in their twin-speak. In his proximity, my mind races with thoughts of our kiss and his whispered words and my temper.

The silence is heavy. Thick. Like the air in summer.

Cordell blurts, "Which one is lantana?" at the exact moment I spout, "What are your niece and nephew into?"

From the corner of my eye, I catch his easy grin.

Ever the gentleman, he says, "You first."

I dip my chin. "Tell me about your niece and nephew."

"They're rascals," he says fondly. "Ryan and Raya. He's eight, she's six. Ryan is all boy. Super into football—go figure—but he's also really into science, especially rocks. I can't wait to see what he grows into."

The pride that lights up his face when he's talking about his family makes me melt.

"And Raya..." His chuckle is a low rumble. "She's the sassiest little tough girl you'll ever meet." He's quiet, and just when I think he's done, he turns to me and says, "Kinda reminds me of someone else I know."

I refuse to acknowledge his implication, but on the inside, I'm a puddle of goo. The way he refers to his niece as *tough* is the highest compliment. He believes girls can be more than one thing. We can be brazen and silly and smart and girly and *tough*.

We can be all those things and find a person who will love and appreciate every facet of who we are.

A warm breeze floats down the street, stirring tendrils of my hair. I tuck the wayward strands behind my ear and covertly observe Cordell as we continue our walk in silence. He's wearing gray basketball shorts and a blue microfiber T-shirt. The outfit is simple, but there's nothing simple about the way the fabric highlights his musculature. He's taking smaller steps, matching pace with me, and his hands are clasped behind his back, the way he paces the sidelines during a football game.

Not that I spend an unreasonable amount of time watching him instead of the game or anything.

As we round the curve in front of the Gregorys' house, I point to the clusters of tiny yellow flowers and thick green leaves that spill out of Mrs. Gregory's flower beds. "That's lantana," I say, answering his earlier question. "Glamma says they're perfect for attracting butterflies. Bees and humming-birds, too."

"Mel-Mel, where's da rudder fry?" Ollie asks.

"Looks like our friend is long gone," I tell my nephew. "But maybe if we stay really still and quiet, we'll see another one."

We pause at the end of the neighbors' driveway and watch for flutters of tiny wings.

"What color would you call those flowers?" I whisper to Cordell, remembering his fascination with crayon colors.

"Oh, they're dandelion, for sure. Even though they're *not* dandelions." He winks after his bad joke.

That's it. I'm convinced that we won't see any more butter-flies today.

Because they're all hanging out in my stomach.

Cordell tilts his head and hums. "Did you know Crayola retired dandelion several years ago?"

"Really?" I narrow my eyes. "And what's involved in a color's retirement?"

"No joke—they gave him a retirement tour." His mouth stretches into a huge grin that shows off his straight white teeth.

"Did you have braces? Your teeth are so perfect." The second the words are out, I wince, wishing I could scoop them up and shove them back in. Why the hell am I having the blurts today?

Tired of sitting still, the boys kick their little legs and demand that I "go, go, go," so I spin the stroller around, and we amble back toward my parents' house.

"I did have braces," he answers. "In fifth grade. I can still feel that ache in my jaw, too. It hurt to chew most things when the orthodontist put them on. My dad dropped by school with a thermos of chicken noodle soup every day that week. He'd stop by the convenience store and pick up a little ice cream cup to put in with it. The ones with a tiny wooden paddle. Remember those?" He chuckles softly and shakes his head. "I was terrified I'd get a splinter in my tongue. He moved his lunch break so he could time it just right with my lunch shift..." He trails off and forces a swallow.

My heart aches for the boy who lost his hero and also for the man who has to navigate life without his father. It makes me so fucking grateful to still have my parents and Glamma.

Rolling the dice that he's the kind of guy who likes to talk about his lost loved one, I clear my throat and peer over at him. "He had a heart attack, right?"

He pulls in a deep breath and lets it out slowly, then nods. "It was what they call a widowmaker. A blockage in the biggest artery in the heart. He was closing up the office for the day. When he never made it home and didn't answer his cell, Ma drove up there to check on him..."

Mr. Watkins was the postmaster. I remember the tall, friendly Black man who doled out lollipops. When he smiled down at me, his kind eyes would crinkle in the corners, just like his son's. When he passed away, my eight-year-old brain didn't fully understand the tragedy, but I remember that the whole town was sad.

Heart aching, I stop and grasp his forearm. "I'm so sorry you lost him."

He bows his head and nods. His eyes are downcast, but there's no hiding the watery sheen.

Unsure about what to say next, I push on, rolling the boys back toward the house. Cordell follows wordlessly, but soon, the heaviness of our conversation drifts away like dandelion seeds in the breeze.

"I hear you're bringing a ridiculously famous visitor to our town."

He barks out a "ha!" and shakes his head. "This town isn't ready for Griffin Lacey."

"Maybe ole Racy Lacey isn't ready for Bennett."

"Probably true," he says, one side of his lips tipping up. "But I've never seen so much interest in one of our camps. Coaches from *Atlanta* are contacting me about sending players."

I whistle. It's a big deal if Atlanta pays even a lick of attention to a place the size of Bennett.

"Is he staying at your place?"

"He is."

"You mean you didn't want to put him up at the Cherokee Rose?"

Cordell rolls his eyes. Our town's lone accommodation choice for out-of-towners is a decrepit Victorian named after

Georgia's state flower that's been converted into a B&B. It's musty, and I'm certain it's haunted.

"He wouldn't last ten minutes without Wi-Fi."

"He'd probably run at the first glimpse of Ms. Myrtle's porcelain doll collection."

He grunts, the ghost of a smile lingering on his lips.

At the end of my parents' driveway, I slow the stroller and lean on its handle to check on the boys, who've gone quiet. They're both dozing peacefully, sweaty and pink cheeked.

"They're a load of fun," he says, smiling down at them. "And you're an excellent Mel-Mel."

I try not to preen at his compliment, though I can't help but lift my chin. I *am* an excellent Mel-Mel. "Thank you."

Hands in his pockets, he scans the street. I follow his gaze, and a thought occurs to me, like a cartoon light bulb blinking on above my head.

"Your date is tonight!" I whisper-shout. "With Destiny," I add. A giggle slips out when I replay the words in my head. *A date with destiny. Ha!*

"It is." His tone is so matter-of-fact I can't get a read on him.

Destiny, on the other hand, texted me again this morning; her excitement was undeniable.

I pull my phone out of my back pocket to check the time. "It's four-thirty. You should probably head out if you need time to shower and change and stuff."

"I didn't know you were in charge of my itinerary." Wow, there's a distinct bite in his voice I don't think I've ever heard.

Typically, I'd snap back, but for reasons still unknown, I ignore his goad. I rock back on my heels and flash him a bright smile. "Let me know when you've found my next date."

His responding grimace is full of so much pain it makes my throat burn. He closes his eyes, as if the sight of me is too much, and takes a breath so deep I can feel the exhale from where I stand. He steps close, his body heat soaking into me again, trapping me in place like I'm caught in his force field. When he reaches up to cradle my cheek, I'm rendered speechless.

"Guess I'll go get ready for my date, then," he murmurs. His dark eyes study every inch of my face. "Can't wait to see if Destiny and I have that *spark*."

I jerk back, and his hand falls away from my face. My glare would be enough to cause most men to cup their balls, but his mouth twists into that damn cocky smirk I hate.

Or hate to love.

"There she is," he says, so fucking pleased with himself.

I'm speechless no longer. "Ugh. You're annoying," I retort, sure to keep my voice low so I don't wake the boys. "And...and —don't touch me. Ever again." I jab my finger into his chest to emphasize the words.

My damn insides quiver in retaliation. My lady-bits (*damn it, Glamma!*) might as well be holding up protest signs. But I stand my ground.

Cordell's responding growl causes goose bumps to skate over my skin. He wets his lips and swallows, and I can't help but watch the way his Adam's apple bobs.

"I won't touch you again, Marshall."

I nod. *Damn right.*

He leans in, his lips so close to my ear his breath tickles my neck, but not touching, like he promised, and rumbles, "Until you ask me to."

After one last arrogant smile, he steps around me. He leisurely strolls across the street, so I taunt, "That'll be a cold day in hell, *Coach*."

Hands shoved into his pockets, he doesn't falter as he hollers back. "We'll see."

# CHAPTER TWELVE

## CORDELL

The drive from Bennett to the bowling alley in Warner Robbins takes an hour. This is one difficult aspect of living in a small town, or dating when you live in one. The amount of time spent in the car on the way to meet up with someone in a place where there are actually things to do is brutal.

The whole way there, I replay my interaction with Mel. Every glance, every word, every smile. The fire in her eyes when I mentioned that word, *spark*, in reference to the date *she* set up...

Getting up in her personal space at the end of our pleasant afternoon was a gamble, but I want to be bolder with her, and I'm sticking to the game plan. I'm determined to wear her down until she admits that we have something.

Something significant and exciting and *memorable*.

Until the day she lets go of past hurts and looks toward the future we can have, I'll play her little dating game, and I'll use each of these setups to move the goalposts.

I play to win, after all.

The final strains of "You Belong With Me" fade out as I pull into the parking lot. "Thanks for keeping me company, Tay." I disconnect my phone and pull in a deep breath, psyching myself up for this date.

I've never met Destiny, but I sure know a lot about her. According to the persistent messages she's sent this week, she's twenty-six, a Gemini, and loves iced coffee. The ten-year age gap did give me pause, but mostly because she *sounds* young via texts. Her connection to Mel is more of a mystery. When I asked her in our exchanges, her response—"I've known Mel a long time"—left me curious. For a minute, I even considered that Mel *is* Destiny, and this whole setup is some elaborate ruse.

It's ridiculous how much I long for that harebrained idea to be true.

Unfortunately, when I step through the doors into the dim lighting of the bowling alley to the sound of my name being squealed at a decibel I'm sure dogs in Bennett can hear, Mel is not the one who greets me. In a number 84 Tors jersey. With braided pigtails and tiny 84 temporary tattoos highlighting her cheekbones.

She's set me up with a *very* enthusiastic jersey chaser. *Touché, Marshall.*

The woman clutching my arm like I'm a rockstar is stunningly gorgeous. And young. Her tawny skin glows, and her warm amber eyes sparkle with excited tears.

"Oh em gee, this might be weird, but can we please take a selfie?"

I flinch at her request.

Did Mel put her up to this?

Though that's my first thought, when I take her in, considering whether to call her out on it, the look on her face is full of nothing but genuine hope. So I affix my best smile and acquiesce. She snaps at least twenty selfies of the two of us, then clings to my side as we walk to the shoe counter.

"I'm, so, like, pumped to meet you," she gushes, the apples

of her cheeks rosy and round. "My whole family *loves* the Tors. Like an unhealthy amount."

"That's cool." I'm kind of in shock at the sheer exuberance of this woman. She's a walking spirit stick. Even the shoelaces in her white Stan Smiths are Tennessee Tors branded.

We give our shoe sizes to the attendant, and while we wait, I ask the question that's been on my mind for days. "So, how do you know Mel exactly?"

Destiny tilts her head, and a sly smile spreads across her face. "She said you'd ask me that straightaway." With a giggle, she squeezes my bicep, completely ignoring the question. "I bet you could toss me around with these."

"Um, okay?" What am I supposed to say to *that*?

"You're, like, really tall." Taking a step back, she sizes me up from head to toe. "I mean, I know you're six-four, but like, you seem taller than that, ya know?"

Fortunately, I'm saved from having to respond when the attendant returns with our bowling shoes. We find the lane we've been assigned and change our shoes, then begin the search for balls. I find one within minutes and return, but when Destiny still hasn't returned several minutes later, I crane my neck, searching for her among the parents and kids and avid bowlers.

I nearly jump out of my skin when she grabs me from behind.

"Boo!" She cackles when I turn around with my hand pressed to my chest. "It's Tennessee Tors blue, see?" she says, holding out a shiny blue ball. "I had to find a blue one." She sets it on the ball return, then bounces into the seat behind the monitor to enter our names. I inwardly groan when my player name appears on the screen above the lane. WR Watkins 84.

"You could've just put Cordell," I mumble under my breath.

"Oh, you don't mind, though!" she cheers, popping out of the seat like she's got springs in her legs.

She steps up to the line, hips swinging far too dramatically, and grins at me over her shoulder. Her ball drops to the floor with a loud thud, then rolls down the lane so slowly I worry that it's going to lose steam before it reaches the pins. At the last second, it veers to the right and knocks down the tenth pin.

"Oh well!" She skips back to the seating area and squeezes my bicep again. "Your turn, big guy!"

When I bowl a strike, Destiny's cheers are so loud, every head in the place whips our way. Her enthusiasm wanes, though, when she continues to knock down one or two pins per frame and I continue to make strikes or spares. She gets a gutter ball in the seventh frame and pokes her bottom lip out like my six-year-old niece.

I handle her the same way I do Raya and ask if she'd like to break for an order of nachos and pop. Her face lights up at my suggestion, and I breathe easy.

We carry our snacks back and settle in at a table next to our lane.

"So," I say between bites of my chili dog, "what's your connection to Mel?" I sound like a broken record, but I need to know how my angry pixie and this peppy, glittery human know each other.

Destiny licks nacho cheese from her finger and mimes locking her lips while she chews. When she picks up her pop, I press her for an answer. "Did she tell you not to tell me?"

She screws her face up and giggles. "No. But she did tell me to make you work for it."

*Of course she did.*

"Are you gonna tell me or not?" I try to keep irritation from leaching into my voice.

"*Maybe...*" She drags out the word, then winks and shoves another cheesy chip between her lips.

Leaning back, I cross my arms over my chest and wait. I'll

stare her down for as long as it takes, but we're not moving from this spot until I get an answer.

She finishes three more nachos before she rolls her eyes and huffs. "Fine. It's not like it's some big secret or anything."

"If it's not a big secret, then..." I trail off, hoping she'll put me out of my misery.

"Okay, okay." She raises her hands in surrender, then spills the not-secret. "The Low Bars. My stepbrother Vance is the lead singer."

My gut drops so violently I worry the chili dog was a bad choice. Of all the ways they could be connected, I for sure didn't expect the ex-husband or his band to be involved.

Destiny keeps talking, unaware of my bewilderment. "I was maybe thirteen when we met? I can't remember for sure. She and Nick had just started dating. She was nice to me. Never made me feel like a nuisance, like my brother did. Well, stepbrother. His dad married my mom when I was seven. He's always seen me as the annoying little sister he never asked for." Her tone may be chipper, but her words are heavy with loneliness. "Of course, I didn't, like, hang out with them or anything. They were the cool college kids, and I was an awkward middle schooler. But they used my parents' garage to rehearse, so Mel was there all the time. She'd leave them to their tunes and come find me in the house. We'd talk about boys I liked, makeup my mom wouldn't let me wear, clothes. She was kinda like a surrogate older sister."

I have so many questions. Have she and Mel kept in contact this whole time? Does Mel still talk to the other members of the band?

Does she still talk to Nick?

She said she didn't know or care about what he does, but from what I've seen, that's not the whole story.

"Y'all have been friends since then?" I ask.

"Oh, no, we only reconnected recently. I mean, after the

*divorce...*" she whispers the word, "we fell out of touch. She moved back home, and I was in high school in Athens. After college, I moved here for work. I found her on the 'Gram a couple years ago." She finishes the last of her nachos and slurps the rest of her pop through the straw.

I shouldn't pry. I should believe Mel when she tells me she's done with Nick. But...play to win, right?

"Does Mel still talk to anyone in the band?" I tamp down the nervousness that flutters in my gut.

She narrows her eyes and studies me for a long moment. "Not that I know of..." But then she drops a bomb that has the potential to ruin my plan. "But the last time I talked to Vance, he mentioned that Nick's still hung up on her. Never got over their breakup."

An icy panic spears through me. Is that why he sent her that postcard? Is he trying to win her back?

"You gonna finish those?" she asks, pointing at the cardboard container of nachos I've barely touched.

I slide them across the table, and she happily digs in while she tells me about the drama going down at her workplace. She's totally invested in whether two of her colleagues will hook up, though I lose track of the story quickly, only catching bits and pieces of the details as my mind becomes a swirling tornado of doubt and worry.

We finish our snacks and drinks and venture back to lane twelve to finish the first game. Destiny pouts when our final scores are tallied, then glares at me like she wants me to feel bad about beating her.

Maybe her abysmal bowling skills will encourage her to suggest that we forfeit the second game.

If only I were so lucky.

As the game goes on, she gets more and more disgruntled. Five frames in, my patience wearing thin, I suggest we call it a day.

She huffs and pokes her chin out in response. "Did *you* quit in that game against Houston when the Tors were down a touchdown with a minute-thirty left in the fourth?"

Baffled, I cock my head and frown at her. "We lost that game."

"Exactly!" she exclaims, triumphant.

"Am I missing some—"

"You!" she yells, loud enough that heads swivel in our direction again. She closes the distance and places her hands on my arms. She leans in—this woman has *no* issue with entering my personal space—and sucks in a breath, her eyes wide and a little crazed. "You. Didn't. Quit." She squeezes my arms to emphasize each word. Before I can ask her to give me some space, she does the last thing I'd ever expect.

She pops up onto her tiptoes, screws her eyes shut, and surges forward. Her lips are only on mine for a heartbeat before my brain catches up. Alarm bells blare, and a neon sign blinks to life before my eyes. The words *You're kissing a girl who's not Mel* flash, bright and insistent.

As gently as I can, I grasp her upper arms and hold her at arm's length. When she opens her eyes, they widen in mortification. A deep blush stains her cheeks, which she immediately covers with her palms. "Oh, God..." she wails from behind her hands. She then whispers something that sounds vaguely like "I did it again."

"Hey." I keep my voice low and soft, hoping to avoid adding to her embarrassment. "We're cool."

I grasp her wrists gently and tug, trying to pry her hands away so she can see my sincerity, but they're suctioned to her face like barnacles. So I wait as she whimpers and collects herself.

A few heaving breaths later, she lowers her hands and fixes her attention on something over my left shoulder. "I'm so sorry."

"It's okay."

She closes her eyes again and shakes her head.

"Do you maybe want to call it a night?" I silently beg her to agree. I have an hour drive ahead of me and Griffin's arrival tomorrow to prepare for.

Her voice wavers and her lips tremble. "You want to cut our date short?"

Great. Now I feel like a jerk.

I wince, but I figure honesty would be the best course of action. "It's just…I'm not sure if I can see us working out in the future. You're a really sweet person, but—"

Her expression goes from despondent to furious so fast my head spins. That alone bolsters my decision. Sure, Marshall can go from one extreme to another in a span of heartbeats, but never have the flames behind her hazel irises sent an actual chill of fear down my spine.

My mother raised me better than to *ever* call a woman crazy, but my date is straight-up giving me crazy-eyes. The ones that make a man hold his breath and dread what comes next.

I ease back slowly, ready to make a run for it if necessary, bowling shoes and all.

"If I'm such a sweet person, then why do you want to leave *early*?" She puffs up in front of me, arms thrown out to her sides. "Huh?"

"I just don't think we're a match," I tell her, using the calmest voice I can muster.

In a blink, she's crying again. "Y-you don't *like* me!"

Oh, Marshall better be prepared, because I am going to rant about this date for *days*.

"Destiny," I try again, still holding to that placid façade.

She wipes her cheeks aggressively, smudging one of the temporary tattoos, and lifts her chin, defiant.

"I think you're a very nice person. You're beautiful and smart. You're going to take one lucky guy's breath away one day." I pause and say a silent condolence for that dude. "But that guy is not me."

*Thank goodness.*

She presses her lips together as she studies me, her brows creased. Then, like a switch is flipped, her expression morphs one more time. With a smirk, she takes a step closer.

It takes all my resolve not to cower.

"You're right, big guy. But at least I can say I dated an NFL player!" With a giggle, she spins on her toes. She grabs her purse from under the seat, flounces to the counter, and retrieves her shoes. Then she skips out of the bowling alley without a backward glance or a care in the world.

Dumbfounded, I stand in the middle of lane twelve's seating area and watch her go.

*Did that really happen?*

A guy in the next lane clears his throat loud enough to get my attention. When I make eye contact, he shakes his head and chuckles. "You dodged a bullet there, my man."

Understatement of the year.

I cut my eyes to the NFL superstar sulking in my passenger seat.

Griffin's slouched against the door, resting his head in his broad palm. His eyes are closed, like maybe he plans to nap on our way into town. He didn't take kindly to my five-thirty wake-up knock on his door.

Racy Lacey is not an early bird.

The headlights of the Porsche Cayenne Seth had waiting for him at the Atlanta airport swept up the long driveway just as the sun was tucking in last night. When I questioned the odd rental choice, he smirked and admitted that he'd told his assistant that whatever make, model, and color he chose would be his after Griffin drove it back to Nashville in a few weeks. "A bonus for putting up with my depressed ass," he'd said.

Gifting a brand-new Porsche to a personal assistant.

I've forgotten what it's like to have NFL money.

Not that I was a heavy spender when I played. I made wise investments, and my only splurges were the house for Ma and SUVs for the both of us. When I built my own place a few years ago, I dipped into that cozy nest egg I'd been growing since my time in the league.

Beside me, Griff's head bobs, then his neck snaps as he jolts awake. He catches my eye and scoots up in his seat, stretching out his long legs. He adjusted the seat as far back as it'll go as soon as he got in, which gives him almost enough legroom.

"You sleep okay?" I ask.

"Yep. That mattress in your guest room is legit." His huge yawn betrays that statement a bit.

"When's the last time you saw six a.m.?"

"Ha. It has been a while," he says, scrubbing a hand through his raven crew cut. "Back home, Donna lets me sleep late. Drives Shaw nuts." He chuckles.

This is the longest conversation we've had since his arrival. After a brief greeting and tour last night, we turned in early.

"How are things in Holly Holler?"

"Hmm." His focus is trained out the window, on the scenery rolling by. "'Bout like round here, I guess. Quiet."

Griffin's hometown is small, tight-knit, and full of memorable characters. A lot like Bennett, I guess. Its official name is Holly Hollow, but according to the Lacey family, no one has called it that since its founding.

"And your family?"

"They're all riding my ass," he says with a laugh. "Donna's busy keeping us all alive, and ole Farmer Fred is still kicking. He's semi-retired, so during the week, he gives tours of the farm to local elementary schools and daycares. He loves it. Even got himself a pair of overalls with *Farmer Fred* embroidered on the front pocket. Wears them for every tour."

I grin at the image of Griffin's burly father showing little kids how to milk a cow or feed goats. Fred and Donna Lacey are the definition of honest, down-to-earth people.

He's still surveying the scenery when he asks, "What made you build out here?"

I scan the rural landscape through the windshield for a solid twenty seconds, letting it settle me the way it always does. "I like having space. Room to breathe. It's the type of place I'd want to raise a family—not that a family's on my immediate to-do list. When I saw the property a few years back, I just knew that's where I was supposed to build."

He hums and finally turns my way. "I get the need for space. And did I see a couple of prime fishing spots when I looked out the window this morning?"

"You did indeed. That was another draw. I do lots of thinking on that creek bank."

He nods and looks away again, this time taking in the road ahead of us.

"So, your parents are doing well. What about your brothers?"

"Those idiots," he says, his tone full of affection. "Shaw spends his days being a grumpy asshole, as usual. And Tucker opened up his own gym."

"Really?" I cock a brow at him. "Good for him. Is he still fighting?" Griffin's youngest brother is a professional MMA fighter.

"Yeah, he's still making events here and there. But he's been focused on getting Club Lacey Fitness up and running."

"Club Lacey. Cashing in on that last name, huh?"

"You know it," he affirms with a wry smile.

"So if your dad is claiming semi-retirement, does that mean Shaw is running the farm now?"

He rubs his close-cropped beard. "He's the top dog these days. And a serious pain in my ass."

Griff and his older brother are close in age but have vastly different temperaments. Broke out into a fistfight after a game once. Their parents stood on the curb and let it play out. I stood right there with them, taking Donna's lead. She just patted my hand and whispered, "This is a regular Monday night for the Lacey family."

As we near the town limits, I update Griffin in on my sister's family and Ryan and Raya's latest adventures. I also fill him in on what to expect at this week's camp. These five days will be busy. High school players will attend morning sessions led by my coaching staff and Griffin. In the evening, the youth camp will be led by all of us, plus my team.

I park in my usual spot beside the gym and do a double take at the smattering of reporters and media waiting beside the fence.

Griffin releases a deep sigh and shoots me an apologetic half smile.

"Dang, I can't take you anywhere."

My joke, thankfully, has the effect I was going for. His shoulders loosen, and he rolls his head from side to side. Gripping the door handle, he pauses. "You know it will be more by the end of the week."

I shrug and give him a reassuring bump with my shoulder. "We'll handle it."

He nods and sucks in a breath, bracing himself. Then he cracks the door.

Instantly, questions are lobbed his way.

*"Griffin, how's the shoulder?"*

*"Griff, what are your plans for next season?"*

*"Any comment on the Tors' decision to part ways?"*

*"Why'd the Tors let you go, Griffin?"*

He stops at the gate and flashes that megawatt Lacey smile.

He's smart. He knows his every movement, his every word, is being captured on the cell phones aimed at him.

"Hey, guys. Thank y'all for being here. I can't wait to be inspired by these kids, to help them learn more about the game I love, and to spend some time with one of my closest friends. Y'all have a good day." With a final wave, he joins me where I wait on the sidewalk.

As we walk side by side, the questions continue, a couple even directed at me. But we leave the noise behind and step into the air-conditioned sports complex.

Clay and Cole stand outside my office door with stars in their eyes.

My assistant coach wipes his palm on his shorts and extends it to Griffin. "Mr. Lacey, it's a real honor."

Griff grips his hand in a hearty shake. "No need for the *mister*. Call me Griffin or Griff." He tilts his head. "I'd tell you to call me what my family does, but it's not appropriate for young ears." He smiles at Cole, who is so starstruck, his father has to nudge him twice to remind him to offer his hand. When he does, Griffin shakes it just as firmly. "What position do you play, my man?"

Cole's face turns beet red, and he sputters, "C-center, sir."

"Ah, center. You gotta be a leader in that spot."

Cole looks like he's ready to pull out a notebook and write down every word out of Griff's mouth.

"My younger brother Tuck played center in high school and college."

"Y-yes, sir. He's MMA now. I've got a poster of him in my room."

Griffin draws his head back. "A poster of that dumba—uh, dummy?" He cuts his eyes to me and smirks like he's proud of himself for his censorship. "So you've got a picture of *Tucker* Lacey on your wall, but not *Griffin* Lacey?"

Cole's face turns an even brighter shade of red. The kid

looks like he's thirty seconds from passing out. "W-well, it's just the fight poster. From when he went up against El Cazador. It's not really a poster. It's just a printout from the school library." He ducks his head. "B-but I do have your jersey, sir. I'd really love for you to sign it."

"I'll sign whatever you got," Griff tells him, a huge grin on his face.

"Oh!" With one quick look at his dad, Cole takes off for his father's office. Seconds later, he's back, a red and blue jersey clutched in his fist.

By eight o'clock, the Bennett High football field is full of players and coaches. We break into defense, offense, and special teams and start work on fine-tuning mechanics. Griffin is in charge of tight ends and wide receivers, and every time I peek over at his group, the kids are hanging on his every word. He looks as thrilled as they are as he gives animated demonstrations and praises each kid's effort. It's like the gray cloud that was hanging over my friend has evaporated.

The sun is high in the sky when we break for the day. Griff is hit up for autographs and pictures, and for over an hour, he obliges every fan's request. Even I get a few autograph and selfie requests from the regional players.

Sometimes I feel so far removed from that life, I wonder if it was all a dream. An alternate reality.

Clay joins me where I watch Griffin interact with the last few kids in his autograph line.

"Successful first morning, Coach."

"Mm-hmm. And we're ready for the little ones this evening, too. The kids have their assignments and groups, and they know what to expect."

"It's cool when they surpass your expectations, isn't it?" He dips his head toward Griffin. "It's fun to watch him on the field —the touchdown dances and charming interviews and outrageous plays. But seeing him with the kids today? The way he made sure every player felt important? He's top notch." He clamps his hand on my shoulder. "Reminds me of someone else I know and have a helluva lot of respect for."

My chest swells at his words, like a balloon has been inflated inside my rib cage. I clear my throat. "Hey, check with Eric and see if he's up for lunch at Ruth's."

"You're taking a two-time Super Bowl champ to Ruth's Diner for lunch?"

"No. *We're* taking a two-time Super Bowl champ to Ruth's. Grab your stuff. And bring Cole."

Clay's face lights up like a Christmas tree, then he's scrambling for his phone and hustling back to the gym.

Lunch at Ruth's is less of a circus than I thought it would be. A few people are brave enough to approach Griffin for autographs and pictures, and he graciously agrees to each one, but for the most part, we eat in peace. Clay, Eric, and Cole bombard him with questions and requests for detailed play-by-plays of his favorite moments on the field. Griff, of course, happily reenacts every one with salt and pepper shakers, a ketchup bottle, and unused utensils.

When we're finished, Griffin insists on paying the bill, no matter how hard the rest of us protest. "I'm bigger than you, Watkins." He smirks as he holds Ms. Peggy's handwritten ticket up over our heads. In his left hand, I notice.

I roll my eyes. "You're one inch taller than me, Lacey."

"I've got twenty pounds on you, too." He smacks my abs with the back of his hand. "Although maybe civilian life has helped with that a bit. You goin' soft there, old man?"

"You eat my mom's cooking and see what happens. You'd be up twenty after a week of her meals. Plus, Clay's wife makes a mean homemade lasagna. I will never turn that down."

Griff arches a brow and regards Clay, who looks pleased as punch. "Her nonna taught her how to make it from scratch."

"Watkins, get us a dinner invitation to the Reeveses' on lasagna night."

"Done." Clay stands a little taller and grins. "I'll call Frannie on my way home."

We go our separate ways for a few hours, since the youth camp doesn't start until seven. Afternoon temps are too high for the kind of physical activities we'll be putting the kids through, and the late start gives parents time to get off work and feed the kiddos dinner beforehand.

I take the long way through town, giving Griff a quick tour, and once we're home, he sets up shop at the kitchen table for a video call with his agent and manager.

I make myself scarce by hitting the treadmill in my home gym. Maybe that "goin' soft" comment got to me.

After I shower, we find ourselves locked in a fierce *Mario Kart* battle. Then, following a quick dinner, we head back to town for the youth camp.

There's a palpable excitement in the air this evening. The stands are fuller than they were this morning, and kids and parents alike cheer when Griffin walks onto the field.

But even with attendance in the stands rivaling that of a Friday night home game, I zero in on her in seconds. She's sitting next to Jane Whitmer, whose son is out here on the field somewhere.

They're at the forty-yard line, about halfway up the stands. Even from this distance, the narrowing of her eyes on me when I lift my chin and shoot her a wink is obvious. She's flipping adorable. Her tickle-me-pink hair is split into pigtails under the same green trucker hat she wore on our fishing trip. She traces a brow with her middle finger, and I can't help but grin.

"Coach."

I startle and slap a hand to my chest at the sound of Clay's voice.

"I need a little help here." He's standing, hands on hips,

next to his daughter. "Cara wants to participate. I've explained that she would be the only girl out there, but..." He huffs out a breath and shrugs.

"Let her play."

Cara beams at me, then gives her father an *I-told-you-so* look that is Frannie Reeves made over.

"But—" Clay starts.

I crouch down to Cara's level. Her expression is nothing but fierce determination. The eight-year-old's ivory cheeks are pink from exertion. Her dark brown ponytail is lopsided, and wisps of hair escape its confines, framing her face. As long as I've known this kid, she's been determined to do everything her older brothers do, and it appears that playing football is no exception.

"You understand that you'll be the only girl out there?"

She nods.

"It's not because girls can't play, Cara. We just didn't have any other girls sign up."

"I know, Coach," she drawls.

"All right, then. Go show these boys how it's done."

She gives me another curt nod, but when I raise my hand for a high five, she grins as wide as the field she's determined to conquer.

When I return to my full height, Clay huffs a dejected sigh. "You know I don't ever want to hold my kids back."

"I know."

He simply hangs his head and walks off to help our players get the kids organized into groups.

Clay and Frannie are amazing parents, but every now and then, they find themselves at a loss for how to parent Cara. She's like Raya: tough one minute, soft the next, and everywhere in between.

I instinctively find Mel in the stands again. She's laughing and bobbing her head. Beside her, Jane's pointing at the field. I follow their line of sight and quickly discover who's capturing their attention: a two-time Super Bowl champ who's busy leading a group of kids in their warm-up exercises.

A trickle of doubt flits through my mind. Maybe setting Mel up with Griffin while he's in town is a bad idea.

Nah.

I shake away my uncertainty. Those two are not compatible in *any* way.

*Right?*

The evening goes the way we envisioned it would. Dozens of excited, energetic kids learning more about football, practicing footwork, and catching passes. I'm beyond proud of our Eagles players. They're attentive and encouraging to the kids every moment of the evening.

Clay, Eric, and I let them run the show and step in where we're needed. Griffin spends most of his time posing for pictures or signing jerseys and footballs, but his enthusiasm never wanes.

When the hour is over, I direct all the high school kids to set up for the morning's session while Griffin finishes up with his fans. Most of the townsfolk, parents, and kids have left, but a few stragglers remain. I'm worn out, but the second I spot pink pigtails in my periphery, my body sparks back to life like I've just downed a double shot of espresso.

Mel waves to Jane and Chase and then strides my way. Every step she takes drags me farther under her spell. She spends lots of time at her parents' pool, and it shows. For someone so tiny, her legs look ridiculously long. The summer tan only adds to the illusion.

Her sun-kissed skin has me thinking about tan lines, and then I'm wondering what color swimsuit she wears and if it's a bikini or a one-piece.

My money's on a bikini. Bright robin's egg blue.

Held up by thin strings tied into loopy bows. What I

wouldn't give to pull those bows loose and unwrap her like the gift she is—

"Hey, I'm talking to you!" Mel shoves my arm.

I shake myself out of the fantasy. The real thing stands in front of me, madder than a hornet.

"What was that?" I do a quick scan of the stadium. It's just us and Griff and one final family who's posing for pictures now.

"I *said*," she emphasizes, "why did you make Destiny cry on your date?" She crosses her arms and juts out a hip. She's wearing army green shorts and a gray T-shirt that reads *I'm not short. I'm concentrated awesome.* As usual, she's got Birkenstocks on her feet, and her toes are painted a vibrant tropical blue.

The exact shade of her bikini in my pool fantasy.

I blink once, twice, a third time to shake the image from my mind, and her words sink in. "Now hang on. She made herself cry."

"Really? That's what you're going with?" Chin lifted, she narrows her eyes.

I have the overwhelming urge to toss her over my shoulder again and make out with her under the bleachers. Instead, I force my mind out of the gutter once more and straighten up.

"That's what I'm going with because that's what happened. She burst into tears because she was embarrassed about kissing me without consent."

She gapes and takes a step back, uncrossing her arms. "She kissed you? Wh-why did she kiss you?" When she homes in on my smug smile, she lifts her chin like she's unbothered.

But she's bothered, all right. Another woman kissed me, and she's spiraling.

*First down.*

I pop a shoulder, nonchalant. "I'm very kissable, Marshall."

Her response is an exaggerated scoff and a roll of her eyes.

"You know better than most."

My attention's still locked on the tiny spitfire in front of me when Griffin wanders over to watch the showdown.

Mel gives him a quick once-over, then skewers me with a menacing stare. "From what I recall, *Coach*, it's what I imagine kissing a dead fish would feel like. No wonder she cried."

I can't help it. I bark out a laugh and turn to Griffin, who's got his arms crossed over his chest and his brows raised like this is the most exciting thing he's seen this summer. He tips his head toward Mel.

The guy gesture for *is this one yours?*

I hesitate, considering how to signal back, and before I can, Mel huffs out a frustrated breath.

That sound is all it takes for me to decide. With a grin, I nod at Griff, claiming her.

Yep, this angry little pixie will be mine. One day.

But today is not that day.

Mel carries on as if we don't have a witness. "You're insufferable."

"Not the first time you've called me that. Perhaps it's time for some new material?"

"Perhaps it's time for you to bite me." The second she spits out the words, she turns an adorable shade of pink.

Oh-ho-ho. My heart leaps at that expression, and I revel in her frustration.

She closes her eyes and takes several deep breaths. "Ugh, just...never mind. I'll update the score. Still tied, zero-zero."

"Cool. Go ahead and make a note for my date. It should read *unhinged jersey chaser*. And for the record, if you want me to bite you, all you have to do is ask."

Griffin whistles low, and Mel whips her head to him. "Hey, I'm Griffin." He holds out his hand, his charismatic smile already in place.

She glares at his hand, then up at his face. "Okay," she says, lifting her hands like *so what?*

When she doesn't take it, he slowly retracts it and rubs his chin. It's the first time he's encountered an unimpressed individual since his arrival in Georgia. His responding bewilderment makes me snicker.

"This one doesn't play well with others." I thumb in Mel's direction.

"And this one is a pompous ass," she retorts. "Who makes girls cry on dates."

"Marshall, how well do you know Destiny?"

"I know her well enough." She clenches her fists and props them on her hips.

"You knew her when she was a kid." I cock a brow, silently challenging her to argue with that statement. "And you know the Destiny she presents on social media today. But you don't really *know her*, know her, do you?"

Mel's brows draw together, and that cute little wrinkle between them makes an appearance. "I mean..." She trails off. "We DM each other all the time." Her voice has lost most of its bluster.

I breeze past that. "If you *really* knew her, you wouldn't think we'd be a match. *Unless...*" I raise a brow and tilt my head.

She purses her lips at my insinuation. "You're delusional, Watkins." With a huff, she spins on her toes and stomps away, muttering under her breath.

I catch words like *audacity* and *cocky football jock-bros* and *kiss* as she hoofs it down the sideline.

When I hear her car door slam, I turn and am met with the biggest grin I think I've ever seen plastered on Griffin's face.

Silently, we watch Mel's car whip out of the parking lot. Then he looks at me and says, "She. Is. *Fun*."

# CHAPTER THIRTEEN

## CORDELL

"Uncle Dell, Mama says it's time for you to get up!" My niece takes a running leap onto the queen-size air mattress and lands in just the right position to knee me in the kidney. Could be worse. I could be a back-sleeper and get forty-five pounds of six-year-old to the gut instead.

I roll to one side, my feet dangling off the end of the mostly inflated air mattress, and snag my glasses and my phone from the desk in the kids' playroom. This is my domain when Ma and I come to Atlanta. Ma gets the extra bedroom, and instead of making Ryan and Raya double up, I spend my nights with robots and Legos and Disney princesses.

According to my phone's display, it's eight twenty-seven. I haven't slept this late since I had the flu two winters ago. I scrub a hand down my face and turn over to sit up. At my feet, Raya is perched on her knees, wearing a Hello Kitty nightgown and a grin that's absent two front teeth. Her wild, dark corkscrew curls surround her head like a lion's mane. She smooths back a coil that's fallen into her eyes and inspects me, her head tilted and her brow furrowed in concentration.

"You have hair on your chest."

"I do." The brutal honesty of young kids never fails to amaze me.

I wish another of my favorite females would be as forthright.

"Will Ryan have that when he's a grown-up?"

My sister appears in the doorway, interrupting our conversation. "It's about time, Sleeping Beauty." Cass's warm smile is a mirror image of mine—it's our dad's smile.

*Does she think of him every time I smile at her, like I do when she shines her smile on me?*

How bittersweet a gift DNA can be.

Ryan and Raya share no DNA with either of their moms or with each other. Cass and Kelly adopted both kids when they were infants. They are a beautiful reminder that love makes a family, not DNA.

"Kell's making huevos rancheros," my sister informs me. "Ma's on the back porch with her coffee, watching Ryan show off his trampoline tricks."

"Trampoline tricks at eight-thirty on a Saturday morning. Gah, to have that kind of energy again."

"Right?" She smirks. "They do keep us young." Her focus drifts to her daughter, then to me. "You need a few of your own."

"Only if they're just like this one." I grasp Raya by the arm and tickle her ribs.

She erupts in a fit of infectious giggles that makes my sister and me laugh. The instant I ease up, she wriggles out of my grasp and takes off, her high-pitched laughter carrying down the hallway.

Cass plugs an ear and winces. "Obviously, there are drawbacks." With one more smile, she follows her daughter down the hall.

I slip on a T-shirt and throw my arms out, relishing the stretch. When I stumble into the kitchen in search of coffee, I find my sister-in-law, Kelly, frying eggs at the stove. Her dark hair is piled on her head in a messy knot, and she's humming that Shakira song about hips.

"Smells amazing," I tell her as I lean in to kiss her cheek.

She smiles up at me. "Almost ready."

All four of Kelly's grandparents immigrated from Mexico when they were young adults and settled in the southeastern US. She and Cass met on a blind date three years before they got married. Within minutes of meeting Kelly, I knew that she and my sister would spend their lives together. They balance each other perfectly—Cass's calm, collected demeanor is the perfect complement to Kelly's passion and big heart.

I pour myself a mug of coffee and sit at the bar while Kelly works her magic. She deftly plates the eggs on top of the corn tortillas and tops each with spoonfuls of homemade salsa. My mouth waters at the thought of the jars that will be traveling home with Ma and me. She usually sends us back with enough to last a few weeks. If they're lucky, I leave with enough to share with the Shipleys and the Reeveses, too.

"Oh!" She spins and points her spatula at me. "Did Cass tell you that Rhonda offered to keep the hooligans tonight so the adults can adult?"

"Did she now?"

She waggles her brows at me. "You know what that means—"

"Mango margs!" we shout in unison.

I clap, being sure to cup my hands just right so it echoes through the house. It's the same clap I use when the kids make an excellent play on the field.

From the other side of the house, Cass hollers, "Mango margs!" too.

After a full day of shopping and a visit to the Georgia Aquarium with the kids, Kelly and Cass and I order mango margaritas and brisket tacos at their favorite Mexican restaurant.

"Oh my *gosh*, I've missed your face." Kelly's holding her giant margarita up to her face and whispering sweet nothings.

"My mother is a saint," Cass says.

"To Saint Rhonda." I hold up my glass, and they clank theirs against it.

"I wish y'all could stay longer than a weekend," my sister whines.

Agreed. School starts next week, so this little weekend getaway is all I can manage at this time of the year.

I pop a loaded tortilla chip into my mouth and chew, then take a long sip of my margarita. "Y'all should come down one weekend for a game while Griffin's still in town." Though it'll be equally hard for them to make the three-hour drive once the kids are back in school.

"Yeah, I need to meet that hunk," Kelly says with a wink.

Cass shoots her a look. "How's he like Bennett? You could've brought him up, you know."

"I offered." I shrug and pop another chip into my mouth. "He's stuck in limbo, waiting for offers. The season is close, and he gets more and more worried as the days tick by."

Teams are deep into the preseason now, and from the way his phone isn't ringing, it seems no one's on the hunt for a veteran tight end.

"He wanted to hang around there this weekend, soak up the quiet without his family hovering over him."

What was supposed to be a weeklong stay for camp has been extended into an indefinite visit. Since he's been a fixture in town for a few weeks, most people greet him with a friendly wave or hello these days and leave it like that. The lack of hoopla surrounding him has been a nice reprieve.

We're polishing off our last bites of taco when Kelly hoists her almost-empty glass in my direction. "What would all your football bros say if they saw Cordell Watkins drinking a girly mango margarita?" She's a lightweight and gets giggly and loud after one drink. Two make her tipsy and bold. I had to give her a piggyback ride to the car and hold on tight while she flailed around like a toddler one night after she downed three piña coladas and a tequila shot.

Cass and I exchange smiles.

"I don't really care what they'd say. Are there really such things as 'girl drinks' and 'boy drinks'? Let the people live, I say. Drink what you want to drink, love who you want to love."

Two margs might make me a bit loose-lipped, too. I'm used to nursing one or two beers at Fuzzy's, and nothing more.

"Here, here!" Kelly proclaims. She brings her marg in close to finish it off but misses the straw twice before she finally captures it between her lips.

"Speaking of loving who you want," my sister chimes in, never one to pass up a segue. "You got anyone special these days, bubs?" She eyes her wife, who, in return, gives her an exaggerated wink.

I shovel three chips into my mouth in rapid succession to buy myself some time to respond. Every time we're together, they inquire about my love life, or lack thereof, but I've always kept my cards close to the vest. It's a strategy that's worked well for me both as a player and a coach. My sister and I are close; she knows almost every secret of mine, but I don't know that I'm ready to reveal my game plan.

In the end, though, the tequila decides for me.

"There may be, possibly, might be...someone."

Kelly squeals and grabs Cass's arm. Both women lean forward in their seats.

"Who is she?" The glint in my sister's brown eyes is all triumph.

I sigh and hold both palms up. "Whoa there, calm down."

"Calm. We're totally calm. Breezy and calm," Kelly

promises, crossing her heart with one hand while still clutching her wife's arm with the other.

Cass has donned her older sister hat if the intense way she's studying me is any indication. Like she can catch every nuance or tell that might flash on my face. Ever since Dad died, she's been like this during serious discussions. The way she looks out for me *still*, even though I'm a grown man and almost a foot taller than her, makes me love her more fiercely than I thought possible.

"You remember that girl I told you about *way* back? The one I met at the bar when I was home for a few weeks one summm—"

"It's her?" Cass asks softly.

This is the one secret I've never shared with my sister.

"How?" she asks. "How'd you find her?"

I blow out a steady exhale. I'm not sure how to explain this or how she's going to react, so I just go for it and hope for the best.

"It's Mel."

"Mel? Who's Mel?"

I swallow past the lump in my throat, but I don't answer. She'll connect the dots if I give her a minute.

"You mean the doctor's daughter?"

"Yes."

"Mel," she says, resting her forearms on the table and leaning in close, "the doctor's daughter, is the late-night dive-bar back-seat hookup you declared, and I quote, 'ruined you for all other girls'?"

"Yes."

Kelly snort-laughs. "*Late-night dive-bar back-seat hookup* would be an awesome band name."

Cass and I raise our brows at each other. How she managed to get all those words out in the correct order after two margaritas is a wonder.

"Let me get this straight." My sister wiggles in her chair and sits a little taller. "Mel, the woman I've caught glaring at you with the fire of a thousand suns on many, many occasions, is the girl you had sex with in the back seat of your Caddy?"

I dip my chin. "She is."

Cass leans back and crosses her arms. "Explain."

So I do. I tell them everything—the mistaken identity at Fuzzy's, the Memorial Day food fight and subsequent truce, the matchmaking competition, the Independence Day kiss and ex-husband reveal. And finally, my plan to win Mel's heart.

They listen, wide-eyed and slack-jawed, until I'm all out of details.

"Damn, I think I'm sober now," Kelly mutters. But the statement is followed by a sappy smile in direct opposition to that sentiment. "Aww, she ruined you for other girls." Like that detail is the most important of them all.

Maybe it is.

My sister tilts her head and scrutinizes me for a solid minute.

The anticipation is killing me. A flutter in my gut makes me regret that last taco. I'm desperate to hear what she thinks, but I'm terrified I won't like what she has to say.

Cass tucks a loose natural curl behind an ear and leans forward to rest her chin on a fist. Still, she's silent.

"Cassidy?" Her name is a question, a request for her to put me out of my misery.

Finally, she presses her lips together and clears her throat. This is it. My moment of reckoning.

"You know what Ray Watkins would say about this messy situation?"

My stomach drops at that word *messy*.

She grabs my hand and squeezes. "Hey, just because it's messy doesn't mean it's wrong." She dips her chin and gives me a soft smile.

With a nod, I steel myself for the rest.

"Dad would ask you if she's the one who sets your soul on fire. That's how he described meeting Ma."

"I remember."

Kelly's dark eyes sparkle with unshed tears. Tequila also makes her emotional.

"If that woman sets your soul on fire, then you'll figure it out." My sister's smile is a little more encouraging now. "I don't know Mel Marshall well, but from the way you describe her, I think Dad would be a big fan of her spunkiness." She looks at her wife with so much love in her eyes, it chokes me up. "Just like he'd be a big fan of this one's kindness." She pulls her wife's hand to her lips and kisses her knuckles.

"That's right, Dell. Sounds like she'll keep you on your toes, but you'll win her over." Kelly's all confidence, smiling through her tears.

Cass flaps her hands in front of her eyes. "Okay, that's enough." She scoots her chair closer to the table and sets her jaw. "Now, let's go over your plan one more time."

"Wait, wait, wait." Griffin's standing at the island pouring milk into a giant bowl of Frosted Flakes.

My temporary roommate eats like a frat boy.

He takes a huge bite and chomps loudly. When he's done, he wipes his mouth with his forearm. "You want me," he asks, pointing his spoon at his chest, "to go on a date with the cute little hellcat who chewed your ass after the first night of camp?"

I'm perched against the counter, one ankle crossed over the other, savoring my morning cup of coffee. Since school started a couple of weeks ago, Griffin has acclimated to an earlier wake-up time. He joins me for breakfast most mornings, though I'm pretty sure he crawls back into bed once my car leaves the garage. Either way, I appreciate his company.

"Yeah. That about sums it up."

He shovels another spoonful. "So you two are...?" he asks, around the cereal.

"In a competition to see who can find the best match for the other."

"How's that going for you?"

"You heard the butt-chewing."

"Right." He narrows his eyes. "So what I'm deducing is that you and the hellcat are setting each other up with duds, on purpose, because you really want to jump each other's bones, but you can't—or won't—own up to that."

I finish the last dregs of my coffee, rinse the mug in the sink, and set it in the dishwasher. When I turn back to Griffin, the grin he's wearing is smug as all get out.

"Don't let anyone accuse you of being nothing more than a pretty face, Lacey." Snagging my keys off the counter, I head for the garage. "I'll be at school all afternoon. See you at the game tonight."

I'm stepping into the Rover when he hollers through the door. "Wait! That makes *me* a dud!"

I chuckle all the way down the driveway, then I spend the rest of my drive revealing game plans—for tonight's opener *and* for Mel Marshall—to my dad.

The school day unfolds like a typical Friday during football season. Clay and Eric ensure the kids' jerseys are in place in the locker room. We hold a team meeting during the varsity football class period, where we go through our last-minute walk-through to prepare.

Our opponent is one we easily defeated last year, but as always, we don't let past successes make us complacent.

Griffin arrives before we take the team out on the field for warm-ups. He's become a fixture at practice for the past few weeks. The kids love to pick his brain. They've moved past his celebrity status, and these days, several of them rag on him the way they do us coaches.

In the locker room, I give one final pep talk. "Remember the game plan, boys. Know your role and do it well. Together, we can win. Together, we *will* win. Let's go out there and be great today!" We huddle up and push our hands to the center. "Eagles on three. One, two, three, *Eagles!*"

Sweat soaks the back of my red polo within minutes of taking the field.

Once I'm on the sideline, I scan the crowd for my people and wave, a pregame ritual I've continued since my first game as head coach. That particular Friday, I was so nervous I threw up in the field house bathroom. Finding my mom and my best friend and his family in the stands was like a tonic for my nerves. They're in their regular spots tonight. As usual, Hannah jumps up and down, waving wildly when she sees me looking their way. My attention is immediately drawn to the shock of pink hair next to Tessa, but Mel is talking to her parents and doesn't notice me.

It only takes a minute for the crowd to realize that the tall stranger wearing an Eagles cap pulled low is Griffin Lacey, and when they do, they erupt. Rhythmic chants of "Racy Lacey, Racy Lacey!" fill the evening air until he raises a hand to acknowledge them.

Once the whistle signals the start of the game, I'm all business. Thoughts of anything other than the field in front of me are stowed away for the next two hours.

The Tigers get an early lead in the middle of the first quarter, but by halftime, we're up fourteen to seven. We make a couple of adjustments during the break, and then we're off to the races in the second half. We complete three scoring drives in the third quarter, and our lead is substantial enough in the fourth for us to sub out some younger players.

Final score: Eagles, thirty-four. Tigers, fourteen.

"That's a helluva way to start the season," Griffin tells me after the final whistle. Our boys and staff head for the field house, but we wait on the field for one final tradition.

Hannah rounds the stairs at the bottom of the stands, her parents several steps behind. She's wearing a huge grin as she runs straight for me, her long brown braid bouncing on her shoulder.

"Good game, Coach!" She launches herself into my waiting arms. I swing her around, pulling joyful cackles from her.

"Banana!" I lower her to the turf. "Did you see Grady's pass to Calvin in the third?"

She nods and hops up and down like a spring.

"Your dad and I had a pass just like that our junior year. I broke away from my coverage and sprinted down the field, wide open, and he gunned one right to me, like—"

"A laser," Luke finishes as he and Tessa join us. "Ah, the glory days." He's wearing a fond smile as he moves in for a bro hug. "Great way to kick off your playoff run, man."

Tessa beams at us, hand on her belly. She's only a month or so from her due date.

"You should have your feet up at the house, little mama."

"I wouldn't miss your season opener, Coach. And don't tell me I'm glowing. I promise it's all sweat."

"You look beautiful," I tell her as I lean down to peck her cheek.

"Good to see you again," Griffin says. "Luke, you're still in for fishing tomorrow, right?"

He gives his wife an apologetic look. "Sorry, I forgot to tell you, Ivy." He uses his nickname for her, no doubt in hopes of softening her response. "We planned to hit the creek behind Cordell's in the morning while you two are at the shower."

"Hope y'all catch some good ones, then," she answers with a wink.

He kisses her cheek in response. The sight of it triggers that familiar pang in my chest—a hurt that hits deep when I'm reminded of what I'm missing.

Griffin's face lights up. "Hellcat incoming," he mutters under his breath.

The whole group turns and watches Mel strut over. Her red Eagles T-shirt has been altered and distressed, the neckline and bottom hem both cut off. One tan shoulder is exposed, displaying the thick strap of a white sports bra.

As usual, just that peek of a flipping sports bra makes my pulse pick up speed.

When she reaches our group, she goes straight for Tessa, only bothering a cursory glance at the rest of us, and I experience an irrational spike of jealousy.

"I'll pick you up at nine-thirty tomorrow."

"You don't have to drive all the way out to get us," Tessa protests.

Mel tilts her head and cocks a brow. "T, tomorrow is *your* big day. We're spoiling you, so get used to it."

Tessa wrings her hands. "Okay, but what if Shanice needs help with—"

"Tessa Shipley." Mel grasps Tessa's hand and gives it a squeeze. "The only thing you need to worry about tomorrow is oohing and aahing over green and yellow onesies. If you'd prefer gifts better tailored to this one," she gently pats Tessa's belly, "then I can give Dr. Singh a call tonight—"

With a sigh and a smile, Tessa shakes her head. "You know better, but good try."

"Are you sure?" That one brow lifts even higher. "My mom has Dr. Singh's number..."

Tessa laughs and swats at Mel's arm.

"Fine. Green and yellow it is." She rolls her eyes, but she's wearing a bright smile. "Now, repeat after me: I do not have permission to stress about my baby shower."

Tessa hesitates, but then obeys. "I do not have permission to stress about my baby shower."

Over his wife's head, Luke mouths *thank you.*

In return, Mel gives him a sly nod.

"All right, folks. We're heading out. It's past my girls' bedtimes." As if on cue, Hannah's mouth opens in a wide yawn. After a round of hugs and handshakes, Luke takes hold of his wife's and daughter's hands, and they stroll off the field.

The spectators have left the stadium, and I need to get inside the field house, but I can't make my feet move that way. Not when striking hazel eyes keep bouncing between me and my former teammate.

They narrow in a calculating way, and then Mel says the worst thing a person could say to a pair of competitive athletes.

"You know what I'm wondering?" She tilts her head. "Which one of you is fastest?"

Griffin huffs a laugh. "Back in his prime, Watkins. But he's gotten soft. I may be coming off an injury, but I'd win. No doubt."

I widen my stance and jut my chin at him. "Watch who you're calling soft, Lacey. I run almost every dang day."

"Yeah, you run for distance. For endurance. You haven't had a cornerback nipping at your heels in a good long while, my man." Griff's smile lights up his whole face.

As for the woman who started it, she bites her bottom lip to keep from grinning. "Seems like there's an easy way for y'all to figure this out," she says, twirling a strand of her hair. "Big, empty field here. I'd be happy to be the starter."

"I bet you would," I growl.

Her smile grows wider, and my heart stutters. I'm about to make a fool of myself. All I can do is hope that any disgrace will be worth it.

That smile would make me do most anything.

"What's it gonna be, Coach?" Griffin goads.

I'm 98 percent sure I can't beat Griffin like I could've ten years ago, but there's no way I'm backing down.

I spin toward the field house and glance at them over my shoulder. "Give me ten minutes."

Behind me, Griff howls. "Let's *go!*"

By the time I finish up with the team and change into gym shorts and a T-shirt, we've collected a small audience. Clay is standing beside Mel in the end zone, along with a few of our players. Griff's out at the fifty-yard line, stretching like he's racing for a gold medal.

I jog out to join him. "I might be too old for this, Lacey."

"Nah," he grunts as he dips into a lunge.

With a laugh, I get to stretching, starting with my quads. With a few bounces on the balls of our feet and a couple of shoulder rolls, Griff and I are ready and getting into position. I'm focused on Mel's figure in the middle of the end zone. She holds an Eagles towel above her head in one hand, ready to give the signal.

Without taking his eyes off the goal, Griffin teases, "A good friend would let you take this, you know."

"Yep."

"But I'm not gonna let you win just because you have a thing for the hellcat."

"I know."

"See ya down there."

The second the words are out of his mouth, Mel drops her arm.

Griffin's reaction time is sharper than mine, but I pull up even with him halfway to the end zone. I'm giddy about it and motivated to pass him, but despite my best efforts, his right foot crosses the line a couple seconds before mine does.

The small crowd that's gathered cheers wildly. Griff gets congratulatory high fives and back slaps while I rest my hands on my knees to catch my breath. Red rubber Birks slide into my view, then there's a towel draped around my neck. I raise to my full height and come face to face with Mel, who's holding a bottle of water in her outstretched hand.

"Not too shabby, Watkins." Her eyes sweep over me appreciatively.

Definitely worth it, then.

# CHAPTER FOURTEEN

## MEL

Discreetly, I swipe at the bead of sweat crawling down my back and rub my hand on my leggings, then once again home in on the two fine male asses on display in the back row.

Two fine male asses attached to two equally fine NFL bodies that are currently sucking all the oxygen out of my yoga studio.

Oh, Fernando, you and I definitely have some business to attend to tonight.

With a heavy swallow, I force my gaze away from the tight, round globes. As I step between the mats, a teenage boy in the middle row whispers, "She's hot."

The comment is followed by Cordell's deep voice whisper-growling the kid's last name. The two boys next to the no-shame cougar-chaser snicker. Keeping my head high, I give the direction for the next pose. In the mirror, I catch sight of Griffin Lacey's broad back, which is shaking with suppressed laughter, too.

Boys will be boys.

I roll my eyes and deny myself another glance in their direction.

For the past couple of years, Cordell has made a point to bring a handful of players to Saturday Flow classes during the season. It helps with the players' footwork, balance, and flexibility. And because he's a great coach, he accompanies them.

That means I should be used to seeing Cordell Watkins's ass in downward dog, and for the most part, I am. Enough to control myself, at least.

But today, he brought a second delicious distraction to muddle my mind and throw me off my Zen game.

Griffin or not, Cordell's been a major distraction these past few months. Food fights and competitions and kisses. Mine and *Destiny's*. Damn, that confession, that Destiny kissed him, haunts me. Every time it surfaces, I burn with the same intense jealousy that engulfed me that evening. That another woman had her lips on his both infuriates and nauseates me.

*Did he kiss her back?*

That question has plagued my thoughts for weeks. My mind is a jumbled mess of confusion and lust and longing. When we're together, thoughts of Nick's betrayal and my reason for closing myself off from relationships and the l-word disappear.

Cordell Watkins makes me *feel* things. Things I haven't felt in a very long time.

Not only do I forget about my tragic relationship history, but I forget that I'm not supposed to *like* him. I'm supposed to harbor a lifelong grudge against him for not recognizing me that night. When I stormed out of Fuzzy's, after he offered me a *selfie*—*twice*, for fuck's sake—I promised myself *never again*.

Never again would I let a man make me feel worthless or forgotten.

Never again would I let a man close enough to even attempt it.

I brush my fingers along my rib cage. Sometimes I can still feel the scratchy burn from that night.

The sound of a low grunt brings me back to the present. Subtly, I scan the class. Arms are shaking in strain all over the place. Shit. They've been in high plank for too damn long.

"Now," I say, keeping my voice calm, "send your hips up and back into downward facing dog, chest facing thighs." I observe them as they move into this rest position. "We're going to stay here for five long ujjayi breaths."

I walk the perimeter of the room and offer suggestions and adjustments where they're needed. When I skirt the back wall, I notice that a certain coach is not in the correct position—a position he can easily hold flawlessly, mind you.

"Your hips aren't right," I whisper.

He doesn't acknowledge me. Either because he's ignoring me or because he's too focused on his breathing. I can't tell. Without thinking, I step up behind him and grip his hips to shift them up and back. A second too late, I realize I've made a colossal mistake. My abdomen is pressed up against Cordell's firm ass. The warmth of his body sends a bolt of heat coursing through me. Glued to the spot, I relish the feel of him, hard and strong and solid.

"Marshall." Cordell's whisper is strained.

It's enough to jolt me into action. I step back and give his ass a playful swat as I return to the front, playing off my blunder.

My face is on fire for the rest of the class. By the time I direct them into Savasana, I'm certain that everyone in attendance knows exactly where my mind has been for the past hour. I can't even make eye contact with Cordell, but soon he, Griffin, and the three teenagers are the only ones left in the room.

"You boys need a ride?"

"Naw, Coach. I've got my truck."

"All right. Drive safe."

With that, the boys tromp out of the room, through the lobby, and out into the Georgia sunshine.

Cordell turns to me, four purple mats rolled up and tucked under his arm. "Thanks for your help with downward dog today, Marshall." His knowing grin causes my face to flame once more. "You remember Griffin."

Six feet and five inches of hotness steps forward to shake my hand. This time, I don't ignore the gesture.

"Racy," I say, all business.

His huge hand swallows mine, but I grip it with a firm shake.

"Hellcat." He goes for serious to match my tone, but it only lasts a heartbeat before a huge smile breaks out on his face. It's so infectious, I can't help but return it.

"Did you just call me 'hellcat'?" Hands on my hips, I peer up at him.

His blue-gray eyes twinkle in merriment. "I would never."

I narrow my eyes, but that grin never leaves his face.

The giants before me are both broad-shouldered and muscly all over. But Cordell's leaner than his friend, his waist trimmer, and he's more graceful in his movements. Griffin's built like a tank, albeit a well-defined one. And they both have tree-trunk thighs you could bounce a dime off. The contrast between Cordell's warm brown skin and Griffin's fair beige makes me again think of those *why choose* books Tessa loves to giggle about.

Maybe those romance authors are on to something.

But I refuse to be intimidated by the gorgeous men in my presence. I pull my shoulders back and address the NFL dreamboat. "How long are you staying in Bennett?"

He's been here for over a month. I've heard through the grapevine—a.k.a. Ms. Daisy—that he's still waiting for the perfect offer, but the season starts next weekend. I'm guessing he's hiding out here to wait for an eleventh-hour phone call.

"Not too much longer, if I had to guess." His smile never

wavers, but his tone is cryptic. Maybe he's heard from a team, after all.

"Since Griff's gonna be around for a few more days," Cordell starts, "I think he should be your next setup."

My stomach drops like it's tethered to an anvil that's been pushed off the side of a high-rise. My next setup? He wants me to go on a date with his friend? The swirling storm of emotions that's been brewing for weeks makes me lightheaded.

*He* didn't want to continue the competition when I set him up with Destiny. That text he sent—*why are we still doing this?*—flashes in my mind. All his nonsense about feeling a *spark*, the hot make-out session on the Fourth of July, the flirty eye-fucking. He had me convinced he wasn't interested in more setups.

And like a fucking fool, I let myself start to *hope*.

Choking back the hurt bubbling up inside me, I search his face for a sign that might explain his sudden change of heart, but his expression is open. Honest. There's no glimmer in his eye or smugness to his smile that would indicate he's got an ulterior motive.

*Maybe he's tired of waiting for you to get over your ridiculous grudge.*

The thought forces me to take a step back and press a palm to my racing heart.

Cordell tracks the movement, and his focus lingers there for a heartbeat before it returns to my face. My pride, that stubborn bitch, stifles any other indication of how upset I am. I shore up, lift my chin, and exhale a ragged breath.

Lips pressed in a line, I look him square in his handsome face. "Perfect. Let's do it."

*Calling your bluff, Watkins.*

I swear a corner of his mouth twitches, but he maintains his composure. Griffin's stupid handsome face is still smiling when I look his way.

"Where are you taking me, Racy?"

"Oh, hellcat, I've got the perfect plan."

I give him a half-hearted glare. He *did* call me hellcat.

"My foundation is partnering with Habitat for Humanity on a build this Friday. What better way to get to know one another than over power tools?"

"Don't worry," Cordell chimes in. "I'll be around to referee. Marshall with a drill or a power saw could be a danger to everyone."

"Wait...*you're* going to be there. On *our* date?" I tighten my short ponytail to give my hands something to do. What the hell is he playing at here?

"It's a community service project for the Bennett athletics program."

"Teenagers with power tools?" I scoff.

"Only juniors and seniors. And they're only allowed to use tools, with supervision, if they're already eighteen."

"Don't worry. My foundation organizes things like this with local schools all the time. We've only had to deal with a couple severed limbs over the years." Griffin's goofy smirk does little to calm the maelstrom of nerves undulating in my gut.

It's not the safety of America's youth that has my insides twisted up like a pretzel.

"The build is early in the day because it's still so hot," Cordell warns.

I shoot him a glare. "How early?"

Cordell gives his friend an *I-told-you-so* look.

Griffin simply grins at me. "I'll pick you up at six thirty, hellcat."

Cordell studies me for a moment, but he doesn't say anything more. Then they're collecting their water bottles and heading for the door.

I silently beg him to turn around and tell me this is a prank. That he's done with the competition and done with my obstinacy and done with fighting how we feel about each other.

Heart hammering, I will him to turn and sweep me up into his arms and kiss the ever-loving breath right out of my body.

But that fantasy comes crashing down when the little bell above the door jingles to signal that both men have left the studio.

And I'm left all alone. Again.

What does one wear on a first date to a construction site?

With a quick survey of my reflection in my bathroom mirror, I decide that my purple leggings and black T-shirt that says *There's nothing I can't do...except reach the top shelf* will have to be good enough. I did take the time to style my pink waves, but that was before I realized I'll have to stuff them under a hardhat.

Did I spend an extra fifteen on my hair for the hunky two-time Super Bowl champ who'll be here in five minutes to pick me up? Negative, Ghost Rider.

I don't let my mind linger on the man I find myself wanting to impress these days. Instead, I swipe my sunglasses off the stack of mail I threw on the counter last night, ready to get out of here. But as I turn to the door, a leafy green corner in the middle of the pile catches my eye. I know what it is before I pull it out.

The postcard features a photo of a fountain in a Savannah park. Heart in my throat, I pinch the edges, ready to turn it over to see which song lyric he's chosen this time, but an image of Cordell's smile flashes in my mind, and I cram the postcard back between the bills and an Ulta catalog.

When I get downstairs, a dark green SUV is idling in the alley. With a grunt, I shove the heavy metal door closed and lock it.

As soon as I sink into the soft, expensive leather seat, I'm enveloped by a warm, spicy scent.

"Smells manly in here," I remark as I pull the seat belt across my body.

"Well, thanks, hellcat. I find a manly scent impresses the ladies more than the smell of my sack of workout laundry." Griffin enters an address in the car's navigation system and slowly eases to the end of the alley.

"I'm not a morning person, either, by the way," he says, leaning in conspiratorially while keeping his eyes on the road.

"What's with the hellcat nickname?"

His gaze cuts to me for a breath, then he's focused on the road again. "The way you gave Watkins hell about making your friend cry? It's a perfect fit."

"Ha." I snicker and rest my head against the seat. "He deserved it."

"Aw, c'mon. Cut the shit. He's the best guy ever, and you know it."

He's annoyingly right, but I keep that to myself. Instead, I study his attire. The loose black track pants and a faded long-sleeved T-shirt are similar to what he's been wearing around town since his arrival. "This your typical first date outfit?" I ask with a sweep of my hand.

He chuckles low. "Quite the opposite, in fact."

"Oh, I'm sure. I've seen how you dress for games and such."

"You approve of my game day fits?" The grin he shoots me is wicked. "That makes me feel all fucking warm and gooey inside, hellcat."

"Please, I hardly pay attention." Yes, I do, but I'm gonna keep that to myself, too. "I just know you aren't usually in track pants and T-shirts."

"Fess up. What's your favorite look?"

"I hardly have a fav—"

"Yes, you do," he laughs. "It'll be our little secret. I won't let Watkins know that you think I'm a better dresser than him."

"Why would I care if he knows that?" Damn, the lie tastes bitter.

Griffin sputters. "Pfft. You care, all right."

I turn my head and take in the buildings as we pass, scared to admit he's right. Crossing my arms over my chest, I mumble, "The purple suit."

He throws his head back and crows. "The plaid one?"

I give a hesitant nod, and that sends him into a gleeful cackle.

"Yeah, that one was pretty sweet."

"I like when you wear hats, too. The beanies or the fedoras. Or that one you wore with the brown suit." I pop a shoulder. "I mean, if I were keeping tabs on that sort of thing."

"Mel the hellcat likes my game day fits." He's silent for a few beats. When he speaks again, his tone is much more subdued. "What was your favorite of Watkins'?"

I open my mouth to protest, but he tuts and gives me a stern look.

"Don't you dare tell me you don't have one. I'd bet good money you have lots of favorites when it comes to him."

My face goes hot at the call-out. I consider arguing, but the thought of denying my confusing feelings for Cordell exhausts me. The man's already cracked my impenetrable walls, so what's the harm if his friend knows?

With a deep breath in, I center myself and focus on keeping my voice steady. "He never dressed as...flashy...as you do. That's not meant as an insult—to either of you."

Griffin ducks his head, affable, his eyes forward.

"But he did take care to look nice on game days."

Hands twisted in my lap, I let my mind wander back to the days when Cordell was still playing and I was infatuated with him. I'd turn on ESPN first thing on Sunday mornings, hoping to catch a glimpse of him leaving the team bus or walking down the ramp into the stadium. I'd watch in awe, mesmerized by him, still blown away at the knowledge that we were from the same hometown.

"He wore this navy pinstripe suit during his rookie season, at an away game in Seattle. He looked so poised, so in the zone, but also so full of joy, like he truly felt honored to be there…" I trail off.

So much time has passed since those days. It seems impossible. And life has changed us in so many ways.

"That was one of my favorites," I say softly.

We're quiet the rest of the drive, but when Griffin turns onto a dirt path that leads to the build site, he clears his throat and sits a little straighter, one arm draped over the wheel. "Thank you for telling me your favorite."

He's not talking about his purple plaid suit.

I turn to him as he pulls into an empty spot. "Why'd you agree to this date with me?"

Through the windshield, he watches the crew gathering outside the wooden-framed structure that will soon become someone's home for a silent moment. "Sometimes a man has to be confronted with what he could miss out on before he'll reach out for what he wants."

I imagine that, this time, he's not only talking about Cordell, but also about his own journey. He pushes the ignition button and flashes me a smile that melts women's panties on the regular. "Let's go have some fun, hellcat."

And that's exactly what we do. We're surrounded by teenagers and school personnel and other volunteers, but Griffin makes sure we're paired up or in the same group all morning. I make a concerted effort not to seek out Cordell, but he might as well be a walking, flashing billboard, for as often as I catch myself looking at him. Most of the time, he's staring at me, too, and I avert my gaze for as long as I can stand.

Griffin flirts shamelessly with me, and his boisterous personality keeps the crew smiling all morning. The only serious expression in the crowd belongs to a certain grumpy coach who shoots daggers our way as he keeps a close watch on the student volunteers.

Midmorning, a couple of reporters and a news crew from Columbus swing by and interview Griffin and a few of the volunteers. I'm standing off to the side watching my date deliver perfect soundbites when he appears.

He sidles up so close I can identify him by scent alone.

"Looks like you're enjoying your date, Marshall." Damn, his tone is bitter.

"Your friend is a good time," I concede with a shrug. And because I'm still confused about his motives behind this setup, I add, "Maybe we'll get to add a point to your column on the scoreboard, after all."

"He's leaving any day now." His angry, gravelly tone does funny things to my insides. I clench my thighs together and will the tingling sensations to simmer. Then I shield my eyes so I can see every perfect detail of his face. His brows are tight, his nostrils flared, and a muscle ticks in his cheek. In fact, his jaw is clenched so tight, I'm kinda worried about his perfect teeth.

Angry Cordell is a fucking masterpiece.

"He is." I dip my head once. "And yet...you suggested this date. Knowing he won't be around much longer. Why is that, I wonder?" I goad, tapping my chin with a finger.

"You. Know. Why," he growls. The fire burning in his dark eyes makes my heart race.

A throat clears beside us, and we turn in unison toward the noise. Griffin has returned, it seems, all done with his interviews. The sunshine highlights the hint of auburn in his dark hair and beard.

"Thanks for keeping my date company, Watkins. I'll take it from here." With a smirk, he pulls me into his side, then he guides me toward the back of the site. When our backs are to the grumpy coach who's no doubt watching our every move, Griffin winks. "I expect that will do the trick, but just to be sure..." He squats low and pats his back.

The sight makes my heart light. This man is ridiculous. With a laugh, I stand behind him so he can lift me, piggyback style. From there, he carries me to where we'll help install siding on the house.

My date plays his part perfectly for the rest of the morning. Innocent touches, tickles, loud laughing that draws plenty of attention. To everyone else here, we look like a flirty couple. But I see the calculated look Racy Lacey gives his friend each time his hands find me. It's a masterful performance. And when Griffin announces in his booming voice that we're heading out a few minutes before the event's end time, he shoots Cordell an obnoxiously scandalous wink that forces me to hide my face.

We talk the whole way back to my apartment. About football, celebrities, and small-town living. Griffin is so laid back and fun, I can't imagine anything ever rattles him.

"I think we're gonna be good friends, Racy."

"For sure, hellcat. Have Watkins give you my number. I'll send you sneak peeks of my game day attire." He says this with absolute confidence that he'll be playing again soon.

"Ooh, insider info. I like it."

He puts the car in park once we reach my building.

"I had fun today," I tell him.

"Me, too." We fist bump, and I gather my purse from the floorboard. I've got my fingers on the door handle when he touches my arm. "Do me a favor." Like a switch has been flipped, his usual happy-go-lucky smile has been replaced with a softer one. "When he reaches out—and there's no doubt in my mind that he will after today—be sure that you reach back."

With a nod, I slide out of the vehicle. Griffin waits until I've opened the metal door to drive away.

Once I'm safely ensconced in my apartment and relishing the cool air, I call Tessa. I need a conversation with my bestie after all the subterfuge at the build site. I kick off my sneakers and curl up on the couch, phone held aloft. Mouse slinks into the living room and hops up to join me.

"Hey, you," Tessa croons when she answers. It's her lunchtime at the library, so she's probably sitting at her desk and nibbling on a lunch Luke packed for her.

"Baby Shipley?"

She's in the weekly appointment stage of her pregnancy, and I haven't had a chance to check on her since her doctor visit yesterday.

"Still baking."

"Really?" I check the date on my phone. Her due date is September twentieth, which is still a week away. "I have a feeling she's going to take her sweet time." I've taken to calling the baby a "she," gender reveal or not.

"He *or* she probably will," she agrees.

I exhale a long sigh, suddenly exhausted and at a loss for how to begin.

"How was your date?"

"T..." That's all I get out before an onslaught of tears chokes me up. "I'm crying sympathy tears again," I moan. My heart hurts in a way that it hasn't in years, so painful that I rub my sternum with my free hand. "I think I really like him."

"You're not talking about Griffin." It's not a question.

"What do I do?" The full force of my years of guardedness hits me all at once, and I haven't a clue about how to navigate this. I've spent so much time fortifying my walls. I never stopped to consider what I'd do if they were knocked down. Never even considered that they *could* be knocked down.

"You tell him how you feel," she says, like it's as easy as breathing in and out.

"Anything but that." I sniffle. The initial deluge of tears has slowed, thank God. Focusing on deep breaths, I rhythmically stroke Mouse's thick, soft fur.

"Honey, I know you go full turtle when feelings are involved," she says. "But I'm afraid that the only way to get to the other side is to go *through* it. You have to open yourself up to the possibility of getting hurt again. Love is a risk. But when it works out...oh, is it worth it."

"Who said anything about love?" I mumble.

I'm being difficult, but she doesn't call me out. My best friend's patience is one of her greatest qualities.

"Mel, sweetie, you've got the biggest heart hidden under all that cynicism. Don't you think it's time to give someone a chance to cherish it?" When I don't answer, she says, "I can't think of a better man for you to offer it to."

"Maybe," I whisper. "But we've antagonized each other for years. I turn into an absolute *child* around him. How can we expect to build a healthy relationship after all *that*?"

She exhales a deep breath. "Second-hand therapy?"

It's what we say when we have a nugget of wisdom to share from our personal talk therapy sessions—me, from the sessions I attended after Nick's betrayal, and Tessa, from the therapist she sees via telehealth to help deal with her anxiety.

I nod, even though she can't see me. "Lay it on me."

"Dr. Patten says that if a person experiences trauma at a young age, he or she will often act out later in life the way they would have when that trauma occurred. In your case, you were nineteen when Nick hurt you, so it makes sense that sometimes, even at the wise, old age of thirty-one—"

I snort. *Wise.* Okay.

"You lash out the way nineteen-year-old Mel would have."

*Fucking Nick.* Messing with my head more than a decade after screwing me over. But maybe it explains why I retaliate so childishly when Cordell irks me.

"*Ugh,*" I drag out my groan. "Adulting is so hard."

Tessa's sweet laughter lightens my mood a fraction. "It absolutely is. But most things worth having are difficult," she reminds me. "And you, my friend, can do hard things."

Her unwavering confidence in me makes me tear up again. All these freaking tears lately. If this is growth, I demand a refund.

"You have class this afternoon?"

"Yeah. At two and four."

"Come have dinner with us. Luke's making fajitas, and I'm taking advantage of a night at home since there's not a game tonight." The Eagles had a rare Thursday night game this week. I don't let myself dwell on the fact that Cordell may be free this evening.

"Thanks, but I think Mouse and I will stay in and be homebodies."

"Are you sure?" My bestie's voice is full of concern.

"Yes. Promise."

"And you promise to think about telling Cordell how you feel?"

My mouth suddenly feels like the Sahara desert, but I force out a "maybe."

"Just consider it, Mel. Please."

"Fine," I huff. "Love you, T."

"Love you, too."

Once I've dropped my phone to the cushion beside me, I follow my best friend's advice and think about Cordell every minute until it's time for me to head to the studio.

# CHAPTER FIFTEEN

## CORDELL

"**H**ow was the build?"

Standing in the doorway, Clay grimaces when I pin my eyes on him.

No doubt in response to the expression on my face. I'm sure it matches the torment lashing my insides. Anger, despair, and disorientation swirl in my gut like the perfect storm. Primed to tip me sideways and pull me under.

I've never in my thirty-six years been the jealous type. Until this morning. Watching Mel laugh and smile at Griffin was pure torture. Seeing his hands on her, even though the touches were innocent, made my blood boil with an intensity that startled me. All morning, I barked at the kids for little things I would usually ignore. My terrible mood gave Darius Jones the bravery to mumble "he needs to get laid" to his teammates when he thought I was out of earshot.

That one I *did* ignore.

No reason to give a teenage boy more ammo, especially if his assessment is spot-on.

Regardless of all the reasons I know Mel and Griff can't possibly be a match, my mind plays every smile she gave him today on a loop, and every dang one adds weight to the doubt plaguing me.

"What happened?" Clay asks, propping himself up against the doorframe.

As much as I'd like to unburden myself of all my romantic woes, midafternoon on a Friday at school is not the time or the place.

Instead, I angle for one of the invites he generously offers all the time. That'll give me a more appropriate opportunity to tell him about how I'm crazy for a woman who refuses to admit that we have insane chemistry. "What's for dinner at the Reeves house tonight?"

Clay's smile is sheepish. "Frannie threatened PB and J sandwiches. She's cooked every night this week, so I told her I'd pick up pizza on the way home. But we'd love for you to join us."

"Yeah. Thanks." I scrub a hand down my face and will myself to focus on the film I've been staring at since we returned from the community service event.

I spend the rest of the afternoon at school and head straight to the Reeveses' at five instead of going home first. I'm not sure how I'll react when I see Griffin. Better to cool my jets before I do or say something I'll regret.

A weight lifts off my shoulders the moment I enter the warmth and chaos of the Reeves household. Frannie's favorite apple-cinnamon candles infuse the air with perpetual fall vibes. She burns them year-round. Says it's the only scent she's found that can mask the odor of teenage boys and a sixty-pound golden retriever. The boys—Cole and his thirteen-year-old brother, Finn—are arguing over a video game in the den while Cara and the dog race from one end of the house to the other.

"Cara, take Sadie outside if you want to play tag!" Frannie yells from the kitchen.

"You're here!" she cheers when I step into the room. She tilts her head to offer her cheek, and after a quick peck and a tousle of her hair, I pull up to the bar and prop my weary body on a stool.

"Clay Reeves!" she hollers as she sets a stack of thick paper plates on the counter. "Round up our hooligans!"

Within seconds, the rest of the family crowds around the kitchen sink to wash up for dinner. Clay hands his wife and me beers from the fridge in the garage, and then we load our plates with pizza and breadsticks.

The tightness that's plagued my muscles since this morning continues to ease the longer I'm here. Listening to Cole and Finn pick on their little sister, who dishes it back with a brutality that's as admirable as it is humorous, goes a long way in quieting my turmoil.

After dinner is cleaned up, the boys gravitate back to their video game feud, and Frannie and Cara take Sadie upstairs for a bath.

Cole leads me out to their screened-in back porch, where we rock in comfortable silence as we nurse a second round of beers.

As much as I love the peace of living in this small town, the quiet gets to me quickly tonight. "I need some advice, man."

"You know how long I've waited for you to ask *me* for advice?" He barks out a laugh.

Ducking my chin, I give my head a dismissive shake.

"I'm serious. You are the most composed person I know. Nothing rattles you. Nothing gets you hot under the collar. I've marveled at this for years. Yet you trust *me* with a problem you can't solve on your own? I feel like I've won the lottery."

I roll my eyes, but he waxes on.

"And if you tell me it's about a woman—"

"It's about a woman," I confess.

Clay's eyes go round, and he sits up straight in his rocker. "Well, I'll be damned." He blinks a few times and shifts his shoulders against the back of his chair, settling in again. "All right. Lay it on me."

"First of all, plenty of things rattle me. *Plenty*," I repeat when he gives me a dubious look. "But my dad taught me to keep that crap locked up tight—not to suppress it until I'm forced to blow, but to protect my image. *Our* image." I take a long pull of beer, relishing the way the cool liquid soothes my throat. "My last name? It's precious. I never want to shine a bad light on it. My dad taught me that there are numerous outlets for my anger, but regardless of which I choose, it should never be handled in public. There are scores of people who'll expect a young Black man to react a certain way, but that my actions would always reflect on him, my mom, and my sister. The last thing I want to do is let my family down. So I keep my cool the best I can. Then I go home and punch the heck out of a bag, or I run like the devil's chasing me on the treadmill."

"Your dad would be so proud of you, Dell." His throat bobs a heavy swallow. If anyone in my life understands how hard it is to carry on a legacy for a loved one taken too soon while missing them with every breath, it's Clay.

I circle back to my "woman troubles" before we both become maudlin. I launch into the details about my relationship, or lack thereof, with Mel. Other than the intimate parts, I don't hold anything back, and it's freeing.

He lets me get everything off my chest so he can process before he chimes in. "You and Mel Marshall, huh?" is the first thing he says after I've spilled my guts.

"Yeah?" I try, and fail, to keep the vulnerability out of my voice.

"No, I like it," he reassures me. "It's not an obvious pairing at first—personality-wise, you're different."

"Understatement," I snort.

"Yeah, but that doesn't mean it won't work. You two clearly

have physical chemistry. Now you just have to figure out the rest."

"You say that like it's simple."

He whistles. "Ooh, boy. It is definitely *not*." He rocks for a few moments, surveying the yard. "It sounds like she's scared of getting hurt again. Like her ex really did a number on her relationship confidence. So you've got to do your level best to convince her that it's safe to take a chance on you."

I nod as I process his advice. I didn't divulge all of Mel's drama with her ex-husband. It's not my place. But he obviously gathered enough about her romantic past from the few details I did share.

"How do I do that? Convince her to take a chance on me?"

"For one thing, stop setting her up with charismatic NFL stars." He gives me the *you're an idiot* look he usually reserves for his children or our players. "Then you show up for her. And keep showing up."

"Simple as that, huh?"

"Simple—and hard—as that." He shrugs.

From there, our discussion turns to what it inevitably does when we're together—football—and we spend the rest of our rocking chair time talking through plans for the remainder of the season. We've got a couple of challenging games coming up, plus the big homecoming game in October.

I say good night to the Reeves fam just as the sun sets, then spend a few minutes in the quiet of my car, ruminating over this roller coaster of a day. With a deep, cleansing breath, I start the ignition, but when I reach the stop sign at the end of the street, I hesitate. Do I make a right and head toward home? Or do I turn left, toward downtown Bennett?

Clay's words float through my mind: *Then you show up for her. And you keep showing up.*

I make the left turn.

The outside door that leads to Mel's apartment is ajar when

I park, so I set an alarm in my phone to remind me to call Mr. Rusty tomorrow. I'll tell him to replace the dang thing if he can't fix it.

The scent of vanilla and sugar hangs in the air at the top of the stairs.

She's baking cupcakes. Her comfort hobby.

A smile splits my face as I picture her in that tiny kitchen, measuring and stirring and mixing. Then the image morphs, and she's in *my* kitchen. *Our* kitchen. Creating something delicious to clear her mind or shake off a bad day.

I knock three times and wait, hoping I don't choke as my heart climbs into my throat.

Soft footfalls sound on the other side of the door. I imagine she's barefoot, flexing up onto her painted toes so she can see through the peephole.

I'm down so bad for her, I might die if she doesn't open this door.

In typical Mel fashion, she makes me sweat a little longer. What's got to be a solid minute later, the door *finally* swings open, and she's there.

She's there, and she's perfect. My first instinct is to close my eyes and commit this moment to my memory, but I don't want to miss a single detail, so I start at her orchid-painted toenails. Her legs are bare, her skin almost back to her natural porcelain shade after months of being sun-kissed. Her oversized Marshall Realty T-shirt stops mid-thigh. Lord, I'd give every one of my yearly coaching bonuses to know what's underneath it. The neck of the shirt is stretched so wide it slouches off a shoulder, but there's not even a hint of a bra strap to tantalize me. The implication there has me half hard in an instant. When I reach her face, I linger, memorizing every centimeter, like I haven't done it numerous times before. I expect to see a hint of her temper in her eyes—I did stop by unannounced, after all. But her bubble-gum lips are parted and her hazel irises reflect a tenderness not typically directed my way. I'm desperate to reach out and brush away the dusting of flour on her left cheek, but our exchange from a couple of months ago comes back to bite me in the backside.

*"Don't touch me. Ever. Again."*

*"I won't touch you again, Marshall. Until you ask me to."*

I brace my hands on the doorframe to hold myself back but push forward so my upper body hovers just over the threshold, like I'm a lovesick vampire waiting to be invited inside. I've done my part—I've shown up—but she calls the next play.

We silently stare at each other like we've forgotten how to speak.

She tucks her hair behind an ear with trembling fingers and says, "Hey."

"What's the flavor?" I tilt my head toward the kitchen.

"Oh, um, funfetti." She shrugs the bare shoulder. "It's the first flavor I made...back then. They're from scratch. I don't use a box mix. I just took them out of the oven." She tilts her head. "Why are you here?" Her voice is so soft, so vulnerable. It's messing with my head.

I force down a swallow. "I needed to see you. After this morning."

"Why?" Her question isn't a challenge; she's genuinely curious.

"Because I acted like a jerk."

"Why did you act like a jerk?"

"Marshall..."

"Tell me why."

"I just..." I sigh. "Watching you with him—"

"You were jealous?"

"Yes," I say, without a moment of hesitation.

Her breath hitches in answer, making my already pounding heart take off at a gallop.

Is her heart hammering against her ribs, too? God, I hope so.

"Are you going to come in?" Her chin's tipped lower than usual—in my presence, she usually holds it high in defiance—and her fingers are twisted in the hem of her T-shirt.

"If you ask me to."

She nods a couple of times. "What will you do? If you come in?" Now her jaw sets, a hint of challenge shining in her eyes. *There she is.*

When I don't respond, she props her hands on her hips, which causes the hem of her shirt to raise a centimeter or two.

Hell. My fingertips tingle with the need to touch her smooth skin.

I flick my eyes back to hers. "What do you want me to do?"

Her upper body tilts forward as a subtle flush shades her neck and face, but she remains silent.

"I told you I wouldn't touch you again until you asked me to."

That defiant chin tilt is back for real now. "I remember."

I push even farther into her space, my knuckles tight where I grip the doorframe. Her lips thin, but instead of stepping back like I expect, she inches closer, too—like her heart's a magnetic pole that's the opposite of mine. That's exactly what we've done all these years: repel and attract, repel and attract.

Mel and I are opposites in many ways, but in the ways that count...we fit.

And I'm done defying the laws of nature.

My muscles strain as I lean in closer. "Use your words, Marshall."

One corner of her mouth lifts, and a shot of wickedness flashes in her eyes. "Get your ass in here and kiss my face off, Watkins."

I freeze. Did I manifest her response? I must've. But no, her lips are stretched in a triumphant grin now, and her hand is fisted in the front of my polo. The next thing I know, she's yanking me into the room and bouncing up on her toes. So I crouch down to meet her. And then we're kissing, and it's pure bliss.

*Touchdown.*

Within seconds, I'm hauling her up so she can wrap her legs around my hips—apparently this is our default make-out position. It's the most obvious choice due to our height difference. My pulse is frantic, but our lips dance in a slow rhythm, caressing and teasing. She nips my bottom lip playfully, and I give her what she wants. When our tongues brush, she loosens a satisfied moan that makes my dick hard as stone.

Keeping my lips on hers, I stumble to the bar and set her on the edge. She keeps her legs wrapped around me, even when she's secure, and drapes her arms over my shoulders. After several breathless moments, we break apart, panting. Her skin is so flushed and inviting, I can't stop myself from trailing my lips along her jaw and down to her neck.

Between kisses, I grate out, "Mr. Rusty will be fixing that dang door downstairs tomorrow. It was open again."

She squeezes my biceps and tilts her head, offering me easier access. "Do me a favor."

I suck on the soft skin right below her ear in response.

With a shiver, she says, "Don't talk about the town handyman while your lips are on me."

"Fair enough," I chuckle.

I pull back and take her in. She's doing the same. We stare at each other in wonder, soft smiles on our kiss-swollen lips.

With her hands framing my face, she examines every inch of it. She rolls her lips, then asks, "Why'd you set me up with him?"

*Because I know he's leaving, and the geography works in my favor. Because he knows how I feel about you. Because I wanted to prove to you that no one else sets you on fire the way I do...*

"Because I'm an idiot."

She flinches, a movement so quick I would've missed it if she wasn't latched on to me the way she is.

I rub soothing circles on her back and dip my chin. "I was an idiot when I didn't recognize you that night in Fuzzy's. I was an idiot when I didn't chase you down and apologize profusely. And I've been an idiot ever since, for letting this drag on for so long."

Brows furrowed, she places her hands on my chest and studies them there. She wets her lips, then gives me a nervous smile. "I-I've been an idiot, too. For pushing you away. For not giving you the opportunity to explain about that night. But now—" Her hands trail around to my nape, and she inches forward until her lips are a hairsbreadth away, so close that they brush against mine when she whispers, "I want more."

The same words she uttered in that dive bar parking lot before we sealed our fate.

I dig my fingers into her hips—God, I'm desperate to know what's under this T-shirt—and murmur, "Where else do you want me to touch you?"

"Everywhere."

Our lips and tongues meet and fall into a sensual rhythm as I carry Mel into her bedroom. My lust-addled brain has enough sense to wave a caution flag. There's still so much more for us to discuss before we have sex again. But the hardness in my khakis wants no part of that. I can give her what she wants right now and worry about the rest later.

All I want is to make her feel good.

Gently, I lower Mel to her unmade bed. She shoves the lilac bedsheets to the far side and gazes up at me, eyes wide, lips parted, full of a vulnerability she's always hidden from me. I caress her cheek, and she leans her head into my palm. It's a signal of her trust.

That small motion sends an ache through my chest I don't ever want to get rid of.

"There's one thing I regret about that night in my Escalade."

Silently, she quirks a brow. The Mel who's always got a retort on the tip of her tongue is subdued.

"Believe me." I snicker. "I regret a lot of things *after*—"

"Like not calling me?" She tosses her head, smirking. There it is. A hint of that fire that I love so much.

"That's at the top of the list, yes." Crouching low, I run my hands up her bare thighs, stopping at the hem of her shirt. "But the one thing I regret from our time together in that back seat... was that I didn't get to taste you...here." I bunch the soft cotton in one hand and push it up, and finally, I'm rewarded with a peek at what's been taunting me—a pair of tight strawberry-print boy shorts.

Her breath shudders. Gaze locked on mine, she leans back on her elbows. An invitation.

With my fingers tucked into the waistband of her shorts, I give them a quick tug. "Up," I command. When she lifts her hips, I take my time peeling the fabric down her body, smiling when goose bumps flare on her skin. I drop to my knees on the fluffy rug by her bed and admire the glorious vision before me. Mel Marshall, bared to me at last. I've touched her here. I've been inside her. But I've never had the pleasure of studying every detail. The neatly trimmed dark brown curls that frame her perfect pink pussy. The plush layers like a flower's petals waiting to be unfurled.

Mel watches me, a hint of nerves skittering across her expression. "I stopped getting waxed months ago." Her words sound like an apology.

"I couldn't care less," I tell her. "I like every single thing I'm looking at."

"Good. Now put that mouth to good use, Coach."

"So bossy," I scold playfully. But I've always been coachable, so I lean in and inhale her primed, earthy scent. Then I taste her for the first time. I swipe my flattened tongue from her opening to the top, right where she wants it.

"Fuck," she whispers, lying back on the bed, one hand fisted in her T-shirt.

I dip back for another taste and keep at it until she's whimpering, her breathy sounds a symphony I conduct with my mouth. Each one signals where to lick—or suck—and how fast or intense she wants it. I take mental notes on every moan, every clench, and commit them to memory like I'm studying the playbook for the Super Bowl.

"I was wrong, all those times before." The words are more for me than for her. I shake my head, dazed. "This is the best thing I've ever put in my mouth."

She whimpers a "please," and that's all it takes for me to double down and get back to work.

Her moans get louder, and her movements more frantic. When she mumbles something that sounds like "so much better than Fernando," I pull away and clench my jaw. I have to blink away the black spots that crowd my vision.

"Who the hell is Fernando?"

She thrashes her head from side to side, gasping. "Top drawer." One of her hands is squeezing her breast through her shirt, and the other is fisted in the sheet. She's absolutely unbothered, while I'm seeing red.

On the verge of losing my mind, I open the top drawer of her nightstand. It's full of random things—a box of condoms that I refuse to give more than a passing thought to, bottles of nail polish, books, hair clips, a TV remote, a fluffy pair of socks, several phone chargers, a bottle of pain relievers. But on top of the junk, easily within reach, is a vibrator, the purple silicone tapered at one rounded end.

*Fernando.* This woman named her vibrator. Why does that endear her to me even more?

I pick it up, and after a quick inspection, locate the tiny button on the side and press it.

At the sound of the soft hum, her eyes fly open, and she lifts her head. "Wh-what's happening?"

"Fernando is joining the party."

"Wait. What?" She blinks rapidly. Her attention bounces all over the room before settling back on me. "You're not intimidated by Fernando?"

"Intimidated? Nah. Way I see it, Fernando and I play on the same team." I hold up the vibrator. "We're teammates, working together to achieve the same goal."

"Teamwork makes the dream work," she teases.

"This a dream of yours, Marshall?" I press the vibrator to her thigh and drag it up to her center. When it touches the apex, she bucks her hips. "Feels good, right? Tell me what you want."

"Y-yesss," she hisses.

I pull the toy away, eliciting a growl from her. She pounds the mattress with both hands and glares. I love teasing her in the bedroom as much as I love riling her up outside of it.

"Tell me. What you. Want."

"To come. I want you to make me come."

"Me? Or Fernando?" Teammates or not, I want to be the MVP. Every time.

"You, Watkins," she breathes, eyes squeezed shut. "You."

I turn off the toy, toss it onto the bed, and then give her what she wants. I use my tongue and my fingers to work her back up, devouring every drop of her desire as I go. She spurs me on with every *yes* and *right there* and *don't stop*. When I close my lips around her clit and suck, she rocks her hips and releases a guttural moan that will play a role in every fantasy I'll have for the rest of my days. Her inner muscles spasm around my fingers as her orgasm breaks, but I don't let up. I flick my tongue against her clit without relenting as she soaks my hand and the aftershocks of her climax fade.

Resting back on my heels, I suck her taste from my fingers.

Sprawled out like a starfish, Mel sighs and covers her eyes with an arm. "You've broken me." Her body is limp and satisfied, so I'd say I did exactly what I intended to.

"Next time, you'll sit on my face." I tense up, then, waiting for her to declare that there won't be a next time. That would've been her go-to comeback an hour ago, but I hope we won't be retreating to opposite corners of the ring like we have in the past.

She hums, and a slow smile stretches her lips. One arm is still draped across her eyes, but she raises the other and wiggles her fingers. "Up, please."

I pull her to a sitting position, and when she's steady, she wraps her arms around my neck and kisses me softly. Peace suffuses every cell in my body. Every cell but the ones that make up one very hard appendage in my pants.

Mel quirks a brow at the unmistakable bulge. "Your turn?" Her tone is almost shy. She snakes a hand down to the fly of my khakis, but I gently grasp it and return it to my neck.

"Not tonight," I tell her. "Tonight was about you."

She bites the inside of her cheek and searches my face, her brows turned down. "You don't want—"

"Oh, I want. Very much." I grip her waist and squeeze. "I want everything with you. Every position. Every surface. Every room."

Her face flames, so pink it matches her hair. I can't keep my lips off her, so I kiss her cheek.

"But tonight was about showing you that you are important to me. Your thoughts, your feelings, your pleasure. Every part of you is special to me."

She lowers her head and presses her lips together, looking almost unsure. I want to rage at her idiot ex, at every man, myself included, who's ever made this woman doubt that she's worthy of being the center of someone's world. I want her to be the center of mine. But Rome wasn't built in a day. I know it'll take time for her to trust, without a doubt, that I won't let her down.

I raise her chin with a finger and press a soft kiss to her lips. "Let's go ice those cupcakes. Funfetti sounds delicious."

She smiles then, a real one that makes my chest feel tight. I help her step into her boy shorts and pull them into place when she stands from the bed. With her fingers laced through mine, she leads me into the kitchen. The whole way there, I chant snap counts in my mind to talk my dick down.

She ices the cupcakes, and I watch on in silence, but we shoot each other flirty looks the whole time. Her lips quirk to the side every time she sneaks a peek, and the spots of color that highlight her cheeks make me grin like a lovesick dummy.

I'm so smitten with this woman it's not even funny.

After the cupcakes are iced, we sample the sweet treats while standing against opposite counters in the kitchen.

"What are you up to tomorrow?" I ask as I snag a second cupcake. I would eat the whole batch if she'd let me.

Mel throws her paper wrapper into the trash. "I have a Flow class and a senior class in the morning."

"What time are you done?"

"Why?"

"Because I'm taking you out, Marshall. Lunch or dinner, your choice."

She looks down at her brightly painted toes, but not before I see the glee in her expression. "I'll be done at eleven-thirty."

"So lunch?"

She nods, the gesture demure.

I marvel at her. She's got such an ooey-gooey center hidden within her prickly, abrasive exterior. Every time I peel away a layer and discover something new, I fall further under her spell.

She's a gift that keeps on giving.

After I polish off a third cupcake, I lead her to the couch. If I stay in the kitchen, I really will eat them all. Initially, when I pull her down to sit next to me, she's stiff, but a few minutes into an episode of *Friends*, her body melts into mine like butter on a hot pancake. Mouse meanders in and curls up tight against her thigh. Mel sighs deeply when I rub soothing circles on her stomach, under her shirt. By the fourth episode, she's asleep; the steady rise and fall of her chest and the softness on her face fill me with a contentedness I haven't experienced in years. Maybe ever.

She doesn't stir when I cradle her to my chest, but the moment her body hits the sheets, she blinks awake in fits and starts. She watches me through narrowed eyes as I tug my polo over my head, then kick off my sneakers to step out of my khakis. In nothing but my boxers, I slip into bed behind her.

"What are you doing?" The raspy sleepiness of her voice softens the accusation.

"We're going to sleep, Marshall. Close those beautiful eyes and dream only of me." I wrap an arm around her waist and pull her into my body—the little spoon to my big one.

"Hmm...fine. But don't think this will be a regular occurrence," she grumbles, already half-asleep again.

"There's my angry pixie," I whisper.

I smirk as she wiggles even deeper into the cocoon of my arms. And with a kiss to her neck, I breathe in her wildflower scent. Then and there, I fall—into sleep, and into something infinite and inevitable.

I can't wipe the grin from my face the next morning. Waking up with Mel wrapped around me like a koala may have been the best moment of my life. When she startled awake and blinked the sleep from her eyes, her confused frown quickly morphed into a soft smile. Though that was replaced by a scowl when I pinched her butt. I laughed into her hair and pulled her closer. Then it was her turn to laugh when Mouse shifted in the spot he'd claimed, unbeknownst to me, near my head on the pillow, and I almost jumped out of my skin.

She found an extra toothbrush for me, and I was sure to place it in the purple unicorn holder next to her sink so it'd be there next time. Then we made out like teenagers until it was time for her to head downstairs for her first class.

Back home, I pull into the garage, right next to Griffin's SUV, and head inside, whistling all the while. I hang my keys on the hook by the door and stroll into the kitchen. At the threshold, I freeze. Before me, Griffin sits at the bar, papers and laptop and phone spread over the surface. His head is down, his face buried in his hands. When he looks up, my stomach plummets. His eyes are red and watery. I've never in my life seen this man cry. My mind whirls with a hundred different scenarios. It must be awful if he's this distraught.

"Griff?" I keep my voice soft.

"It's the Blues."

Relief floods my body so violently I have to grab the edge of the counter to keep myself steady.

The Blues. These are happy tears. Happy, relieved tears.

"Tell me," I rasp, dropping my elbows on the counter.

"Delvecchio was injured in Thursday night's opener. He's out for the season. They want a veteran tight end on the roster with Greenway and their rookie."

Devon Greenway is only in his second season, so it makes sense that the Blues would be on the hunt for someone with experience like Griffin.

He swipes a hand down his face. "It's a one-year contract. It's a good offer. As good as an old-timer like me is going to get coming off an injury. And it's the Blues, man." Tears well in his eyes again.

The Memphis Blues is Griff's hometown team. Holly Holler is an hour outside of Memphis, and the Lacey brothers grew up wearing Blues jerseys and going to games with their parents. That *this* team has offered him a contract for what is possibly his final season? It's a last-second Hail Mary in the fourth quarter that results in a touchdown.

It's a flipping football miracle.

"Dang, Griff, I'm so happy for you." I round the counter and pull him into a bone-jarring hug.

He pounds my back with his fist and pulls in a couple of deep breaths, working to rein in his emotions.

"Have you called Donna and Fred yet?"

"Yeah," he says as I step back, his voice wobbly. "They're over the fucking moon. Donna said 'oh, I get to keep my boy at home.' Like I won't get a place in the city. They'll get to come to all my games, Dell. I still can't believe it."

"Kevin came through," I say with a laugh.

"Kevin came through."

"When do you have to head out?"

"Today." The frown he shoots me isn't all that heartfelt, but it's tinged with regret. "Seth reserved a room for me in Birmingham for tonight. I'll make the rest of the drive tomorrow. I meet with the owners and coaches Monday morning."

"Dempsey's got an arm." The Blues' quarterback is damn impressive.

"He does. I'm stoked, man." A brilliant grin lights up my friend's face, filling me with relief all over again. That he gets to play another year. That he'll get to live his dream a little longer.

"Now it's time to discuss the elephant in the room." He closes the laptop and stacks the papers neatly on top. "Don't think I didn't notice that you didn't come home last night, mister." He wags his brows at me. "Did you close the deal with the hellcat?"

He knows I won't disrespect Mel by answering that, but though I try like hell, I can't fight a smile.

"Woo hoo!" The whoop he lets out echoes through the room. He raises both arms in the touchdown signal. "You're welcome, by the way."

"How's that?"

He tilts his head. "Dude. Like you would've made the move without my magnificent performance yesterday."

Until this moment, it didn't register. His distraught expression when I walked in, then his big news, have distracted me. I haven't seen him since the community service project. Where he was flirting with Mel, touching her and laughing with her. "I'd call you an a-hole, but I already owe Ma forty for the swear jar from last week."

He smirks. "I don't see Mama Watkins around. Let 'er fly."

"Ha!" I bark. "The next time I see her, she'll know. It only takes one look at my face."

He lets out a deep laugh but quickly sobers. "Damn, I'm gonna miss you, Watkins." With a thick swallow, he rolls his lips together. "I can't tell you how much it's meant to me—to just get to *be* for a while. It's brought me back to life." He presses his palms to the island and leans forward. "I'll never be able to thank you enough for opening your home to me, for letting me into your world. It's an honor to have met all the people who've shaped you into the man you are. I swear I'll dream about Frannie's lasagna for the rest of my life."

We both chuckle.

"You've got something special here, Watkins. This life suits you, my man. I hope you know that."

I blink to quell the emotion welling inside me. He's spot-on. This place, these people, are special. For maybe the first time, I'm grateful for the concussions and the injury. For the difficult path that led to my current one. If I'd never been forced to move home, would I be as close as I am with my mom? With Luke and Clay? Would I have had the chance to reconnect with Mel?

"You're welcome here anytime, Lacey. Honorary Watkins for life."

He nods and swipes at a stray tear. "I'd love for you to come see me in Memphis. Bring Mel. She'll love Beale Street."

"You got it."

I angle in to hug it out, and when I pull back, the suitcases and duffel bag waiting by the couch catch my eye. Griff and I load them up, and after one more bro hug, he climbs in. With my hands in my pockets, I watch him back out of the garage. But before he starts down the driveway, he rolls down his window.

"Hey, Watkins?" He's wearing that million-dollar smile, and as usual, it makes me beam right back. "You and the hellcat? That's a sure thing. I'm shipping y'all so fucking hard, man." With that, Racy Lacey rolls up the window and speeds out of my life—for now.

## CHAPTER SIXTEEN

MEL

F ifteen minutes before the kickoff of the game between the Bennett Eagles and the Rutland Hurricanes, Tessa sends me a four-word text:

Contractions heading to hospital.

Do I respond in a cool, calm way and tell her to keep me posted and to call me when she's settled at the hospital? No, I do not. With shaky fingers, I immediately hit that call button and bounce in place while it rings.

She answers on the fifth one. "Mel, calm down." Why the hell is her voice so soothing?

"Oh my gosh, I can't!" I may be shouting. I can't tell. "My hands are shaking. T, you're having a *baby*!" I force myself to sit on the couch, but I pop up again seconds later and pace the length of my living room rug. I need to steady myself before I send Tessa into panic mode.

"I'm aware," she says wryly.

"What do you need me to do? I know y'all have your plan and blah, blah, blah. But I need something to do."

"Mel," she says, still ridiculously patient. "Take a breath. We've got a long way to go. Luke's being overly cautious and insisting that we make the drive over to the hospital. Yes, I'm having contractions, but they aren't close. I highly doubt we'll meet Baby Shipley tonight."

I deflate like a flat tire.

"Jelly Bean's spending the night with the Shipleys. They'll be at the game, in fact. And that's where you need to be, too. Go support Cordell. I promise to let you know immediately if anything changes."

"Fine," I grumble. "He knows?"

"Luke texted him. We'll see you both tomorrow."

"Okay." The word leaves my mouth with a huff. I sound like a petulant child. "I want frequent updates from Luke, T. I mean it."

Her soft laughter muffles the line. "Of course."

"Thanks, bestie. I'm so happy for you. You're going to be amazing." My voice catches on the last word.

Tessa sniffles in answer. "Thanks, Mel. See you soon."

At the game, I sit in Tessa's spot next to Hannah so we can talk about her new sibling. We've both been firmly Team Girl since her parents announced they were expecting.

"Have they told you any name ideas?" I probe the eight-year-old beside me. She and I have speculated about this topic before, but now that we're hours away from the birth, it's fun to rehash.

"No. They say they have two boy names and two girl names, but they won't choose until the baby's born. It's not fair." She crosses her arms and puckers her lips. But in an instant, she's grinning again. "I can't believe I'm gonna have a little brother or sister, like, tomorrow!" She beams.

"You're going to be the *best* big sister in the history of big sisters, JB."

"She sure is." On Hannah's other side, Ms. Marj wraps an arm around her and squeezes.

Hannah grins up at me. "JB is the *best* nickname for me, Ms. Mel. Cause it goes with Jelly Bean, which is what Mama calls me. And it also goes with what Nana calls me: June Bug."

In the row in front of us, Ms. Rhonda twists at the waist. "Gracious, I wonder if little brother or sister will have as many nicknames as you, sweet girl." She winks at me.

I'm certain my face must be as red as the players' jerseys. How can I look that woman in the eye knowing her son's head was between my thighs last weekend?

Just the thought of that night causes a throbbing ache at my core. I focus on steady breaths and cross my legs to ease the inconvenient reaction. Every single moment of his surprise visit was perfect. He said all the right things, did all the right things. And then he treated me to lunch the next day, where we talked about the most important things right along with the most random things. I'm really in trouble with him. The good kind of trouble, yes, but the kind of trouble I've spent most of my adult life avoiding.

He's in full coach mode, among the throng of high schoolers, coaches, and officials on the sideline, and he's so fucking hot wearing that red visor and headset. The way he leads this team is a major turn-on. After a player drops a pass that likely would've resulted in a touchdown, Cordell consoles him with a hand on his shoulder pad. The kid nods, his full attention locked on his coach and his directive. When Cordell's done, he smacks his helmet and sends the kid back out. On the next play, that same kid makes a catch that leads to a key first down for the Eagles.

We haven't seen each other since he walked me home and kissed me against the newly installed door after lunch last Saturday. This week has been busy, but we have talked on the phone a few times, and we've texted several times. Not an insult in the bunch.

I press my fingers to my lips and watch him. Is it jarring that we've shifted from snarky insults to flirty touches? For sure. But it feels *right*, even if I can't explain why. We've yet to define what *this* is, and we haven't gone public, either. For now, I'm good with cautiously exploring this undeniable attraction.

The Eagles come away with a thirty to eighteen win, and after a round of hugs, I leave the Shipleys, who are all still chattering in excitement. Tessa started a Baby Shipley group text, and her latest update indicated they had settled into a private room and were waiting for things to progress.

Mouse and I are snuggled up in bed watching *Friends* when my phone buzzes from somewhere in the sheets. Giddiness bubbles up when I see the name of the caller.

"Good game, Coach."

"Thank you, Marshall." There's a smile in his voice. "Have you gotten any new Baby Shipley updates?"

"Not since that last group text. I thought I'd be too excited to sleep, but I'm nice and cozy, so I don't think it'll be a problem."

"Hmm," he rumbles, sending a wave of goose bumps skittering up my arms and legs. "Cozy, huh? What are you wearing?" There's a teasing lilt to his question, but it scorches me anyway.

I push the sheets and comforter down to my waist and tease back. "You want to come over and find out?"

A heavy sigh crackles through the phone. "There's nothing I'd like more, but I just passed Thigpen. Put me out of my misery and tell me, please."

I push down my disappointment. He's almost home, and we're both wiped from this week. Postponing the sexy times won't be that bad, right?

Resigned to our reality and ready to lighten the mood, I tell him the truth about my nighttime attire. "So picture this...fuzzy purple socks."

He hums. "Sexy. Tell me more."

"Turquoise pajama pants covered with pictures of Mouse. A Christmas gift from the twins, of course."

Cordell groans. "You're killing me, Smalls," he says seductively.

I bite back my laughter. "And to complete the ensemble, a faded extra-large UGA T-shirt that I'm pretty sure belonged to my brother at one time."

His responding exhale is so heavy and pained it sends me into a fit of giggles.

"You really know how to get a man going, Marshall."

"Master seductress." The following snort is quickly overpowered by a yawn.

"You should sleep," Cordell murmurs. "I'll be home in five minutes."

"Okay," I whisper. I don't want to hang up, but sleep will win out every time.

"Can I pick you up after your classes tomorrow? We can grab a bite and head over to the hospital if things are moving along."

"Yeah, let's do it."

"'Kay. Good night, Marshall."

A soft smile splits my lips in response to his tender tone. "Good night."

In minutes, I'm asleep, dreaming of gentle brown hands and soft pink lips and a brilliant white smile.

Early Saturday morning, between my Flow and senior classes, I catch up on office business and update membership spreadsheets. I'm in the middle of adding the final new member's contact information when the studio's landline rings.

"Go With the Flow-Ga, this is Mel."

There's a pause, and then a deep chuckle. "Catchy name, Melly."

My heart lurches, but then I get annoyed. With a palm to the face, I groan. "Why are you calling my business, Nick?"

"If you'd answer your damn cell, I wouldn't have to," he huffs. I've been careful not to answer calls from unknown numbers lately. "I just want to catch up for a few minutes, babe."

"Ugh, don't call me that." *Asshole.*

"Don't be like that. I called to tell you about my new job. It's at a dealership in Athens."

"Wait." I let my head fall back against the wall. "You're selling cars? What happened to that office job you told me about?"

"Oh, uh, it...didn't work out. But yeah, babe. I'm a salesman right now, but my boss says I have real general manager potential."

I roll my eyes so hard I'm afraid they might stick that way. Nick's resume consists of playing guitar in a band and working odd jobs for shady bar owners. Factor in his unreliability, and it's a recipe for disaster.

Thank goodness it's not *my* disaster.

He's the opposite of the steady, dependable man who's picking me up this afternoon in so many ways. That thought is immediately followed by an epiphany. One that might rid me of Nick's lingering presence for good.

He's jumped into a monologue about how great his sales were last month, but I cut him off.

"Hey, Nick. Um, I don't think you should call me anymore. Or send postcards."

"Melly, babe, don't say that." That raspy voice that once sent shivers through me when he whispered sweet, seductive lyrics in my ear does nothing for me.

"I'm seeing someone."

Nick's silence stretches on for so long, I consider just hanging up. But as I'm pulling the phone away from my ear, he clears his throat. "Who is it?"

I huff a laugh. "None of your business. As I've told you *many* times before, I stopped being your business when you fucked Kimber in our bed."

"Damn it, Melly. Why you always gotta bring that shit up? It's ancient history."

I drop my chin and shake my head. The audacity of this man. "You're absolutely right, Nick. You know what else is ancient history?" I don't give him a chance to respond. "You. I've moved on and I'm happy. I highly recommend you do the same." And with that, I hang up on my ex-husband for what I hope is the last time.

By the time my last class is over, I'm so Zen that Nick's phone call is nothing more than a blip on the radar. I brush all thoughts of him away easily and focus on the man who makes me breathless.

Cordell picks me up after class as promised and takes me to a roadside shack in the middle of nowhere that he claims has the best barbeque in Georgia. After my first bite of brisket sandwich, I'm a believer. I have to hold back more than one moan as I devour the thing. He doesn't gloat too much. Instead, he leans across the tiny, rickety table to kiss me.

The group chat has been quiet for a while, but we decide to drive over to the hospital in Americus and wait with the Shipleys anyway. Cordell stops for gas, and while he's filling up, I do a little snooping. His Land Rover is immaculate. Not a speck of dust or a stray straw wrapper in sight. My perusal quickly sends me back to our night in his Escalade and the condom he procured so easily. I hold my breath and pop open his glove box. Instantly, a whoosh of air leaves my lungs. Inside, all I find are the owner's manual and a package of tissues. Satisfied, I move on to the center console. The one in my car is a hot mess, but Cordell's is as tidy as the rest of the vehicle. I find another package of facial tissues here, along with a small hand sanitizer, a neatly coiled USB cord, and a few other odds and ends. I roll my eyes and grasp the lid, ready to shut the thing, but a sparkle at the back of the bin catches my eye. It's a light blue sparkle, and when I push aside a mini flashlight to get a better look, my heart stutters.

An icy chill spreads from my core and through my limbs as I pinch the small rhinestone hair pin between my thumb and forefinger and hold it up to study in the sunlight. The blue jewels that make up a flower's petals are the exact shade of the cornflower bridesmaid dress I wore for Mark and Lisa's wedding.

He kept it. All these years.

This isn't even the same vehicle. He had to have transferred the hair pin to this one when he bought it.

The driver's side door opens. "All right, passenger princess, I got you a drink…"

Cordell's voice trails off when he catches sight of the tiny object I'm still holding aloft. It's featherlight, but oh so heavy at the same time.

"Mel—"

His face is stricken. His eyes dart from me to the hair pin, then back to me. It takes a few seconds to register that he called me Mel instead of Marshall. He so rarely uses my first name, but the devotion behind the single syllable makes me want to cry.

"Get in the car, Watkins," I whisper as I roll the end of the pin between my thumb and pointer, watching how it sparkles in the sunlight streaming through the windshield.

With a sigh, he places two sodas in the cupholders, then he hauls his tall frame into the car. When the door is shut behind him, he twists his upper body my way. "I'm not sure what's going through your mind right—"

"Why'd you keep it?" I blurt, eyes locked on his.

My heart gallops away from me at the emotion staring back at me.

"I wanted to keep a piece of you with me. To remember that night. To remember you."

He didn't a few months later. That still stings. But not with the ferocity it once did. He's apologized more times than necessary, honestly. And I've come to recognize that the Mel who bumped into him in Fuzzy's that night was not the Mel who hooked up with him in a back seat. And neither of those Mels is the same as the one sitting next to him today. I've been so many versions of myself over the past decade as I've stumbled along, figuring out who I *really* am. Not just Greg and Beth's daughter, Mark's little sister, or Owen and Ollie's aunt. Not just Nick's ex-wife. I've carried pieces of each one of them, and others, with me as I've grown and learned and lived. And the Mel I am today is a compilation of all the versions who came before.

I love the *me* I am these days—one who lets herself feel emotions instead of boxing them up. One who's begun to believe that she's capable and deserving of *love*—the romantic kind. And the man beside me has had a profound influence on my quest to become my best self.

Caught up in the sweetness of him, I lean in and press my lips to his. His brows are raised when I break our kiss. I pull down the sun visor and regard myself in the mirror. Then I stick the hair pin next to the barrette that holds a chunk of my hair away from my face. "Now you have the real thing," I tell him, "so you won't need this anymore."

Cordell closes his eyes for several seconds, but when he opens them, the smile he gives me is the same one I fell in love with when I was eight. The same one I looked for through my teenage years and hunted for on a television screen when he was far from home. It's his happiest, most genuine smile, and when it shines on me, I'm happy, too.

"Let's go meet the newest member of our family," he says as he shifts into drive.

"Perfect." Taking his right hand, I twine my fingers through his, then I rest our hands on my lap all the way to the hospital.

When we meet up with the Shipleys in the labor and delivery waiting room, Hannah's proudly wearing her *Big Sister* shirt, and according to Ms. Marj, Tessa is fully dilated and ready to push. It's close to dinnertime, so Mr. Tom takes fast-food orders and makes a food run for us.

We spend the next couple of hours eating, talking, and keeping Hannah entertained. Cordell and I take turns playing tic-tac-toe with her, and we all listen as she reads us a few chapters from her library book about dragon warriors.

A few minutes after seven, Luke wanders into the waiting room wearing a triumphant grin. His eyes are red rimmed, and his usual stubble is approaching beard status, but the happiness emanating from him immediately chokes me up.

"Daddy!" Hannah launches herself into her father's waiting arms. He hugs her tightly, then looks around at the rest of us.

"Baby's here," he announces. "Perfect and healthy. Mama is doing great."

"What is it, son?" Ms. Marj swipes at her happy tears and clings to Mr. Tom's arm as she waits for her son to reveal the answer.

Luke smirks. "You'll find out when you meet the baby." Ignoring our protests, he sets Hannah on the ground with a kiss on her cheek. "I'm gonna head back so we can do the golden hour thing. I just wanted to update y'all first." After giving his parents quick hugs, he pushes through the double doors that lead to the maternity rooms.

"I can't believe I still don't know!" I wail as I stomp over to the upholstered chair I've occupied for the past few hours.

"Marj, our kids sure do like to drag out a surprise," Mr. Tom huffs. It's probably the most frustrated I've ever seen him. "Come on, June Bug. Let's go ride the escalators."

Hannah takes her papaw's hand, and they stroll down the opposite hall. Ms. Marj stares a hole in the doors Luke walked through moments before, like she can manifest X-ray vision and use it to discover the baby's sex if she tries hard enough.

By the time Luke returns to collect his parents and Hannah an hour later, we're all on the edge of our seats. He takes one look at his best friend's grouchy expression and grins. The four Shipleys start for Tessa and the baby, all smiles and anticipation. I smack Cordell's abs to get his attention when Mr. Tom sidesteps in front of his wife to keep her from sprinting to the room.

"And then there were two." Cordell stretches his long, jean-clad legs out and crosses them at the ankle.

"Your dad was tall," I remark without much thought.

I feel his eyes on me when he responds. "He was six-one."

"And your mom's tall."

He nods. "Five-nine."

I nod and blurt, "Do you want kids?"

I slap a hand over my mouth as soon as the words escape, and my eyes shut. Damn, I wish I could reverse time so I could go back twenty seconds, to when I didn't sound like a desperate hussy.

*Why* did I ask him that? And so soon into whatever *this* is?

My ribs are crushing my lungs with such ferocity I'm thankful the emergency department is so close.

Cordell gently pulls my hand from my mouth and holds it in his. He swipes his thumb over my knuckles—back and forth, back and forth—until I force my eyelids open.

"I do want kids," he says, nonchalant.

Meanwhile, I mentally practice yoga poses to calm my heart rate.

"I'd love to have two or three," he continues. "Biologically or through adoption. What about you? Do you want kids?"

Somehow, I pry my tongue from the roof of my mouth to answer. "Yeah. Someday."

Marj, Tom, and Hannah push through the doors, startling us. In a heartbeat, we're both on our feet. The smiles on their faces are blinding.

Hannah stops in front of me, her little face tired but excited. "Mama said I can put you out of your misery, if you want."

On instinct, I grasp Cordell's hand and squeeze. Then I give her a nod.

Hannah giggles, but then her face contorts and tears spill over her lashes. "I have a sister!" She wraps her arms around my waist and buries her head in my shirt.

"Oh Jelly Bean," I choke out, clinging to her. "I'm so happy for you."

Cordell's warm hand rests on my back. A steady comfort.

Hannah nods against my stomach, then pulls back to look at her Uncle Dell. When she moves to hug him, he crouches low, lifts her off the ground, and holds her tight.

"Shh, Banana," he soothes, rubbing circles on her back. "You're already the best big sister. Think of all the things you get to teach her. She's going to be an amazing human because of *you*."

Ms. Marj is full-on sobbing, but we all laugh when she says, "We're crying more than that baby girl will during her whole first year."

Mr. Tom steps up to Cordell and holds his arms out. "Let's get this June Bug home so she can get some rest. She's had a big day."

Ms. Marj grasps my forearm. "Go meet her. They're in room five." With a peck to my cheek and a hug for Cordell, she heads out behind her husband and granddaughter.

I knock softly, and we wait to be invited in. When Cordell

pushes the door open and guides me into the room with a hand at my back, Luke is standing next to where Tessa's reclined on the bed, a tiny bundle in his arms.

I pop up on my tiptoes to get a look, and Cordell hovers close, peeking over my shoulder at the tiny, swaddled baby sleeping in her dad's arms. She has a full head of thick, dark hair and a tiny pink face with the cutest little button nose.

I squeeze Luke's bicep. "She's perfect."

His proud smile makes me tear up again.

"You did it, T!" I whisper-shout.

She watches us meet her daughter through exhausted eyes, but her smile is luminous.

After a careful hug, I prop my hip on the edge of her bed and clasp her hand.

Cordell gives his friend a hearty slap on the back. "Beautiful girl you've got there, Dad."

Luke nods and painstakingly passes his newborn daughter over. "Meet Emma Rose Shipley."

Cordell cradles her in his muscly arms like she's the most precious thing on the planet, and my ovaries wave white flags.

Damn, that man looks good holding a baby.

Somehow, my lustful and emotion-addled brain remembers to capture a few pictures with my phone.

After I've pocketed the thing, I hold my arms out and bounce in front of Cordell. "Hand her over, Watkins."

With the utmost gentleness, he passes Emma to me.

"So nice to meet you, Emma." I marvel at her tiny features and her glossy dark hair. "Hannah's over the moon," I tell her parents as I sway from side to side.

"Yeah, uh, she was a tad emotional," Luke says, his tone full of affection.

With a wince, Tessa scoots over to give her husband room to perch beside her.

"And this one was a champ." He kisses Tessa's temple and runs a hand down the back of her hair.

When it's time for Emma to nurse again, we take our leave, promising we'll visit after they get settled back at home.

I angle in close to give Tessa a goodbye hug. "I'm so fucking proud of you."

She smiles, her eyes watery. "That pink hair really worked." She laughs quietly along with me but sobers quickly and grasps my hand. "It's your turn," she whispers, tilting her head to where Cordell's handing the baby back to her father.

A smile spreads across my face, and warmth blooms in my chest at the sight. "You know, T? I think it just might be."

# CHAPTER SEVENTEEN

## CORDELL

It's nearly ten by the time we leave the hospital. Mel holds my hand in her lap again on the drive. The ride is silent; no doubt she's thinking about the tiny miracle we held in our arms the same as I am.

Emma Rose Shipley.

A beautiful name for a well-loved baby girl.

My heart is full of joy and pride for Luke. For the man he is and the challenges he's overcome. Witnessing all the ways my best friend is living his best life makes me so hopeful about my own future. I want that. I want it so badly.

And I want it with the woman in the passenger seat.

Mel watches the scenery pass by, her head resting against the seat. Every streetlight we pass illuminates her pink waves and that sparkly blue flower she's stuck in her hair. My stomach dropped to my feet when I found her twirling it between her fingers. I thought for sure she'd freak out when she realized I've been holding on to it, that she'd use it as an excuse to run away from me again—physically and emotionally.

I won't let it happen. Not again. Because with every passing day, Mel Marshall owns another piece of my heart. If she runs, I'll have no choice but to chase her.

But she didn't run. She didn't pick a fight or shut down. In fact, her response—*Now you have the real thing, so you won't need this anymore*—felt like a declaration.

Even so, I don't know that I actually *have* her. Not *all* of her. Though we're moving in the right direction, I can't shake the fear that something will crop up and set us back. And I have no interest in going back to how we were before. The setbacks I've endured in my lifetime have been so numerous and so heavy that when things are great, I can't help but wait for the other shoe to drop.

When another shimmer of blue flashes in my periphery, I make a snap decision. Instead of heading straight toward the highway, I veer off to the right and take us down a side street. After another turn, Mel notices we've changed course.

"Where are we going?"

"Do you trust me?"

She gives me major side-eye, but when she whispers "yes," I press my lips to the back of the hand that's been holding mine since we left the hospital.

It doesn't take long to get to our destination, and when I pull into the dark, empty lot, a niggle of worry eats at me. But then the neon sign flickers. The name is different, but it signals that the place is open, despite appearances.

Mel scoots forward and eyes the sign, her muscles still and tight. She turns to me and blinks slowly a few times, silent.

I raise my hands in surrender. "You said you trusted me."

"I'm rethinking that," she smirks. But then her fiery eyes soften. "Why are we here?"

"I thought it was time for a little walk down memory lane." I turn toward her as best as I can and brush my fingers along her collarbone, then run them under her hair and squeeze her nape. "A chance for me to get it right. A chance to do what I should've done ten years ago."

She swallows audibly, searching my face. "What should you have done?"

"I should've gone home with the pixie I met that night. I should've called her the next day. I should have pursued her, wooed her until she had no choice but to fall for me."

"Better late than never," she whispers, a ghost of a smile on her lips.

"C'mon. Let's grab a beer."

The inside of the place hasn't changed much. Same decor, same scent, same dark atmosphere. We pull up to the bar and order.

"I'll have a Terrapin, please."

"Blue Moon for me, with the orange slice."

I raise my brows. "Sunshine and happiness?"

The smile that splits Mel's face is incandescent, lighting up the dark space around us. "Thought I'd give 'em a try."

I raise my cold beer bottle. "To sunshine and happiness."

Mel clinks hers against it. "To us."

*Ten years, three months, and fifteen days ago...*

I scrub my hand down my face. My vision blurs as I squint into the headlights of oncoming traffic. My contacts are dry and suctioned to my eyes. I promised Luke one more day of fishing tomorrow before I leave for Tennessee and training camp, so I really should be heading home.

Leaving my mom, my sister, and my best bud is always hard, but I'm dreading the goodbyes even more than usual this summer.

I've been driving around lecturing myself, trying to will my heart to accept the restlessness I've been feeling since supper with my mom. I'm stuck between two worlds: the homespun, small-town vibes of Bennett, and the glitz and glamor and punishing schedule of life as a professional football player. As I drive toward the highway that will lead me back to Bennett, a neon sign catches my attention. Not allowing myself a second thought, I turn into the parking lot, where one lonely car is parked.

Bottoms Up is a terrible name for a bar, but I could go for a beer about now, and from the looks of things out here, this place won't be crowded. Which means I won't be hounded for a picture or autograph.

The dark bar smells, weirdly enough, like motor oil and pine-scented cleaner. The cool air is a welcome relief; even the short walk from my Escalade to the entrance was enough to make my shirt stick to my skin.

Like I suspected, the place is empty, save for a woman sitting at the bar. The bartender looks up from his phone long enough to notice me and take my order.

"Can I get a Terrapin, please?"

With a nod, he wanders over to the tap. I post up at the middle of the bar, leaving an empty stool between myself and the woman to my left, and place my phone face down on the lacquered bar top.

Just as I'm raising the cool glass to my mouth, a feminine voice pipes up. "Terrapin, huh?"

I twist toward the owner of the voice, instantly gobsmacked. She's gorgeous and petite, and she's smirking at my beer choice. Her hazel eyes narrow at me, then quickly widen. With that one look, it's clear she knows who I am. But she plays it cool, and I respect the hell out of that. I scan her from head to toe, cataloging the heavy makeup and the blond updo, noting the sparkly blue flower thing pinned in her hair. Her made-up top half is a total contradiction to her worn cutoffs and brown sandals.

"When in Rome," I tell her. And because I'm intrigued, I can't help but flirt. "What do the pretty Georgia girls go for these days, beer-wise?"

"Blue Moon, sans orange wedge," she says, raising the glass to a pair of pretty pink lips.

"You don't like oranges, or…"

"They taste too much like sunshine and happiness."

Her answer surprises me, which intrigues me even more. Who doesn't like sunshine and happiness?

But I keep my attention fixed on the rows of liquor behind the bar. "And those are bad things?"

Her eyes are on me as she studies my profile. I want to stare back, but I refrain, though I desperately want to continue talking to her.

"I'd need *way* more of this before we get into *that*." In my periphery, she tips her beer in my direction and swivels back to the bar.

Who is this woman? She's far too young to be so jaded. What's her story, and why does she seem familiar? Determined to learn more about her, I give her my first name and hold my hand out, hoping she takes it. Hoping she gives me her name, her attention, her life story, while we're at it.

She slides her delicate hand into mine. "Mel."

Her name is enough to make me smile for the first time all night.

Mel. It suits her.

Short. Sweet. No nonsense.

Then she tilts in and surprises me again. "I know who you are, by the way."

My stomach twists. "Don't hold that against me."

She tells me that her brother got married today. That explains the fancy hairdo and professional-looking makeup.

When I ask her if she's a fugitive on the run from a

bridezilla, she smiles big and tells me all about her brother's new wife. Her eyes light up when she's talking about Lisa, like a ray of sunshine has broken through the gray cloud that hovers over her.

"How'd they meet? Mark and Lisa." I give myself a mental pat on the back for remembering their names. But then again, I kind of suspect I'll remember every syllable this woman utters tonight.

"They met during their freshman year. Like two weeks after classes started. They were at a party and locked eyes across the room. Boom. That was it."

*Boom.*

"That was it."

Damn, she's beautiful. Expressive eyes and pouty pink lips. I'd really like to know how those lips would feel against mine.

Her brother's meet-cute reminds me of the story of my parents' first meeting. They told it so often they each had specific parts memorized, and they'd jump in and take over for one another, like reciting a beloved play. Cass and I could probably retell it even now, word for word.

"To Mark and Lisa," I say, raising my glass. A love like that deserves a toast.

"To Mark and Lisa." She taps her glass against mine.

Our conversation goes on, and although she's vague about her folks, she does divulge that she's "Georgia born and bred."

I like knowing that she's from around here.

When I give her my patented *it was a good place to grow up* soundbite, she narrows her eyes. "C'mon, what do you *really* think about your hometown?"

"You don't want to ask me about football? About being drafted?"

That's a first.

I signal for another beer and continue to grill her, failing to keep the bitterness out of my tone.

"You don't want to ask about my *way* more famous team-mates? My QB? My money?"

We're facing each other now, so I watch her reaction carefully. The last thing I need is for some stranger in a bar to run her mouth to the media. I've worked so damn hard to keep my image spotless. I had to do the responsible thing and ask, try to suss her out, but deep down, I don't think I'll have to worry about Mel. From her demeanor, it's obvious she's not even a bit impressed by my day job. It's like she really wants to know *me*.

It only adds to her allure. Only fuels my desire to take this further.

"Who *are* you, Mel?"

She juts her chin out like she's daring me. Daring me to give her my truth.

So I'm honest with her about Bennett, a place that wears its small-town distinction proudly. I'm proud to be from there, but for every high I experienced in my hometown, there've been twice as many lows. I stick with the positives, though, as I fill her in. Bennett is the place that welcomed my family with open arms when we were new to town. Where my mom is surrounded by kind, salt-of-the-earth people. It's the place I met the best friend a guy could ask for.

What I don't mention? That Bennett's the place where my dad took his last breath.

When she asks what I'm doing at Bottoms Up, I go with honesty again. I tell her that sometimes I need to be alone, to find a place where nothing is expected of me.

"I'm glad I came here tonight, though." And I mean it. Because this impulsive decision led me to this woman. With her fancy makeup and hair and sad, jaded attitude. That's the thing that's kept me rapt the whole time we've been talking.

Why is she sad? What's *her* truth?

Was it a man who muted her colors?

"Oh, yeah?" she asks.

I nod. "Yeah. I've got peace and quiet. There's no one around to butt into my personal space or ask for a picture or an autograph. Cold beer. Plus, I met this pixie of a girl who intrigues me. That'd be you, by the way." I lean in and catch a whiff of something floral and feminine. It reminds me of the field of wildflowers that Luke, Cass, and I would play in behind the school during the summer.

Her brows pull together, forming a tiny wrinkle between them that's as cute as she is. "Me? Why in the world are you intrigued by *me*? Oh wait, it's because I'm not in your personal space, right?"

Hell, I'd love her in my personal space. She can move on in, put up wallpaper for all I care.

I don't pick up women in bars. Or at restaurants or clubs or parties or any other place professional athletes frequent. I can count the number of women I've slept with on one hand and have digits leftover.

But this one draws me in, makes me want to be reckless. Makes me want to shed my good-guy image, if just for an hour. So I give her more of my truths. "First of all, I wouldn't mind *you* in my personal space. At all."

The way her lips part in response to that confession makes my groin ache.

"But you intrigue me. Because under that updo and makeup highlighter, I think you're sad. You're trying like hell not to let it show, though. And I know a little something about the outside not matching the inside."

She scoffs at my knowledge of highlighter, but her response is a defense mechanism. I hit a nerve. I still can't explain *why*, but I want to be alone with Mel. At least for a little while. To take away the sadness behind her gorgeous eyes.

So when she tells me she wants to forget, I can't deny her. I won't.

I pay our tab and lead her out of the bar. Our first kiss is electric, and before I know it, we're in the back seat of my Escalade. Mel straddles my lap with her firm, silky thighs, and then she tells me to make it memorable. We won't have a chance to do all the exploring I'd like, though. This will be a rough and rowdy hookup.

The first of my life. In all my twenty-six years, I've never had a one-night stand. As we kiss and explore each other, one thought won't leave me alone: I don't *want* this to be a one-night thing. I want to get to know the gorgeous woman who's grinding on my lap, to take her in different positions, in different locations, but that's not what she's looking for tonight.

And one night is all I can offer her, anyway.

So I'll enjoy this for what it is.

When Mel pulls off her tight blue tank top, I freeze. Her tits are perfect. Perky and round, with nipples already pointing in my direction like tiny arrows. I swallow hard when she grasps my wrists and places my hands on her warm flesh.

This woman is so *freaking* unexpected.

When I lift up to pull my shorts and boxer briefs down, I push her straight into the headliner, causing her to hit her head. I panic that she's truly hurt, but her response is to laugh. The poof of her updo probably softened the blow.

We work together to remove the pins from her hair, and when it's loose around her face, I take her in. God, is she stunning.

I don't get to admire her for as long as I'd like, because a second later, she's gasping at the sight of my cock, and I'm chuckling at the reaction. I'm six-four and have huge hands and feet; what did she expect? But my laughter quickly fades when she questions whether she can take me.

"It'll fit," I insist.

And it does, after I make her good and wet with my hand. She rides my fingers, and when she leans back to give me access to her bouncy breasts, I almost blow too soon.

When she comes on my hand, I tell her she's breathtaking. There's no better word to describe her with her head tipped back and her mouth open, her skin flushed pink. I file that memory away so I can revisit it later.

My heart twists when she traces the letter M on the window, and then it trips over itself when she does the same to me. Like she's marking me as hers. And damn if my stupid heart doesn't keep on flipping.

*Cool it, Watkins. This is a one-time thing.*

The way she wantonly positions herself above me and slides down my shaft forces a grunt to escape my lips. She's warm and wet and tight and perfect. I don't mean to call her *babe*; it slips out as I'm lost in the moment. Lost inside her.

Then she's riding me with abandon. I'm holding on for dear life, loving every second of it. I make sure she comes again, gripping her hips so she can grind on me until she climaxes. And when we've both found that relief, we're a sweaty, sated mess.

After we put our clothes back on and climb out, Mel pops up on her tiptoes. I dip my face low and meet her for a sweet, slow goodbye kiss. And damn if our lips and tongues don't already know the perfect way to slide together.

"Thanks for helping me forget," she tells me.

"No problem, little pixie." I shoot her a wink.

She lights up in response, her eyes bright and a genuine smile splitting her face. There isn't a hint of the sadness I saw earlier. Like those muted colors have sprung back to life.

My heart beats double-time when she pulls out a pen and a crumpled-up receipt out of her bag. She holds the receipt to her thigh and jots her number down, and when she hands it to me, I tuck it into my pocket, wishing like hell I could use it. But I'm going back to Tennessee, and she'll be here. And for the foreseeable future, football will be my life. I'm a jerk for even taking it from her, even when she swears there's no pressure to call.

Because she's exactly the type of woman I'd choose for myself if I had time to pursue a relationship. She's beautiful and bold and brilliant. And undeniably memorable.

That smile of hers keeps one on my face—despite the knot that's formed in my gut—as I drive home to Bennett, well after one. I'm happy I could offer her an escape for the night, but something tells me I'm going to regret letting her get away.

These days, when I think about that night—the night we gave each other an escape—I can't help but be grateful for all the ups and downs that followed. Because every single one led us to this moment.

Led us here. Brought us together.

I let Mel get away that night, and I regretted it even more than I thought I would, but I won't make the same mistake twice.

I am coachable, after all.

We finish our beers, and without a word, she laces her fingers through mine. This time, she leads *me* out of the bar.

And I gladly follow.

# CHAPTER EIGHTEEN

## MEL

Cordell parks in the alley, and my insides erupt in a million sensations: swarms of butterflies in my stomach, electric tingles in my fingertips and down in my toes, heavy tightness in my breasts, a dull throb between my legs. It's like every cell in my body is holding a rave to celebrate what comes next.

And there's no doubt in my mind what comes next. He made his intentions clear the minute he steered us into that dive bar parking lot.

When we exit the car, he's clutching a leather Dopp kit.

I quirk a brow and tease him. "Someone is feeling confident."

He winks but says nothing, sending the butterflies in my belly into barrel rolls.

He *is* confident. And he has every right to be. This man is *so* getting laid tonight.

Every look and touch is charged. When he places a hand on the small of my back to lead me up the stairs, I have to bite my lip to keep from whimpering. The sound of our footsteps on the stairs is a staccato beat that matches the rhythm of my heart. When he takes my keys to open my apartment door and his fingers brush mine, my pelvic muscles clench in response.

The moment the door is closed and locked behind us, Cordell fakes a yawn. "Well, it's been a long day, and it's really late." He checks his smartwatch. "Look at the time. It's after midnight, Marshall. Would you be terribly upset if I offered you a rain ch—"

I whirl and point my finger at his chest. "Don't you *dare.*"

"Didn't think so." He grins, and before I can blink, he hoists me up on his shoulder, the same way he did on the Fourth of July.

A high-pitched squeal escapes me as he carries me into the bedroom. I give myself a mental high five for sorta making the bed and kicking the stray, unmated shoes underneath it this morning.

He lowers me to the floor same as last time, a slow glide down his body as gravity pulls me back to earth, and when I'm steady, I bury my face in his shirt, overcome with a sudden shyness.

"Hey," he says. "We don't have to—"

I lean back so he can see the sincerity in my face when I assure him. "I want to."

With a nod, he grasps the collar of his faded gray LSU T-shirt and yanks it over his head. I make a mental note to pen a declaration. It'll assert that this is the hottest way for a man to remove a shirt, and it will proclaim that it should henceforth be standard undressing protocol.

I drink in the chiseled chest in front of me. His smooth brown skin beckons me, and when I heed its call and lightly trace his muscles with my fingertips, he shivers. A grin overtakes me at the growl that works its way out of him when I rake my nails through his sparse chest hair.

He tips his chin. "Shirt. Off."

"So *bossy*," I chide, but I quickly whip off my shirt, never breaking his stare. My chest heaves as I unhook my bra and let it fall to the floor. Though I hate myself for the insecurity, I brace for the sliver of disappointment that's sure to flash in his eyes when he's met with the sight of me topless. I've always been self-conscious of my small boobs, and that was only compounded after Nick asked if I'd ever thought about getting implants.

But Cordell's inspection remains desirous, and when his calloused thumb grazes a nipple, I close my eyes in relief.

"So responsive," he murmurs. "These are as beautiful as the rest of you." With both of my breasts cupped in his hands, he leans down and takes my mouth. Our tongues advance and retreat, advance and retreat, and he matches the rhythm with his hands.

He pops the button on my jeans and lowers the zipper, teasing me with the deliberateness of his movements. I'm lost in the sensations, too far gone to even consider grasping his waistband, when suddenly, his hand is in my cotton panties and he's discovering how turned on I am.

"Soaking. Wet," he grunts. Without letting up on his teasing, he sits on the edge of the bed.

My body has no choice but to follow. My knees hit the mattress between his spread thighs, but I keep myself upright by clutching his broad shoulders.

"I want you to come like this, Marshall. On my fingers." He plunges two inside me, pulling a moan from deep in my chest. "You're perfect like this. Dripping for me. Skin flushed such a pretty shade of pink." With his thumb, he rubs my clit in perfect circles.

I dig my nails into his rock-hard traps and suck in a sharp breath. In this position, Cordell's face is level with my chest, so he takes full advantage and nuzzles my boobs with his beard. The scrape of his wiry scruff against my soft, sensitive skin heightens his ministrations between my thighs.

"Fuck. Cordell…"

"Mmm, sweetheart." He moves from one breast to the other, dropping soft kisses along the way. "I love to hear you say my name like that. Like I'm the only man who can make you feel this good."

"You are."

As if he's rewarding me for that admission, he wraps his lips around the tip of my left breast and tortures my nipple with hot lashes of his tongue.

I clutch his head to my chest as I chant "yes, yes, yes" over and over. My boobs might be small, but they are hella sensitive, and when he gives the other side the same attention, that telltale throb begins deep in my core. He circles my clit twice, and I detonate. My legs turn to jelly, but he holds me up with a strong arm around my waist.

That was one of the most powerful orgasms of my life, and I'm still wearing my jeans and shoes.

"Good girl," he praises, still peppering kisses to my torso. "That's a view I could get used to—you coming apart for me. Every day."

"If you give me an orgasm like that every day, then I guess I'll let you hang around." With a teasing smile, I brush my lips against his.

His lips tip up, and his shoulders shake in silent laughter.

Damn. That reaction makes me feel like I'm floating.

I toe off my Chucks, and Cordell peels my jeans down over my hips, and then I'm standing before him in nothing but my popsicle-print panties.

He tilts his head as he studies them. "Are these a subliminal request, Marshall? Your way of asking me to lick your pussy?" One dark brow lifts, and he rakes his teeth over his bottom lip. "I already told you it's the best thing I've ever had in my mouth. I'd devour it morning, noon, and night if I could."

I bark a laugh, even as my cheeks heat. "Coach Watkins. You have a filthy mouth."

His responding smirk is wicked. "I've been saving it for you. You're the only one who'll get to hear it."

"Good." I kiss his brow and step back, ready to get this show on the road.

But when Cordell's focus veers to the left side of my torso and he squints, icy tendrils coast over my skin like I've been caught in a deluge of freezing rain.

I don't know how he missed it earlier, and I was so deep in the fog of lust that I didn't think about it myself. We were caught up in our passion, and my upper arm likely hid it from his view. But now, he's going to see it and question me about it.

"What's this?" With his hands on my hips, he twists my upper body so he can get a better look at the tiny tattoo inked into my skin. Its location on my ribcage is always covered by a bra or a bikini top. Cordell rubs his thumb along the black ink, less than half an inch tall and about an inch wide.

LXXXIV.

"They're Roman numerals," he muses.

Yes. And it won't take him more than a couple of seconds to understand the meaning behind them. He's smart.

He flicks his eyes to mine, then back to the tattoo. "It's eighty-four."

"Yeah," I breathe. The urge to run hits me full force. But that's what I would've done in the past. So despite the rush of panic coursing through my veins, and despite the way my heart pounds against my ribs, I hold my position.

He's got his lower lip pulled between his teeth, and his eyes are searching every inch of my face, waiting for my explanation.

But I'm at a loss. How the hell do I explain why I have his jersey number tattooed on my body? I could go with the lesser of the two evils: chalk it up to being so infatuated with him once upon a time that I impulsively had it inked on my skin. It makes me sound like a stalker, but it's not that far-fetched, considering I *was* infatuated with him back then. But it's not the truth.

After everything we've gone through to get here, I owe it to the both of us to be 100 percent honest. I move back, just out of his reach, and I brace myself for the fallout.

"I had it done right after...after you didn't recognize me at Fuzzy's. I was so hurt and angry and..." I take a breath to collect my thoughts and calm my racing heart. "I let a lot of outside forces dictate my self-worth back then. And you not remembering me added fuel to my *I'm-so-worthless* fire. My parents were on a cruise that week, so I raced home from the bar and got wasted in their kitchen." I swallow back the bile rising in my throat. The memory of the epic hangover I had the next day still makes my stomach roil. "I hung out with this guy back then—we were just friends, but I think he was hoping we could be more. Anyway, I called him, blitzed out of my mind, and demanded that he pick me up and take me to see this buddy of his who lived in Oglethorpe and did tattoos in his garage."

Cordell winces.

"I know. Not the most sanitary. I'm lucky my skin didn't rot off."

I'm so exposed at this moment—literally, since I'm wearing nothing but my freaking underwear—but also emotionally. Regardless, I don't hold back. "It was definitely a rage tattoo. Back then, at least. It was meant to be a reminder to never again let a man make me feel worthless and forgettable."

Cordell closes his eyes and slumps. "Mel..." His voice is nothing but pain and regret.

Though I'm the one who broke contact, suddenly, the need to be connected to him as I bare my soul is a physical ache. "Will you touch me?" I blurt. "Please."

I lift a hand, and he does the same. He threads his long,

strong fingers between mine and holds on tight, instantly warming me with his touch.

"It wasn't only you. It was fucking Nick. And, to a certain extent, my brother."

His brows raise at that.

"Mark has never knowingly made me feel worthless, but it was hard growing up in his shadow. He was always meticulous and perfect and dignified. Not to outshine others, but because that's who he was. Who he still *is*. It took me a long time to realize that his success should have no bearing on how I see myself."

He rolls his lips between his teeth and nods. "I get that. I've lived in my father's shadow since he died. I had the pressure of carrying my family name on my back when I played. Hell, I still carry it, in the way I coach those boys and how I conduct myself. Even though all I would've had to do to make my dad proud was live an authentic life—remain true to myself. Like Cass has. I don't have to make decisions based solely on what I think he would've wanted. *My* opinions and judgment matter most. I'm the one who has to live with my choices, after all."

He brings our joined hands to his lips and kisses my knuckles.

"Mel, I'm so sorry—"

"Stop. No more apologizing, Coach. You've made amends tenfold by now."

He breathes out a heavy sigh. I hope he believes it, but if he still harbors even a tiny kernel of doubt, I'll do my damnedest to rid him of it.

"Please don't tell my brother I felt that way when I was younger." A sliver of guilt snakes through me. "He's the *best* big brother, and he would be devastated."

"All your secrets are safe with me, Marshall."

I believe it. The look in his eyes assures me that not only are my secrets safe with him, but my heart as well.

I shiver when he presses his lips to the tattoo and holds them there, like he can kiss away the hurt associated with the permanent reminder.

"Hey." I gently pull his face away and cup his cheeks. "It doesn't represent that for me anymore. The meaning of a tattoo can change over time, just like *we* can."

"What does it mean now?"

"Now? Now it means *you*. You've inked yourself into my life, and I like how that feels."

He wraps his arms around me, hugging me so tight that his face is smashed against my chest, and like he's breathing me into his lungs, he takes a long, deep breath and holds it.

"So...that was kind of a downer in the middle of the sexy times," I joke. "Do you...want to postpone the rest?"

*Please say no. Please say no.*

"Not a chance. Do you?" He straightens and assesses me, probably to gauge my reaction.

I shake my head and bite down on my lower lip.

With a thumb, Cordell presses on it, releasing it from my teeth, heat swirling in his stare. "Nuh-uh. The only one who'll be marking your flawless skin like that tonight will be me."

And with that one proclamation, my nipples harden and my pussy pulses with a wet heat.

Our mouths fuse, a twisted tangling of licks and pulls and nibbles that send waves of pleasure through my body. In a flash, my panties are gone and I'm stepping back, giving him room to stand and shed the rest of his clothing.

He chucks his shoes and his jeans to the side, but I get to his boxers before he can. So what if I'm eager? His very prominent erection gives me pause, though. I haven't forgotten the sheer size of him or his grumbled "*it'll fit*" all those years ago. Hands trembling with a mix of desire and nerves, I reach into the nightstand for a condom and a bottle of lube.

"Slow down, sweetheart."

His tone is so damn soothing, yet here I am, frantically working at the condom wrapper.

He gently pulls it from my fingers. "I've been waiting a long time to be inside you again. I want to savor it."

While part of me wants to stamp my foot like a brat, another part melts like molasses at the sweetness of his words.

He sits and pulls me onto his lap so I'm straddling his thighs. With gentle touches, he ghosts his fingers over my brows, my lips, my jaw, then he traces my collarbone. His eyes follow the path his fingers take across my skin, down to my breasts. He smooths concentric circles around my areola until he reaches my nipple, which stands at attention for him like a good little soldier.

"I want to memorize every inch of you," he whispers as his exploration moves farther south, down to my navel. His fingertips skim the skin beside it, and I shiver at the sensation. When he dips between my legs and grazes my clit, I buck against him, desperate to ease the ache that's built up again.

I slip a hand into his boxers and grasp him, reveling in the feel of his hard length. With a firm grip, I smooth my hand up and down, up and down, until his breath catches. He tips his chin, a silent request, and I press my lips to his. For a long moment, we share passionate kisses while we touch each other's most intimate parts. I've never felt closer to a person than I do right now. With him.

He doesn't stop teasing me. He gives me moments of bliss but pulls away abruptly when I'm teetering on the edge. "Cordell...please," I whimper between kisses.

"I've got you," he pants. "Condom."

Eager to please, I get the wrapper off and roll the condom down his cock, taking my time assessing its beauty where it juts up between us.

"How do you want it?" he asks. Though I'm still wrapped around him, he stands and uses one hand to shove his boxers down those tree-trunk thighs while the other holds my bare ass.

He ducks low and plants open-mouthed kisses along my throat, waiting for my answer.

"On top."

He said he wants me "in every position," and here he is, giving me the first choice.

Not once in all the times Nick and I slept together did he ask me what position I wanted.

With a toss of my head, I banish all thoughts of my dumbass ex and every other man from my mind. All my attention should be on the one in front of me.

He presses his lips to the place where my neck slopes into my shoulder, and I gasp when he bites my flesh there. It's not a painful bite, but it's hard enough to send a message to my brain and to my nether regions: *I claim you.*

If anyone other than Cordell had done that to me, they would've received a punch to the dick in return. But for him, this isn't an act of possession, but one of passion.

"You're so sexy, Marshall." He reclines on the mattress, bringing me with him.

I roll my hips, sliding my wetness along his shaft. He grunts in pleasure, and I feel like I've been given a gold star.

"Not so bad yourself, Watkins."

From this vantage point, I take in the glorious naked man underneath me, letting my eyes rove over every inch of him. I love the way his muscles bunch when I trail my hands down his torso, so I let them linger in his curves and trace the planes of his body at my leisure. I duck low and swipe my tongue over a dark brown nipple, and I'm rewarded when his cock twitches against my stomach.

"God, I've wanted you so badly, for so long." He watches me, lips parted in awe, as I move over top of him. He kneads one breast, and with his other hand, he grasps my hip and digs his fingers in like a brand.

When he traces an M over my heart, mirroring my action during our first time, tears spring to my eyes.

"Let's make it memorable, sweetheart."

All I can do is smile and nod. I'm so overcome; a riot of sensations bubbles to the surface and overwhelms me. Passion and lust and excitement and fear and nervousness and...*oh my God*. Love.

Shit. I love him. Like, really, *really* love him.

Not the love of a besotted kid or an infatuated teenager or a dazzled football fan. No, I love him as a woman who's finally figured her shit out. One who is whole and happy with who she is.

My love for him is soul deep.

The realization is terrifying, so rather than telling him, I do the next best thing: I show him with my actions.

I squeeze a dollop of lube into my palm and work him from root to tip. I'm plenty wet, but he's a big boy, and some extra glide won't hurt. On my knees, I position him at my opening and let gravity help us along. Slowly, with his hands on my hips for support, I work myself onto him. I squeeze my eyes shut and buck to take the last of his length. When he's fully seated inside me, he releases a throaty groan that makes me even wetter.

We watch each other, gazes locked, a silent look that communicates so much. The bickering, the flirting, even the damn matchmaking, all of it led us to this.

"You feel incredible," he whispers, breaking the spell we're under.

Tentatively, I roll my hips, and when all I feel is pleasure, I do it again. As I buck faster, he continues to whisper encouragement. Every *yes* and *that's it* and *look at you take me so well* spurs me on, makes me want to please him while pleasing myself.

I go to plant my hands on his chest for better balance, but Cordell senses what I need and holds his hands out, his elbows locked at his sides. I lace my fingers with his and brace myself on his hands, letting him hold my weight while I rock my hips even faster. I grind down on his pubic bone to give my clit the friction it needs.

"*Oh*, right there. Yes." My breathy moans are met with sharp grunts from him. The sounds are so damn hot. I want to record them on my phone for later use. *Maybe next time...*

My inner muscles pulse once, then again, followed by a throbbing sensation that rises to the surface in short bursts. Finally, it spills over as waves of ecstasy flood my body. I tip my head back and savor each thrum that vibrates through me.

When the swells of desire ebb, Cordell lowers our entwined hands to the bed, and I collapse on his chest, breathless and spent. He kisses the top of my head as I try to catch my breath. "Freaking. Goddess."

I blush at his description but prop my chin on his chest so he can see my smile.

"Thank you."

"No, thank *you*. I'll be thinking about that on my deathbed," he vows.

I snort, and his chest rumbles with laughter.

Splaying my hands on his chest, I lift up and clench my inner muscles around his cock. A reminder. "It's your turn, Coach."

He thrusts his hips. A promise. "Yes, ma'am."

After a scorching kiss, I sit up and rest my hands on his lower abdomen. In turn, he grips my hips and holds me in place. When I'm secure, he bucks up gently, assessing my expression each time, and when all I feel is bliss, he thrusts deeper, filling me completely.

His grunts become more frequent, and when he grates out "touch yourself. Come again," I do as he says and resist the urge to tell him that I've never, not once, had *three* orgasms in the span of a couple of hours. That shit only happens in Tessa's romance books. Even so, I want him to lavish all the praise on me, so I rub circles on my clit with two fingers.

"*Yes*," he hisses. "So hot and tight. So perfect. God, Mel, you —" His voice breaks, and when he thrusts home one final time, euphoria washes over his face. He holds there, his cock pulsing, and empties into the condom. I don't get to soak in how stunning he is for long, because another climax sneaks up on me. Not as intense as the first two, but still wholly pleasurable. I ride it out by circling my hips once, then twice, and on the third roll, I crumple against him again.

"I think we just fucked each other's brains out," I gasp.

The laugh that leaves him is rich and deep. Damn. I *might* enjoy that sound a tad more than even his passionate grunts. I'll record that one, too, and listen to it on my sad, mopey days.

"I'm okay with being brainless with you." He maneuvers my pliant body so that I'm draped across him and takes a tissue out of the box on my nightstand. Once he's dealt with the condom, he rubs soothing circles on my back.

A contentedness I don't know that I've ever felt settles over me as I snuggle into the warmth of him. We lie like that for a while, quiet, letting our pulses return to normal. Then we take turns using the bathroom. When he comes out sporting a pair of dark-framed glasses, my mouth drops open and I squeeze my thighs together.

*Holy hell.* Cordell Watkins in glasses might be the death of me. But what a way to go.

He cocks his head to the side when he catches me gawking.

"Umm, this"—I wave a hand, gesturing to his face—"should be illegal."

"What?" The frown he aims at me is pure confusion.

"You. Looking like a buff Clark Kent in those glasses."

His lips twist in a smirk. "They're just glasses, Marshall. I don't like to sleep in my contacts."

"Pfft. They're just glasses, my ass. Those things are panty-droppers."

"The only panties I'm interested in dropping are yours. Now scoot over." He crawls under the covers next to me and places the panty-droppers on the nightstand.

Cuddled up to his strong, hard body once again, I let out a sigh. I drape a leg over his thigh and trace random patterns on his chest.

Within minutes, he's asleep. His breaths are deep and even, and the arm wrapped around me has gone slack. I continue my ministrations, though my eyelids grow heavy. I drift off nestled in the arms of the man who was once my nemesis but has become the star of my sweetest dreams.

When I blink awake on Sunday morning, Cordell and I are still wrapped up in each other, my body tucked into his side and his hand cupping my butt. I raise my head from his shoulder to get a look at his sleeping face and notice that we have company. Mouse sleeps soundly on Cordell's broad chest, curled in a tight gray coil. An *aww* slips from me before I can stop it. Dang, I wish my phone was within reach so I could capture the two of them like this.

Cordell pats around the nightstand until he finds his glasses, and once he's got them on, he rakes his fingers through Mouse's soft fur.

"I think he likes you," I whisper.

"I think I like *you*." With that, he plants a kiss on my temple. "Want me to run down to the coffee shop for provisions?"

"Ooh, please." Easy access to fresh gourmet coffee is a major perk of my apartment's location.

"Sorry, buddy," Cordell murmurs, gently lifting Mouse off his chest. With a scratch behind the cat's ear, he sets him in the warm spot he vacated. Then he scoots to the edge of the bed to put his boxers on. The glimpse of his delicious booty I get when he stands to pull them up makes my toes curl. Right then and there, I devise a plan to leave my own teeth marks on that bubble butt during our next naked session.

While he takes care of his bathroom business, I luxuriate in bed, sated and boneless. Mouse bumps my shoulder with his head, and his loud purrs fill the silence when I indulge him with ear scratches. When Cordell opens the bathroom door and leans against the frame, toothbrush in his mouth and wearing only his boxers, I revel in the moment.

A girl could get used to mornings like this.

He dresses, then leans over the bed to kiss me. When he pulls up straight again, he waggles his brows. "Will you still be naked when I get back?"

"Maybe," I tease.

He winks and starts for the door.

"Oh, get a chocolate croissant, please! And a muffin!"

"You got it," he calls over his shoulder.

To his utter disappointment, I'm dressed in a tank top and leggings when he returns from DejaBrew. We enjoy our morning coffee and baked goods at the bar while he tells me story after story about his niece and nephew and I crack him up with highlights from Glamma's long and colorful life.

After breakfast, we make out on the couch, and his warm hands feel me up under my shirt.

He pulls back, his lips kiss-swollen, and checks his watch. "I have to go, Marshall. I help my mom with her grocery shopping on Sundays."

I melt like icing on fresh-from-the-oven cupcakes. Of course he does.

"But tonight is Griff's debut with the Blues. Why don't you come over to watch the game? I'll grab dinner supplies while I'm at the store with Ma."

"That sounds perfect," I tell him. "I'll make dessert."

"What flavor?" he asks.

"I'll surprise you."

After a few more languid kisses, Cordell leaves Mouse and me alone in my apartment. I survey the quiet space and nod, determined. First, I grab the Savannah postcard that's been lingering in my stack of junk mail like a bad smell. Then I stomp to my closet and pull on the cord dangling from the ceiling. With the light shining in the small space so I can see what I'm doing, I pull down the shoebox that's been mocking me for years. In goes the Savannah postcard, joining ones from Pensacola and Charleston and Atlanta and Mobile and Athens. Years of bright, colorful locations and song lyrics written by a hand that no longer has a hold on me.

And hasn't for a long time. That hand might have once held my heart, but I'm ready to give it to a man who won't crush it, who will hold it with tender loving care and will never make me doubt my worth.

The bright September sunshine greets me when I step into the alley. And when I chuck that box of postcards into the nearest dumpster, the last of my already-crumbled walls are razed to the ground.

# CHAPTER NINETEEN

## MEL

Five uncomplicated, blissful days later, I'm in danger of fucking it all up.

If this were a story about my life, this chapter would start something like: *And on the fifth day, Mel Marshall spirals into sheer panic and ruins the best thing that's ever happened to her.*

The day started like every other this week: with Cordell and me tangled together in the bedsheets, peaceful and dreamy and warm. I spent the night at his place after we played a few intense rounds of strip War with a deck of cards I found in his annoyingly organized kitchen junk drawer. Seriously, instead of tossing in random things indiscriminately like a normal grown-up, he uses a plastic organizer to keep it all tidy. Like a psycho. I teased him relentlessly until he snatched the cards out of my hand and challenged me to a game.

This morning's shower turned into sexy time. Then he kissed me and sent me on my way so I could change before my first class at the studio. "See you this afternoon," he said, all gruff and satisfied, and I drove into Bennett with a huge grin on my face.

After my morning classes, I ran to the grocery to grab a box of tampons for my impending visit from Aunt Flo. To save time and avoid small talk, I cut through the stationery aisle to get to the health and beauty section. When familiar green and yellow boxes caught my eye, I doubled back to grab one. As I stood in the middle of the store, holding a box of crayons for a man I'm desperately in love with, I started to panic.

Who knew a small box of crayons could be so frightening?

Why they triggered a full-body meltdown is a mystery, but there I was, having one in the middle of aisle seven.

My lungs seized, making it impossible to pull in more than shallow breaths as I trudged my way to the checkout line. The girl at the counter frowned when I placed the lone box of crayons on the belt, but I managed to swipe my card and get out to my car before the real fear kicked in. I couldn't stop the deluge of tears that flooded my cheeks and I couldn't make my heart calm. Deep, cleansing breaths would have helped, but I was still struggling to get enough oxygen.

Things with Cordell are real. Like, *really* real. I've never felt this way about another man, not even Nick, and that has me shaken. What if he gets tired of me after a few weeks? What if I piss him off, and we can't come back from it? What if he pisses *me* off, and my first instinct is to run again? I haven't been in a relationship in a decade. What if I don't know how to do it? What if I can't be what he needs? What if this whole thing has been a pretty lie and I'm really not meant to have this kind of love?

Then, even more terrible thoughts assaulted me. What if something happens to him, something terrible like what happened to his father?

I made a mental note to ask Mom for the name of the best cardiologist in the state.

When my heart rate returned to an almost normal rate, I drove back to the studio, shaky hands at ten and two on the wheel, but the fear hasn't dissipated. It wasn't until I walked into the building that I realized I didn't even get the damn tampons.

Now, that ninety-six count box of rainbow sticks is hidden under the shelf behind the counter, and I'm frantically scrubbing the same spot on the countertop.

Glamma always says, "If you ever catch Melanie with a sponge or a broom, hunker down, because the end times are nigh!"

Right now, she just might be right.

I clean and organize and work through a pile of papers that need to be shredded until my four o'clock Flow class, but the whole time, all I can think about is how my body feels feverish and my hands won't quit shaking. Skipping lunch was a bad idea, but the grocery store freak-out left me feeling nauseous.

I'm about to stick the *Namaste Out Here Until I Return* sign in the window and go next door for an ill-advised caffeine fix when the little bell on the door jingles and a six-four football coach steps into the space.

"Wh-what are you doing here?"

It's three fifteen. School's just let out, but he usually stays on campus on game days. The Eagles have an away game tonight. It's in a town half an hour from Bennett, but those buses will probably be leaving soon.

He shoots me that easy, happy smile that usually makes my heart flutter. But today, the sensation is more of an uncomfortable tingle.

"Just wanted to see you before we head out." He leans across the counter for a quick kiss. I let him give me a peck, but when he pulls back, his brows crease. "What's wrong?"

"Who says something's wrong?" I ask as I focus back on the spotless countertop.

His big, warm hand covers mine to stop my frantic scrubbing. "Hey." His voice is gentle and low and full of concern. It makes me want to curl up in the fetal position. "Talk to me, please."

Full turtle Mel activated. No way do I want to confess to my epic meltdown, so I deflect with the first thing I can get my hands on.

"I got something for you." I slam the crayon box down on the counter with more force than I intend.

He blinks at me several times before he picks it up. "A ninety-six pack. They didn't come in boxes this big back in my coloring days." Deftly, he pops the cardboard lid open and removes a wax stick, then he holds it up next to my face. "Tickle me pink. That's the color of your hair." His voice is deep and husky now. "And your lips." The wink he sends my way makes me want to burrow into his pocket and force him to carry me with him always.

When I don't snark or flirt back, he returns the crayon to the box and sets it on the counter between us. "Why are you freaking out?"

"I'm not freaking out," I insist, but the high squeak in my voice makes a liar out of me.

He crosses his arms. "You are. And it's okay that you are. I just need you to tell me why so I can fix it."

Fix it? Of course he wants to fix it; that's who Cordell Watkins is. He's a lot like my brother in that way. But what if I *can't* be fixed?

I lick my lips and roll them together to buy some time. But with one look at his concerned, gorgeous face, I blurt the first thought that comes to me. "What are we even doing here, Watkins?"

He closes his eyes and sighs, clearly understanding the true meaning of my question. I'm not referring to what we're doing at this moment or even existentially.

"You want a clear definition of what this is." It's not a question. His dark eyes pierce me, like laser orbs ready to demolish my doubts and insecurities. "*This*," he emphasizes, "is a consensual relationship between two adults. It's a partnership. We're teammates, lovers, and friends. You are my *girlfriend*."

"We're in our thirties. Aren't we too old to use 'boyfriend' and 'girlfriend'?"

Yeah, I'm grasping for something—anything—to help me remain contrary. He's saying all the right things, but my heart isn't convinced. Not yet.

He snorts a laugh. "There's no age limit for relationship terms."

"But that's what you'll call me? To others? Your girlfriend?" I jut my chin.

"I'll call you whatever you want me to call you. But we're dating. Exclusively."

"What if I don't know how to be a girlfriend?" I fire back. I have very little experience, so it's a valid question.

He cups my shoulders and gives a reassuring squeeze. "I'd say you're doing an excellent job so far. You bought me a meaningful gift because you thought of me." He inclines his head toward the crayons. "And you're fulfilling the other girlfriend duties quite well, I assure you. On your knees in the shower this morning, for example. That was an A-plus girlfriend experience."

I blush like a sunset, but I appreciate his efforts to add levity to my mental spiral, even if it is of the R-rated variety.

He's humoring me while I'm being ridiculous and difficult. Even so, I can't stop myself. "But our names *rhyme*!" I whine. "Is that weird?"

"Who cares if our names rhyme?" He narrows his eyes and shakes his head, fired up. "Nope. No way are you using that dumb excuse to deny what this is, Marshall. I will freaking change my name if it bothers you that much."

His brow is furrowed and his muscles are tight. There isn't an ounce of humor in his expression now. He's serious. He would actually change his damn name if I asked him to. Just like that, the panic and worry from this morning melt away like a popsicle on a hot Georgia sidewalk.

My heart is putty in this man's hands, and he has the power to mold it any way he sees fit. I already trust him with it. Now I simply have to trust myself with his. And trust that we have what it takes to go the distance.

I bite the inside of my cheek to stanch my brimming tears. Cordell sweeps his hands into my hair and cradles my head. When a lone tear escapes, he swipes it away with a thumb.

"Mel. Sweetheart. We're *together*." His emphasis on that last word steals my breath and leaves no room for doubt. "I want all of it—baking cupcakes and going fishing and downward dog and family pool days. Arguing as foreplay." That particular item on his list is accompanied by a smirk. "I want you in the stands at our games and in my bed every night. Or me in yours."

A laugh bubbles up from my chest. My knees shake with nerves, but I do it anyway. I tilt my chin higher, swallow past the lump in my throat and give him my truth. "I love you."

His lips part and his eyes go wide. "You—" he breathes.

"Yep. Love you. Even though our names rhyme."

My heart pounds painfully when he straightens and doesn't speak right away. My skin grows hot, like I'm burning from the inside. *Oh, God.* Does he not feel the same way? Is it too late to play it off as a joke? *Ha, ha. Just wanted to make you sweat! There's no way I could be in love with the man I once flung potato salad at.*

Cordell removes his cell from his back pocket and taps out a text message.

"What are you doing?" I place my tightly clenched fists on my hips to keep from throat punching him. I confess that I love him, and not only does he not *say* anything, but he has the gall to keep me hanging while he texts a friend?

"Oh," he says, head down as he types. "Letting Clay know

that I'm going to be a few minutes late for the bus because I want to tell the woman I'm crazy about that I'm undeniably, catastrophically in love with her, and I need a little extra time to make it memorable."

I scoff. "You—wait. What?"

He lifts a brow. "Catch up, Marshall."

"Stop bossing me, Watkins." My grin is so wide my cheeks hurt.

"Come here." He takes my hand and leads me around the counter and out the door, right into the middle of Central Street, which is surprisingly empty for a Friday afternoon.

"What's happening?" I ask when he faces me.

"This place." He takes a deep breath and glances around. "It's always felt like home to me. But I never knew home could be a person, too. Not until you."

I don't even try to stop the tears flowing like the Flint River down my face.

Cordell cups my cheeks, his expression so, so soft. "I love you, Melanie Jane Marshall. I know you don't like people to call you Melanie—"

"I'll allow it," I say, laughing through my tears.

"Good." He smiles, bright and happy and beautiful. "I wanted to use your whole name the first time I said it. Because I love *all* of you."

"And I love you. So, so much. Kiss me like you mean it, Coach."

"Now who's being bossy?" He studies me as he wipes away my tears. Then his arms are around me and he lifts me off the ground, and when our lips touch, it's a moment I'll never forget.

A perfect and memorable one.

We kiss in the middle of Central. The world around us disappears. That is, until an obnoxious series of honks breaks the spell.

When we pull apart, Ms. Daisy is cackling, her gray head

poking out the window of the yellow Bronco she uses to deliver flowers. "Ha! I *knew* it! I knew you two would figure it out!" She wolf-whistles loud enough to be heard in Montezuma and honks obnoxiously as she steers around us. The sound still rings in the air well after she turns the corner onto a side street.

"And now the whole town will know, too," I say with an eye roll.

"Is that so bad?" He tilts his head, a wrinkle forming between his brows.

I smooth it with a finger. "Nope. Not at all."

He grins and lowers me to my feet. "There's one more thing I want to do before I have to catch the bus. Grab your keys and meet me at the back door."

My eyes widen. "Um, sir, I don't think we have time for *that...*"

He huffs and gives me a flat look. "Keys, Marshall. Do it." And with that, he smacks my ass and strides to the corner.

We meet up in the alley and hurry up the stairs. Once I get the door open, Cordell marches into the kitchen and wrenches the junk drawer open. He pulls out the notebook where we've documented each of our matchmaking attempts. Pages rustle, and then he flips it around.

I arch a brow. "Still tied. Zero-zero."

"Hmm." He takes a pen and draws a line from left to right under the last set of zeros. "Only time in my life I'll ever be happy with a tie."

Emma's sweet cries float on the air all the way out to the front porch. When I knock twice, Chipper's bark and Luke's voice hollering "Hannah! Door!" add to the cacophony.

Hannah opens the door, hair disheveled, and grins. "Welcome to the madness."

Inside, Tessa's standing by the couch, bouncing a squalling Emma in her arms. She smiles when she sees me but doesn't pause her efforts. Chipper, the Shipleys' boxer, trots up to me wagging his whole backside, with what looks like a burp cloth in his mouth.

"No, Chip." Hannah extracts the cloth from his mouth and replaces it with a stuffed donut squeak toy.

"Hey, Mel," Luke calls out as he descends the stairs carrying a loaded laundry basket.

When he passes us on his way to the laundry room, Hannah tosses the cloth onto the pile.

"Banana, help Mel with that stuff," he says over his shoulder before he disappears down the short hallway behind the kitchen.

Hannah is wandering toward the kitchen with the foil-wrapped loaf of French bread and the bagged salad when Luke reappears and takes the heavy pan from me.

"God, this smells good," he says, holding it up and inhaling deeply.

"Frannie said to pop it in the oven at three-fifty for half an hour."

"Bless her," Tessa says, still bouncing.

"I bet I've gained a solid fifteen pounds since this meal train started." He preheats the oven and slides the pan inside, then approaches his wife. "Let me try, baby."

Tessa passes a red-faced Emma to her father, frazzled. "She nursed not too long ago. Maybe she's hungry again?" She worries her lip and tucks back the hairs that have escaped her ponytail.

Luke carefully but expertly maneuvers his daughter so that her tiny arms are tucked against her chest and resting in his big palm. His other hand is under her bottom so her legs are hanging free. As soon as he starts softly bobbing her up and down in this position, she quiets.

"Whoa, Shipley. You're like the baby whisperer," I tease, though I can't hide the awe in my tone.

He gives me a good-natured eye roll. "Nah. A nurse showed me this trick when Banana was a baby. First time I've had to use it on this little pumpkin, though. She's been happy as a clam this week." Tipping his head low, he kisses the back of Emma's dark hair, then carries on with the calming rise-and-fall motion.

"Got an interesting text a little while ago," he says to me. "My best friend couldn't hold back from spilling the beans about how he'd finally gotten a certain yoga instructor to use the l-word."

"Eek!" Tessa, who'd just slumped back against the couch, pops up and clasps her hands against her chest. "I want to know everything. All the things."

Luke beams at his wife's reaction. "He said it back, by the way."

Tessa is squealing again when Hannah bounds back into the living room with Chipper. "What's happening?" she asks with one finger holding her place in a chapter book.

"Your father is a bigger gossip than Ms. Daisy. That's what's happening." I cross my arms and try to look put out, but my cheeks are warm, and I can't wipe the big goofy smile off my face.

"Hey," Luke says, suddenly serious but still bouncing. "I'm happy for y'all. He's the best guy I know, and he deserves to be happy. You'll keep him on his toes, that's for sure."

"She sure will," Tessa declares.

"Y'all have come a long way from that food fight in my parents' kitchen," he jokes.

Tessa snorts. "That was their version of flirting, handsome." She settles back into the cushions with a sigh. "A frenemies-to-lovers romance. How perfect."

I hold my arms out to Luke and make grabby hands, ready to move on from the teasing and get my Emma snuggles in.

Luke transfers a sleeping Emma into my arms, then joins his wife on the couch.

"Can you stay for dinner?" Tessa asks around a yawn.

I shake my head. Frannie's lasagna is the bomb, but I've got other plans. "No. I'm picking Ms. Rhonda up for the game."

"What's a frenemy?" Hannah drops to the cushion beside Luke and snuggles in close when he tucks his arm around her. "Is that like a friend who's sometimes an enemy? 'Cause I definitely have one of those." She cuts her eyes up to her father, but he's resting his head on Tessa's, eyelids heavy like he's minutes from conking out.

"Mm-hmm," Tessa hums, her eyes droopy, too.

I sway, keeping Emma settled, as I wander to the wall of windows that looks out over the back porch and yard. "You'll be running out there before we know it, sweet girl," I whisper to her. I press my nose to her hair and inhale her delicious baby scent. "I can't get over all this hair, Emma Rose."

She puckers her tiny rosebud lips, her mother's lips, in response, and I place a soft kiss on her forehead.

"You're going to have an amazing life, you know that?"

My phone buzzes in the back pocket of my jeans. I swipe it open with one hand and smile at the text.

COACH MCHOTSTUFF

Ma said she'd be ready to go at six thirty.

COACH MCHOTSTUFF

I love you.

COACH MCHOTSTUFF

And your face is my favorite face.

I type a quick one-handed reply.

Tucking the device back into my pocket, I survey the yard, picturing all the future barbeques and birthday parties and sprinkler days and family gatherings. Not so long ago, I was certain that a life full of backyard cartwheels and skinned knees and potty training wasn't in the cards for me. But as I stand here holding this precious new life, I let myself imagine it: Cordell. Me. A couple of tawny-skinned, curly-haired giggle boxes who are the perfect combination of their father's calmness and their mother's sass. I don't care which one of us they favor more; all I know is that our kids would be happy and loved.

They'd have the best father, after all.

I want that life with all my heart, and for the first time, I let myself hope for it. And I do it with abandon.

I turn back to the living room, tiny baby nestled close to my chest and tears in my eyes, and smile at my friends. They're nothing but a pile of exhausted happiness, all three asleep on the couch.

Letting the new parents and big sister sleep, I soak in the quiet minutes with Emma. When the oven timer dings, I hug the Shipleys goodbye and head back to Bennett.

Ready for whatever comes next, with my man by my side. Turns out I found my safe place to land, after all.

# CHAPTER TWENTY

CORDELL

September melts into October, which passes by in a blur of colors: goldenrod leaves, orange pumpkins, emerald turf, red pom-poms, rose-gold tresses that fan across my pillow. Now that Emma has arrived, the tickle me pink is no more. Mel's hair is almost back to its natural color—the dishwater blond it was the night we met at Bottoms Up—but with subtle rosy strands blended throughout. I couldn't care less what color her hair is, but this shade fits her best. It's soft with a bit of an edge, just like the woman I love.

We're deep into fall and deep into each other, and I'm deeply happy. We've spent lots of weekend time with our families who, thankfully, though unsurprisingly, get along like peas and carrots. When Mel and I are alone, no one exists but the two of us. It doesn't matter what we're doing—baking cupcakes, fishing in the creek on my property, rewatching *Gilmore Girls*, or making love or even arguing. When we're together, all is right in my world.

Football has been phenomenal, too. The Eagles are on track to end the regular season undefeated, and a win tonight will give us home field advantage for the playoffs. We've already faced the biggest competition on our schedule, so it's almost a given that we'll host some tough teams here in Bennett as the playoffs get underway.

My life's firing on all cylinders: Mel and I are building a solid, passionate relationship. The team is focused and primed for a strong playoff run. Ma is healthy and living her best life.

Yet a sheer jolt, like a shot of pure adrenaline, blasts through my body every now and then. It's hit me a few times since Mel and I declared our love for each other. Each time, it's sudden and unexpected, and I've yet to figure out what triggers it.

I shake off the thought as I stroll to the parking lot outside the stadium, choosing instead to focus on the scents of grilled meat and popcorn and cotton candy that float on the breeze. The Taco Tuesdays food truck is parked on the edge of the lot next to the football booster tent, where Frannie and several other football parents are selling snacks and drinks. Tiny superheroes and princesses and monsters dart from car to car, holding out plastic pumpkins or canvas bags for fun-size chocolate bars and bags of Skittles. All the vehicles that line the east side of the lot have trunks open or tailgates down or rear doors lifted.

The Bennett Tailgate Trunk or Treat is in full swing.

Our hometown lives for Halloween, but usually, it's the downtown area that's swarmed with kids and parents in costumes. Only for their beloved Eagles football would these folks consider altering tradition.

This town's dedication and attention to detail are impressive. The costumes are as inventive as ever, and the vehicle decorations are beyond elaborate. One looks like the open mouth of a monster. Several are decked out with orange, purple, and black balloon arches. One even has an underwater theme, complete with streamer jellyfish and a pool noodle coral reef.

The Shipleys are stationed at the back of Luke's truck, which is decked out in a safari theme. The tailgate is draped with a tiger-print blanket, and several of Ms. Marj's potted ferns decorate the truck bed, along with blow-up monkeys and several of Hannah's stuffed animals. All four Shipley adults are dressed in khaki safari gear, complete with hats and prop binoculars. In Tessa's arms, a baby giraffe sleeps peacefully, despite the noise and chaos around her.

"Boys ready for tonight, Coach?" Mr. Tom asks when I reach them.

"Yes, sir" is all I give him.

They know my stance. I never reveal too much about our players or our games. Anything can happen out on the field, so I keep my answers vague.

Plus, a little superstition can be a coach's, or player's, best friend.

"Where's Banana?" I ask.

Luke bends to toss a package of animal crackers into a cowboy's open sack. "With Mel. They're waiting in the Taco Tuesdays line."

"They've been gone a while," Ms. Marj pipes up.

I nod. The line was snaked through the lot and down to the back of the visitor's side bleachers when I walked through earlier, but Mel wanted her costume to be a surprise, so I didn't spot either of them in line.

"I'll go check on 'em." Mr. Tom pushes his safari hat back a little. "They might need help carrying stuff, too."

Ma wanders up, arm in arm with Ms. Rita, wearing a witch hat. But that's the extent of her costume. Rather than witchy wears, she's donned the same Eagles T-shirt she's worn to every game since I became head coach.

Sometimes, superstition is a football mom's best friend, too.

Ms. Rita's costumes are always historical in nature, and this year she's decked out as a suffragette; a *Votes for Women* sash drapes across her body, and her long gray hair's tucked up in a wide-brimmed hat.

"Dell, what are you doing out here?" Ma only glances my way when she asks. She's too busy taking a sleeping Emma from her mother's arms. Willing cuddlers are never in short supply.

I check my watch. Kickoff is in an hour, so I do need to head back to the field house to finish last-minute prep, but I'm dying to see Mel's costume before the game.

"He's waiting for me to put a little pep in his step." Like I summoned her with my thoughts, Mel appears, with Hannah and Mr. Tom in tow. She's got a cardboard tray full of street tacos in both hands and a red and white pom-pom tucked under each arm.

She's dressed as a zombie cheerleader.

A slow grin spreads on my face as I check her out. It looks like she managed to get her hands on an old Eagles cheer uniform. It's identical to the ones the girls wore when I played for the Eagles. She's aged it, with slashes and cuts on the skirt and top. Her black tights are shredded, like a wild animal had a field day with them. Her hair is pulled up in two high pigtails, red bows adorning each one, and she's done her makeup to look like she's the living dead, pale foundation and dark smudges under each eye.

The best part of her costume? The component that heats my blood? It's what she's wearing over the cheer top.

*My* high school letterman jacket.

She must've asked Ma for it.

It nearly swallows her. She's rolled up the sleeves several times, but dang, the sight of her wearing my jacket, with 84 stitched on the arm, does something to me.

Makes me proud and horny at the same time. Can't say I've ever experienced that combo before, but it's heady.

Mel sets the tray of tacos on the tailgate and steps over to me while the rest of the crew doles out the food and drinks.

"You like it?" The way she tilts her head is all shy, like there's even the slightest possibility I'll say no.

"I love it," I growl, my lips brushing the shell of her ear. "I want you to wear this later." I pinch the white leather sleeve of the jacket. "Only. This."

Her cheeks turn rosy under the pale makeup as she bats her lashes up at me. "You got it, Coach." She rises on her tiptoes and plants a quick kiss on my lips. "Now go give 'em hell."

"Just one thing before I go." I twist her upper body so that I can get a glimpse of her back. The name Watkins has never looked so good. The sight of it emblazoned across her back has me weak in the knees.

Think I'd like to see my last name attached to her in a more permanent way.

I give her a wink and dole out goodbyes to the rest of our crew, then head back to make final preparations for the game.

Clay and I tag team the final pep talk, and then it's time. We run onto the field as the marching band plays the Eagles' fight song and burst through the giant paper sign the cheerleaders hold up. The boys get a kick out of seeing their families and friends decked out in Halloween costumes in the stands. As always, I find my people first thing. They're even easier to spot than usual because of the way Hannah's lion mane headpiece bobs up and down as she bounces in excitement. Ms. Marj is absent, probably on Emma duty for the night, but the rest of my favorites cheer wildly as we start the penultimate game of our season.

We get off to a slow start and end the first quarter with only three points on the board. But our defense holds the other team to only two field goals by the half, and the break gives us time to make some key changes. On the opening drive of the third, Grady puts up a beautiful pass on third down that gets us in the red zone. We run in a touchdown on the next play.

By the two-minute warning in the fourth, we've got a comfortable ten-point lead, and the crowd's chant of "Go Eagles, go!" is electric. The Panthers get a late penalty on third down that pushes them back well out of field goal range and forces them to punt. From there, all we have to do is run out the clock to secure the win.

After a quick victory speech and a reminder to be safe and smart tonight, I release the team. Once the boys are showered and headed out, Eric, Clay, and I lock up and follow them.

On the short drive from campus to Mel's downtown apartment, another pang of worry attacks me, deep in my gut. I had my yearly physical last month, plus I have annual heart checks with a cardiologist due to my family history, so it's safe to say the episodes aren't physical. No, these twinges that make me suck in deep breaths like I had a hard hit on the field are mental.

All facets of my life are working in perfect harmony. Thus, my brain must be preparing my body for the other shoe to drop. Because no way will the universe let me have all this sweetness without sending some sour to counterbalance it.

Of all the ways my life could go sideways, football is the only area I'd be willing to sacrifice. It would hurt like hell, but my mom's health and my relationship with Mel are far too precious to me.

I shake off the what-ifs and knock on the door. And when Mel opens it, fresh-faced and wearing nothing but my letterman jacket and a saucy smile, everything else fades away.

~

"I'm sorry your daughter and her family couldn't join us, Rhonda." Wearing a sympathetic smile, Mel's mom places a huge bowl of mashed potatoes on the table. "But Thanksgiving on the beach has got to be a special treat."

"Mashed toes!" one of the twins shouts out from his booster seat.

I still have a hard time telling Owen and Ollie apart, but I get it right over half the time, so...progress. Mel squeezes my thigh under the table in an attempt to not laugh at the little boy's outburst.

"I hate it, too. It's Kelly's parents' turn for Thanksgiving, but that means that *we* get Christmas, so I'll take that as a win." My mom's expression is bright as she passes the basket of dinner rolls to Mel's father.

Greg takes it from her and adds two to his plate before he turns to me. "Y'all ready for tomorrow?"

"Yes, sir. Our practices have been productive this week, the kids out of school and all."

Tomorrow night, the Bennett Eagles face the Thomson Bulldogs in the quarterfinal round of the state playoffs. It's the furthest we've ever advanced.

In the history of Bennett High School.

No pressure, right?

"Thomson's defense is elite," Mark adds.

Mel shoots her brother a scowl, and he busies himself by serving one of his sons a spoonful of potatoes.

Greg nods. "That's why they're the reigning two-A champions. But our boys can hold their own." Though his words are meant to be reassuring, they make my stomach knot with nerves.

"Dad, maybe less football talk at dinner, okay?" Mel suggests.

Greg rubs the back of his neck and gives me a sheepish smile. "Sure thing, honey."

"Great. Now someone pass me the mashed toes. I can't have Thanksgiving without them."

Both Owen and Ollie cackle at their Mel-Mel, and the rest of us dig into the feast.

Through dinner, my phone buzzes in my back pocket. Texts from Clay, I'm sure. His nerves manifest in the form of unnecessary reminder messages he'll send at all hours of the day and night. This started two weeks ago after we breezed through the first round. That was when we entered what we're affectionately calling no-man's-land since no team in Bennett's history has ever made it past the first round.

"Clay?" Mel whispers when that telltale buzz starts up again.

I nod and shove a bite of dressing into my mouth. I'll deal with him later.

"Melanie, I need you to bring this hunk of yours around more. Stop keeping him all to yourself." Mel's eighty-two-year-old grandmother playfully squeezes my bicep. When she eases up, she keeps her hand tucked in the crook of my arm and shoots me a wink.

"Mom. Behave." Greg's words are a reprimand, but his tone is full of nothing but fondness.

Glamma angles her head so close it's practically resting on my shoulder. "Oh. pooh. These people never let an old woman have any fun. I ain't gettin' any younger. But I am lettin' them throw me a big birthday bash next month. Tell me *you'll* be there, Coach."

"Glam, stop flirting with my man," Mel scolds with a laugh.

That term—my man—makes me puff out my chest. Just a little.

"I wouldn't miss it," I tell Glamma. She wags her head from side to side and returns to her dinner.

We spend the rest of dinner laughing at the twins and discussing anything but football. When it's time for dessert, Mel places her apple pie cupcakes next to my mom's pecan pie, and I silently hope that every Thanksgiving from here on out will be like this one. Delicious food, family, laughter, love.

Everyone's stuffed, but no one forgoes either dessert.

"Glad I wore my stretchy pants." Beth leans back in her chair with a moan.

"When you're my age, all your pants are stretchy," Glamma retorts. "There are perks to getting old, my loves."

While several conversations start up around the table, Mel perches sideways on my lap with her dessert plate in hand, giving us a quiet moment alone.

"Did you have a good Thanksgiving, Coach?" The way her tongue darts out to catch a glob of pecan pie that's in danger of falling from her fork has me sucking in a breath. If I'm not careful, she'll feel exactly what that move does to me.

I wrap a hand around her thigh, right above her knee, and tug her closer. "The best."

"Mmm, you might change your mind when you get your ass kicked in soccer here in a few."

"Soccer?" I quirk a brow. "No one said anything about soccer."

"Marshall family tradition. After dessert, it's backyard soccer. Nets and everything."

"Oh," Lisa chimes in, "these Marshalls are very serious about their Thanksgiving soccer." She grabs one twin's empty plate, then the other, and stacks them on top of hers. "And Mark and Mel refuse to be on separate teams, so you're stuck with me."

"You can't break up the dream team," Mark scoffs. "We win every year."

"Until this one." There's no stopping my challenge. What can I say? I'm competitive.

The table breaks out into a round of *oohs* and whistles.

"A bold claim, Coach." Mel lifts her chin, and with a glint in her eye, she stands from my lap and helps her mom and Lisa clear the table.

Trash talking ensues and gets more heated by the second until finally Greg holds up both hands to referee.

"Let's save it for the game," he says. "While y'all clean up in here, Cordell and I can set up the nets. We'll meet out back and rock-paper-scissors for teams."

Mark opens his mouth to protest, but Greg cuts him off.

"We know. You and Mel are a package deal."

I follow Greg toward a shed at the edge of the backyard, certain that he wants to have "the talk."

That's confirmed when he hands me the first net and pauses in front of me, hands on his hips. "So, you and my daughter..."

When he doesn't continue, I clear my throat and stand a little straighter. "Yes, sir?"

"You probably know you're the first man she's brought home since Nick."

"I do."

He turns and moves a few lawn chairs out of the way. When he's got the second net in hand, he looks me square in the eye. "It's really good to see her happy again, Cordell. *You* make her happy."

A rush of air escapes my lungs. Though I know he's right, it's daunting to hold such a sacred gift as her happiness in my hands. "I'm in love with your daughter, sir."

He presses his lips together and searches my face for a long moment. Finally, he nods. "I'm rooting for you two. Mel's a modern woman; she can certainly love who she wants to love without her old man's blessing, but you have it, nonetheless."

My throat thickens. "Thank you, sir. That means a lot."

I start for the yellowed grass on the far side of the pool area, but Greg stops me. "Oh, one more thing. I love my daughter more than life, but...well, she's her own person. I'll never forget the day she came home from her first day of fifth grade and declared that she'd no longer go by Melanie, that from then on, she expected us to call her Mel." He smiles and shakes his head at the memory. "She's five-foot-one, but her attitude is six-one most days. Don't let that scare you away."

I bark a laugh at the accuracy of his description. "I can handle Mel and all six feet of her sass."

Greg's face lights up with a smile that matches his daughter's. "Good man." He extends his hand, and we shake, a gentleman's agreement.

I keep my grip firm, hoping to convey to him that he'll never have to worry about his daughter with me.

Owen and Ollie's laughter draws us back to the patio, where Glamma is tapping her hot toddy to Ma's glass of wine, and the rest of the Marshall family is arguing over teams. For the next couple of hours, I put aside the pressure and nerves that have assaulted me all week and enjoy the moment.

And later that night, alone at last, Mel distracts me in a wholly different way.

Black Friday starts crisp and clear, without a cloud in the sky. I drop Mel at her apartment before I head to the school. Clay, Eric, and I decided to start this day like we would any other game day, so we meet in the boys' gym a little after eight and run through our game plan and playbook for what feels like the hundredth time. Both men join me in the weight room for a few quick reps, and then I change into my running gear and head for the track. I need a few miles to clear my mind.

The steady rhythm of my feet pounding the rubber soothes my nerves a bit. Talking to Dad in my head for a good portion of the run does even more good.

Frannie and Eric's girlfriend stop by at lunchtime with

sandwiches, but I only get a couple bites down before my stomach flutters in warning. I haven't been this keyed up for a game since my first as head coach. And there's a *lot* more riding on this one.

The kids drift in after lunch, and we put them through a modified workout before we go over key reminders. We do our best to keep them calm with our "business as usual" plan, but it only makes me restless.

By late afternoon, I'm about to come out of my skin, so I pop my head into Clay's office. "Hey, I'm going to run by Mel's real quick."

He does a double take, then checks his watch. He frowns, like he wants to question my decision, but he won't. "Boosters have dinner set up in the gym. They'll start serving at four thirty."

"I'm not hungry."

That frown deepens. "I've never seen you turn down food, Coach."

I nod at the floor a few times and sigh. "I'll be fine. I'll only be gone a few minutes."

What I don't tell him is that I *need* her. I need to see her and hear her voice and run my fingers through her hair and hold her close.

A few months ago, I couldn't have imagined seeking Mel Marshall as a source of comfort and calm.

But here we are.

Clay opens his mouth, probably to give me another reason to stay put, but I tap his doorframe twice and stride out of the building.

The cool November air is refreshing, so I opt to walk. Her building is only a few blocks, and I have time, so I zip my pullover all the way to the top and trek downtown.

Downtown Bennett looks like an Eagles pep rally. Red and white balloons, banners, and streamers are strung on anything upright. Life size cut-outs of Aquilo, the school mascot, peek out of storefronts along Central Street. Gordo's even hung a tarp over the Fuzzy's sign that reads *The Nest*. The streets are crowded due to the after-holiday sales. Every person I pass wears an Eagles T-shirt, jersey, or jacket, and every shop window in town sports a red poster with the word *Believe* in white block letters.

I see him when I turn the corner. He's standing in front of Mel's studio, looking up at the sign above the door, twirling a key ring on his finger.

Mel's ex-husband. Nick Hayes.

I'd know him anywhere. I googled the heck out of the Low Bars after I found out about him. About what he did to her. There were plenty of images online: professional shots of the band in front of an abandoned house or next to graffiti-covered train cars or under a sprawling oak tree. Then there were the amateur shots, ones taken by fans in dark clubs with neon spot-lights illuminating them mid-song. I even perused the band's Instagram page, making sure to pay special attention to the list of upcoming shows they pinned as a top post.

There were no venues listed close to here.

As he pulls the studio door open, a chill spreads from my head to my toes, like I've been drenched in a Gatorade bath.

This is when the other shoe drops.

Mel doesn't have classes today—Black Friday is practically a holiday—but she had some bills and paperwork to catch up on. I imagine her, behind the counter, head down and focused on her business, when that little bell trills. She'll lift her head at the sound and come face to face with the man who not only cheated on her but also wrecked her trust in men and relation-ships for over ten years.

Of their own volition, my feet are moving. I pause outside the coffee shop next door so I can peek into the studio and assess the situation. Will I catch them in an embrace? God, the thought makes me want to hurl up the pathetic excuse for a lunch I consumed. But no, Mel wouldn't do that to me. To us.

*Right?*

Even through the window, Mel's anger rolls off her body in waves. She's wearing a workout tank under an unzipped jacket. The skin above her breasts is a mottled pink that matches the hue of her cheeks. Those striking hazel eyes narrow at the man in front of her and then flash with rage when he places his hand on the counter between them. He's trying to placate her, and she's having none of it.

For his part, Nick appears unbothered. He's at ease in a T-shirt and jeans. His golden-brown hair is pulled into a messy knot at the back of his head, and a day or two of scruff covers his jaw.

They aren't shouting. Mel can handle herself. Like her dad said, she's her own woman. So I hold back. But when Nick reaches across the counter and grabs her upper arm, I couldn't stop my body from moving in their direction even if I tried.

I swing the door open a little too forcefully, causing the bell above to jingle violently.

Both heads swivel.

"Wh-what are you doing here?"

"Take your hand off her," I tell Nick. I'm not a violent man, but the second he made physical contact, my pulse pounded in my ears and adrenaline coursed through my veins. I won't hesitate to knock this joker on his ass if I need to.

Nick releases Mel's arm more slowly than I'd like, so I take a step closer.

"Cordell. I'm handling it."

I blink at her. She can. Absolutely. But she shouldn't have to. Not on her own. And now that he's put his hands on her, I'm not leaving until he does.

Nick runs his tongue over his teeth. "Who's this, Melly?"

I'd give my car to knock that cocky smile off his face.

She huffs a breath. "This is Cordell."

When she doesn't follow up with *my boyfriend* or *the man I'm seeing* or *the idiot I sleep with every night*, my chest tightens.

She sweeps a hand toward Nick. "And this is my asshat ex-husband, Nick—a man-child with a man-bun."

"Aw, you always liked my hair long, Melly. I grew it out just for you."

The familiarity he's using with her makes the blood simmering in my veins boil.

For her part, she's not charmed by it. Arms crossed, she stares me down. "You need to go, Coach." She taps her phone, likely to check the time, and her eyes widen. "Now."

Maybe she's concerned about me getting back for pregame routines, but the command feels more like a dismissal.

Why the hell isn't she taking advantage of my presence and demanding that her ex leave? Because she wants him here? Did she arrange to meet him? At a time she expected me to be occupied?

The list of negative thoughts grows and spirals through my mind until I'm lightheaded.

Or maybe it's the lack of food to fuel my body.

"Coach, huh?" Nick smirks. Then, like a dim light bulb has been illuminated in a dark cave, his eyes round. "Wait a second...Cordell. You're that football guy Melly was obsessed with back in the day."

"For the love, stop calling me Melly. And he's the head coach who's going to be in serious shit if he doesn't get his ass back to campus." The corners of her lips dip in a frown.

"I'm not going anywhere until *he* leaves, Marshall." I point at Nick and widen my stance.

The idiot gives Mel an incredulous look, but he doesn't leave. In fact, he drops an elbow to the counter and crosses one ankle over the other. Making himself at home.

"Ugh. I've had it with the machismo. You both need to go."

"Mel—" I start.

"No." Her tone is sharp, but her eyes soften when they lock with mine. "I'm fine here. I promise. I don't need you to fight all my battles for me. Go to the game. I'll see you there."

My heart sinks, and I deflate. There's nothing left to say, I suppose. She doesn't want me here. I want to forcibly remove him from his spot—in this room and in her life—but she has to do it herself.

This is how I show up for her today. I show her that I can step back and let her fight the good fight alone, when she needs to.

I hang my head for another moment, but when I look back at the woman I love and she mouths *go*, I do as she wishes, even though it kills me. Swallowing my frustration, I spin on my heel and pull in a deep breath through my nose, working to mentally prepare myself to coach this game.

I make it back to the school in time to run through our last-minute prep and get the boys fired up. Clay keeps shooting nervous glances my way, but I do my best to tune out all distractions.

"Coach?" He sidles up beside me minutes before the announcer is set to call the team onto the field.

"I'm okay." I turn and drop a hand to his shoulder. "I just need a minute."

Without a word, he nods and joins the rest of the team huddled inside the doors of the field house.

For the third time in my football career, I lock myself in a bathroom and throw up from nerves. After a quick rinse and a swish of mouthwash, I join the team, and we take the field, the frenzy of the crowd pulsing through the night air.

When we reach our sideline, I do my customary sweep of the stands. I find Ma first, and when we lock eyes, she grins and yells louder. Then I move up a row to the Shipleys, minus baby Emma and Tessa. Hannah, standing on the stands between her nana and her father, has red *B*s on both cheeks, and she's shaking a red and white pom-pom stick so frantically every other movement causes her to whip one of the people flanking her in the face. My search continues, moving back to the row that Ma sits on. I skim over Greg and Beth Marshall, but their daughter is not beside them. She's not next to Luke in Tessa's spot either. I give my best friend a questioning look, one that translates to "where is she?" His response is an apologetic shrug.

She's not here. The biggest game of my coaching career, and my girlfriend is not here.

My brain immediately goes to a place I shouldn't let it. Questions I shouldn't entertain plague me. Is she still with him? Did he manage to worm his way back into her good graces?

With a shake of my head, I tune it all out. Every thought but the ones revolving around the field in front of me, the players who've fought hard to get here, and the coaches who've worked tirelessly to prepare for tonight.

The Bulldogs won the toss and defer, so our offense is up first. And man has their defense come to play. Our O line struggles to protect Grady, and he's sacked on third down. Good field position after the punt and a lucky chip shot down the sideline mean the Bulldogs are up by seven within the first five minutes of play.

Our night doesn't improve from there. The hype of this big game has rattled some of the boys. No matter how diligent we were about keeping things "normal," nerves lead to stupid mistakes and dropped catches and penalties we rarely made during the regular season. At halftime, we're lucky we're only down by ten points.

As I stand in the locker room and take in the sea of defeated faces, I decide against a rousing pep talk or making crash-course game plan corrections. Instead, I look Cole

Reeves in the eye. "Who or what are you playing this game for, Cole?"

He lifts his head. "Coach?"

"Why do you play football? And I don't mean this specific game tonight. I mean this *game*."

His eyes dart to Clay, who's standing by the door. "For my father, Coach. He loves this game, and he taught me to love it, too."

I nod a few times and then step farther into the room. "What about you, Jones? Why do you play this game?"

Darius Jones: heck of a talent, terrible attitude. He's given Clay hell all season. But he looks around at his teammates and raises his chin. "Football keeps me alive. Keeps me out of trouble. If I didn't have it, I'd end up like my brother—serving time for bad decisions with the wrong people."

Clay and I lock eyes across the room.

We continue until every player speaks. I'm humbled by every single answer. They have little to do with winning and glory, and everything to do with family and love. I say a silent thanks to my dad for strapping those pads on me and driving me to practice all those years ago.

When it's just about time to return to the field for the second half, I take over again. "I want you to go out there and play this next half for the reasons you just mentioned. I want you to go out there and show this town how much you love this game. Win or lose, play with heart, boys."

In the end, the Bennett Eagles succumb to the Thomson Bulldogs, thirty-five to twenty-seven, but our boys sure left it all out on the field. They played the second half for the love of this game and this town, and we hold our heads high as we congratulate the Bulldogs on their victory.

When our act of good sportsmanship has been fulfilled, the field is swarmed by both Eagles and Bulldogs fans, members of the media, marching bands, and cheer teams. Disoriented by the events of the day, I drift through the chaos, lost until Clay tugs on my shoulder.

He gives me a hearty hug, and chokes out, "Hell of a season, Coach."

I grasp the back of his ball cap and keep him close. "Wouldn't want to do it with anyone else. We'll get 'em next year."

"You got it."

While he melts into the crowd to find his family, I stand alone, surrounded by a sea of people. A few players stop to give hugs, and our principal pats me on the back and congratulates me on the season.

Emotional and drained and ready to call it a night, I move through the crowd toward the end zone near the field house. And like the sun breaking through the clouds on a dreary day, the crowd parts, and she's there.

Mel Marshall stands in the end zone, waiting for me. Wearing ripped jeans and a gray T-shirt that says *Dibs on the coach* in bold red letters.

She's so perfect, it's hard to breathe. My eyes brim with tears, and her smile wobbles as we regard each other. And then she runs. Not away from me, but *to* me.

I catch her in my arms and hug her so tight I'm afraid I might crack her ribs.

"I'm so sorry, Coach," she says into my ear, her warm breath on my skin. "But I'm so fucking proud of you, too."

She wraps her legs around me and lets me hold her, lets the press of her body to mine communicate all the words we can't say right now. The crowd, the loss, the disappointment all fade to nothing when she's in my arms.

I pull back so I can see her beautiful face. "When I looked in the stands—"

"I know, Luke told me. I'm so sorry I was late. I only missed the first two plays."

"And Nick?" I'm scared to know, but I can't move forward until I do.

She blows a raspberry and rolls her eyes. "That loser. He's long gone...for good, I think."

"For good?" I can't hide the doubt in my tone.

She frames my face with her hands. "Cordell. I didn't want you caught up in the Nick drama. I didn't want his idiotic attempt to wear me down to cause you to lose focus tonight. He's my past, but you're my future."

I swallow hard and study her face. "I know you can fight your own battles, Mel. But I *will* be the man standing beside you when you do. If you ever need me to tap in, I'll be there for you."

She grins. "Aww, just like *Friends*." She brushes her lips against mine. "I'll be there for you, too. I love you, Coach."

"I love you, sweetheart." I press my lips to hers for a lingering kiss, then squeeze her hips, silently signaling her to release her hold on my legs.

Once she's steady on her feet, we thread our fingers together and walk toward the field house, the Friday night lights beacons that guide our path.

We might've lost the game tonight, but with her hand in mine, I see nothing but wins on the horizon.

# EPILOGUE
## MEL

*One year later...*

The grip I have on Tessa's hand is so fierce my knuckles are white. I've had a death grip on her since the start of the fourth quarter. My best friend has tears in her eyes—from excitement and not pain, I hope—and on her other side, Luke has his hands on the top of his head. Over and over, he looks from the Jumbotron in the rafters above us to the field and back.

The Bennett Eagles have a three-point lead with one fifteen left in the game. But the reigning two-A state champs have the ball at the Eagles' forty-five, and our defense is worn out. Our boys have played with heart and toughness all game, and they're so close. So close to upsetting the Bulldogs and winning their first ever state championship.

The Bennett faithful are raucous in this Atlanta stadium. Every fan wearing red and white is on their feet and yelling at the top of their lungs, hoping to give our boys one last boost. Almost the entire town made the trek up here this weekend to cheer the Eagles on. Ms. Marj, Mr. Tom, Emma, and Glamma might be the only Bennetians holding down the fort back at home.

The Bulldogs use their final time-out, and the crowd quiets.

"That second corn dog might be coming back to haunt me," Tessa laments, rubbing her barely noticeable baby bump. She and Luke got the surprise of their lives the week of Emma's first birthday. This baby Shipley is due next May, and yes, they want the sex of the baby to be a surprise again. No matter how much I bribe them.

"Uncle Dell looks nervous." On my other side, Ryan clings to the railing in front of our seats while his sister and Hannah hold up a giant cutout of Cordell's head—best money I've ever spent. When he saw us waving it wildly at the season opener in August, he doubled over in laughter on the sideline. We've had "Big Dell" with us at every game this season. Hannah swears it's a good luck charm, and seeing as how we're here today, I think she's right.

"We're all nervous." Cass gives me a tight-lipped smile and reaches around her son to take my other hand. She tugs on it gently and leans in as close as she can. "No matter what happens in the next minute, he'll be okay. He has you."

She's right. Cordell will be fine no matter the outcome. But he wants this win so badly. He wants it for his boys and for our town. He'd never admit to anyone but me or his family, but he's worried about letting our hometown down two years in a row. But he doesn't see what I see when we mingle with the people of Bennett. They hold him in the highest regard; even if he lost the championship ten times in a row, their respect for him would remain.

As the game resumes, I can't take my eyes off where my man paces on the sideline with his hands clasped behind his back. Cool and collected. On the surface, at least. My arms tingle with the need to hold him close, heartbeat to heartbeat. The way we woke up in our hotel room this morning.

The Bulldogs gain eight yards, and my heart feels like it's trying to break through my ribs. They're close enough for a field goal to tie the game, but they decide to run it on fourth and two in hopes of victory. One of our boys tackles their running back, and the hit dislodges the ball before he hits the turf. A fumble. The ball spins in the air, like it's suspended in slow motion, rotating end over end over end...and lands square in the hands of Darius Jones. Jones takes off, and the Bennett sideline and fanbase erupt.

He makes it all the way to the Bulldogs' twenty before he's tackled by their quarterback. The excitement is at a fever pitch as our offense takes the field and runs the clock down. When Grady takes a knee on the last play, he's mobbed by the rest of the team.

We won. The Eagles fucking *won*.

Tears pour down my cheeks as we hug and celebrate in the stands. It's bedlam down on the field, but I find him immediately. He shakes the opposing coach's hand, and as he turns to move on, Clay snatches him up in a bone-crushing hug. I spin, searching for Frannie. She's a couple of rows up from us with Cara and Finn, whose faces are wet but deliriously happy as they cling to their mom. When our eyes lock, she mouths *they did it*, and we grin at each other through our tears.

Thank goodness for waterproof mascara.

My phone buzzes in my back pocket, and I cackle when I read the text.

> RACY LACEY
>
> B and I are watching online. Eagles victory!
> Give your man a kiss from me, hellcat!

After the trophy is presented to Cordell and the team, we're allowed onto the field to celebrate. I stand back and let Cordell hug his mom, Cass, Kelly, and the kids, but his eyes are on me through every embrace. My cheeks hurt from grinning so wide, and my tears have surely washed away every trace of makeup. My voice is hoarse from all the screaming, too, but when he finally wraps me up in his arms, nothing else matters.

"You did it, Coach."

Cordell's voice cracks. "God, I love you so much, sweetheart." He cradles the back of my head tenderly, causing even more happy tears to rain down my face. I'm overwhelmed with excitement, with loving him. Overwhelmed by how perfect our lives are these days. I don't think anything could top this pinnacle.

But then Cordell lowers me to the ground and takes my hand. He sinks to one knee, and that's when I see the small purple velvet box in his free hand.

"Mel—"

My head whirls at the sight in front of me. This plot twist. My heart stutters and then speeds up double-time. *Is this really happening?*

I know it's real when the circle gathered around us comes into focus. We're surrounded by the people who love us most—Ms. Rhonda, Cass and her family, my parents, the Shipleys, the Reeveses. Their happy grins and wet eyes reflect my joy as Cordell grips my shaking hand and looks up at me with utter devotion.

"Mel," he says again. "You're the best thing that has ever happened to me."

My grin stretches wider and my heart splits, making room for more love than I ever imagined I could feel.

A lone tear tracks down his cheek, and I swipe it away with my free hand. "You're a kaleidoscope of colors that lights up my world. You're my favorite person." He swallows harshly. "Mel Marshall, I want to make a memorable life with you. Will you marry me?"

My head nods my answer before my lips can form the word. "Yes," I choke out. "Yes, I'll marry you, Coach."

The cheers and whoops and whistles that sound out around us as Cordell slips a gorgeous pink diamond ring on my finger are deafening. My cheeks heat at the attention, but I can't take my eyes off him. He lifts me in an embrace, and when he spins me around, I tip my head back in laughter.

I'm lightheaded when we stop, when he whispers "we're getting married" in my ear.

"I already have the something blue." I tilt my head so he can see the tiny blue flower I pinned in my hair that morning.

I kiss him without a care in the world that we're in the middle of a crowd. And when he kisses me back, it's full of promise and hope and forever.

He smiles, big and bright and blinding, and I'm delirious with happiness.

And so, so thankful that this last time I fell in love with Cordell Watkins, it stuck.

# ACKNOWLEDGMENTS

I'm so incredibly thankful I get to do this again!

To all of the readers who read *Between the Lines* and expressed a desire for Mel and Cordell's story...thank you. When the words wouldn't come or it felt like I had to mine the depths to get their story finished, I thought of YOU, and it made me dig even deeper because I didn't want to let you down. They are yours as much as they are mine, and I hope you love their story as much as I do.

To the Bookstagrammers who reviewed, posted about, created content for, and recommended *Between the Lines*, or slid into my DMs about my first book baby...gosh, I love y'all. You've made me feel like a legit author, and you made me smile and happy-cry on hard days. Forever thankful that you took a chance on an unknown rookie author's debut.

Heather, Mallory, Melanie, Kayla, Nicole, Laura, Lily, and Tanisha, aka the lovely humans who beta read *Keeping the Score*: thank y'all for reading an early version of this story and for giving me the best feedback. I'm so grateful for your suggestions, excitement, and beautifully unhinged comments.

To my dear friend Kourtney, who gave her time to be a sensitivity reader for this manuscript to ensure that I got Cordell's journey right...I'm so freaking proud of you and those three Cordells you're raising. Thank you for being so dependable and honest. Forever #royal

To my amazing editor, Beth, I meant it when I said I don't want to put a book out in the world without your eyes looking at it first. Thank you for making this story the absolute best it can be, and for helping me with that pesky blurb again. I'm manifesting a trip to Michigan so I can buy you a coffee, and we can spend time discussing our love for Xaden Riorson and debating which dragontail is the best.

To Mel (the one who doesn't live in my head), I can legit say that *Keeping the Score* wouldn't have happened without you. Thank you for hashing out the plot and characters with me before I even wrote the first line, and for reading the completed manuscript and offering valuable feedback and advice. Mel (the one who *does* live in my head), Dell, and I are big fans of yours! Looking forward to working together again! (A certain tight end needs his own HEA, right?)

Lorissa, you are insanely talented and wonderful to work with, and this cover is a dream come true! I'm sure it was a challenge to match the vibes of a cover done by a different artist, but you took my vision and created magic. I big puffy heart love every single detail. Thank you so much!

Kristen, book formatter and magic maker, it was so great to work with you again! It's so comforting to have someone in my corner who will work tirelessly to make sure my words look fantastic. You're the best!

To the many friends who asked for regular updates on the progress of this book, your cheerleading means the world to me. Thank you for being so excited to get your hands on Mel and Cordell's story. And for being so genuinely enthusiastic about my little author journey. I'll never forget or take for granted how amazingly supportive you've been throughout all of this. I love y'all.

My precious Graham fam, you are so special to me. That quote "friends are the family you choose" could not be more true, and I'm so grateful we've chosen each other. Jocelynn, I owe you so much for this book—ideas and band names and endless encouragement. Thank you for loving Mel and Cordell right from the jump. For telling me that this book is better than my first one, even though you were worried it would hurt my feelings. You can be my alpha reader for life, even though you skim over the saucy parts! Matt, so many thanks to you for your coach's point of view. Grateful that you put up with my million and one sports questions. You put so much thought into your advice, and my work is better because of it. And to Parker Reese, thank you for letting me hijack your parents' attention sometimes. I love being your Aunt Brandy.

To my favorite yogi and future podcast co-host: Leigh, thank you for being my unpaid therapist and for being a Cordell stan. And for letting me imbue Mel with shades of your awesomeness. You can also be my alpha reader for life, especially because you *don't* skim over the saucy parts. Thank you for believing in and loving this story (even if you wanted me to kill off Glamma.)

To Sonic #3621, thank you for the bacon breakfast burritos and large Dr Peppers that fueled this endeavor. (And to the ten pounds I gained while writing this book: eff you.)

Finally, to quote my favorite celebrity Snoop Dogg, "I want to thank me. I want to thank me for believing in me. I want to thank me for doing all this hard work...I want to thank me for never quitting." Writing this book was such a struggle. I agonized over every sentence and doubted that I had the talent to write a second book. I worried that the only reason I was able to write the first one was because it was so closely tied to my day job. Imposter syndrome became my constant companion. I army-crawled through some dark mental health moments in the weeks it took me to finish this story, but I didn't give up. I'm so damn proud of myself for that, and I can't wait to see where this journey takes me next.

# ABOUT THE AUTHOR

Brandy Pelletier spends her days as a reading specialist and her nights and weekends reading anything she can get her hands on. She's wanted to become a published author ever since second grade, when her original story "How the Giraffe Got Its Long Neck" was published in her school district's annual writing anthology.

When she's not blasting Taylor Swift or attempting to tackle her ridiculously long TBR, she can be found collecting book boyfriends and dreaming of living in a witch cottage with her miniature schnauzer, Pippa. *Keeping the Score* is her second novel. She reckons that indicates it's okay for her to start calling herself an *author* and actually mean it. Probably also time for her to get a website or start a newsletter. In the meantime, follow Brandy on social media.

instagram.com/thebrandyland

tiktok.com/@thebrandyland

threads.net/@thebrandyland

9 798988 068730